MARGOT HUNT

BEST FRIENDS FOREVER

A NOVEL

mira

ISBN-13: 978-0-7783-3113-1

Best Friends Forever

For questions and comments about the quality of this book, please contact us
at CustomerService@Harlequin.com.

MIRABooks.com

BookClubbish.com

Printed in U.S.A.

Friends have drifted in and out of my life over the years.
This book is dedicated to those special few that stuck around.

BEST
FRIENDS
FOREVER

IMAGINE YOU'RE SHIPWRECKED on an island inhabited by only Knights and Knaves. Knights always tell the truth. Knaves always lie. There is no way to distinguish between the two just by looking at them. The only way to separate the liars from the truth-tellers is by asking them questions.

For example, suppose you encounter two islanders. Let's call them A and B. You ask A, "Are you a Knight or a Knave?"

A responds by saying, "At least one of us is a Knave."

B is silent.

Who is a Knight and who is a Knave?

The answer is easy. A cannot be a Knave, because if so, his statement would be truthful, and Knaves always lie. Therefore A must be a Knight, and telling the truth. Which would mean B is a Knave.

In real life, of course, there are no such things as Knights, those absolute keepers of the truth.

Everyone lies about something.

1

IT WAS A perfectly normal school morning in the Campbell household—disorganized, chaotic and at least one of my children was running around half-naked—right up until the moment the police arrived at our front door to question me in connection with the death of Howard Grant.

Before the doorbell rang—before everything changed—my most pressing concern was not to overcook the eggs I was scrambling for our breakfast.

I had learned through practice and error that the key to perfectly scrambled eggs was to keep the heat low. As I slowly stirred the eggs with a flat whisk, a flash of movement outside caught my eye. I turned to glance out the kitchen window, which overlooked our side yard and the street beyond. Our next-door neighbor Judy Ward was walking her fat dachshund, Rocket, down the sidewalk. Judy was carrying a green plastic bag of dog poop in one hand and Rocket's leash in the other. The dog was panting so heavily, he looked like he was about to keel over.

"Mom, where're my shorts?" Liam yelled from his room, which was located on the other side of our one-story house. When I didn't answer, he shouted again. "Mom! I can't find my uniform shorts!"

I drew in a deep breath and counted to five to stop myself from yelling back that if my son needed something, he should walk across the house and ask me politely. Sure enough, the *thud-thud-thud* of large thirteen-year-old feet stampeded across our ceramic tile floor. Liam appeared in the kitchen, wearing only a navy polo shirt with his school logo on it and white cotton briefs. Liam had my husband's unruly dark curls and lopsided smile, but his wide, pale blue eyes and long, straight nose came from me. He was getting so tall, officially a teenager, but still child enough to run around in his underwear. I loved him so, this wild boy of mine.

"I can't find any clean shorts," Liam said. He balanced on one leg like a crane and began to hop in place.

"Why are you hopping?"

"Because I can," Liam said carelessly. "Have you seen my shorts?"

"Did you look in the dryer?"

Liam snapped his fingers. "The *dryer*," he repeated, drawing out the word and then hopping out of the room. I smiled, watching him go.

"Breakfast will be ready in five minutes. And don't forget your belt," I called after him. Despite going to the same school with the same dress code for seven years, Liam still forgot to put on a belt at least every other day.

"I know!" he yelled back.

I turned the burner off under the eggs, pulled out a loaf of whole wheat bread from the pantry and started on the toast. I noticed that the pears in the wire fruit bowl were starting to look bruised. I picked one up, and the flesh gave way, my fingers sinking into the rotten fruit. I shuddered and tossed it in the garbage.

"Mom?"

This time it was my daughter calling for me. Bridget, at eleven, was more organized than her older brother would ever be. She was already dressed in her school uniform, the same blue polo with the crest embroidered on the left chest, tucked neatly into a knee-length khaki skirt. Her long strawberry blond hair—just a shade lighter than mine—was tied back in a low ponytail, and she was holding a piece of white poster board with pictures and snippets of text neatly glued to it. It was her state capital report, which she had diligently worked on for the past two evenings.

"How are you going to bring that into school?" I asked as I turned to the sink to wash my hands. "I don't think it will fit in your backpack."

"It won't," Bridget confirmed. "But it's going to get all bent if I carry it in like this."

"Maybe we can roll it up and put a rubber band around it," I suggested. "Go see if Dad has one in the office."

"Okay." Bridget trooped off toward our home office. Todd habitually checked his email on the desktop computer there every morning as he drank his coffee.

"Liam, did you find your shorts?" I called out.

"Oh, right. I forgot to look," he responded. There was another flurry of heavy footsteps, the metallic *thwack* of the dryer door being opened and slammed closed. "Got 'em!"

Bridget returned, this time with Todd trailing her. My husband was a tall, broad-shouldered man with milk-pale skin and dark eyes. Todd's dark hair was still thick, but it was becoming increasingly streaked with gray. I'd also noticed that lately he'd started wearing his tortoiseshell reading glasses more frequently.

"I don't have any rubber bands," Todd said.

"Oh, no! What are we going to do?" Bridget asked fretfully, her voice thin and sharp. Yes, my daughter was far more organized than my son, but her moods shifted so much faster. Joy one moment, tears the next. I worried constantly that the stormy emotional seas she traversed each day would one day capsize her.

"Don't worry," I soothed her. "Can't you use a hair elastic?"

Bridget brightened at this suggestion. "Oh, yeah! I didn't think of that!" she said and scuttled off to the bathroom the children shared to find one of the four million hair elastics that lived in the flotsam and jetsam of the drawers there.

Todd smiled at me. "Good save," he said, crinkles appearing at the corners of his eyes. He rested a hand on my shoulder.

"I have my moments," I said, turning back to the sink so that his hand fell away.

Todd had been trying lately. I had to give him credit for that, even if I wasn't particularly charmed by his efforts. I wondered, fleetingly, if our marriage would ever return to the warm, secure place it had once been.

But then, before I could become too maudlin, remembering past happiness and the unlikeliness of its return, the doorbell rang. I looked up, wondering who it was. No one ever rang the doorbell before nine.

"Who do you think that is?" Todd asked.

I bit back my involuntary response. *How should I know?* Censoring oneself was necessary to a happy marriage. Or, in our case, to keeping an unhappy marriage from spiraling even further downward.

Don't mess with one another, Dr. Keller, our marriage counselor, had suggested. *Don't drink too much. Don't pick fights.*

Don't be too truthful, I'd privately added to the list. Honesty was overrated, especially within the boundaries of a troubled marriage. Actually, these days, I was starting to think that couples therapy itself was overrated. Was it really necessary to pay Dr. Keller an exorbitant rate just so we could have someone watch as we salted each other's wounds once a week? Nothing ever scabbed over and healed when you kept picking at it. There was an undeniable wisdom to the old saying *Least said, sooner mended.*

I made a mental note to cancel our next session.

"It's probably one of the neighbors," I said. "Maybe someone has a dead car battery and needs a jump."

Todd nodded and went off to answer the door just as the toast popped up. Whoever was at the house, they were arriving just as breakfast was ready. I checked the toast and decided to drop it down for further browning.

I heard the low murmur of Todd as he spoke, but I didn't recognize the voices that responded. One male, one female, I thought. I couldn't hear what Todd said in reply, but something about his tone sounded off. The smell of burning bread filled my nose. I popped the toast up. It was now charred black. I swore softly, feeling another flash of irritation at the interruption to our morning routine.

"Are you okay, Mom?" Bridget asked, appearing in the kitchen.

"I'm fine."

"Gross," Bridget said. "Burned?"

"Burned," I confirmed.

"I'm not eating that," Bridget said, pointing an accusatory finger.

"No one's asking you to." I plucked the bread out of the toaster and tossed it in the garbage can. "I'll make some more."

"Who are those people Daddy's talking to?"

"I'm not sure," I said. "Why?"

"He looks worried," Bridget said.

I inserted a few fresh slices of bread into the toaster and put a lid on the pan of eggs to keep them warm.

"I'll find out what's going on," I said. "Are your hands clean? No? Go wash them. Breakfast is almost ready."

I passed through the open-plan living room with its well-worn brown leather sofas and floral wool rug, all overdue for replacement, out to the front hall. Todd was standing slightly to one side of the open door, so I had a clear view of the man and woman on our front step. Both were dressed in suits that looked too warm for a sunny April Florida morning. The automatic sprinklers switched on then and began spraying water across the browning lawn with *rat-a-tat-tat* efficiency.

"Who is it?" I asked.

Todd turned to me. Bridget was right, he did look worried.

"They're police officers," he said. "Detectives..." Todd's voice trailed off as he turned back to look at our visitors. "Sorry, I've forgotten your names."

"I'm Detective Alex Demer." The detective was tall and bulky and had dark, pockmarked skin and a closely cropped beard. "And this is Sergeant Sofia Oliver."

"I'm Alice Campbell," I replied. Neither of them offered a hand to shake, so I followed their lead.

Oliver was the younger of the two. She was petite and fine-boned, and her auburn hair was cut short in a pixie style. Her lips rounded down, and her eyes were flinty. My best friend, Kat, would call it a "resting bitch face." In Oliver's case, it was an accurate description.

"Th-they want to talk to you about Howard Grant," Todd stammered.

Howard Grant. Kat's husband. Or, to be more accurate, her *late* husband. Howard had died three days earlier. The shock of his death still hit me anew every time I thought of it.

"Oh, right. Of course. You're with the Jupiter Island Police?" I guessed. Kat and Howard lived—or in Howard's case, *had* lived—on tony Jupiter Island. While their home was close geographically to where we lived, in the Town of Jupiter, the island was its own separate and quite exclusive municipality.

"The Jupiter Island Public Safety Department," Sergeant Oliver corrected me, her tone needlessly officious.

"Actually, Sergeant Oliver is with the Jupiter Island Public Safety Department," Detective Demer said. "I'm with the Florida Department of Law Enforcement based in Tallahassee. I've been temporarily assigned to look into Howard Grant's death."

"I thought Howard's death was an accident," I said.

Detective Demer gazed down at me, his expression inscrutable. "That's what we're looking into. And that's why we need to speak with you."

"Of course. Please, come in," I said, stepping aside to give them room.

Todd shook his head, and I could tell from his expression that I was missing something important.

"Alice, they want you to go *with* them," my husband emphasized. "To the police station."

"Really?" I looked at the police officers. "Why?"

Demer held up a placating hand. "It's nothing to worry about, Mrs. Campbell. Your name came up in the course of our investigation, and we have some questions for you. It's all very routine."

I nodded slowly. I didn't understand why the conversation couldn't take place in our living room. And if they wanted me to come to them, why hadn't they just called? What was the point of showing up on my doorstep first thing in the morning?

"What's going on?" Liam asked, appearing behind me. He had his shorts on now, thankfully, but was still not wearing a belt.

"Nothing," I said. "The eggs are ready. Go serve yourself. I'll be right in. And don't forget to put on a belt."

"I'm sorry if we've come at a bad time," Demer said. He did look as though he regretted the imposition. Maybe he had children of his own back in Tallahassee and knew how chaotic the mornings could be. I nodded and smiled faintly to signal that I understood he was just doing his job.

"When would you like me to come in?" I asked.

"As soon as possible," Oliver snapped. In contrast to her colleague, she didn't seem at all sheepish about appearing on my doorstep before 8:00 a.m. and disrupting our routine. "In fact, we'd like you to come with us now."

I shook my head. "That's impossible. I have to finish helping my children get ready for school and then drive them in. I can meet you after that."

"How long will that be?" Demer asked.

In truth, it took me only twenty minutes to complete the school run. But I was currently wearing a ratty old T-shirt of Todd's and a pair of jogging shorts. I'd never put much thought into what one wore to a police interview, but I was fairly sure this was not the ideal outfit.

"Where is the Jupiter Island Public Safety Department located?" I asked, wondering why it couldn't just be called a police department. Was that somehow offensive to the extremely wealthy residents of Jupiter Island? Were police necessary only for regular citizens? The marked differences between the very rich and everyone else reared up at the oddest times, even in our so-called equal society.

"On Bunker Hill Road in the old town hall building," Oliver said.

I mentally calculated how long it would take me to get the kids off to school, get dressed and drive there. "I could be there in two hours."

The police officers exchanged a look, but Demer nodded.

"We'll see you then," he said.

Once the front door was closed and we were alone again, my husband looked anxiously at me.

"What's going on? Why do the police want to talk to you?" Todd hissed, keeping his voice low so Liam and Bridget wouldn't hear. Children have superhuman hearing when it comes to picking up on any brewing parental conflict.

"I have no idea," I said. "But Howard's death was...odd." An understatement, to say the least. "I'm sure they have to investigate. Make sure there wasn't any...I don't know, foul play."

Foul play. It was such a melodramatic phrase, like something out of an Agatha Christie novel. Murderous vicars and little old ladies who put arsenic in the tea.

"But why do they think you'd know anything about it?"

"I'm sure they don't." I shrugged. "But they obviously know that Kat and I are friends."

"I don't think you should speak to the police without having an attorney present."

"What? Why? I'm not a suspect," I said.

"How do you know?"

"Because that would be insane," I said. I shook my head. "Look, I'm sure they have to investigate, even when the death was clearly accidental. It's certainly nothing to worry about."

"Then why are the police at our door at eight in the morning," Todd pointed out.

"I have no idea, but there's no reason to overreact," I said, turning away. "I have to go check on the kids. If I don't pay attention, Liam eats all the toast and none of his eggs, and Bridget doesn't eat anything at all."

My husband grabbed my arm and spun me back toward him. He leaned forward, his face close to mine, and whispered, "What's going on? Did Kat have something to do with Howard's death?"

His breath was hot and smelled of coffee. I pulled my arm out of his grip and took a step back. "Don't be ridiculous. Of course she didn't."

Todd wasn't sure if he should believe me. I could tell by

the way he was searching my face, looking for some trace of a lie in the way I blinked my eyes or clenched my jaw.

Like a visitor to the island of Knights and Knaves, Todd wanted to try his hand at ferreting out the liars.

I felt a stab of fear and hoped I was more convincing when I spoke to the police.

2

JUPITER ISLAND WAS a long, narrow barrier island north of Palm Beach. There were only a few access points to reach it from the mainland, which I assumed was by design to ensure the privacy of its well-heeled residents. I approached it from the south, driving up US Highway 1, taking a right just past the Jupiter Lighthouse, then heading north up the island on Beach Road.

I drove past the tall condo buildings of Palm Beach County. They abruptly stopped, signaling that I'd passed into Martin County with its more stringent zoning laws. I passed through the Blowing Rocks Preserve, where the road was lined with short palm trees and bushy sea grape shrubs. Just past the preserve and tourist parking, the private houses began. Some were visible from the road, others sheltered behind gates and privacy hedges. All were large and ostentatious. The houses to the east fronted the Atlantic Ocean, while the ones to the west faced the Intracoastal Waterway. Each property had a twee white sign set by the curb, displaying the family name or the name of the house—Sand Castle or Shangri-La—or the more practical, if somewhat pointed, Service Entrance.

Kat's house was on the left about a mile past the preserve, set back at the end of a gravel drive. I wondered if she was home, and I thought about stopping and checking on her before I went to the police station. I'd called her twice on my way over to the island, but she hadn't picked up. This wasn't entirely unusual. Unlike most people of the modern world, Kat had only a tenuous connection to her cell phone. She didn't always pick up when I called, and she frequently ignored texts for hours, or even a day.

We'd spoken only once, briefly, since Howard's death. Kat had been in London to meet with several artists whose work she was considering carrying in her gallery. She'd called me from Heathrow while she was waiting for her flight home. Kat had been subdued, which wasn't surprising. The police had tracked her down at her hotel in London only hours earlier to notify her that Howard was dead. The housekeeper had found his body lying facedown on the back patio.

"Are you okay?" I'd asked.

"No," she'd said. "But I will be. At least, I think I will."

"I wish you didn't have to be on your own right now."

"I usually hate the flight back from Europe, but I'm sort of glad that I'll have this time to pull myself together. There will be so much to do once I get home," Kat said.

"Have you spoken to Amanda?" I asked. Kat's daughter was in her first year of medical school at Emory, in Atlanta.

"I'm going to wait until I get home," Kat explained. "She's studying for a big test in her anatomy class. I don't want to upset her."

"You probably won't be able to avoid upsetting her," I said as gently as I could.

"I know, but I'd like to at least put off telling her until after her exam is over." Kat sighed. "Marguerite was apparently hysterical. It must have been awful for her, finding him like that. What does it mean when the housekeeper has shed more tears for my dead husband than I have?"

"It probably means you're in shock," I said.

Kat's flight had been called then, and she had to hang up. I hadn't spoken to her since. I'd tried calling and texting her a few times, but she hadn't responded. I knew she was probably busy planning the funeral and dealing with her relatives. Stopping by now, uninvited, at a house in mourning seemed intrusive. I drove by.

I arrived at the Jupiter Island Public Safety Department. It was located in a charming yellow building with green shutters, lush landscaping and neat hedgerows, and across the street from one of the holes of the Jupiter Island Club's pristinely manicured golf course. I parked my ancient Volvo in a small lot just to the left of where the island's two fire trucks were housed.

I checked my phone, but Kat still hadn't responded. I sent her a text:

At Jupiter island police. They asked me 2 come in 4 interview about Howard. Not sure what's going on, but will try to be helpful. Hope ur ok. xx.

I dropped my phone into my bag and climbed out of my car into the Florida sunshine. It was an unusually warm morning, and I had dressed for it in a light blue linen shirtdress and flat brown sandals. But the fabric was already starting to wilt in the heat, and perspiration beaded on my forehead. There was a flagpole in front of the building with an American flag at full mast. A light breeze caused the pulley to bang with a metallic rhythm against the pole.

As I entered the police station, a frigid blast of air-conditioning hit me. The waiting room area was small and, apart from some chairs and a table scattered with magazines, empty. Jupiter Island did not appear to be a hotbed of criminal activity.

I walked up to the middle-aged woman sitting at the reception desk. She wore a floral dress rather than a police uniform, and her glasses hung around her neck on a beaded cord. There was a small brass dish shaped like a pineapple and filled with candy on her desk.

"How can I help you, dear?" she asked.

"I'm here to see Detective Alex Demer. My name is Alice Campbell," I said.

"Of course," she said, smiling up at me. "He's expecting you."

I had deliberately not asked for Oliver. I hadn't liked her, and I hoped she wouldn't be there for the interview. But then I remembered the whole good cop–bad cop phenomenon. Maybe she'd been purposely rude so I'd open up to the more sympathetic Demer. Or was that just something from the movies?

The receptionist told me to take a seat, but I waited only a few minutes before Detective Demer came out to greet me, holding a paper coffee cup in one hand. His height should have made him imposing, but for some reason, he wasn't. Perhaps it was his rumpled suit or his ugly tie, or the fact that his eyes looked tired and bloodshot. I wondered if his unkempt appearance was a result of living out of a hotel or if he always looked like this. Did he have a wife at home who did his laundry and picked up his dry cleaning? Or did he live in a bachelor pad with dirty dishes piled in the sink? I glanced at the detective's left hand. He wasn't wearing a wedding band.

"Mrs. Campbell, thank you for coming in," he said, extending the hand that wasn't holding the coffee cup.

I stood and shook his hand. "Of course."

"Come on back. I'm working out of the conference room," he said, nodding toward the hallway he'd just emerged from.

I followed him. The building didn't look anything like the police stations did on urban cop movies, with the huge cement-floored rooms furnished with rows of industrial desks and perps handcuffed to chairs. Instead it looked like the office of an insurance company, with subdued furnishings and a low-pile beige carpet. We passed a few small offices, most of which were empty. Sergeant Oliver sat in one, and she looked up when we passed.

"Mrs. Campbell is here," Demer said to her.

"I see that. I'll be right in," Oliver replied.

The detective led me to a small conference room and gestured for me to sit at a rectangular table with a shiny cherry finish. Sun was streaming in through two windows, and Demer adjusted the blinds so the light wouldn't be in my eyes.

"Can I get you anything to drink?" he asked. "Coffee? Although I wouldn't, if I were you." He held up his Starbucks cup. "I'm not a coffee snob by any stretch, so you can imagine how bad it would have to be to get me to spend five bucks on this. We also have soda and bottled water."

"Water would be great," I answered.

"Sure thing. I'll be right back."

Demer left just as Oliver strode in. She had removed her suit jacket and rolled up the sleeves of her blue oxford button-down. Her face was bare of makeup, and the only jewelry she wore was a pair of small gold hoop earrings. She took a seat across from me, dropping a notebook on the table.

"You took your time getting here," she said. The bad cop was officially on the scene.

I wondered if she was always this bad-tempered or if there was something about this particular case bothering her. Was it contempt for the extremely wealthy area her department policed? But if so, why choose to work here over a grittier but surely more exciting law enforcement agency, like in West Palm or even Miami? Or did her anger stem from Demer's presence? Maybe she was angry that he had been brought in from Tallahassee to work on an investigation that she had expected to take the lead on.

I chose not to respond to her comment. Instead I looked

back at her steadily, wanting to make it clear early on that I would not be bullied.

"I heard you're some sort of a writer," Oliver said, folding her arms over her chest.

I nodded. "I'm the author of a series of books of logic puzzles for children."

"How'd you come up with that idea?"

"It's my background. I was an associate professor in the mathematics department at the University of Miami."

The sergeant's eyebrows arched.

"But you're not a professor now?" she asked.

"No."

"Did you, like, get fired or something?" She gave a contemptuous snort. I knew she was purposely trying to needle me, but I didn't know why. Either she was just an unpleasant person or she wanted to see how I'd react to her barbs.

I smiled without warmth. "I stopped teaching after my daughter was born."

"And why was that?" Oliver leaned forward, her elbows braced on the table.

"Personal choice." There hadn't actually been much of a choice, but I wasn't about to get into that now.

The door opened and Demer came in. He glanced from Oliver to me and back again.

"Everything okay in here?"

"Sergeant Oliver has been asking me about my work experience," I said. "But I assume that's not what you wanted to talk to me about."

"No, it's not," Demer agreed. He handed me a bottle of water and sat down next to Oliver. The detective placed a folder on the table and flipped it open. "Thank you for taking time out of your schedule to come talk with us."

"Of course. Although I'm still not sure how I can help you."

"Why don't you let us worry about that?" Oliver interjected.

I pressed my lips together and folded my hands in my lap. Demer's eyes flitted in the direction of his partner. I sensed that he wasn't on board with her interview technique. Maybe he didn't like the good cop–bad cop dynamic any more than I did. Or maybe this was part of their act, too.

"As you know, we're investigating the death of Howard Grant..." Demer began.

I nodded.

"As I'm sure you know, the cause of his death was unusual," the detective continued. He glanced up at me. "I'm assuming you know how he died."

"Yes." I couldn't help but shiver. "It was pretty awful."

"How well did you know Mr. Grant?" Demer asked.

I paused, not quite sure how to answer this. I had actually spent very little time with Howard over the years. But Kat had confided so much to me about her husband and their marriage that in some ways I knew him intimately.

"I knew Howard, of course, and we would occasionally be at social events together," I said carefully. "But Kat was the one I was friends with—*is* the one I'm friends with. I knew Howard only because he was married to Kat."

"So you consider yourself and Mr. Grant to be, what— social acquaintances?" Demer asked.

I nodded. "I suppose that's the best description."

"Were you ever alone with him?" Demer continued.

"No." Then I hesitated, realizing this wasn't quite true. "I mean, there were a few times when I was at their house and Kat would leave the room for one reason or another. But we never spent any significant time alone together."

"Would you say that Howard Grant was a heavy drinker?" the detective asked.

"Yes."

"How would you define that? What a heavy drinker is, I mean," he qualified.

"I'm not an expert on the subject, but from what I observed, I'd say that Howard was an alcoholic," I told the detective. "Almost every time I saw him, he was drinking."

"But you just said that you saw Mr. Grant only at social events," Oliver cut in. "Times when drinking alcoholic beverages wouldn't be unusual."

"That's true. But even then, he drank quite a bit more than I would consider a normal amount. And Kat and I are close. She was concerned about how much he drank." It felt odd disclosing this confidence—Kat and I had always guarded each other's secrets—but I didn't see any way around it. "Wasn't he drinking the night he died?"

"At the time of his death, Mr. Grant had a blood alcohol level of .30. Do you know what that means?" Demer folded his hands on the table and looked steadily at me.

"That sounds high."

"It is. For a man his height and weight, he would have consumed around eleven drinks in a three-hour period. Most people would have passed out by that point."

I nodded. "I guess that's how he fell off the balcony."

"But, see, that's the thing we keep going back to. Why was he even out on his balcony? If he'd had that much to drink, so much that he should have passed out, why was he outside in the first place? Did he suddenly get the urge to go look at the stars?" Demer said.

"And more to the point, how did he fall over the railing?" Oliver chimed in.

I frowned. "You just said he was so drunk, it was surprising he was even conscious. Maybe he leaned over the railing and blacked out."

I shifted in my seat. I might not have liked Howard, or been close to him, but I certainly didn't enjoy conjuring up the gruesome image of him toppling off the second-story balcony of his and Kat's lavish Mediterranean-style house.

The thought of his body falling heavily to the patio below, smashing against the Italian travertine, and the ambient lights around the pool illuminating his blood as it spread outward from his broken body made me queasy.

"Have you ever leaned over a railing?" Oliver stood. "The automatic tendency would be to brace yourself like this." She demonstrated falling forward and splayed her hands out in front of her, catching them on the table. "It would actually take some effort to go over the railing. Even if you were drunk." She shrugged. "Especially if you were drunk, since your coordination would be impaired."

"So, what...you think Howard jumped?" I asked, arching my eyebrows. "You think he committed suicide?"

"No." Demer leaned forward slightly, his brown bloodshot eyes fixed on me more intensely than I was comfortable with. "We definitely *don't* think Howard Grant committed suicide."

This stark statement hung between us. I felt a frisson of fear.

"Let's start from the beginning," Demer said. "How long have you known Katherine Grant?"

3

"ATTENTION, PASSENGERS ON Flight 523 to West Palm Beach. We are experiencing mechanical difficulties with the aircraft that will cause a delay in our departure time. We will update you as soon as we get additional information. Thank you for your patience."

I closed my eyes and breathed in deeply through my nose. It was the third time a delay had been announced over the crackling airport intercom.

"How much longer are we going to be stuck here?" Liam whined.

"Forever," Bridget moaned.

I privately agreed with my daughter that it certainly did feel like we would be stuck there forever in airport purgatory. The terminal at JFK was crowded with holiday travelers. Everyone looked grumpy as they slumped on uncomfortable seats, their luggage and possessions scattered around them. When the announcement had begun, the herd had raised their heads hopefully, ears pricking up. At the news of another delay, shoulders sagged and groans rang out all around.

"Mom, my tablet is almost out of power," Liam said, waving the device at me for emphasis.

Like most modern mothers, I firmly believed that my children should spend less time on electronics, staring at screens, and more time in the real, nondigital world. Looking at the scenery, interacting with real people, reading actual books. I was, however, willing to abandon these scruples completely when we were in crowded airports, only halfway through our journey, with no hope of being home before—I checked my watch and stifled another groan—midnight.

"Let's find a place to charge up." I looked around.

Liam nodded toward a bank of high stools in front of a counter equipped with touch screens and electrical outlets. Most of the spots were occupied, but miraculously one of the screens was free.

"Hurry. Let's grab those stools." I moved swiftly, pulling my small wheeled suitcase behind me. The kids took longer to gather up their belongings, so by the time they joined me, I had already claimed three stools, by sitting on one and putting bags down on the other two.

"Are you, like, using *all* of those?" a twentysomething girl asked, her voice a contemptuous squawk. She had squinty eyes ringed with black eyeliner and long, straight hair in an odd shade of pink-streaked blond.

"Yes, I am." I nodded toward my approaching children. "My children are sitting here."

The girl let out an exasperated snort, rolled her eyes and turned away. I felt a surge of petty pleasure at this small victory.

Once seated, Liam and Bridget were keenly interested in the touch screen. After they each plugged in their devices, they started tapping and discovered the screens offered very slow internet access as well as the ability to order food and drinks from a nearby restaurant in the terminal.

"Hey, Mom, can we get fries?" Liam asked.

"Only if there's something resembling dinner on the same plate," I said. "Do they have hamburgers?"

I got out my credit card while Liam tapped at the screen. He frowned. "It's not working."

"Maybe you're tapping it too much," I said. "Give it a chance."

"It's really slow," the woman sitting next to us said. "It takes forever to place your order."

"Did you get it to work?" I asked.

"Yes, finally. And not a moment too soon," she said as a waiter arrived, bearing a single martini on a tray.

I looked at the drink and smiled—I loved martinis, and a drink seemed like the perfect antidote for the too-bright, too-crowded airport terminal.

The woman, I noticed then, seemed incongruously glamorous to the disheveled mass of weary travelers. I guessed that she was a bit older than I was, probably in her mid to late forties. She was very thin and had shiny dark hair cut into an angled chin-length bob. I'd always coveted a sleek bob, but it was a style I'd never be able to tame my wavy hair into. Her eyes were a startling bright blue, and her face was made up of interesting, strong lines—a long nose, full lips, square jaw. Her features were too angular to be truly pretty, but she was a very striking woman.

"A vodka martini, straight up, with a twist?" the waiter asked, setting the drink in front of her.

"Perfect," the woman said, trying to give him a five-dollar bill.

The waiter raised his hands. "All tips have to be done electronically."

The woman crinkled her nose. "Really? I didn't know." She tried to hand him the bill again. "Please, take it. I didn't add one on my total, and I already checked out."

The waiter shrugged and turned away.

The woman looked at me with a smile. "I guess I'll have to order another one and double the tip."

I looked at her drink again, this time covetously. "I'm jealous. That looks delicious. I wish I could have one."

"You can," she said. "Just tap the martini picture on your screen once it stops freezing up. And voilà! A drink magically appears."

"I can't," I said, glancing over at Liam and Bridget. The screen was cooperating with them now, and they were entertaining themselves by ordering far more food than they would eat. I would need to delete half their selections before I swiped my credit card. "I'm here with my kids."

"I've been there. Traveling with children should come with hazardous duty pay," the woman said. "Trust me, you need a martini even more than I do."

I hesitated. A drink sounded wonderful, but I was on my own with the children. We had spent the New Year with my parents in Syracuse. Todd had begged off the trip, claiming he had too much work to do. Although when I'd spoken to him the day before, he'd sounded deeply hungover from whatever party he'd been to on New Year's Eve. It was not the first or the last time I would wonder how unfairly the parental burden fell. Men could get away with bacchanalian nights out, while their wives usually couldn't unless it was preplanned under the pink polka-dotted banner of a Girls' Night Out. In any event, on New Year's Eve, my straitlaced academic parents had gone to bed early, as was their custom. I'd spent the night watching the ball drop at Times Square on television while my children—who'd insisted they were old enough to stay awake—slumbered heavily on the couch.

I decided this woman was right. I *did* deserve a martini.

Besides, Liam and Bridget were old enough that I didn't

have to monitor them like toddlers. And once we reached the airport in Florida, Todd would be there to drive us home.

"Are you on the flight to West Palm?" she asked.

"Yes," I said. "If there ever is a flight to West Palm, that is. I'm starting to worry that we'll be stuck here all night."

"I'm on the same flight. And we're not going anywhere anytime soon. Here, let me order you a drink," she offered.

"No," I demurred. "I can order one through my screen."

"I don't know, Mom," Liam said dubiously. "It's freezing up again."

"I insist," the woman said. "And you'd be doing me a favor, because now I can tip the waiter. How do you like your martini?"

"You really don't have to buy me a drink," I protested weakly.

She smiled, displaying two rows of very straight, very white teeth. "If you don't tell me, I'll have to guess, and I'll probably get it wrong. *That* would be a tragedy."

I laughed. "I like my vodka martinis straight up and very dirty," I said.

She began tapping at her touch screen. It seemed to be working better than the one my children were using.

"Done and done," she said.

"That's very kind," I said. "Thank you."

"I'm Kat." She extended a hand.

I shook it. "Alice."

"Do you live in West Palm?"

"Close. I live in Jupiter."

"Me, too!" Kat exclaimed. "Small world."

"We're practically neighbors," I said.

Later I learned that Kat actually lived on Jupiter Island, which boasted the highest per capita income and highest median home sale price anywhere in the country. Higher than Manhattan. Higher than Marin County. It was where mega-rich sports stars lived. We weren't anywhere close to being neighbors.

"And these are your children?" Kat inquired.

I introduced Liam and Bridget, who were, thankfully, very polite. Bridget even remembered to extend a hand, which Kat shook solemnly. Then there was a flurry of activity as the touch screen finally started working properly. I was able to edit the children's dinner orders and swipe my credit card. By the time I turned my attention back to Kat, the waiter had appeared with my martini. He held out the tray and, with a flourish, neatly set the martini in front of Kat. She slid it over to me.

"Thank you," I said to the waiter. Turning to Kat, I said, "And thank you."

"Cheers," Kat said, raising her glass to mine.

I took a sip of my drink. It was delicious and cold. A blue cheese–stuffed olive speared through the middle with a bamboo pick bobbed inside. I fished the olive out and bit into it.

"How long have you lived in Jupiter?" Kat asked.

"Eight years," I said. I nodded at Bridget. "We moved there from Miami when my daughter was a baby."

"Miami to Jupiter. That's a big change."

"It was. But a good change. I wanted to take some time off work while my children were little. And then my husband got an excellent offer to join an architectural firm in West Palm, so it all seemed, well, serendipitous."

This was the Facebook version of our life, the one we liked to put on display, in which we appeared smart and in control of our lives. It left out the grittier details, like the real reason I'd left my job. And how every time I thought about the career I had left behind—probably so far behind by now I would never be able to get back to it—the pain of failure still cut deeply. That although it was true Todd *had* gotten a decent job offer from S+K Architects in downtown West

Palm Beach, the job was not all he'd initially hoped it would be. Eight years later, he still hadn't made partner or even received the large bonuses they'd hinted at when they hired him. The Florida real estate market had rebounded somewhat since the 2008 crash, but it had never gotten back to where it was in the early 2000s. Anyway, the partners at S+K had an inflated sense of the sort of projects their firm attracted. Most of their work was residential, with a few small but decent office building contracts. No one was hiring them to design the airports or shopping malls or museums Todd had once dreamed of. We had reached our late thirties with our marriage and family intact, but with most of the hopes and dreams of our younger selves in tatters. Life had not turned out as either of us had expected.

But this was not a conversation one had with a stranger in an airport.

"What are you taking time off from?" Kat asked, looking at me intently over the rim of her martini glass.

"I was an associate professor at the University of Miami," I said. "I taught in the math department there."

"Wow," Kat said, looking impressed. I could feel my cheeks growing hot. "What did you teach?"

"Logic."

"You mean like Mr. Spock?" Kat asked.

I smiled. "Not exactly, although he always was my favorite *Star Trek* character. I taught systemic reasoning." Kat's eyebrows knit together, and I knew she wanted an example. "Problems like…all humans are mortal. Kat is a human." I gestured toward her with a wave of the hand. "Therefore Kat is mortal."

Kat wrinkled her nose. "I don't think I like that problem."

"Sorry," I said.

"I'm just kidding," Kat said. "I think it's fascinating. So these days you're, what—illogical?"

I laughed. "Pretty much. That's what being a stay-at-home mother feels like a lot of the time. But, no, actually I'm writing a book of logic puzzles for kids." I surprised myself by telling her this. Hardly anyone knew about my little project, as I thought of it. I looked at it much like not telling anyone you're pregnant until you get past the risky first trimester. I didn't want everyone asking me about it if I failed to finish or publish the book. So why had I told Kat? Was I trying to show off?

Kat looked impressed. "Good for you."

"What do you do?" I asked. I had already clocked her Louis Vuitton carry-on, her navy cashmere sweater, the diamond studs sparkling in her ears that I suspected were not cubic zirconia, like the pair I was wearing. If she was a stay-at-home mom, it was on a different level than the one I lived on. "You said you have kids?"

"Kid. One daughter, but she's all grown up now. She's premed at Vanderbilt. She obviously didn't take after me, since I faint at the sight of blood." Kat smiled. "I have an art gallery, which is probably about as far away from medicine as you can get."

"Wow," I said, intrigued. "What kind of art do you sell?"

"Mostly modern and contemporary, although my real passion is sculpture," Kat said. "That's why I came up to New York after Christmas. To tour some galleries, follow a few leads. Nothing panned out, but what are you going to do? How about you? Were you staying in the city?"

"No, we were in Syracuse, visiting family," I said.

"You're smarter than me. I don't know what I was thinking going to Manhattan on New Year's." Kat rolled her eyes. "The crowds were insane. I finally gave up and spent the last two days holed up in my hotel room, eating room service and watching reality TV, which I really don't get at all. Why does anyone find watching grown women wearing far too much makeup, going to awkward social events and throwing temper tantrums entertaining? It's so bizarre. And why would anyone want to have someone following her around, filming her? That would be my worst nightmare."

Her trip sounded incredibly glamorous to me. The idea of having two days to myself to luxuriate in a posh hotel, ordering room service and watching mindless television shows sounded like sheer decadence. I couldn't remember the last time I had traveled without my husband or children.

"Total nightmare," I agreed.

"Anyway—" Kat sighed and took a large sip of her drink "—New Year's Eve is my least favorite holiday. I much prefer the cozy ones like Thanksgiving and Christmas, when you can curl up and relax at home all day."

"Me, too," I said, although I wasn't sure about the relaxing part. Every year, the weeks that stretched from mid-October to late December devolved into a marathon of shopping, cooking, baking, sewing costumes and wrapping endless piles of presents, all while having to attend a never-ending series of school performances and holiday parties for every extracurricular activity the children were involved in.

There was another pause in our conversation as my children's food arrived. A hamburger and fries for Liam, fried chicken tenders and fries for Bridget. Not a vegetable in sight. But then, my view on airport food was much like my view on airport electronics: anything goes. I took a moment to open Liam's ketchup packs and cut Bridget's chicken up with the dull plastic knife provided. By the time they were settled in, munching happily, and I turned back to Kat, she was grinning at me.

"What?" I asked.

"I just ordered us another round," she said, tapping a short manicured nail against her martini glass.

"You didn't!"

She giggled, and her girlishness surprised me. I almost demurred. My head was already starting to swirl from the first drink. But then I felt an uncharacteristic rush of recklessness. Why shouldn't I have another cocktail? My children were safe and accounted for. I wasn't driving.

"If we're going to have another round, let me get it," I said, digging out my wallet.

Kat waved me away. "Too late. Besides, you're doing me a favor. I was bored to tears sitting here by myself before you came along."

Over our second round of drinks, which I was careful to sip much more slowly, Kat and I got to know one another. She grew up in Palm Beach, and her parents and brother still lived there. She had studied art history at Tulane, and after graduation, she had landed a plum job with the Hirshhorn Museum at the Smithsonian in Washington, DC. She had worked there for two years before returning home to Florida to open her small art gallery near Worth Avenue in Palm Beach. She'd met her husband, Howard—who, she said with a dismissive wave of her hand, did "something in finance"—when he came into the gallery looking for a painting.

"He didn't have any interest in art. He just had blank walls in his condo and was looking for investment pieces to hang there," Kat explained.

"Did he end up buying one from you?"

"Yes, but at that point, he was more interested in trying to impress me than he was in the art." Kat smiled, again displaying her straight white teeth. "It didn't work, of course. But he eventually wore me down."

"How long have you been married?"

"Eighteen wonderful years," Kat answered, holding up her martini glass. "Or more like two wonderful years and sixteen mediocre ones. Oh, well. How about you?"

I thought Kat was probably kidding, since her tone was

light, and I could already tell she had a sardonic sense of humor. But I had the feeling there was some truth hidden inside the joke.

I told her that I'd grown up in Syracuse and gone to the university there and then Cornell for graduate school. After I graduated, I accepted a job as an assistant professor at the University of Miami. Unlike Kat, I didn't have a cute story about how I'd met my husband. Todd certainly didn't woo me by buying expensive artwork, or whatever the equivalent would be in my line of work. Instead I'd met him at a rather pedestrian birthday party for one of my work colleagues. We chatted over plastic cups of boxed red wine and paper plates of previously frozen lasagna. A week later, Todd called and asked me out. On our first date, we went to the movies.

"Sometimes I wonder if the concept of marriage to one person for the rest of your life is unrealistic," Kat mused.

I glanced at my children. They were both immersed in their electronic handheld games and weren't paying any attention to us.

"I know what you mean," I said, making sure to keep my voice low. "Everyone always says that marriage is something you have to work at. But I don't think it's possible to grasp what that means until you've been married for a while. The constant grind of it."

"On my wedding day, my mother told me the secret to a happy marriage is to develop a blind eye and a forgiving heart," Kat said. She rolled her eyes dramatically. "As you can probably imagine, that gave me all sorts of unwanted insights into my parents' marriage."

"She told you that on your wedding day?" I laughed. "I'm surprised you went through with it."

"I know, but I really liked my dress," Kat confessed. "I thought it was fabulous. It had this high neck and huge puffy sleeves." She demonstrated by drawing circles in the air away from her arm. "Looking back, it was hideous, of course."

"We are ready to begin boarding Flight 523 to West Palm Beach," a female voice announced over the loudspeaker. A cheer went up from the ragged horde of travelers waiting by the gate. "We would like to invite our first-class passengers to board now."

"That's me," Kat said, hopping off her stool and shouldering an expensive-looking orange leather handbag along with her designer carry-on. She was shorter than I had expected, even in high-heeled boots. Kat looked at me expectantly. "Are you coming?"

I laughed. "Oh, no. We're not in first class. The Campbell family always flies steerage."

"What a bummer," Kat exclaimed. "I was hoping we'd be sitting near each other. It's been fun talking to you."

"You, too," I said, feeling incredibly flattered by her warm words. "Bye."

Kat strode off, seemingly unaffected by the alcohol. The two martinis had made me light-headed, and I fumbled with our bags as I got the children organized to board. When we walked onto the plane, Kat was comfortably ensconced in her plush first-class seat, studying a magazine. She didn't look up as we passed by.

I probably would never have seen Kat again if not for a mishap at baggage claim when we reached Palm Beach International Airport.

Todd met us at the security checkpoint, kissed me hello and hugged Liam and Bridget. The family Campbell made our way to the baggage carousel just as it ground into motion and began spitting out suitcases. I noticed Kat on the other side of the carousel, standing alone while she waited for her bag. I wondered why her husband hadn't met her but shrugged it off. Maybe he was out of town, or she had a car waiting to pick her up. Either way, it really wasn't any of my business.

I watched as Kat grabbed her suitcase off the conveyor belt, snapped the pull handle up and turned to stride off in what I was already recognizing as her signature walk—a little faster than necessary, as though it perplexed her that everyone else was moving so slowly. Then I saw something fall out of her shoulder bag. Kat didn't notice it.

"Kat," I called after her, but she didn't hear me. I turned to Todd. "I'll be right back."

Before my husband could respond, I darted forward and around the conveyor belt before anyone saw the dropped item. It was a wallet, made of leather and stamped with the same Hermes brand as her handbag. It probably cost more money than Todd and I currently had in our checking account. I bent down to pick it up just as a man—white-haired, pot-bellied and grunting with the effort—was moving toward it.

"It's my friend's," I explained. "She dropped it."

The man gaped at me, but I was already turning away to hurry after Kat. I reached her just as she got to the sliding glass exit doors.

"Kat!" I said. "Wait! You dropped your wallet."

Kat turned, her eyes wide with surprise. I held up the Hermes wallet.

"Oh, no!" Kat exclaimed, taking it from me and pressing it to her chest. "I can't believe I did that! Can you imagine what a disaster it would have been if I lost my wallet? All of my cards are in here. And my license. I can't believe I was that stupid. Thank you so much, Alice."

"It's no problem. I'm just glad I saw it before someone else grabbed it."

"I am, too! I can't thank you enough."

I waved her apology away and smiled. "It was nice meeting you earlier," I said, and just as I was about to turn away and head back to my waiting family, Kat rested a hand on my arm to stop me.

"Let me take you to lunch," Kat said. "So I can properly show my appreciation."

"You really don't have to do that. It wasn't a big deal at all."

"It is to me. Besides, I liked talking with you, too. It would be fun to get together again." When Kat smiled, the angles of her face softened, and she looked suddenly younger and prettier.

"Okay," I said impulsively. "I'd love to."

We made vague plans to have lunch the following week and exchanged phone numbers. Kat squeezed my arm. "I'm looking forward to it."

Todd and the children had retrieved our suitcases and were waiting for me back at the luggage carousel.

"Who was that?" Todd asked.

"Just a woman I met while we were delayed at JFK," I said. "We might get together for lunch or something."

"Aw, look at you. You made a friend," Todd teased me.

I gave him a whack on the arm. "Come on, let's get home. We're exhausted."

4

Three Years Earlier

THE K-GALLERY WAS located on Highway A1A on the island of Palm Beach, not far from Worth Avenue. It occupied the ground floor of a five-story building that was painted peach with elaborate white cornices. I probably would have missed it if the GPS in my car hadn't insisted that I had arrived at the correct address. The only signage was a simple brass plate next to the door.

Feeling a little nervous in a way that strangely reminded me of being the new kid at school on the first day of classes, I opened the large glass-paned door, setting off a chime as I entered. K-Gallery had white walls and a dark hardwood floor. It was spacious and airy. Small sculptures of twisted metal wire were displayed on white pedestals. A series of large abstract canvases hung on the walls, painted in moody blues and stormy grays. They reminded me of the finger paintings my children had made when they were little, although I thought I probably shouldn't mention that to Kat.

"Alice!" Kat called, sweeping into the room. She gave me a quick hug, which I returned. "I'm so glad we were able to get together."

"I am, too." I had been surprised but pleased when she called me a week after our flight back to West Palm Beach and invited me to lunch.

Kat was wearing an immaculate sleeveless white shift dress and black heeled sandals. I was glad I had opted to dress up for our lunch, wearing a cotton sweater and skirt I'd bought on clearance at J.Crew, instead of my usual uniform that consisted of a T-shirt and yoga pants.

Kat noticed that I was admiring the wire sculptures. "Aren't they exquisite? They were done by an artist in Miami who welds in a storage locker with no air-conditioning, if you can believe it. I think he's going to be the next big thing."

"The paintings are incredible, too."

"You think?" Kat tipped her head to one side, regarding the closest one, which featured wild swirls of olive green paint. "They're by an English artist named Crispin Murray. He's quite successful, and they sell wonderfully. But I have to admit, his paintings always remind me of the ones my daughter brought home when she was in preschool."

I laughed. "I actually thought the exact same thing but was afraid it would sound gauche if I admitted as much. Especially since I don't know anything about modern art."

"Not at all! I can't stand it when people get pompous about art, as though there's only one valid opinion. Art is supposed to elicit a reaction from you. Or at least, good art is. And your reaction is as valid as anyone else's." Kat waved a hand. "Enough with the art talk. Let's go eat. I'm starving."

Kat suggested we eat at Renato's, an Italian bistro on Worth Avenue. It was a glorious day, cool and sunny, so we decided to walk to the restaurant.

Even though Palm Beach was only a short drive from Jupiter, I hadn't spent much time on the tony island. As we strolled down the sidewalk, I was struck by how picturesque it was, from the neat rows of royal palms to the luxury stores housed in Mediterranean-style buildings to the Rolls-Royces and Aston Martins parked on the street. My earlier nerves dissipated, replaced by a frothy, bubbling sense of well-being. Here there were no dishes to wash, no homework assignments to check over, no piles of laundry to fold. Only a delicious lunch to look forward to and, possibly, a new friendship.

We decided to sit in the elegant outdoor courtyard, which was filled with round tables dressed in starched white linens and surrounded by flowering bougainvillea. Our waiter, who was young and handsome with a slight build, beamed at Kat as he handed her a menu.

"Welcome back, Mrs. Grant." He spoke with a slight Italian accent. "It's nice to see you again."

"You know I can't stay away," Kat said, returning his smile. "I'm craving the risotto."

The waiter rolled his eyes upward. "It is sublime, no? Shall I bring you the wine list?"

Kat looked at me and asked mischievously, "What do you think? Should we?"

I almost never drank wine at lunch, other than the occasional indulgence on vacation. But I was suddenly feeling festive.

"Why not?" I said.

Kat ordered a bottle of something white and imported, and the waiter swiftly returned with the bottle in hand. After he went through the presentation of uncorking it, offering Kat a taste and filling our glasses, he set the bottle in a silver bucket of ice. Kat raised her glass to me.

"Cheers," she said. "To new friendships."

We clinked our glasses together. The wine was cold and crisp and delicious.

"Your gallery is beautiful," I said.

"Thank you," Kat said. I would later learn that Kat always

accepted compliments with a simple thank-you. She did not brush them off with the self-deprecating remarks many women, including myself, fell back on. Kat was not an especially vain woman, but she was perfectly willing to accept compliments on her appearance, her taste, her home, as nothing more than an obvious truth.

"How long has your gallery been open?" I asked.

"It's hard to believe, but nearly twenty years. I opened it when I was pregnant with Amanda, and she turned nineteen in November," Kat said.

"I thought you said you met your husband at your gallery." I immediately regretted this intrusive remark. The details of when she'd met her husband and when she'd given birth to her daughter were none of my business.

But Kat didn't seem put out. She just smiled and said, "You have a good memory. Yes, I met Howard after Amanda was born."

"I'm sorry. I didn't mean to pry."

"You didn't. It's not a secret. Well, it's not a secret that Howard isn't Amanda's biological father. The truth is—" Kat leaned forward and dropped her voice to a conspiratorial whisper "—when I was living in DC, I had an affair with a married man. A politician, if you can believe it. I know, it was reckless. But I was young and selfish, and foolish enough to believe that my feelings were more important than his family." She shook her head. "Looking back, I want to slap my younger self for being such a brat."

"Don't be so hard on yourself," I said. "Everyone makes bad choices when they're young."

"Yes," Kat agreed. "But trust me, I deserve to be hard on myself. I did my best to convince him to leave his perfectly nice and blameless wife and their two young children. All because I was in love."

"He was the one who was breaking his vows," I said. "So he was more at fault than you were."

I wasn't sure why I was arguing the point. Of course, Kat was right. What she had done was selfish and destructive. But at the same time, twenty years of self-flagellation seemed a heavy price to pay. I'd also noticed that she hadn't named her daughter's father. I wondered if he was someone I would've known from the news.

"I'm sure you won't be surprised to learn he didn't turn out to be a good guy in the end," Kat said. "When I told him I was pregnant, he ended the relationship. Actually, first he tried to talk me into having an abortion, and then, after I refused, he said he never wanted to see me again."

"Wasn't he worried you'd bring a paternity suit against him?"

"No." Kat shook her dark, glossy head. "He knew I'd never do that. Anyway, I decided it was time to leave DC and headed home to Florida. My mother was horrified, of course—she's easily horrified—but my father was more pragmatic. He said if I was going to be a single mother, I needed to have a business to support us, so he encouraged me to open K-Gallery."

"Had you always wanted to open an art gallery?" I asked.

"Not really. Before I got pregnant, I was working at the Smithsonian and thought that if things didn't work out with the married man, I would probably move to London or Paris, where I'd work as a curator for one of the great museums." Kat rolled her eyes. "I'm sure whatever I imagined that life to be like was something out of a movie and not in any way rooted in reality. Romantic dinners at a Paris café, cocktails at the glamorous hotel bars, love affairs with handsome foreigners. I certainly wasn't calculating in the long hours, toiling away in an office to build the sort of career I imagined myself having. It's not like they hire twentysomethings to buy

Renoirs or organize Rodin exhibits. And the simple truth is that I wasn't ambitious or driven to succeed in that sort of world. There are too many hungrier candidates for those positions out there. So in the end, having my own gallery has suited me very well. I can exhibit art that interests me and close early for the day when I feel like it. And, of course, I had Amanda. The affair was a bad choice, obviously, but having her was not."

I listened to Kat's story with interest. I was impressed that she was self-aware enough to recognize and accept her limitations. But it was also true that unlike most of those hungrier would-be art curators, Kat had enough money to open her own art gallery in Palm Beach.

Our conversation was interrupted by the return of the handsome waiter, eager to take our order. Kat ordered the lobster risotto. I chose a decadent-sounding dish of fettuccine with grilled chicken in a light cream sauce. The waiter effusively praised our choices and hurried away.

"Amanda was just a few months old when I met Howard. So he's the only father she's ever known," Kat said. She paused to take a sip of her wine. "Actually, Amanda is probably what brought us together. Howard was definitely not my type. But between having a baby and getting the gallery up and running, I was so overwhelmed. Hormonal, too, I suppose, and still nursing a broken heart. And Howard was just so—"

She stopped abruptly, searching to find the right word. I expected her to say something like *kind* or *supportive* or *nurturing.*

But instead she said, "Forceful."

"Forceful," I repeated. It did not seem, to me at least, to be a foundation for romance. Sexual excitement, perhaps, but that usually wasn't enough of a basis for eighteen years of marriage. At least, I didn't think it was.

"Yes. Howard's primary motivation in every aspect of his life is to get what he wants when he wants it. He's unapologetic about it." Kat lifted her wineglass to her lips again. "And at that time, I was just so tired. Tired of making the decisions, tired of being in charge of everything, tired of my mother's endless badgering that I needed to get married for Amanda's sake. Not that Howard was ever all that interested in being a father." Kat laughed. "But he was more than happy to step in and straighten out my life. Suddenly I was hiring an assistant for the gallery and a full-time nanny for the baby and then, somehow, planning a wedding. I think if I had ever stopped to catch my breath and really thought about what I was doing, I would never have gone through with it."

"Which part?"

"The part where I married a man I wasn't in love with," Kat said. She lifted one shoulder in a shrug. "But I did. And here I still am eighteen years later."

"Why are you still married?" Then, realizing that I might again be dangerously close to crossing a too-personal line, I raised a hand. "I'm sorry. That was intrusive. You don't have to answer."

"No, it's fine. I just don't have a good answer. A divorce would be messy and expensive..."

"And you had your daughter to think of," I offered.

"Actually, I'm not sure how much our divorcing would bother Amanda. She and Howard have never been close. I've often wondered if that's because she wasn't his, at least not biologically," Kat said.

"Did Howard adopt her?"

Kat nodded. "When Amanda was twelve. I thought it might bring them closer together, but..." She trailed off and shrugged. "It didn't work out that way. I think Howard always resented the time and attention I gave to Amanda. And Amanda's a smart girl. I'm sure she sensed it."

I couldn't imagine happily living with a man who resented

my children. Todd might've had his failings, but he adored our Liam and Bridget as much as I did.

"Anyway, it's not like I have any interest in joining the local singles scene. Online dating and all that," Kat continued. She gave an exaggerated shudder. "It's always seemed easier to keep the status quo. Anyway, that's enough about me." She smiled. "What about you?"

"I don't have any plans to get divorced in the foreseeable future, either," I said lightly.

"I meant your career. You said you used to teach at the University of Miami, right?" Kat said. "Logic, but not the Mr. Spock kind."

I laughed, flattered that she'd remembered. "That's right."

"Why did you give it up?"

I hesitated. It wasn't that I wanted to conceal the truth from Kat, especially when she had just been so forthcoming with me. But sharing my past would cast a pall on what had been until now such a lovely day.

Kat seemed to sense my discomfort. "Am I being intrusive?" she asked, borrowing my earlier line.

"No, not at all." I took a deep breath. It was never a good idea to start any relationship with lies. "It's just… It's a sad story. My daughter Bridget had a twin sister. They were both born prematurely. Bridget was fine—*is* fine—but my other daughter…she didn't make it."

I had told this story dozens of times over the past eight years. It had gotten easier in some ways. The dark, suffocating grief that had crippled me in the days and weeks following my daughter's death had eventually receded. I could now talk about my lost baby without instantly dissolving into tears. But the heavy weight of her absence in the world was still there. In a way, I treasured this. If I ever stopped missing her, it would mean that my daughter, the one who left the world before she could ever make her mark on it, would be forgotten forever.

Usually when I did tell people about her death, this was the point when they would lean forward, face creased with horrified sympathy. They would pat my arm and tell me how sorry they were, how much it must comfort me that Bridget survived. This was true, of course. I was lucky in many ways—I had two healthy children, and that was something no parent should ever take for granted. But it was also true that no bereaved parent ever wanted to hear that her living children made up for a dead one. It didn't work that way.

But here again, Kat surprised me. "What was her name?"

"Meghan." My voice cracked a bit. I cleared my throat. "Her name was Meghan."

"Meghan," Kat repeated. "That's a beautiful name. Were she and Bridget identical twins?"

I nodded. "We were so surprised when they did the ultrasound."

"Do you know what caused you to deliver early?"

"Placental abruption, although my doctors didn't know what caused it. Everything was fine, all my checkups were great...and then suddenly everything wasn't fine, and I was in labor two months ahead of schedule. But even then, even after the delivery, both babies were doing well at first. They were small, of course, and we knew they'd have to spend some time in the NICU. But the doctors kept reassuring us that they were doing well, that they'd be able to come home soon, so I wasn't worried."

I stopped and took a sip of wine to steady myself. That lack of worry, that blind trust in the doctors' feckless pronouncements, still haunted me on the nights when I lay awake. Kat was silent, still looking at me, her focus absolute.

I continued. "Then Meghan had a brain hemorrhage. And she just...died."

My mouth was suddenly unbearably dry. I reached for my water glass and took a large gulp from it. I could feel the pricks of unshed tears gathering in my eyes. I willed them away. If there was one thing Meghan's death had taught me, it was that crying didn't fix anything. It certainly didn't bring back the person who was gone forever.

"That," Kat said, "is a fucking nightmare."

The unexpected profanity made me laugh and then choke slightly on the water. I dabbed at my mouth with my napkin.

"Are you okay?" Kat exclaimed, reaching a hand out.

I waved her off. "No, you're right. It *was* a fucking nightmare."

Kat relaxed back in her seat. "I'll say. You were not only experiencing one of the worst things that can happen to any mother but also taking care of a newborn." Kat shook her head and drained the rest of her wine. She reached for the bottle and poured each of us another large glass. "I'm so sorry you had to go through that. No wonder you left your job. It would have been too much for anyone to cope with. I can't even imagine. I think I'd have a hard time just getting out of bed in the morning."

"Oh, I struggled. That's the thing about grief. It's just… suffocating. Like you're being buried alive. And even the easiest tasks, like showering or eating or even brushing your teeth, suddenly seem insurmountable." Then I shook my head and smiled regretfully at Kat. "I'm sorry. This isn't a very cheerful topic of conversation. I'm putting a damper on our lunch."

"No, you're not, not one bit. I asked you a question and you answered it honestly. Frankly, it's refreshing to talk to someone who doesn't feel the need to bullshit her way through life." Kat patted my hand. "I'm glad I called you. I'm usually terrible about following through on things. But I have a feeling that you and I are going to be good friends."

She raised her glass, and I clinked mine against hers.

"To new friendships," I toasted.

"I am home and I have pizza," I called out, using my foot to push open the back door that led into our house from the garage. My hands were filled with a grease-stained pizza box. Half cheese, half sausage and onion, with a side order of garlic knots.

"Mom's home!" Liam hollered, not looking up from the Xbox game he was absorbed in.

"No, don't get up," I told him. "You don't have to eat any pizza. There'll be more for the rest of us."

Liam rolled his eyes but grinned. He hopped up, gave me a quick hug and headed toward the kitchen. Bridget was there, sitting at the kitchen table, frowning down at her homework.

"Hi, honey," I said, trying to remember if I'd even had homework in elementary school. I didn't think so. Some in middle school. Both of my children came home from school every day with their backpacks full to bursting. "What are you working on?"

"Science," she said moodily. "And it's really hard."

"Where's Dad?"

"Right here," Todd said, coming into the kitchen. He kissed me on the cheek and plucked the pizza box out of my hands. "We're all starving."

"Sorry I'm late," I said. "Thanks for picking the kids up from school."

Once I'd realized that lunch was extending into the late afternoon, I'd texted Todd from the restaurant and asked him to handle the school run. It meant that both kids had to wait in aftercare until Todd arrived.

"I hate staying late at school," Bridget complained. "Where were you, anyway?"

"I was having lunch with a friend."

"You've been at lunch all this time?" Liam asked. "It's dark out!"

"After lunch, we went shopping, and then we had coffee." I shrugged. "We started chatting and lost track of time."

"Stop giving your mom a hard time," Todd said. "She gets to have a day off every now and then."

I smiled at my husband, feeling a surge of affection for him. "It was nice to do something out of the ordinary."

"Lunch in Palm Beach compares favorably to laundry and the school run?" Todd teased.

I laughed. "Surprisingly, yes, it does."

Todd grabbed plates and napkins while I poured glasses of water for everyone. Once we were seated at the table, I got reports from the children on their days. Liam shrugged and said his was okay, which was pretty much what he said every day, and then returned his attention to stuffing pizza in his mouth. Bridget launched into a very long story involving hurt feelings and drama over a game of four square played by her classmates that, in the end, had nothing to do with her at all, because she was on the opposite side of the playground when it happened.

"But if you weren't participating in the game, why do you care that Annalise got so upset?" I asked. "I thought you didn't even like Annalise."

"I don't like her. That's the whole point," Bridget said hotly.

I looked at Todd to see if he had any insight into these third-grade dramatics, but he just shrugged and shook his head. After dinner, the children cleared the plates and headed off to their nightly bedtime routines. Todd got a beer from the fridge.

"You had a nice time today?" he asked, sitting back down at the kitchen table.

I poured myself a glass of red wine and joined him.

"Yes, I did. Kat's great. I'm glad she called me."

"What's she like?"

"She's smart and funny and really has her act together. She owns the most beautiful modern art gallery."

"You're smart and funny," Todd said loyally.

I smiled and put my hand on his arm. "It was nice having someone different to talk to. Almost everyone I know here I've met through the kids in one way or another. Moms from school, women from the playgroups the kids were in when they were little. Don't get me wrong, they're nice ladies. Or at least, most of them are. But every time I get together with any of them, the conversation revolves around the children. What the moms are doing at the PTA. Whom they're friends with, whatever the latest drama is at school. It just gets so tedious."

Todd's eyebrows arched, but he didn't speak.

"Don't judge," I said. I loved being a mother, but there were so many aspects of it, especially when my children were little, that I found mind-numbing. Singing the same cloying songs every week in the Mommy & Me class. Sitting on the cold tile floor during bath time. The hours spent at playgrounds being commanded over and over to "Watch me! Watch me!"

Having children was a wonderful, miraculous, soulful experience. Just not each and every moment of it. I found motherhood easier to cope with now that Liam and Bridget were older and more independent.

"It was nice to talk to someone about other things. About art and work and life," I said.

Todd nodded and took a sip of his beer. "Does Kat have children?"

"Yes, a daughter, but she's in college."

"Kat's older than you, then?"

"A bit, although she did say she had her daughter when she was young," I explained. "I think she's in her mid to late forties."

"Do you think you'll get together with her again?"

I rolled my wineglass in my fingers, the way I'd once been taught at a wine-tasting class, and watched the bloodred liquid stream down the inside of the glass.

"Yes," I said. "I think I will."

5

Present Day

"I'M CURIOUS ABOUT SOMETHING," Sergeant Oliver said. "Why did you think Howard Grant was suicidal? I thought you said you weren't close."

"We weren't. And I never told you I thought he was suicidal. I thought that's what Detective Demer was suggesting."

"I don't think he suggested that at all," Oliver said, fixing her eyes on me. They were dark and flat, like a shark. I wondered again why she was being so hostile. Had she met Kat, not liked her and extended her dislike to me? Kat could be charming and funny, but I had also seen her turn suddenly cold and imperious, especially when she was challenged. It was not hard to imagine Oliver affecting her that way.

"I have a question," I said. Oliver just stared at me, but Demer nodded, so I addressed him. "You said you were brought in from Tallahassee. Why was that?"

Demer glanced at Oliver. "It's not uncommon for a small police department not to have any detectives on staff. Sometimes when there is a situation that requires a more in-depth investigation, they'll request a detective on loan."

"So, I'm not sure how this works. Are you and Oliver partners in this investigation?" I asked. "Or are you in charge, and she's reporting to you?"

I knew instantly from the sour expression on Oliver's face that they were not, in fact, partners. Demer was the lead, Oliver his unhappy subordinate.

"I'm taking point on the investigation for the time being," Demer said mildly. "Let's go back to your friendship with Katherine Grant. How long have you known each other?"

"Three years."

"And you're close friends?"

"Yes," I said. "Very close."

"How would you describe Katherine Grant?" Demer asked.

It was odd hearing Kat constantly referred to by her full name. She had always been Kat to me.

"How would I describe Kat?" I repeated. How did you distill someone you loved down to a few words? "She's funny. Smart. Thoughtful. Loyal. Generous... Solid."

Solid? Was that really Kat? I wasn't so sure. Kat was more like quicksilver, shimmering and changing. You'd think you knew her, were sure you could predict absolutely what she'd do, and she'd still somehow find a way to surprise you. Oh, well, I had already said it. I couldn't exactly take it back now, could I?

Oliver didn't actually roll her eyes at my description, but I think it took all her willpower to avoid doing so. I sensed that she was not the sort of woman who'd ever had a best friend. Certainly not the kind of best friend who rubbed her pricked finger against yours to become your blood sister. I actually could relate. I had never been that sort of a woman before, either.

"Would you say that Howard and Katherine Grant had a happy marriage?" Demer asked.

I hesitated. The truthful answer would be no, they certainly did not. But I also didn't see any benefit in telling the police that.

"I don't think anyone on the outside ever truly knows what goes on inside a marriage," I said carefully.

Demer smiled patiently. "No, probably not. I'm just asking for any impressions you might have formed from being around them."

"That's just it. Whenever I saw the two of them together, well, I was there, wasn't I? Most married people behave differently when there are other people around. I know my husband and I do."

It was a nonanswer, but if it frustrated Demer, he hid it well. Oliver, on the other hand, looked like she wanted to slap me.

"Fair enough," Demer said. "Did Katherine ever complain about her husband?"

"Kat," I corrected him.

"Excuse me?"

"She goes by Kat, not Katherine."

"Okay. Kat, then. So, did she?"

"Complain about her husband?" I repeated. He nodded. "Sure, from time to time. I hate to break it to you, Detective, but most women complain about their husbands to their friends."

The wonderful thing about this statement was that it had the benefit of being the absolute truth.

"Let's get back to Howard Grant," Demer said.

My patience was starting to fray. "I've already told you, I wasn't close with Howard. I was friends with Kat. I suggest you talk to her if you want to know about her husband."

"Oh, we've already talked to Katherine Grant," Oliver inserted.

Something about this bald statement caused a flicker of concern at the edges of my consciousness. I wasn't sure what exactly about it bothered me. Of course, it only made sense that they would interview Kat as part of their investigation, even if she was out of the country at the time of Howard's death. But then, suddenly, I realized what the problem was. Kat hadn't told me the police had been to see her. And we told each other everything, or almost everything. I knew when her insomnia was acting up, and when the dry cleaner ruined her favorite dress, and usually what she'd had for dinner the night before. So why didn't she call to tell me the police had questioned her about her husband's death?

"When did you speak with Kat?" I asked.

Demer shot Oliver a glance. She shrugged but didn't say anything more. I suddenly had the distinct feeling that there was something more going on here. That the police had not asked me to come in simply to give them background information.

"What is this all about, anyway? Why are you asking me about Kat and Howard's marriage?" I pressed.

"Like I said, we're looking for background," Demer said. "We're just trying to make sure we've covered everything."

"And they brought you all the way down here from Tallahassee to do that?" I asked.

Demer looked at me steadily but didn't answer my question. It was clear there was something going on, some reason they had for questioning me, and I didn't know what that was.

"Why don't you tell us about when you first met Howard Grant?" Demer suggested.

"I'm not sure if I remember," I said, thinking back. "It would have been three years ago."

"Try," the detective said. "Take your time."

6

Three Years Earlier

"WHAT ARE YOU doing in here?" Todd asked.

I started violently but managed not to scream. I was sitting in our home office, working on the computer with my back to the door that led off the front hallway. Our garage was on the opposite side of our one-story house, so I hadn't heard Todd come home. I had always hated being startled. Horror movies, haunted houses, practical jokes—these were not among my favorite things. I also didn't like the idea of someone entering my house without my being aware of it, even if that someone was my husband.

"Don't sneak up on me like that," I said, willing my heart rate to return to normal.

"Sorry," Todd said mildly. He dropped a kiss on the top of my head, and I could smell the scent of sweat still clinging to his body.

"How was your match?" I asked.

"First, ask me this… Who is the king of tennis?"

"Who is the king of tennis?"

"Me! I am the king of tennis. I just pulled out the win in a third set tiebreaker." Todd raised two triumphant fists over his head. "I ended the match with an ace. It was so sweet. Maybe the best match of my life."

"Good job," I dutifully supplied.

"Good job? Is that all you can say?"

"What else do you need from me?" I asked. "Congratulations on your win? Yay you?"

"A little enthusiasm would be nice. That's the first time I've ever beaten Joe Hammond. He's owned me until now."

Todd was a tennis fanatic and competed weekly in a local league. It was basically a bunch of middle-aged men playing at night after work, but they took it so seriously that you might have thought they were training for Wimbledon. Still, I was glad Todd had an outlet. When work started to overwhelm him and he wasn't able to play, my husband became tense and moody. Far better he took his stress out on a little yellow ball. However, there were some downsides to his hobby.

"Speaking of tennis," I said, "I was going over the bills, and I wanted to ask you about something. Did you really spend $224 at an online tennis store? I was hoping that was a mistake on the bill."

I could see from my husband's sheepish expression that it was not. My spirits plummeted.

"I know, I know," he said, holding his hands up. "It was an impulse purchase."

"What was?"

"A new racquet. But it's the racquet Federer plays with. I was just going to try it out—they let you take it out on a test run and then return it if you don't like it—but I couldn't *not* keep it. It's the best racquet I've ever played with. It's the racquet that helped me finally beat Joe Hammond! Anyway, it was on sale."

Tension tightened my shoulders, and acid roiled in my stomach. I took a deep breath, trying to contain the anxiety, not to lose my temper.

"We can't afford a purchase like that right now." I pointed to the Visa statement I had pulled up on the computer. "Have you seen this lately? Our balance is over ten thousand dollars. That's the limit. We're now officially maxed out."

I could have continued with a full accounting of our current financial struggles. We were a few weeks late paying the mortgage because the majority of Todd's last paycheck had been swallowed up by an expensive car repair. The school tuition bill was due. Liam's birthday was in two weeks and he had been begging for a laser tag party, which we couldn't afford at the moment.

It was times like these, the nights when I was poring over the bills, trying to figure out where I could cut our already tight budget, that I tried to remember why I had ever given up my job. But almost as soon as the question floated up into my consciousness, I would remember anew, with a fresh jolt of pain. It hadn't been a choice to stop working but a necessity. The grief I experienced after losing Meghan was a dark, smothering force that robbed me of my will to do just about anything. Eating, sleeping and showering were all equally unappealing options. But I had a three-year-old and a newborn to take care of. Falling off a cliff wasn't a luxury I could indulge in.

I had arranged for a three-month maternity leave before I gave birth to the twins. When that time was up and I was still struggling, I went to see the dean of the math department. He suggested I take the rest of the semester off. But even when the grief started to recede and I slowly rejoined the world, going back to work still seemed like an impossible task. Then Todd was offered a job in West Palm Beach, which at the time seemed to offer a fresh start for our family.

But it also meant that we suddenly went from enjoying a comfortable two-income existence to living on one. We learned to make do while we waited for the raises and bonuses

Todd had been promised when he was hired. We made up the difference with a series of credit cards we were paying only the minimum on each month to cover the unexpected expenses. A repair to the air-conditioning unit at our house. A cavity that needed filling. Tennis club memberships.

"It was only $200," Todd said. He crossed his arms over his chest. "Besides, how much have you been spending on all of those lunches out with Kat?"

"I don't spend $200 on lunch," I retorted.

"No, but $30 a couple times a week adds up."

"So it's okay for you to burn through money on your tennis hobby, but I'm not allowed to have a social life?" I hated how thin and brittle I sounded. But I resented more that we couldn't have the simplest conversation about our finances without it turning into a fight.

"I didn't say that. Jesus, why do you have to be such a..." Todd struggled to find the proper word to describe just how awful a person I was.

"Bitch?"

"I did not say that," Todd said, pointing at me. "I would never call you that."

Bridget appeared at the door to the office, looking anxious. She was wearing ladybug-print pajamas, and her hair was tousled. She was clutching Leo, her well-loved plush lion, to her chest.

"Are you fighting?" she asked in a small voice.

"No, we're just talking," I said at the same time Todd was saying, "No, honey, everything's fine."

"You were shouting," Bridget said. "It woke me up."

"We weren't shouting. We were just talking a little... loudly," Todd said.

Bridget's lower lip trembled. "It scared me."

"We'll keep our voices down," I said, hoping the smile I gave her looked more genuine than it felt.

"Come on, Monkey, I'll tuck you in," Todd said, holding out his hand.

"Good night, sweetheart," I called after them.

Todd didn't return to the office to continue our fight after getting Bridget settled. I found him in the kitchen, a beer in his hand while he flipped through the mail on the kitchen counter. I rubbed a tired hand across my face and decided to leave the argument about the Visa bill for another day.

"Don't forget Kat invited us over for dinner tomorrow night," I reminded him.

"Oh, right. To celebrate your book," Todd said. His face relaxed. "That's some good news, for a change."

I had gotten the word a few days earlier. My book of logic puzzles would be published by a small university press. The advance I was getting was nominal—certainly not enough to make much of a dent in our current financial woes—but it was still an exciting development. Even this small success—or at least, small compared to the publishing I'd hoped to accomplish in the course of my academic career—made me feel a little more like the Alice I'd been before Meghan's death.

"So I'm finally going to meet the mysterious Kat," Todd said. He lifted his bottle of beer in a mock toast, then brought it to his lips.

"She's hardly mysterious," I said, annoyed by his flippant tone.

"She is to me," Todd said. "What's her husband like? What's his name?"

"Howard, and I'm not sure. I've never met him."

"But you don't like him?"

"Why would you think that? I just said I've never met him."

"Yes, but right after you said it, you did that thing you do when you disapprove of something or someone. You twist your lips up."

"I don't do that." As I said it, I could feel my lips starting to twist. What a horrible habit to have developed.

"Yes, you do. You do it all the time," Todd said. "You did it a few minutes ago when you were asking about the charge on the credit card."

I hated the idea of having a tell and decided that I would not allow my lips to twist ever again.

But Todd was right. I wasn't at all sure I was going to like Howard. Whenever Kat talked about her husband, which wasn't very often, she hadn't exactly extolled the positives. Howard was selfish, she'd told me, and people often found him abrasive.

"I finally get to meet the mysterious Kat and her apparently unlikable husband. That should make for an interesting night," Todd mused. He took another long draw from his beer.

I used to find my husband's insouciance charming. I wondered when that had stopped.

7

Three Years Earlier

I KNEW BY then that Kat and Howard were very wealthy. Kat drove a sporty new Porsche convertible with creamy leather seats. Her clothes were all impeccably cut and clearly not purchased at The Gap, where most of my wardrobe came from. The bag she carried was probably worth more than my car. And she had already disclosed that her house wasn't in the town of Jupiter, where I lived, but on the far tonier, far more expensive Jupiter Island.

But Kat was my friend. My very good friend, the person I was starting to confide in even more than my husband. When I received the email from the publisher to tell me that they wanted to publish my book, I had called Kat before Todd. Although, to be fair, she'd been far more excited for me than my husband had been. The difference in our respective net worths shouldn't have mattered. It *didn't* matter. All it meant was that Kat was quicker to pick up the lunch check and more likely to splurge on a nice bottle of wine for us to share.

But then I saw where she lived, and I realized just how different our lives really were.

Todd pulled our Volvo wagon into the crushed-stone

driveway, the tires crunching on the gray gravel. We got out of the car and stared up at the building in front of us. The house, which would more accurately be called a mansion, was certainly impressive. It was white stone and built in a U shape around a neatly manicured front courtyard featuring elaborate topiaries. It had casement-style tile windows and a red Spanish tile roof. A detached garage, which looked more like a stable and was large enough to store five cars, was set off to the right of the driveway.

"Holy cow," Todd said, staring up at the house.

"Is that your professional assessment of the architecture?" I teased.

"I think the whole point of that house is for people to look at it and say 'Holy cow.' It isn't exactly subtle. I wonder who designed it."

"You don't know whose work it is?" Todd had an encyclopedic knowledge of the architects behind much of the real estate throughout South Florida.

"No, but it's a fantastic example of the Spanish Colonial Revival style," Todd said. "It's really very nicely done. Look at the detailing around the windows."

We walked up to the front door, an enormous wood-and-glass affair surrounded by a decorative casing nearly two stories tall. I rang the bell and realized suddenly that I was nervous. Why? I wondered. Was it about meeting Howard? Or were my nerves jangling because I wasn't sure Kat and Todd would like one another? But then I heard footsteps echoing against a hard floor and the front door opened.

Howard Grant wasn't at all what I had pictured. For some reason, I had envisioned Kat's husband as a tall, fair man with broad shoulders and a cleft chin. I had no idea where I'd gotten this mental picture, since as far as I could remember, Kat had never described her husband to me.

The real Howard was of average height and very slim. He

had thick dark hair speckled with gray, an aquiline nose and deep-set brown eyes. He wore a black T-shirt and slim-fitting dark blue jeans with soft, expensive-looking brown loafers. When he smiled at us, the expression didn't reach his eyes.

"Howard Grant," he said, holding out his hand to Todd.

"It's nice to meet you. I'm Todd Campbell."

Howard looked at me but did not offer his hand.

"I'm Alice," I said. "Kat's friend."

"Right. The *author*." Howard spoke the word ironically, as though I didn't quite qualify to be called one. I had been predisposed not to like Howard, and so far, he wasn't doing anything to change my mind. But before I could respond, he had turned. Walking away, he called back over one shoulder, "Come on in and let me know what you like to drink."

Todd and I exchanged a look. Todd mouthed, *What the fuck?* which made me laugh and feel a surge of affection for my husband. We did not always have an easy marriage, it was true, but these moments of connection were our saving grace.

We followed Howard through the airy, expansive foyer with marble floors and soaring ceilings. The exterior of the house had been over-the-top, but the interior was austere and curated—more like the K-Gallery. This was especially true when we reached the living room, which featured two black chesterfield sofas, a pair of low-slung white leather chairs and a few tall sculptural potted green plants. It was clear that the furnishings, while lovely, had been left intentionally understated so that the art was the star of the room. I was still not well versed in modern art, but even I could appreciate the visual impact of the large colorful canvases that hung on every wall.

Howard headed for a large and well-stocked glass-and-chrome bar cart set behind one of the chesterfields.

"What can I get you, Todd?" Howard asked. "I have a fantastic twenty-five-year-old Glenmorangie whiskey."

Todd did not drink whiskey. His drink of choice was almost always beer, with an occasional glass of red wine with dinner. But he smiled, squared his shoulders and said, "That sounds great. Thank you."

I had a feeling there was some sort of a man-test at work, where whiskey was a line that had been drawn in the sea grass rug.

Howard had poured them each a glass of whiskey but hadn't yet asked me for my drink order when Kat strolled into the room. As always, Kat was impeccably dressed, tonight in a long red strapless sundress that set off her smooth shoulders and pale arms.

"Alice!" she cried, folding me into a hug. Then she turned to Todd and smiled. "And you must be Todd. Unless, of course, Alice decided to pick up a date for the evening."

I could tell that Todd was charmed by Kat, and also that he hadn't expected to be. I suspected that he wanted to categorize Kat as a "bad influence," a snake charmer who seduced his wife away from her domestic life into wasting time and money over long, gossipy lunches. But if there was one word that could entirely sum up Kat's character, it was that she was, more than anything else, charming.

"Don't tell me you started pouring whiskeys for you and Todd before you got Alice a drink," Kat exclaimed, turning to her husband.

Howard winced and said, "Oops," while Kat turned to me with an exasperated sigh.

"He always does this. He makes sure the men have drinks and leaves us women to fend for ourselves," Kat complained.

Howard gave a theatrical eye roll. "Women," he said in a mock-withering tone. "Can't please them."

I knew we were supposed to take the exchange as witty banter, a cocktail-hour performance for our benefit. But I sensed a real simmering antagonism behind their words.

Howard and Todd found some common ground over a discussion of professional tennis, of which Howard was also a fan. While they debated the merits of Nadal versus Federer, Kat and I slipped off to the kitchen, which was another huge space featuring dark cabinets and a dramatic marble island with gold stools lining one side. A wonderful aroma of cooking food mingled with the smell of exotic-scented candles burning on the counter.

"Your house is amazing," I said, looking around in wonder.

"Thank you."

An older woman wearing a tan uniform came into the kitchen. She was small and plump and wore her short gray hair feathered back from her face. I shouldn't have been surprised—of course, anyone who lived in a house like this would have domestic help—but Kat had never mentioned having staff.

"Excuse me, Mrs. Kat," the woman said in accented English.

"Marguerite, this is my friend Alice Campbell," Kat said. "Alice, this is Marguerite Sampson, our housekeeper."

Marguerite smiled and nodded. "Nice to meet you."

"You, too."

"If you don't need anything else, Mrs. Kat, I'm going home."

"No, thank you, Marguerite. Good night."

"Have a good night, Mrs. Kat."

Once the housekeeper had left, Kat smiled at me.

"Mrs. Kat?" I teased.

"I know, it's so silly. She's been with us for fifteen years, and for fifteen years, she's refused to call me Kat. Anyway, I hope you like short ribs. I've never made them before, but the butcher swore they would be easy and delicious. He was right on the easy part, at least. I just plunked them in the oven hours ago and haven't touched them since."

"They smell fantastic," I said.

Kat pulled a bottle of chilled Pouilly-Fuissé from the enormous stainless steel refrigerator. She poured us each a glass.

"Cheers!" Kat tapped her wineglass against mine. "I'm so glad you came tonight."

"Thank you for inviting us," I said. "It's such a treat to have someone cook me dinner."

"Todd isn't at all how I pictured him." Kat pulled out a plate of cheese and crudités from the refrigerator and put it on the counter. "He's much taller than I thought he'd be."

"Really? That's funny. I was just thinking the same thing about Howard."

"But Howard's not at all tall! What, did you think he was a midget?" Kat exclaimed.

I laughed and relaxed. "No, actually he's shorter than I thought he'd be. I just mean I'd pictured him differently. For some reason, I thought he'd be blond."

"Oh, no, I've never gone for blond men." Kat gave a humorous shudder. "Or redheads. No offense, because your hair is gorgeous. But it doesn't translate well to men."

"Really? I've actually always been attracted to redheads," I admitted. "And Scots."

"And kilts on men?" Kat teased.

"I draw the line at men wearing skirts."

"Good Lord, what are you two talking about?" Howard asked as he strode into the kitchen. Much like his wife, Howard's pace was a few notches faster than average. I wondered if they were both naturally quick walkers or one had influenced the other over the course of their marriage. "Tom, watch out. Our wives are talking about men in skirts."

"Todd," Todd said, coming in behind him.

"Right. Todd. Sorry." Howard picked up a slice of cheese and popped it into his mouth. He chewed and swallowed it before turning his intense gaze on me. "I can't believe your husband is such a tennis fan and he's never been to the Miami Open."

"What's that?" I asked.

"It's a huge tennis tournament held every year down in Key Biscayne. All the top players go. I never miss it," Howard said. "Kat's father's company has a box there."

"Your father owns a company?" I shouldn't have been astonished, but I was.

Kat had mentioned her parents to me only in passing. I knew they lived nearby, but I didn't think she'd ever mentioned what they did professionally.

Howard had just bitten into another slice of cheese, and my question clearly caught him off guard, since he nearly choked. He coughed and hammered at his chest with one fist.

"Are you okay?" Kat asked. Her tone was casual as she poured a glass of water from a carafe on the marble countertop and handed it to her husband.

"You don't know who Kat's father is?" Howard asked, ignoring his wife's question but accepting the glass of water. "How is that even possible? He's *Thomas Wyeth*."

The name sounded vaguely familiar, but I couldn't place it. I wondered if he could possibly be an artist or maybe a writer. But, no, I didn't think an artist would have corporate box seats at a tennis tournament.

"You're a Wyeth?" Todd asked.

He had clearly caught on sooner than I had. In fact, he was staring at Kat, his mouth agape. It was almost as though she had been unmasked as a celebrity, like a member of the English aristocracy or a Kennedy.

"No, she's a Grant," Howard said irritably at the same time Kat smiled and said, "Guilty as charged."

Howard and Kat glanced at one another. Howard seemed annoyed, but Kat merely arched her eyebrows and looked amused.

"You don't mind me being a Wyeth when it comes time to use the company's box seats," she said lightly.

Howard opened his mouth as though he wanted to say something, but then thought better of it. "Of course I don't *mind*. Don't be ridiculous," he said.

"I'm sorry. I feel like I'm playing catch-up," I said. "Is your father famous?"

Kat let out a peal of laughter. "No, he's not famous," she said. "He just owns a construction company."

"But he is actually famous," Todd said.

"You only know his name because you're an architect," Kat said, patting Todd's arm.

"No, my dear, he probably knows the name because your father is worth… What is he worth these days? Has he hit a billion dollars yet?" Howard asked in the same ironic tone he'd used to offer whiskey to Todd.

Kat rolled her eyes at me. "Not even close. He's not Bill Gates," she said.

"He's not far off," Howard said under his breath.

Kat shot her husband a sour look. "It's tacky to talk about money."

"Yes, you're always quick to tell me how much I need to work on my manners," Howard retorted.

Suddenly it all became clear. Kat wasn't just wealthy. She came from capital-*M* Money. The sort of money that doesn't last just a lifetime but through multiple generations thereafter. It would be nothing to a multimillionaire to set up his daughter in a Palm Beach art gallery. Just a carrot to tempt his headstrong bohemian daughter to return home to South Florida.

I had never thought of myself as a covetous person and firmly believed jealousy was wasted energy. There would always be someone with more than you, any way you chose to measure it—intelligence, beauty, wealth, talent, happiness. Even so, it was hard not to look around the beautiful home of the woman who was quickly becoming one of my closest confidantes, remember the pile of unpaid bills on my desk at home and not whine silently, *It's not fair.* Of course, life wasn't fair. But sometimes the sheer magnitude of the unfairness could stick in your throat like a bitter pill.

The dinner was fantastic. It did not surprise me that Kat, who seemed to do everything well, was a wonderful cook. The short ribs were tender and flavorful. They paired perfectly with the creamy garlic mashed potatoes and green beans tossed in olive oil and lemon zest. Howard had uncorked several bottles of cabernet sauvignon, which I thought at first was foolhardy—there was no way the four of us would drink through three bottles of wine. That was, until I saw just how much alcohol Howard was able to put away all on his own. He poured himself glass after glass, drinking until his eyes were unfocused and his manner increasingly aggressive.

"I think we should have a toast to Alice on the publication of her wonderful book." Kat raised her glass in the air.

"Absolutely," Todd said.

"Oh, don't. It hasn't been published yet," I protested weakly. I did not share Kat's gift for gracefully accepting compliments.

"And it's not a novel, right?" Howard asked. His lips were stained red from the wine. "I thought Kat said it was just a book of puzzles for children."

The truth was, it *was* just a book of puzzles for children. But something about the way Howard said it rankled me.

"That's right," I said, striving to keep my tone neutral.

"It's a *book*!" Kat said. "A book that Alice *wrote*. That's what's so exciting. How many people can say they've written a book?"

"These days? As far as I can tell, just about anyone," Howard said with a condescending smile. "Haven't you ever heard of e-books? Self-publishing? Anyone who ever fancied himself the next Ernest Hemingway suddenly has a platform. Not that any of these so-called writers have actually read Ernest Hemingway."

Kat looked at her husband coldly. "And what about you? Have *you* ever read Hemingway?"

The words hung between them in an icy silence, until Todd waded in.

"Alice wasn't trying to write the Great American Novel," he said. "She's a logician. Her book is meant to teach children how to solve logic puzzles."

I know I should have appreciated his defense. But when I saw Howard shrug and splay his hands in front of him as though he couldn't be bothered to keep up with the nuances of my career—not that anyone was asking him to—I became irrationally annoyed at my husband. Why did he need to put me into my little box, to put a label on me that Howard would find less threatening?

"I think what Alice has done is amazing," said Kat, my staunchest supporter. "To you, Alice."

She raised her glass again and blew me a kiss. I smiled back at her and felt my irritation recede.

Despite Howard's temperamental mood, Kat rallied to make the dinner a success. I could tell that one of her goals for the evening was to win Todd over. Not that it was hard. Like most people, Todd found it easy to like someone who was nice and funny and seemed delighted to be talking to him.

"So, Todd," Kat began, topping off his wineglass. I'd already had so much wine, my head was spinning a little. I hoped that Todd would be okay to drive us home. "Are you an only child, like Alice?"

"Unfortunately, no," Todd said, which made Kat laugh. "Seriously, if you met my younger brother, you'd understand. His greatest accomplishment in life is that he can chug a beer and then burp the alphabet."

"But that's an incredibly useful skill!" Kat exclaimed. "You could hire him out as an entertainment for children's parties."

Todd chuckled. "That's an idea. Maybe he can fall back on it if his current career selling energy drinks online isn't a success."

"Just the one brother?" Kat asked.

I glanced at Todd and wasn't surprised to see a shadow cross his face.

"Just one I grew up with," he said. "I had a half brother from my father's first marriage. His short-lived and ill-fated first marriage."

Kat nodded, her expression understanding. She knew all about children who were born of short-lived and ill-fated relationships.

"They were divorced when Brendon, my half brother, was a baby, and it was pretty contentious," Todd continued. "Afterward Brendon and his mother moved to Georgia, where I guess she was originally from. We didn't see a whole lot of him growing up. He was eight years older than me, so when he did come to stay for a few weeks in the summers, he didn't want much to do with me."

"So you're not close," Kat concluded.

"Well, no, we weren't. Unfortunately, he passed away last year," Todd said.

"I'm so sorry," Kat said. "He must have been very young."

Todd nodded in thanks. I thought he'd end the story there, but the wine was making him verbose. "It was actually pretty terrible. We were there at the time. Alice, myself, the kids. We were all at my parents' house for Thanksgiving. Brendon was drunk, as he often was, and he fell down the stairs. The fall killed him."

"Oh, my God," Kat exclaimed, looking at me. "How horrific."

"It really was," I said, shaking my head. I didn't like to

think about that night. "We called the paramedics, but it was too late to save him. I was so worried the children would wake up and see him...well, lying there. Luckily they slept through the whole thing. But it was an awful night."

"I thought drunks never got hurt," Howard cut in. On the word *drunks*, he slurred the *r*. "That they always walk away from car accidents."

"It's hard to walk away from anything when your neck's broken," Todd said.

There was a brief moment of silence.

"Why don't I bring in dessert?" Kat suggested.

"What an asshole," Todd said once we were in our car.

"Are you sure you're okay to drive?"

Todd waved me off, and he did seem sober enough, so I let it go. He pulled out of the drive, sending a spray of gravel in his wake.

"How did those two end up married? They seem like complete opposites," he continued.

I shrugged. "It happens. Maybe he was less grumpy when they met."

"Grumpy? Is that what you'd call him? You make him sound like one of Snow White's seven dwarfs."

"Well, how would you describe him?"

"I thought he was a dick," Todd said.

I laughed and leaned back in my seat. "He really was awful, wasn't he? From what little Kat has told me about him, I certainly wasn't expecting Howard to be genial. But I also wasn't expecting him to be so hostile. I got the feeling he resented our being there, and his having to play host."

"He spent the entire night trying to one-up me," Todd said. "When I told him I play tennis, he claimed he was good enough to play for his college team. When I told him what I do, he said he'd thought about being an architect but decided he'd make more money in finance."

Todd's tone was unusually bitter. I imagined I was not the only one who had been impressed by the size and scope of the Grants' house, particularly against the backdrop of our current financial crisis. But that wasn't something either one of us wanted to get into. And even if we had no choice but to discuss our money woes periodically, we rarely addressed Todd's lack of career success directly. If he was frustrated by the lack of traction he'd gained in his field over the years, he dealt with it by whacking tennis balls. As for me, I didn't think I was in any position to comment on Todd's or anyone else's career failures, considering how I'd unceremoniously left my cushy academic job.

"Howard played tennis in college?"

"No." Todd laughed. "He just said they tried to recruit him, but he decided he didn't want to play, which is such bullshit. I think he really just wanted to tell me he went to Yale. Jesus. You know how I feel about people who name-drop their alma maters."

"I know, you've always hated that. I guess future double dates are out of the question."

"I liked Kat," he said. "I can see why the two of you hit it off. You're very much alike."

This surprised me. "We are? How so?"

"You're both smart. You have similar senses of humor," Todd said. He glanced over at me, the streetlights casting an odd green glow on his face. "Why? You don't think you're alike?"

"I never really thought about it," I said. "I mean, don't get me wrong, I love Kat. But she's so much more—" I faltered, trying to think of the right word "—poised than I am."

Todd let out an incredulous bark of laughter. "You can't be serious."

"What?"

"Alice, you are, without exception, the most poised person I have ever met."

It is not often that your spouse of over a decade can shock you. I'd seen my husband out of his mind with grief after the loss of our daughter. I'd washed out the bowl he threw up into for three days when he had food poisoning. I knew he hated eggplant but loved foul-looking peanut-butter-and-bacon sandwiches. But I never knew he, or anyone else, thought of me as poised. After all, I experienced myself through the maelstrom of my own swirling thoughts and emotions, through joy and grief, worry and hope. I had moments of peace, but I certainly never felt poised.

I was quite pleased to know that I put up such a convincing front.

8

"IT'S SAFE TO say you weren't a fan of Howard Grant," Detective Demer said.

"No, I wasn't," I agreed. "But then, Howard went out of his way to be unlikable."

At this, Demer gave me a quizzical look.

"That's an interesting observation. Why do you think he did that?"

"I'm not sure. His antagonism always seemed pointless. In my experience, it's almost always easier to get along with people than it is to aggravate them," I explained.

Oliver let out a snort. I glanced over at her.

"Clearly not your life philosophy, Sergeant," I said drily.

Demer raised a hand to his mouth, but not before I caught the smile he was trying to cover. Oliver was too busy fixing me with a hostile stare to notice his amusement.

"Do you know who the prime suspect always is in a homicide investigation?" Oliver asked.

"Homicide?" I asked, startled by the word. "You're investigating Howard's death as a homicide? Based on what?"

Oliver ignored my question.

"The spouse or partner of the victim is always the prime suspect. Almost always, unless the homicide is committed during the course of another crime, like a robbery," Oliver said. "And there's no evidence that the Grants' house was burglarized on the night of Howard Grant's death. Do you see where I'm going with this?"

Sergeant Oliver didn't seem to expect an answer, so I didn't bother giving her one.

"Kat Grant was the only person who benefited from her husband's death," she continued.

"That's ridiculous," I cut in. "It doesn't benefit Kat that her husband is dead. She loved him. She's devastated to have lost him, especially in such a sudden and terrible way."

"She's devastated?" Demer asked. He sounded mildly interested. "She told you that?"

"I've spoken to her only once since Howard's death. But, yes, she was very upset."

"We've heard from other witnesses that the Grants' marriage was on the rocks," Oliver said.

"Who told you that?" I asked sharply.

Oliver ignored my question. "Their marital net worth is estimated at being somewhere in the neighborhood of sixty-three million dollars. Do you see where I'm going with this? That's a lot of money. If Howard and Katherine Grant were headed for a divorce, Howard Grant's death couldn't have come at a more convenient time for Mrs. Grant."

I stared at her, momentarily stunned. Sixty-three million dollars? I knew Kat and Howard were wealthy, of course, but I never knew the extent of their wealth. The amount was staggering.

"Let's go back to the state of the Grants' marriage." Demer clearly wanted to get the interview back on track. "You just said that Katherine Grant loved her husband. What do you base that impression on?"

"Don't most married people love one another, at least to some extent?"

Demer laughed. "In my experience, no, marriage in and of itself is no guarantee of love."

"As I've already told you, I'm not an expert on Kat and Howard's marriage."

"But you and Katherine are close friends. You must have had some idea about her state of mind," the detective persisted.

"I know she wasn't planning on divorcing him."

"You're sure about that?"

"I think if she had been, she would have mentioned it to me at some point. You know she was in London when Howard died?"

"Yes," Demer responded with an affable nod.

"Unless she's some sort of superhero who has the power to teleport, I don't see why you're investigating her." I shook my head, becoming exasperated with what was clearly a fishing expedition. They didn't have evidence against Kat. They didn't even have confirmation that Howard's death was anything other than an accident. As far as I could tell, the investigation was based entirely on neighborhood gossip and the large amount of money at issue. I pushed my chair back from the table, ready to stand and leave. "If those are the only questions you have for me, I think continuing this interview will be a waste of our time."

Oliver's eyes narrowed. She placed her hands palms down on the table and leaned forward in a way I think I was supposed to find intimidating. But before she could say anything, Demer again signaled to Oliver to tone it down. Her face pinched with anger.

"I don't know about that," he said mildly. "I think it would be mutually advantageous if you stayed and cooperated with our investigation."

I surprised myself by laughing. But really, it was a ridiculous statement. "How is this in any way advantageous to me?"

"You said yourself that Katherine Grant is your close friend. It would be in her interest to be cleared of any suspicion."

"True," I said. "But all you seem interested in is whether Kat and Howard were getting along at the time of his death. It doesn't sound like you're hoping to clear her name. And you're ignorng that she has a pretty fantastic alibi. You know she was in London when—"

"She could have hired someone to kill him," Oliver interrupted.

"You mean like a hit man?" I laughed again, this time incredulously. "So we're leaving reality and jumping into an Elmore Leonard book?"

She shrugged. "It's been known to happen. And Mrs. Grant certainly has the means."

"I am absolutely sure that Kat would have no idea how to go about hiring a hit man," I said. "It's not like they advertise online. Or do they? Are there hit men out there with Facebook pages?"

Demer laughed. "I suppose it's possible, but I can't imagine they would stay in business very long if they advertised on Facebook."

"Katherine Grant's father is Thomas Wyeth," Oliver said.

"Yes, I know."

"There have been rumors about connections between Wyeth Construction and organized crime for years," Oliver added. She leaned back and spread her hands out in front of her, palms up. "If I was looking to hire a hit man and my daddy knew some mobsters, I think I know where I'd go."

"Then maybe your husband should be worried." I had lost all patience with the sergeant.

Oliver looked at me coldly. "There was a witness."

"Excuse me?" I asked.

"Someone saw Howard Grant pushed off the balcony," Oliver snapped. "I think it's about time you dropped this Little Miss Innocent act and start telling us what you know."

Demer stood abruptly.

"Sergeant, let's step outside." The detective was no longer genial. Instead he looked angry and, for the first time since I'd met him that morning, a little intimidating.

"Fine." Oliver spat out the word. She stood, too, crossed her arms over her chest and stalked out of the room. A moment later, after first casting a lingering glance in my direction, the detective followed her.

I sat as still as I could long after the door had shut behind them. I had no idea if anyone out there in the Jupiter Island Public Safety Department—Christ, what a name—was watching me. I didn't see any obvious two-way mirrors in the so-called conference room, but that didn't mean I wasn't being observed. For all I knew, they had cameras on me. I had to assume that a Jupiter Island police station had the very best tech available to them. It was important that I remain calm with my senses sharp. I needed to figure out what was going on.

I was also starting to suspect that the fact Kat hadn't returned my phone calls was more significant than I had first realized.

9

Two Years Earlier

"WOW, YOU LOOK FANTASTIC," Todd said as I emerged from the bedroom.

"Thank you," I said, fighting my customary impulse to deflect compliments. I had learned well from Kat's example.

We had been invited to Kat's parents' annual holiday party. They lived on the island of Palm Beach, so I knew it would be a swanky affair. I was wearing the black beaded cocktail dress I had worn to a wedding Todd and I had attended a few years earlier, and I'd twisted my hair into a low chignon. Like most redheads, I couldn't pull off heavy makeup—it looked garish against my pale, lightly freckled skin—but I did put on eyeliner, mascara and a swipe of rose lipstick.

Our babysitter, Emma Vanover, had arrived while I was dressing. She was a not-very-bright but sweet-natured fifteen-year-old, and she was currently the children's favorite sitter. Bridget liked her because Emma had a limitless enthusiasm for tedious make-believe games. *"You be the evil stepmother and the dragon and the pet goat, and I'll be the princess and the unicorn."* Liam liked Emma because she left him alone to play video games without the annoying time limits his parents imposed on him.

"Our cell phone numbers are on the fridge," I told Emma after I'd greeted her. "We're going to a holiday party. I don't think we'll be out past midnight, but I'll text you if our plans change."

"No problem," Emma said perkily.

I ran through the basic house rules for the evening—bedtimes, allowed snacks, time limits on computer games—and Emma nodded enthusiastically along with each one. I knew she'd ignore almost all of the parameters I was giving her. Bridget was a startlingly honest child and always told me when the babysitters didn't follow the rules. I was just happy if they didn't drink our booze or invite their boyfriends over to have sex on the living room couch.

"What's this evening going to be like?" Todd asked once we were in the car, driving south.

It may seem odd, but on the rare nights when we did go out, I almost enjoyed the ride there more than the event itself. The novelty of being dressed up and out on our own, unencumbered by children. The chance to talk over whatever the issue of the day was, whether it was our own domestic matters or something weightier on the news. My feet didn't yet hurt from walking in the unaccustomed heels, and my head was still clear and sharp.

In response to my husband's question, I shrugged, not that he'd be able to see me in the darkness.

"I'm not sure. Kat said her parents throw this party every year. I doubt we'll know anyone there other than Kat and Howard."

"Ah, Howard. My favorite," Todd said. He had never forgiven Howard for his rudeness, not that he had seen him since the dinner party all those months ago.

"Kat's dad is a builder, so I'm sure you'll have plenty in common with him."

Todd laughed. "Babe, her dad isn't a builder. He's a mogul. There's a big difference."

"Is there? You're both in the construction business, albeit from different angles. I'm sure you'd have plenty to talk about."

Todd glanced at me. "Are you trying to get me to audition for a job?"

"No, of course not. Why would you think that? Does he hire architects?"

"Wyeth Construction has anywhere from ten to fifteen architects on staff. It's a lucrative and soul-sucking position."

"Why soul-sucking?"

"Because all they do is design the same cookie-cutter houses for the various subdivisions Wyeth develops."

"And that's bad because...?" I asked.

"Because that's not what I went to school to do," Todd said tersely. "That's not the kind of architect I want to be."

I nodded but didn't say anything. What was the point? If I commented that he wasn't setting the world of architecture on fire now, it would start the evening on a sour note.

The Wyeths lived in a large house on Lagomar Road, with southern views of the Intracoastal. It was two stories and featured lots of columns and double glass doors. The grounds were as manicured as those of a high-end country club, with decorative shrubs and tall palm trees. Todd turned onto the circular brick-tiled driveway, the mouth of which was flanked by two stone lions. We slowly followed the line of cars curving up toward the front door, where valets were stationed to relieve drivers of their cars. Everyone I could see was dressed to the nines. A few of the women were even wearing gowns. I felt a prick of concern, wondering if my little black dress was dressy enough.

"This all looks very ritzy," Todd commented.

"What did you expect?" I asked. "A family-style barbecue with hot dogs and hamburgers?"

"If so, I think I'd be disappointed," Todd said.

We reached the top of the driveway. The valet, a young man with military-short hair and a white jacket, opened the door for me.

"Welcome," he said politely.

"Thank you," I said.

I waited for Todd to join me and then took his arm. We walked into the house.

I'd never been a particularly social person. I preferred quiet nights at home reading a book or watching a movie to attending parties. I'd looked forward to the children's school's annual auction fund-raiser with equal parts of dread and resignation. (The year that Liam contracted stomach flu the night before the event, thus giving us a good excuse not to attend, was cause for celebration in our house.) But I had to admit, I had been looking forward to the Wyeth Christmas party ever since the engraved Crane invitation arrived in the mail a month earlier.

I knew the party would be glamorous, and a departure from our usual holiday social schedule, which revolved heavily around school concerts and cookie swaps. But I was also especially interested in meeting Kat's family. I was curious to see how they matched up with her descriptions. Her mother, controlling, haughty and easily disappointed. Her father, warm and lovable toward his daughter, but a tough and ruthless businessman. Her older brother, Josh, who was smart and successful, but also humorless and self-centered.

Todd and I walked into the grand foyer, a vast, high-ceilinged space. It was already crowded, with many different generations represented. I didn't recognize a single person.

"Alice! You made it!"

I turned to see Kat sweeping toward me, her arms open. She looked beautiful in a gold sequined A-line dress and very high heels. She gave me a huge hug and Todd a kiss on the cheek, leaving behind a smear of red lipstick.

"I'm so glad you came," Kat said, beaming at us both. She leaned toward me and whispered, "Maybe this year I'll actually have fun for a change."

"Why? Is it normally awful?" I whispered back.

Kat rolled her eyes comically. "I didn't want to tell you ahead of time in case you bailed, but *yes*. It can be brutal. Come on, let's get you both a drink, and then I'll introduce you to my parents."

Kat hailed a passing waiter and snagged us each a flute of champagne off a silver tray.

"I need to introduce you to the Dragon Lady so we can get it out of the way and start having fun," Kat said.

"You call your mother the Dragon Lady?" I asked with a laugh.

"You will, too, after you meet her. Come on, let's get it over with."

Kat shepherded us into a formal living area, which was slightly less crowded than the foyer, but only because there wasn't much space to stand. I couldn't help notice that quite unlike Kat's spare, modern taste, the theme in this room was glamorous excess. There was barely an inch where some sort of overstuffed chair, couch or occasional table hadn't been crammed. Portraits hung on the walls, including one that I thought must be of Kat when she was a girl. The effect of the room would have been overwhelming even when it was empty of people. Filled with a crowd, it was claustrophobic.

Kat grabbed my hand and pulled me along, while Todd trailed behind us. "Mother, I'd like you to meet my friend Alice, and her husband, Todd."

I found myself face-to-face with a tall woman—taller than

Kat—with steel-gray hair pulled back from a surprisingly youthful face. She was wearing a column of white silk, and her only makeup was dark red lipstick. She must have been beautiful in her youth. Even now she was an incredibly handsome woman.

"It's a pleasure to meet you," Mrs. Wyeth said. She shook each of our hands in turn, somehow infusing this most pedestrian of greeting with a sort of grandeur. Her grip was firm, and her chin tilted upward.

"It's so nice to meet you," I said.

"Thank you for inviting us," Todd added.

"You're quite welcome," Mrs. Wyeth replied.

Eleanor Wyeth was cool and crisp and utterly devoid of warmth. It felt a bit as though we'd been brought before a queen. I could feel Kat tense beside me.

"I've told you about Alice," Kat said. "Remember?"

Eleanor Wyeth studied me. "Oh, right. The logician."

I glanced at Kat, surprised she had described me this way, but nodded.

"I gather you teach?" Eleanor Wyeth asked.

"I was a professor, but I stopped working once my daughter was born. These days I'm just a standard stay-at-home mom," I answered.

Kat looked from me to her mother. "Don't be so modest, Alice. She *wrote* a *book*. Isn't that amazing?"

"A book," Mrs. Wyeth repeated without even a hint of interest. "I don't suppose it's something I would have read?"

"It's a children's book of logic puzzles."

"Then probably not," she said with a tinkle of dismissive laughter. She looked at someone over my shoulder. "Judge Barnes, how nice of you to join us."

Our audience with the queen was over. Mrs. Wyeth held out a hand to the judge, and I edged to the side to get out of their way. In the process, I banged my knee against a coffee table.

"Ouch."

"I know. Let's get out of here. There isn't any room to breathe, much less stand," Kat said too loudly.

I glanced at Eleanor Wyeth just in time to see her cast a disapproving look in her daughter's direction.

Kat either hadn't noticed or didn't care. Or maybe she was used to her mother's disapproving looks. "Are you hungry?"

"No," I said just as Todd said, "Starving."

"There's a huge spread in the dining room." Kat pointed the way to Todd. "We'll be out on the patio, by the pool. Get a plate and come find us."

"Do either of you want anything?" Todd asked, but Kat and I both shook our heads, and he headed off toward the food.

"What's on the patio?" I asked.

"My dad, probably. He likes to hide out there and smoke cigars, which he's been expressly forbidden to do." Kat fake-coughed. "Come on. I can't wait for him to meet you."

I nodded and smiled, feeling a flush of pleasure at Kat's warmth, especially in the wake of how coldly her mother had dismissed me. I've never had much interest in the pursuit of social power. I've watched the alpha school mothers jockey for positions on the PTA and felt only mild curiosity over why anyone would care that much about who got to be in charge of the book fair fund-raiser or the field day activities. Even worse, though, were the betas, the sycophantic toadies who would do anything to cozy up to and curry favor from the alphas. The whole dynamic both confused and exhausted me. I was only too glad to avoid it.

Still, perhaps my own disinterest in such social politicking had made me naive about what these women did once they achieved such positions. Kat's mother, who certainly occupied a far higher place on the social ladder than the PTA Queen

Bees, wielded her position as a weapon. Warm smiles for the lucky favorites, icy disdain for the rest. I wasn't exactly sure what had put me in the latter group. It could have been simply that I was a friend of Kat's. I knew their relationship was strained. Or perhaps Eleanor Wyeth was a snob who believed that a middle-class suburban mother was not worthy of her attention. Maybe a little of both.

I followed Kat out onto the veranda, which was very large and grand and had a spectacular view of the water. Kat, who lived several miles to the north, could have boated down to her parents' house if she wished. The veranda had a pergola overhead and was furnished with navy upholstered patio furniture, glass tables and large potted palm trees. Off to one side was a rectangular pool surrounded by statuary. There was a chill in the air, but it felt good after the crush of the crowd inside.

Kat looked around for her father.

"He's not here." She looked disappointed. "Oh, well, he's bound to come out eventually."

She plopped down onto one of the rattan chairs and kicked her heels off. I took the chair next to her.

"I'm sorry about my mother," Kat said. "I should have warned you that she can be... What would be a polite way of saying this? Difficult, I suppose. Although even that might be sugarcoating it."

"It's fine." I sipped my champagne. "I'm sure it's not personal. I didn't take it that way."

"Oh, but it is personal." Kat let out a humorless laugh.

"What?" I asked, startled.

"I mean, no, of course it's not personal about *you*. She obviously doesn't know you. But she's always been predisposed not to like any of my friends. She always warned me when I was younger that the people who wanted to be my friends might have ulterior motives," Kat explained.

"What kind of ulterior motives?"

"Money," Kat said simply. "That's part of it. But also access to the family. Which really means access to Daddy. Mother does it to my brother, Josh, too, but nowhere near the extent she's shoved it down my throat. I think in her twisted view of the world, it's normal for men to use money to attract women, friends, business, whatever. Not so for women."

"Wow," I said. "That's equal parts sexist and paranoid."

"That's my mother," Kat agreed, holding up her mostly empty flute of champagne in a mock toast. "A paranoid sexist. It should say that on her gravestone. It's as accurate an epitaph as any."

"The entire time you were growing up, you were worried that anyone who was nice to you had an ulterior motive?" I asked.

Kat put her champagne flute down and leaned back in her chair, tucking her feet beneath her. "Not exactly. I had some good friends, people I trusted. And I knew from a fairly young age that my mother was full of shit. But sure, it did make me wonder sometimes. It affected me more when I was a little older and started dating, especially after I graduated from college. I'd wonder if the men who asked me out were really interested in me, or if they were just hoping to marry into the Wyeth family. I think that's part of the reason I fell so hard for the senator." Kat still hadn't told me the name of her ex-lover and Amanda's father. "He had no intention of ever leaving his wife, so I knew that he, at least, wanted to be with me for me. Or at least, that's how I rationalized it after he broke my heart."

"What about Howard?"

Kat turned to look at me, her eyes large and unreadable. "Howard," she mused. "To be honest, I've never been entirely sure—" She stopped abruptly, and then her face brightened. "Daddy!"

She hopped up and, without bothering to put her shoes back on, hurried across the veranda to a squarely built man with snow-white hair. Thomas Wyeth smiled down at his daughter and folded her into his arms. Kat hugged him back fiercely, then broke away to wave me over.

"Daddy, I want you to meet my friend Alice. Alice, this is my father, Thomas," Kat said, tucking her hand in the crook of her father's elbow. He extended his other hand to me.

"It's very nice to meet you finally, Alice. Kat has been raving about you for months. She said that you are the smartest person she's ever met." Mr. Wyeth smiled down at me. His eyes, which were the exact same shade of blue as Kat's, crinkled pleasantly at the corners.

"That's very nice of Kat and almost certainly not true," I protested.

"Don't listen to her, Daddy. She *is* brilliant and she's funny as hell, too," Kat insisted.

"My kind of gal," Mr. Wyeth said. He laughed and patted me on the back.

Much as I'd been struck when I met Howard for the first time how mismatched he'd seemed with Kat, it was equally hard to imagine how a man who seemed as jolly as Thomas had ended up with the icy Eleanor. Had Eleanor once been a carefree young girl, and only hardened into a stiff-backed matriarch in her later years? Or was this yet another confounding example of opposites attracting?

"Did you sneak out here to smoke?" Kat asked.

Her father adopted an expression of innocent surprise. "Does that sound like something I would do?"

"Absolutely. That's why Alice and I came here in the first place. I thought I'd find you here," Kat said.

Thomas Wyeth winked at his daughter and slipped a cigar out of his pocket. "Just don't tell your mother."

"As though I would." Kat rolled her eyes.

"That's my girl." Mr. Wyeth lit his cigar with an engraved jet lighter and took a deep, satisfied drag on it. The cigar smoke was spicy and earthy as it swirled in the cool air.

"Is there some sort of family reunion going on out here?" a voice asked. "And if so, why wasn't I invited?"

I looked up and saw a lanky man with thinning hair and wire-rimmed glasses. He was followed by a blonde woman who was so painfully thin, her head looked like it was two sizes too large for her body.

"Oh, we make it a point to never invite you to family reunions, Josh," Kat said drily as her brother joined us.

"Kat the Kidder." Josh reached out to rumple her hair.

"Stop it!" Kat swatted his arm away. "Alice, this is my annoying brother, Josh, and his wife, Ashley."

I shook each of their hands in turn.

"Why are you all out here? It's freezing." Then Josh noticed the cigar in his father's hand. "You know Mom's going to kill you if she catches you smoking again."

Mr. Wyeth waved a dismissive hand. "I can handle your mother."

"Famous last words," Kat murmured.

Mr. Wyeth chuckled and turned to join a gathering of men who had clearly come out to the patio with the same idea. They were all lighting cigars while engaging in lighthearted conversation.

"Hey, did you know Zach Harris is here?" Josh turned toward his sister.

"Zach came?" Kat seemed surprised. "Where is he?"

"I saw him inside. He and his wife just got here."

"Come show me." Kat grabbed her brother by the wrist. She looked at me. "Zach is an old friend of mine. We used to date in high school. I'm just going to say hello. I'll be right back."

"Sure, take your time," I said. I didn't want Kat to feel like she had to babysit me.

"Okay, I'll see you in a bit," Kat answered over her shoulder.

I watched Kat and her brother disappear into the house. Kat was still barefoot, having left her shoes behind on the veranda.

I wanted to find Todd, but it seemed rude to leave Ashley on her own.

I smiled at Kat's sister-in-law. "This is a great party."

"How long have you known Kat?" Ashley asked.

"Just about a year."

Ashley was pretty in a lacquered-over way. Her blond hair had been ironed straight, and her makeup had been applied with an expert if rather heavy hand. When she spoke and smiled, her face remained strangely flat and waxy, the telltale signs of Botox.

"Kat's something else, isn't she?" Ashley offered in a high, almost singsong voice that betrayed just a touch of a Southern twang.

"She's great."

"She has quite a habit of collecting people." Ashley smirked. "I guess you're the latest addition to the collection."

The smile slid off my face. From the slight slur of her words, I guessed that the glass in Ashley's hand did not represent her first drink of the evening. Then again, she was so wisp thin that it might not take much to make her tipsy.

I arched my eyebrows. "I have no idea what you're talking about."

"You don't? Well, let me tell you something about my sister-in-law. She comes across as, like, the coolest girl ever, right? And she's *so* much fun and *so* put-together, and you're *so* flattered that she wants to hang out with you all the time... and then, as soon as she gets what she wants out of you—" Ashley tried to snap her fingers, but in her lubricated state she wasn't able to pull it off "—you never hear from her again. That's Kat. She's uses people, and then she discards them."

"I should probably go find my husband." I turned away from Ashley, wondering if Kat knew just how much her sister-in-law despised her.

Ashley grabbed my arm, pulling me back around toward her with a surprising and somewhat disturbing strength. I looked down at her bony hand gripping me with its long, red-painted nails. It reminded me of a claw.

"Ask Kat about Marcia Grable," Ashley hissed, pushing her face far too close to mine. "Just ask her. I *dare* you."

I twisted my arm out of Ashley's grip and took a step back from her. "Excuse me," I said coldly.

I turned away and headed back into the house. But I did hear her singsong voice, the Southern accent even more pronounced than before, call after me, "Don't say I didn't warn you."

"What's wrong?" Todd asked when I found him standing near the buffet on his own, holding a plate piled with an assortment of hot hors d'oeuvres.

"What do you mean?" I realized I was holding my arm where Ashley had grabbed me. I saw Howard Grant across the room, standing too close to a pretty brunette woman laughing flirtatiously up at him. He either didn't notice me or, if he did, didn't acknowledge that he recognized me. I wasn't surprised. Howard hadn't grown any friendlier toward me over the months since I'd first met him.

"You look a little freaked out," Todd said. "Are you feeling okay?"

"Yes, I'm fine. I just had a… Jesus, I don't know what that was." I plucked a mini crab cake off Todd's plate and bit off half of it. It was delicious. I popped the rest of it into my mouth.

"What?" Todd asked. "Did someone grab your ass?"

I choked on the bite of crab cake I'd been in the process of swallowing and pressed a hand to my mouth while my eyes watered.

Once I'd recovered my composure, I said, "Don't do that!"

"What?"

"Make me laugh when I'm eating."

"Asking if someone grabbed your ass makes you laugh?" Todd smiled down at me. Whenever he was amused, his eyes squinted up into two half crescents.

"This isn't exactly an ass-grabbing sort of crowd," I said, making sure to keep my voice a low murmur, aware of the heads that had swiveled in my direction when I was coughing.

"What happened, then?" Todd asked.

Before I could fill him in on my run-in with the unpleasant Ashley, Kat appeared in front of us, smiling, her face flushed.

"Here you are! I've been looking for you everywhere," she said. "Todd, I see you found the food."

Todd raised his plate in answer. "Everything's delicious," he said.

"Yes, nothing but the best for my mother." Kat's voice was heavy with irony.

"I'm going back for another round," Todd said. "Alice stole all of my mini crab cakes."

"I did not! I only had one."

"It's your word against mine." Todd winked at me and then turned and headed purposefully toward the buffet table.

"Todd's great," Kat commented. She sounded almost wistful. "You're so lucky."

"Why, because the man appreciates a buffet?"

"You know what I'm talking about. He's a good guy." I followed Kat's gaze and saw she was staring at her husband, who was still chatting cozily with the brunette. Howard touched the woman's bare shoulder, and she giggled in response. Kat tensed. "Better than most."

If Howard's flirtation and Ashley's venom were common occurrences at her parents' holiday party, I could see why Kat dreaded it. And she hadn't even heard what Ashley had said to me. I wondered if I should tell her, but decided against it. Kat was in a good mood, happy and vivacious, or at least she had been until she spotted her husband ogling another woman. I didn't want to spoil her night. Besides, Ashley was clearly a poisonous person, I decided, and she'd probably been jealous of Kat for years. Kat was certainly brighter and more personable and definitely more attractive than her aging sorority-girl sister-in-law.

No, I decided, I wasn't going to play the part of Ashley's tattletale. And I certainly wasn't going to ruin Kat's evening. Instead I was going to enjoy the party and drink champagne until my always-overworked brain was comfortably numb. To hell with the headache I'd have tomorrow.

"What did you think of Ashley?" Kat asked, almost as if she was reading my thoughts. "I saw you two chatting."

I shrugged. "I think she's had too much to drink. She wasn't making much sense, and she was slurring her words."

"That seems likely. She usually is."

"Really? How does she stay so thin?" I asked.

"She never eats. She lives on a diet of wine and bitterness," Kat said, which cracked both of us up.

"What are you two ladies laughing about?" Todd asked, joining us. He slid an arm around me and cupped his hand on my waist.

"I'm just so happy I met Alice," Kat told him. She squeezed my arm. "She's exactly who I needed in my life."

10

I DREW IN a deep breath, and then another. I'd always told Bridget, my child prone to anxiety, that worrying never helped anything. Worse, outright panic led to stupid mistakes. It's always better to clear your mind of any distracting noise to appraise a situation once you're calm.

Here was my current situation:

I had been brought into the police station to be interviewed about Howard's death. The police believed that Howard had been murdered.

The police also believed that Kat had a financial motive for wanting Howard dead.

Sergeant Oliver was oddly hostile toward me. There was—or at least, Sergeant Oliver claimed there was—a witness who had come forward.

I hadn't heard from Kat.

I set my logician's brain whirring on the problem, but I got back…nothing. There were too many loose ends, too many unknown factors.

For example:

Was Oliver telling the truth about a witness who had seen

someone push Howard off the balcony? I wouldn't have put it past her to lie just to gauge my reaction. She clearly didn't like me and had been adversarial throughout the interview. And if there really was a witness, who was it? Someone who knew the Grants, or a stranger?

And then there was the staggering amount of money that was presumably now Kat's, and Kat's alone.

There were a lot of factors to process before we even got to the meat of the matter. Which was—at least, to my mind— where was Kat in all of this? It was impossible to know, since I hadn't heard from her since that singular conversation we had when she was at the airport ready to board a plane home to bury her husband.

I wondered if I should insist on stopping the interview until I had the chance to consult with a criminal attorney, as Todd had urged me to do. And yet I still thought it was highly unlikely that the police considered me a suspect in Howard's death. It was far more likely that Demer had been telling the truth when he told me their purpose in interviewing me was to gain background information on Kat and Howard. And I had to think that the more I found out about the focus of the police's investigation, the better it would be for Kat.

The door to the conference room opened. Detective Demer entered and closed it behind him.

"Sorry about that," he said. He pulled out his chair and sat down heavily in it.

I nodded. I hoped that my husband was right, that I did possess an inscrutable face. I needed one now.

"I don't think Sergeant Oliver likes me very much," I remarked.

Demer paused for a moment. Then, raising his eyebrows, he nodded. "I think you might be right about that." He gave a rueful chuckle. "I wouldn't take it personally. I'm not sure she likes anyone."

"Why is she so convinced that I know what happened to Howard?"

Demer looked at me thoughtfully, tapping a pencil against the table. I got the feeling that he was trying to decide how much to tell me.

"What she said was correct. A witness has come forward," he finally replied.

Goose bumps were rising up on my arms and shoulders. It was just the air-conditioning, I told myself.

"What kind of a witness?" I asked. "You can't see into the Grants' backyard from any of the abutting properties."

"You seem quite sure about that," Demer said, as though my observation might have some significant meaning.

"I've been to their house many times."

I pictured the view from the Grants' back patio, where Kat and I often sat, lingering over a glass of wine while watching the boat traffic pass by. There was a combination of high walls and manicured hedges that blocked any view into her backyard from the neighbors to both the north and south. And while you could see the houses across the Intracoastal— no one would block a multimillion-dollar water view with a privacy fence—they were far enough away that you could see only their facades. Maybe the witness had been on a boat? It seemed the only plausible possibility, although even then, it was hard to imagine anyone on the water would have a good view of the Grants' house at night.

"The witness lives on the opposite side of the Intracoastal," the detective said.

"On the other side of the water? But that has to be, what? Over a thousand feet away? How would they be able to see anything?" I asked.

"The man is an amateur astronomer," Demer said. "He was looking through a telescope."

"Pointed at the Grants' house?" I asked, feeling my eyebrows arch.

Demer shrugged. "Maybe he had other hobbies, as well..."

"Okay. So you have a pervert who was hoping to see a free show and he instead saw...what?"

"He said he saw someone push a man over the railing."

"Howard," I clarified.

"Our witness couldn't identify the victim, but as no other bodies turned up that morning, that seems the most obvious guess."

"Did he see who pushed him?"

The detective again hesitated. "He didn't see who it was."

I stared at the detective, absorbing these words. The door opened and Sergeant Oliver strode in. She did not look chastened. If anything, her expression was almost smug. Demer glanced up at her and she nodded back at him.

"Mrs. Campbell, do you have a key to the Grants' house?" Oliver asked.

I shook my head no. "Why?"

"But you know where they store a spare key. You know the code to the house alarm," Oliver continued. These were technically questions, but she was stating them as facts.

Actually, I did know where Kat stored the spare key. It was in the garage, hidden behind the light box. Kat and I had gone shopping one day, and when I dropped her off, she hadn't been able to find her house key. She'd shown me where she kept the spare key and how to disarm the security alarm.

"Just in case you ever need to get in," Kat had said at the time.

"Why are you asking?" I looked to Demer.

"Just answer the question," Oliver snapped.

"No," I said, crossing my arms. "Not until you tell me why you want to know. Because if you are attempting to implicate me in this in any way, I'm going to terminate this interview."

Demer raised a placatory hand. "There wasn't any sign of a forced entry, so at this point, we're just trying to exclude all persons who knew how to access the household."

"How many people fall into that category?"

Demer and Oliver exchanged a look.

"Just two of you," Demer said. "You and the Grants' housekeeper."

"What about Kat's family? They must have keys or know where the spare is."

Demer shook his head. "According to Katherine Grant, you were the only two."

According to Katherine Grant.

They were the most chilling words I had ever heard. Unless I was misreading the situation, or unless the police were purposely misleading me, it sounded very much like Kat had deliberately cast police suspicion on me.

Except that Kat would never do that.

I took a deep breath, quelling the anxiety that was starting to ferment. I needed to keep my head clear.

"I may be one of the only people whom Kat told where the spare key was," I said. "But what about Howard?"

"What do you mean?" Sergeant Oliver asked.

"He might have told any number of people about the key and the alarm code."

"We've spoken to Mr. Grant's assistant, Ellen Propst, who frequently ran errands for him. He never gave her a key to the house or the alarm code, and she couldn't think of anyone else he might have told. His only living relative other than his wife and daughter, who were both out of town at the time of his death, is an elderly mother, who lives in a nursing home."

I drew in a deep breath. "He might have told his girlfriend."

Detective Demer set down his pencil and looked at me. "His girlfriend?" he repeated.

"I thought you said that as far as you knew, the Grants had a happy marriage," Oliver said. "I thought you said they weren't headed for a divorce."

This wasn't information I had planned to share with the police or anyone else. But they, and Kat, had left me no choice.

I ignored Oliver and instead looked directly at Detective Demer. "Howard Grant was having an affair."

11

—————

Twenty Months Earlier

KAT HAD ASKED me to meet her for lunch in downtown West Palm Beach. Somewhat unusual for her, she'd called at the last minute and, even more strange, had asked if we could go to Brio Tuscan Grill at CityPlace. We usually chose lunch spots that were closer to one of our homes or to Kat's gallery. I was happy to make the drive, though. Kat had spent the summer in Nantucket, and I hadn't seen her since she'd returned home a week earlier.

Kat was already at the restaurant when I got there, sitting at a high-top near the bar. She waved at me.

"Hey," I said once I'd reached her table. I noted that Kat had already ordered a bottle of wine, set in a marble cooler on the table.

"Hey, you!" Kat grinned and stood up. She opened her arms to embrace me warmly. She smelled, as always, like her favorite lemon verbena–scented soap.

"I've missed you," she exclaimed. "Thanks for meeting me."

"Are you kidding? I've missed you, too! I'm so glad you're

back. Having lunch with you is much more fun than spending the day folding laundry."

"Ah, the glamorous life of a mother," Kat said, and I smiled, even though I was fairly sure she had never folded laundry in her life, before or after she became a mother. "Would you like a glass of wine? I hope so, because I went ahead and ordered a bottle."

"Sure."

Kat plucked the bottle from its cooler and poured me a glass. The waiter had already brought a bread basket and dipping oil.

"This is a new spot for us," I said. "Were you down here running errands?"

"I suppose you could call it that," Kat replied. "An errand of sorts."

"That sounds mysterious." I took a sip of my wine.

"No, I'll tell you all about it. But first, what have you been up to?"

"Nothing much," I said. "Same old, same old. I'm just glad the kids are back in school."

The truth, which I had already decided I was not going to share with Kat, was that the summer had been simply awful. There was the heat, which had been stifling and muggy and made any midday errand a misery. My children had participated in a few camp sessions—basketball for Liam, sailing for Bridget—but those had ended in mid-July, and anyway, at over $200 a week per child, they had stretched our budget to its breaking point. I'd spent most of August tripping over the kids while they bickered endlessly. Then our ancient Volvo wagon had suffered the dual insults of a blown tire and, a week later, a broken radiator. The subsequent repair bills meant that we were now a month behind on our mortgage payments. Just thinking about it made my chest tighten and my breathing shallow. I knew I needed to go back to work, but Palm

Beach Atlantic University didn't have any openings in its math department. There were more universities down south, but there was no way I could swing the commute to Miami and still get back in time to pick the children up from school.

I decided to see if I could pick up some work tutoring students in math. I'd spent the past two weeks since school had started circulating flyers to everyone I knew with middle school–aged and older children. True, it was not exactly my dream job, but if it helped keep my debit card from being declined at the grocery store—which had actually happened at one point in mid-August—I would be…well, no, not *happy*. That would be an overstatement. But at least I might get some sleep at night.

While Kat and I might tell each other everything—or at least, most things—I wasn't going to tell her about our financial problems. At best, she'd pity me. At worst, she'd judge me. I could just about manage to cope with the difficulty of our current situation as long as I wasn't forced to explain it to anyone else.

"I thought you went out of town for a few days," Kat said. Kat wasn't much of a texter or emailer, so we'd been mostly out of touch while she was gone.

"We only drove up to Jacksonville to visit my in-laws. It wasn't exactly a dream vacation."

"You should have come with me to Nantucket," Kat said. "My parents' house there is huge. There was more than enough room, especially since Amanda only ended up staying for a week before she went back to Vanderbilt for summer session."

This struck me as an odd comment, since Kat had not invited me to go to Nantucket with her. Did she expect me to ask myself? To show up without warning, husband and kids in tow, hoping for a free vacation?

I just smiled and replied, "Maybe next time."

"Anyway, it was nice to get away from the heat. And from my darling husband." Kat smiled icily.

"I thought Howard went with you." I was surprised by her disclosure.

"He did. For the first weekend. But then he supposedly had some sort of 'crisis' at work, and so he just *had* to fly home," Kat explained, making quotation marks with her fingers on the word *crisis*. Her lips twisted, and it was clear just what she thought about that.

"Maybe he really did have a work crisis." I was no fan of Howard's, it was true, but for Kat's sake, I wanted him to be a better man than I suspected he was.

"Maybe. Or maybe he was fucking that blonde bartender over there." Kat nodded toward the U-shaped bar. I followed her gaze.

The young woman tending the bar was one of the most beautiful women I had ever seen outside a magazine or a movie. She was curvy in a lush, almost old-fashioned way, with a small waist and full breasts and hips. Her face was a perfect oval with no sharp angles. Just large, round eyes and full, pouting lips. She couldn't have been much older than twenty.

"Jesus," I said.

Kat laughed, spluttering her wine and then raising a hand to wipe her lips.

"I knew there was a reason I loved you," she said. "You always know the perfect thing to say."

I smiled, but for just a moment. "You think she's sleeping with Howard?"

Kat shook her head. "I *know* she's sleeping with Howard."

"No!"

"Yes."

"That girl—" I pointed my chin at the goddess "—could have anyone. Why would she pick Howard?"

Kat tilted her head to one side and looked at me quizzically. "Why do you think?"

I considered this question. There was, of course, only one answer. Howard could be considered handsome if you completely ignored his personality. But even then, Howard could really be considered attractive only *for his age*. How could he have caught the attention of a girl this gorgeous?

Except for the obvious fact that Howard was very, very rich.

Actually, I wasn't even sure how accurate this was. I knew by now that Kat came from an exceedingly wealthy family, and that Howard had some measure of professional success. But was he as wealthy as Kat? I had no idea. Kat never talked about it. And if I didn't know, I was pretty sure the blonde bartender didn't, either.

"Tell me," I said.

And so Kat did.

She had been suspicious even before their trip to Nantucket. There had been a lot of unexplained absences, times when Howard was supposed to be home or somewhere with Kat and had begged off at the last minute, claiming work emergencies or last-minute client dinners.

"My darling husband thinks he's much cleverer than he really is," Kat mused. "He assumes that if he tells me he has a client meeting, no matter what time of day or night it is, I'll believe him, even if he doesn't get home until midnight. But besides that, he was acting odd even before we left for Nantucket."

"How so?"

"I can't put my finger on it, really. Moody. Distant, I guess. And his temper was awful." Kat sighed, picked up a bread stick from the basket and crumbled it onto her plate. "Worse than usual, which is saying something. He's fine if he sticks with wine, but when he starts knocking back the scotch, he gets ugly."

"Because he drinks more of it?" I asked.

"No, I don't think so. I'm not sure there's science to back me up, but I do think that certain types of alcohol affect him differently. He doesn't get argumentative—or at least, not more so than usual—when he's drinking wine or rum or vodka. But once he gets deep into the scotch—" Kat shook her head and exhaled deeply "—it's not pretty."

"Why did he go with you at all if he was going to bail after one weekend?"

"Who knows? It's not like he's going to tell me the truth about any of this."

After they'd been at her parents' Nantucket house for a few days—Kat threw in some random descriptions here, including beachside cocktail parties, a clambake and leisurely hours spent lounging on the beach, all of which sounded wonderfully glamorous, especially in contrast to the miserable summer I'd just endured—Howard had suddenly announced that he had a work emergency that required him to return to Florida immediately. When Kat pressed him for details about the nature of the emergency, Howard had been defensive.

"He didn't even have a convincing story planned," she said, tucking a strand of dark hair behind one ear. "When I asked him why he couldn't deal with the problem remotely with his laptop and cell phone, he went into a rage. He said I had no idea how difficult it was to run a business. I pointed out that I've run a successful art gallery for twenty years, and he rolled his eyes in the most patronizing way possible and told me it was hardly the same thing."

I was not on Howard's side in any of this, of course, but I did think he might have had a point there. While I didn't know anything about his financial investment business, I was pretty sure that in all the time Kat had been running her gallery, she never truly had to worry about whether it was making a profit. This was not to say that she didn't run it in a professional manner, or that she wasn't successful. But it was not like she wondered how she'd keep the lights on and her family fed if K-Gallery went under.

In any event, Kat had not been able to convince Howard to stay in Nantucket and work out his business emergency from there. Instead he departed quickly, booking a flight back to Florida that very night. On his own. To an empty house, unencumbered by either wife or daughter. Free to do whatever he wanted.

"And I take it this all made you suspicious."

"Yes, it did," Kat agreed, raising her wineglass to her berry-glossed lips. "My husband has never been one to give up a vacation in favor of work. Especially a free vacation."

"How did you find out what he was up to?"

Kat hesitated, toying with the gold bangle on her wrist. "It's actually a little embarrassing."

"You don't have to tell me if you don't want to," I said, although, of course, I was dying to know.

"I hired a private investigator," Kat said.

"Seriously?" I asked. Kat nodded. "How did you find one?"

"My father gave me the referral," she said, as though everyone's father knew a private detective or two. I was fairly sure that my father, who was a retired history professor, didn't know any.

"What was the private detective like? Did he call you a dame and keep a bottle of whiskey in his desk?" I asked, picturing Humphrey Bogart in *The Maltese Falcon*. I had gone through an old black-and-white noir film phase when I was in my twenties.

Kat looked at me blankly. "I have no idea. I didn't go to his office. I hired him over the phone, and then he emailed me his report. Which, by the way, included photos."

"Of Howard and—" I stopped and tipped my head discreetly in the direction of the bar.

"The very same," Kat said, her lips curving in a humorless smile. "Her name is Alana. Can you believe that? A-la-na Dupree." She sounded it out, exaggerating the vowels. "Doesn't that sound like something a stripper would be called? Nineteen years of marriage and building a life together, raising a child, and my darling husband decides to turn me into a cliché just so he can bang a woman half his age."

Kat smacked her wineglass down so hard, I was surprised it didn't shatter. She lifted one hand to flag down our waiter. As always when Kat summoned pretty much anyone to do anything, he hurried over. I'd never been able to figure out how she was able to command such instant attention. Certainly she was an attractive woman, but was that the only reason? It was as though Kat was able to communicate silently her status to the world around her, and it responded as it should. In the time I had known her, I'd witnessed people fawn over Kat's clothes, her jewelry, her car. It still struck me as strange that the mere owning of things should somehow be so praiseworthy.

"This wine is terrible," Kat said, pointing to the bottle. "I think it's gone off."

"I'm so sorry," the waiter said obsequiously. He was wearing a name tag that read STEVE. Steve took the bottle without commenting on the fact that it was half-empty.

"It's not your fault," Kat said, smiling warmly at him. "I'm surprised the bartender didn't notice it when she opened the bottle. It's practically turned into vinegar. The cork must have been degraded."

"The bartender is young and, unfortunately, not very experienced. I'll let her know that in the future, she can't miss things like this. And I'll have a replacement bottle out for you immediately," Steve promised.

"Thank you so much," Kat said.

Once Steve had rushed off to berate Alana for her neglect, I looked at Kat.

"There wasn't anything wrong with that wine," I said softly.

"Oops." Kat smiled, pleased with herself.

"How did he not notice that we drank almost half the bottle?"

"I'm sure he doesn't care. It's not like it's costing *him* anything. And by taking care of this problem for us, he's basically guaranteeing himself a good tip." She looked over at Steve berating Alana the bartender. I followed her gaze. We watched as Alana sniffed the wine and shrugged. Steve shook his head in disgust. He spoke louder, although still not loud enough for us to hear what exactly he was saying, but he waved his arms demonstrably.

"I think he's enjoying this," Kat commented. "He probably thinks she's a stupid little twat, too."

"Kat!" I said, mildly shocked at this coarse language. To be honest, I was almost amused. This was not how the PTA mothers at school described one another, even when they were ready to scratch each other's eyes out.

"What?" Kat said mildly. "Do you have a better term for a grasping little gold digger who sleeps with married men?"

I did not.

"Have you told Howard that you know?" I asked.

"Not yet," Kat said.

"Why not?"

"I haven't decided what I'm going to do yet."

I tried to imagine myself in her position. Would it be possible for me to know Todd was having an affair and continue to live with him—handing him mugs of coffee, making dinner, chatting about the children—without confronting him about it? I was surprised to realize that it might be. If I'd been asked this when I was a new bride, I'm sure I would have said that I'd never be able to tolerate infidelity. That cheating would automatically be the end of my marriage. Any woman who chose to look the other way was foolish and weak. But now...now I wasn't so sure. It would depend on the details, of course, and I wouldn't just ignore the affair. But I didn't think I would be too quick to put my children through the trauma of a divorce.

"Is this the only time Howard's been unfaithful?" I asked.

"No, it's not," Kat said. But then she paused, thought about it and qualified her response. "At least, I don't think it's the only time. I've had my suspicions over the years, but Howard's always denied it."

"What sort of suspicions?"

"There was a woman he worked with a few years ago, someone in his office, who was just...overly present in his life. They'd go to lunch all the time and she would call him her work husband."

"Gross," I said.

"I know, right? But I thought the fact that they weren't sneaking around, and would even joke about people thinking they were having an affair, meant they couldn't possibly actually be having an affair." Kat paused, looking down at the table. "I suppose that sounds idiotic."

"No, it doesn't," I assured her.

"If that doesn't, this will—a woman once came into the gallery and told me that she and Howard were in love."

"Are you serious?"

"Unfortunately."

"Who was she?"

"Her name was Beth. She was a chiropractor. Howard saw her for some back issues he was having, or at least that's what he claimed at the time. Anyway, she came to the gallery that day to announce that they wanted to be together, and to beg me to let him go. According to her, Howard had told her I'd hurt myself if he left me. She thought I was standing in the way of their true love."

I shook my head, speechless.

"Howard denied the whole thing, of course. He insisted she had a unrequited crush on him, but that he'd never led her on, and he'd certainly never slept with her. And I believed him." Kat sighed. "Dumb as that may sound."

"He's your husband. You're supposed to believe in him," I said, although I was pretty sure that was bullshit. Howard had cheated before, and he was cheating now. I wondered yet again why Kat stayed with him.

"Then there are all of the business trips he's taken over the years." Kat gave a mirthless laugh and shook her head. "I have no doubt he took his opportunities when they arose."

"I'm so sorry. I can't imagine how hard this is for you," I said.

"What would you do in my position?" Kat asked.

"I was just wondering the same thing," I answered. "It would be different for us, of course. Todd and I have two young children, and that would obviously affect our decision. And we really couldn't afford to separate. I would have to go back to work, maybe even move out of town to find a position in my field, which would be even more traumatic for the kids. But that doesn't mean I wouldn't seriously think about leaving him."

"It's not that I can't afford to divorce Howard. Not exactly. But..." Kat began as Steve reappeared with a new bottle of wine.

"That was our last *chilled* bottle of the Sonoma-Cutrer," he said, the emphasis making clear his disdain of Alana the bartender and her inability to keep the wine at the proper temperature. "Please accept this bottle of the Duckhorn chardonnay on the house instead."

"Thank you very much," Kat said, displaying her straight white teeth as she smiled.

Steve uncorked the wine and waited while Kat tasted it.

"Delicious," she pronounced.

Steve beamed at her, as though she were the source of all that was well and good in the world, and proceeded to pour us each a glass. "Are you ladies ready to order?" he asked.

"I think we might need a few more minutes," Kat said.

"Take as long as you need. I'll check back in a bit," Steve said. He bowed his head and departed.

"This is excellent. And it costs twice as much as the first bottle," Kat said. She leaned forward in a conspiratorial way. "And even better, it's *free*."

It wasn't the first time in my friendship with Kat that I was able to observe how much she—who could afford any bottle of wine in any restaurant in the world—reveled in the pleasure of being comped something. I was also sure that if I had been the one to send the wine back, which I would have done only if it had actually turned into vinegar, the waiter would not have reappeared with a free bottle of a more expensive wine.

"I think I might have caused a bit of a scene," Kat said, looking over at the bar. I followed her gaze. Alana was staring back at Kat, her young, lush face stricken and pale. Kat raised her wineglass in the young woman's direction, which caused Alana to start and turn quickly away. "I wonder if she recognizes me. Look at that. She already has her cell phone out. Gee, I wonder whom she's texting? Do you know she's barely older than Amanda?"

"I don't know what Howard was thinking," I said.

"You don't? I do. Look at her. That face, that body. I'm sure Howard's not too interested in her witty conversation or her insights into nineteenth-century literature," Kat said, taking a large swig of her wine. I didn't blame her. The discovery that your husband of many years was sleeping with a woman slightly older than your daughter would have made anyone want to dull the pain.

"So, what now?" I asked. "Are you going to try to work it out, or are you going to…" I trailed off, not wanting to make any assumptions.

"I don't know what to do. If we…*separate*…" Kat began. She, too, seemed reluctant to say the word *divorce*. "I would stand to lose quite a lot of money. Howard and I didn't have a prenuptial agreement."

I nodded but stayed quiet. Kat rarely talked about her fortune or the rarified position in the world she held because of it. She also knew that I was not wealthy, but we never talked about that, either. I think by that point, we both treasured our friendship. Neither one of us wanted to spoil it.

"You're lucky you have Todd," Kat said.

Kat had made similar comments to me a few times in the past about my marriage, and they always irritated me.

"Kat," I said, setting down my wineglass, "I love my husband, and I don't doubt that he loves me. But don't make the mistake of thinking that every marriage other than your own is a happy one."

"You're not happy?" she asked, sounding surprised.

I considered this. "I'm not *unhappy*," I said. "But we have our own issues. Everyone thinks that other people, other couples, have it all figured out. That you're the only ones who struggle. But there really is no such thing as a perfect marriage. In fact, I've been thinking Todd and I should talk to a marriage therapist."

Kat leaned forward, looking concerned. "Is anything serious going on?"

"I don't know." I shrugged. "We just haven't been connecting lately on any level. The only thing we have in common these days are the kids. I'm starting to think that marriage should have a ten-year term limit."

"And how exactly would that work?"

"After ten years, you sit down and decide if you want to keep going for another ten or not. If so, great, you sign a new contract. If not, you shake hands and go your separate ways."

Kat laughed and shook her head. "That's not very romantic."

"No, but then, neither is marriage."

"At least your husband isn't fucking a twenty-two-year-old bartender," Kat said sourly.

I nodded, acknowledging the truth of this. "No, he isn't. Or at least, I don't think he is."

She gave me a long look. "You would know."

"Maybe I would, maybe I wouldn't," I said. "It would depend on how good a liar Todd was."

But Kat just continued to stare at me through slightly narrowed eyes.

"You would know," she repeated. "And what's more, Alice, you wouldn't put up with it. Not for one minute."

12

Present Day

IF DETECTIVE DEMER was surprised by my statement regarding Howard's infidelity, he didn't show it. His face remained expressionless other than a slight flicker in the depths of his dark brown eyes, which I might have imagined. Sergeant Oliver's response, on the other hand, was more predictable. She slammed one open hand down on the table, uttered an expletive and then fixed me with a hard stare that I suspected she practiced in front of a mirror.

"Do you think this is some sort of a game? It's not. It's a murder investigation, and it's time you started cooperating," Oliver snapped.

I stared back at her, impassive. It occurred to me that someone this volatile was probably not cut out for police work. It was a job that required logic and problem-solving skills but also a certain level of detachment. Indulging in this level of vitriol toward someone you were investigating seemed like it would only backfire.

"I am cooperating," I said.

"A few minutes ago, you told us that Katherine and Howard Grant had a happy marriage. Now you're claiming that he was having an affair."

Oliver leaned across the table, her eyes narrowed into angry slits. "Were you lying then or are you lying now?"

This struck me as a particularly moronic question. As though lying once, twice or multiple times somehow insulated you from lying again.

"It wasn't a lie," I said. "I do think that, for the most part, Kat and Howard's marriage worked for them."

"Except for the fact that he was sleeping with someone else," Oliver retorted.

"Relationships aren't that simple." I shrugged. "Of course Kat was hurt by Howard's infidelity. But it wasn't the end of their marriage."

Oliver was about to respond, but Demer lifted a hand in her direction without taking his eyes off me. The sergeant pressed her lips together into a thin line, her nostrils flaring.

"Who was Howard Grant having an affair with?"

For a moment I considered not telling him. Despite her solid alibi, the police clearly considered Kat a suspect in Howard's death. But perhaps giving them an alternate suspect—or a bunch of alternate suspects, since it wouldn't surprise me if Howard had brought more than one woman home when Kat was out of town—would help Kat. At the very least, the police would have another line of inquiry to follow.

"Her name is Alana Dupree," I supplied. "She's a bartender at a restaurant in CityPlace. Or at least, she used to be. I don't know if she still works there or not."

Demer jotted down a few notes on the lined pad in front of him.

"How long had the affair been going on?" he asked.

"I'm not sure." Then, catching Oliver's look of disbelief, I said, "Really, I don't know when it started. Kat found out about it over a year and a half ago. I know she confronted

Howard and he promised to end it. But…" I stopped and shrugged again.

"You don't think he did end it," Demer said.

"I saw them together recently," I admitted. "I was driving home from a committee meeting at my children's school. They pulled up next to me at a stoplight."

"Grant was with—" Demer checked his notes "—Alana Dupree?"

"It was definitely Howard. He drives—" I began and then stopped. "I mean, he *drove* a red Mercedes convertible, which I recognized at once. It's very noticeable. The girl with him looked like Alana—Kat pointed her out to me once—but I suppose I couldn't definitively say it was her."

"Did they see you?"

"No." I remembered looking over, registering that it was Howard and then watching as he turned to the blonde sitting next to him and began kissing her. Howard clearly hadn't mastered the art of discretion, which was rather surprising for a serial adulterer. I'd have thought he'd have been more skilled at it by then.

"When was this?" Demer asked.

"Just last week. It was the last time I saw Howard."

"Did you tell Katherine Grant about what you'd seen?"

I shook my head. "No. Kat had already left for London. It's not the kind of thing you text someone. And then…well, the only time I've spoken to her since was when she called to tell me that Howard had died. As you can imagine, I didn't think that was the best time to bring it up, either."

Demer nodded, looking only faintly disappointed. It would have fit the narrative he seemed to be favoring if Kat had recently learned Howard was still cheating on her.

"Do you have an alibi for Monday night?" Sergeant Oliver asked.

Monday, I realized, was the day Howard had died. I felt another frisson of unease.

"An alibi?" I repeated. "Do I need one?"

"It's standard procedure," Demer assured me. "We're asking everyone who had access to the house or who was a frequent visitor. Friends, family, yard and housekeeping services."

"I was at the beach," I said. "Alone."

"At night?" he asked, looking surprised for the first time that morning. "In the dark?"

"It wasn't that dark. There was a full moon…" I thought back again to the witness who claimed to have seen Howard pushed off the balcony. The moon had glowed low in the sky that night. It had been both beautiful and eerie.

"Do you often go out for late-night walks? That doesn't seem like a very safe habit," Demer commented.

"No, not often," I said. "But my husband and I had an argument that night. I didn't want the fight to escalate, especially since our children were home. It upsets them when we fight. So I left. I drove to the beach and walked until I calmed down. Then I went back home."

"What were you arguing about?" This from Oliver.

I pressed my lips together in a tight smile before responding. "That's private."

"This is a homicide investigation," Oliver retorted.

"Which my marital dispute has nothing to do with," I countered.

"Why don't you let us decide what is and is not relevant to our investigation?" Oliver pointed a finger at me as she spoke. It was a gesture I had never liked. I liked it even less coming from her.

The door to the conference room swung open. All three of us looked up to see a slim man with snow-white hair slicked neatly back off his face. He was very dapper, wearing a sharp navy blue suit over a starched white shirt, with a light blue tie knotted perfectly at his neck.

"It looks like I'm interrupting something," he said cheerfully.

Demer raised a hand. "Sir, if you could return to the lobby, I'm sure someone will be there to help you momentarily."

"No, I'm here to interrupt. John Donnelly," he said, holding out his hand to the detective.

"Alex Demer." The detective shook his hand. "And this is Sofia Oliver."

Sergeant Oliver did not shake John Donnelly's hand, but this seemed only to amuse him. He grinned at her, then looked over at me.

"And by the process of elimination, I take it you're Alice Campbell?" he quipped.

"I am."

"Excellent." Donnelly nodded toward the door. "Let's go, Alice Campbell."

"Hold on, one minute," Sergeant Oliver sputtered. "Who the hell do you think you are?"

"I didn't say? My apologies. I'm Mrs. Campbell's attorney, and she's leaving with me."

"Mrs. Campbell is here of her own free will. She's cooperating with our investigation." Demer spoke in his calm, deep voice. I wondered if anything ever rattled him.

"And now she'll be leaving of her own free will," Donnelly said. "This interview is over. Mrs. Campbell?"

I stood, glad for my white knight, whoever he was. I'd had enough. Enough of the questions, enough of Oliver's rudeness, enough of how suffocating the small, bland room had become. Mr. Donnelly held the door open for me and I headed toward it. But before I made my escape, Detective Demer spoke.

"Loyalty is an admirable trait. You just have to make sure it's not misplaced."

The detective was right, of course, but it didn't persuade me to stay. I didn't know what was going on with Kat, although I intended to find out as soon as possible. But if there was one thing I was sure of, it was this—over the past three years, Kat had more than earned my loyalty.

I turned and walked out the door.

13

Eighteen Months Earlier

I WAS CARRYING three heavy bags of groceries into the house when I heard the sound of a dog barking inside my handbag. Liam, who thought it was hilarious to steal my cell phone and change the ringtone, had clearly been up to his old tricks. At least the dog was preferable to the fart sounds he had once programmed in.

I struggled to drop the shopping bags on the counter and grappled for the phone, which was, as always, at the very bottom of my handbag. Caller ID reported that it was the children's school, Seaview Country Day. I managed to hit the accept button just before it went to voice mail.

"Hello!" An orange rolled out of one of the grocery bags and fell to the floor with a dull thud.

"Am I speaking to Mrs. Campbell?" a nasal male voice said in my ear.

I recognized the caller at once from the endless back-to-school nights, awards ceremonies and school plays. It was Phil Douglas, the principal.

"Yes, it is." I was never sure whether to call him Phil or Mr. Douglas, so I usually tried to refrain from doing either.

"This is Principal Douglas from Seaview Country Day."

"Is everything all right?" Calls from the school always caused me a surge of anxiety. "Are Liam and Bridget okay?"

"They're fine." Principal Douglas sounded unusually terse. He normally affected a jovial manner that he never quite pulled off. "That's not why I'm calling."

I waited, and after a brief pause, he continued. "I'm calling about your tuition bill."

"What about it?"

"It's overdue."

"What? No, I'm pretty sure we paid it just last week." I knelt to pick up the orange.

I specifically remembered asking Todd if he'd mailed in the tuition check, and his affirmative reply. Todd had insisted on taking over paying the bills a few months earlier, claiming the chore stressed me out. It actually didn't. I liked organizing the bills, then methodically going through them. What stressed me out was never having enough money to pay them all. I had agreed to let Todd take over, but only because I hoped it would help him finally see the reality of our finances and curb his compulsive spending habits.

"We haven't received a payment from you since the beginning of the term," the principal corrected me. "You have a past due balance of nearly six thousand dollars."

"What?" I gasped. I suddenly realized I was still crouched on the ground and slowly stood back up, the orange clutched in one hand. "No, there must be a mistake. We're on a monthly payment plan."

"That's just it. You haven't been making your monthly payments." He cleared his throat with an unpleasant phlegmy cough. "This shouldn't come as a surprise to you, Mrs. Campbell. Our school accountant, Ms. Davies, has spoken to your husband several times about your outstanding balance."

"That may be, but this is the first I've heard of it." I was surprised at how calm I was managing to sound. I wondered if Principal Douglas was a gossip, whether news of our financial troubles would spread through the PTA. "Let me look at our accounts and get back to you. I'll try to make at least a partial payment by early next week."

The principal sighed, sounding aggrieved. At least he didn't seem to be enjoying this conversation any more than I was, cold comfort though that was.

"You don't understand, Mrs. Campbell. We've already given you *several* extensions. You're going to have to pay off the outstanding balance immediately or Liam and Bridget will not be allowed to continue coming to school."

I absorbed this. "When do you need the payment by?"

"Tomorrow," he said.

"By *tomorrow*?" I repeated. My voice sounded high and sharp, so I drew in a deep breath to steady myself. "That seems awfully harsh. I'm very sorry the payments are late, but the children have been going to your school for years. Surely you can grant us an extension, at least until I figure out what's going on. There must be a mix-up somewhere."

"I'm sorry, but it's impossible. We've already given you several extensions," Principal Douglas said.

I hung up and sat down shakily at the kitchen table. I had precisely one business day to find six thousand dollars to pay to the school, and I had no idea what was going on. What had happened to the tuition money we budgeted each month? Why hadn't Todd paid the bill? Why had he told me he had?

I picked my phone back up and dialed Todd's number.

"Hey." He picked up after one ring. Wherever he was, it sounded noisy. I could hear ambient music and background voices.

"Where are you?"

"Work," he said. "Why?"

"It sounds noisy."

"Oh, well, actually I just stopped by a Starbucks on my way back to the office," Todd said.

"Then why didn't you just say you were at Starbucks?"

"I did."

"No, you said you were at work."

"I guess in my mind I am at work. Just stopping for some caffeine in between the job site and the office. Did you call for a reason?" Todd asked, now sounding irritable.

It was this, his petulant, touchy tone, that cut through the fog of disbelief and sparked my anger.

"Yes, actually," I said. "I just got off the phone with the school."

Todd hesitated. "Is everything okay?"

"No. No, it's not. Apparently we owe the school nearly six thousand dollars. Apparently we haven't made a single payment since the beginning of the term. And apparently you've known about this but for some reason neglected to tell me." I bit the words out.

Todd went silent. The background music—a dreary female vocalist crooning along to a lackluster guitar accompaniment—seemed to swell louder in my ear.

"Hello?"

"I'm here." Todd took a deep breath, and when he spoke again, his voice sounded strange, as though it had been hollowed out. "I haven't known how to tell you."

"Tell me what?"

There was another long pause. "I lost my job."

"You... Wait, *what*? When did this happen?"

"Stop shouting."

"I'm not shouting. I'm... Jesus." I struggled to contain my emotions. "When did this happen?"

"Three months ago."

Now it was my turn to go silent. I stared down at the table, focusing intently on the grain of the light pine wood. There was a scatter of toast crumbs left over from breakfast and a white circular ring that meant someone had set a cold glass on the table without using a place mat or coaster. I tried to remember the tip for getting water stains out of wood. Was I supposed to rub it with mayonnaise? Or was that the trick for removing candle wax spills?

The shock seemed to be having an odd effect on me, because all of a sudden, my anger and fear had drained away. It felt like I was floating in a bubble, safe and self-contained. It was almost as though I'd had the sense that something was wrong, had been tensing for the blow to come for months, and now that it was finally revealed to me, I could relax. It was impossible to solve any problem without knowing all of the facts, no matter how unpleasant they might be.

"Alice?" Todd's voice was insistent in my ear.

"What?" I still stared at the water ring.

"Say something."

"What have we been living on for the past three months?" I had quite a few students I was tutoring regularly, but the money I made was laughably small. We didn't have any savings to speak of. What few valuables we owned had not disappeared from the house. But the power was still on and my debit card had not been rejected at the grocery store again, so money was coming in from somewhere.

Todd hesitated again, which made me brace for information I didn't want to hear.

"I cashed out my retirement account," he said quietly.

I could no longer hear the wailing music and suspected that he had stepped outside of the Starbucks.

"You have to pay a penalty for cashing out early." I swiped the crumbs off the table and onto the floor.

"I know, but...I didn't have a choice."

He didn't have a choice? That wasn't true, I reflected. He'd had lots of choices. Like, for starters, the choice he'd made not to tell me he'd lost his job.

"How much do we have left?"

"Not much."

I exhaled, closing my eyes. "Why didn't you tell me?"

"I kept thinking I'd get another job. I've gone on a few interviews. They all went well, but… I just need some more time."

"We don't have more time."

"What do you mean?"

"The school said that if we don't pay our bill by tomorrow, Liam and Bridget won't be allowed to stay at the school."

Todd was silent. Suddenly the bubble was gone, and my anger was back. My hands were starting to shake, and my body had gone simultaneously hot and cold, which was an odd sensation. Even so, I sensed that the feelings I was experiencing now weren't anything in comparison to what I would be feeling later, tomorrow, the following week, when I'd had time to process it all. But in the midst of that anger, I had just the slightest twinge of compassion. I knew Todd hadn't kept this hidden because he enjoyed deceiving me. No. He'd done it because he'd felt scared. Helpless. Humiliated.

It just wasn't a good enough excuse.

"I have to go," I whispered.

"Alice, wait—"

But I didn't wait. I disconnected and dropped the phone on the now crumb-free table. I buried my face in my hands, bracing my elbows against the wood. Panic, hot and acidic, flooded over me.

We'd had money problems for years, had become pros at juggling bills and unexpected expenses, but Todd's regular income had given us some security. What would happen now? How would we pay for our mortgage and our groceries? And where would Liam and Bridget go to school on Monday? We had opted to enroll the children in Seaview Country Day, even though we'd barely been able to afford it, because of how favorably it compared to the local public school system. And it certainly wasn't a decision based on snobbery. We were zoned for the worst public middle school in town. Just last week, there had been a stabbing there. An actual stabbing.

But now we wouldn't have a choice.

I laid my hands flat on the table and forced myself to draw in several deep breaths, not to panic. True, this was a problem, but like all problems, it had a solution. Todd would get another job. I would find more tutoring work.

I suddenly remembered my conversation with Todd all those months ago, when he'd sneered at the idea of working for Kat's father. Was that a possibility? Or did asking Kat to put in a good word for Todd, perhaps even to set up an interview for him, cross the line of what one could reasonably ask from a friend? Even a friend as close as Kat.

My phone rang again, startling me. I assumed it was Todd calling me back and was just trying to decide whether I wanted to take the call when I saw the caller ID. It was Kat, almost as though she'd known I was thinking about her. I accepted the call and lifted the phone to my ear.

"Hey," I said, trying to adopt a tone of casual nonchalance.

I didn't want Kat to know how upset I was. I needed time to think through all the murky layers of this latest catastrophe before I talked to her about it. What if she agreed to set up an interview for Todd and he refused to go on it? That seemed insane. Surely he would not be so picky or so dismissive of the so-called cookie-cutter houses Wyeth Construction built in the face of this looming financial disaster. But then again, I would never have thought my husband would lie to me for several months about losing his job. Maybe I didn't know him at all.

"What's wrong?" Kat asked. "You sound weird."

I cleared my throat. "I'm fine. Maybe I'm coming down with a cold."

"Alice, I know you. I can tell there's something's wrong. What is it?" Kat pressed.

And then I surprised both of us by bursting into tears.

An hour later, I was at Kat's house, sitting on the back patio by the pool. It was still warm out—not unusual for Florida in October—but the sticky heat of the summer had passed. I closed my eyes and tipped my head back, enjoying the feel of the sunshine on my face.

"Here you go," Kat said, appearing with a chilled bottle of white wine and two glasses. She poured a generous glug of sauvignon blanc into each and handed one to me.

"Thanks," I said. I took a sip. It was delicious, of course. Kat had wonderful taste in wine.

"Now, what's going on?" Kat sat in one of the large wicker chairs, tucked her feet underneath her and looked at me intently. Her attention was absolute.

"I don't know where to start."

"You don't want me to sing that song from *The Sound of Music* about starting at the very beginning," Kat joked. "I have a terrible singing voice. It'll just make you feel even worse."

I smiled weakly and looked out at the Intracoastal. The water changed color depending on the currents or the amount of pollution seeping in from Lake Okeechobee. Today the water was bright aqua and rippled with sunlight. A large motorboat puttered slowly by. The passengers were lounging on deck, drinks in hand. They all looked as though they had no worries in the world. Of course, they might have been looking back at Kat and me reclining outside Kat's beautiful house, thinking the same thing. Everything looks better from a distance.

"It's embarrassing," I finally said.

"More embarrassing than finding out your husband is having an affair?"

I shrugged helplessly. "In a way. I don't know how to quantify the different levels of humiliation."

Kat took a sip of her wine and fixed her startlingly bright blue eyes on me.

"You can tell me anything," she said. "You and I will always keep each other's secrets safe."

So I told her. All of it. I told her about the call I'd gotten earlier that day from Principal Douglas, about Todd losing his job and not telling me about it, about our myriad of money troubles that had suddenly become as large as a gaping chasm ready to swallow us whole. Kat listened attentively without interrupting.

When I finally ran out of words, she shook her head.

"You have had an incredibly crappy day. I'm so sorry you had to go through that," Kat said.

"Thanks." I exhaled loudly. "And thanks for listening. It helps. I don't know why, but it does."

"Probably because you needed to get it out. You can't keep things so buttoned up."

I nodded, acknowledging the truth of this. I'd always been self-contained and had never related to the modern confessional culture. I didn't want to know everyone's emotions the moment they felt them. Like those drama queens who posted regularly on Facebook—*"Having a tough day. Please send hugs!"* or *"I hate toxic people. I can't say more than that here, but it's time I start putting myself and my own needs first."* I found this oversharing repulsive.

And though talking to Kat meant my problems weren't weighing as heavily on me as they had earlier in the day, there was also something present that hadn't been there before. A faint, oily sense of shame. I supposed it was the price I paid for my own oversharing. I didn't care for it at all.

"Now the question is, what are you going to do?" Kat asked.

"I don't have a choice. I'll have to pull the kids out of Seaview and enroll them in public school." My voice was calm, but my stomach clenched painfully.

"You can't do that."

"I don't have a choice," I said. "The elementary school we're zoned for isn't so bad, I guess. But the middle school is a nightmare. I'm going to go down to the district office tomorrow to see what our options are."

"But the school tuition is the easiest piece to solve," Kat said. "It's just money."

"Money I don't have," I pointed out.

Kat stood suddenly and, without explanation, padded barefoot into her house. She returned a minute later with a slouchy white leather handbag that probably cost as much as two months' tuition. She reached into it, pulled out her checkbook and looked up inquiringly at me. "How much do you need?"

"No," I said, shaking my head. "No way. I'm not taking your money. That's not why I told you all of this."

"I know that!" Kat exclaimed. "Think of it as a loan."

I held up a hand, warding her off. "Which I'm in no position to repay," I said. "Not in the near future. Or the far future, for that matter."

"I don't care if you repay it or not. I want to help, Alice."

"Nothing poisons a friendship faster than borrowing money."

"No, nothing poisons a friendship faster than sleeping with your friend's husband," Kat retorted. "Money is meaningless."

"It's not meaningless when you don't have it."

"I know. I'm not trying to be flippant." Kat sighed. "But I love you. You're my best friend. And you have some large, pressing problems that I can help solve for you."

"No, I can't accept it. It wouldn't be right," I said, holding up both hands, palms facing out.

"Fine. I know you wouldn't take it for your own sake. But you have to take it for the kids. What middle school would Liam go to if he had to transfer?"

I hesitated and then admitted, "MacArthur."

"MacArthur?" Kat yelped. "Wasn't there a shooting there just last week? I could swear I read something about that in the paper."

"It wasn't a shooting. It was a stabbing."

"Alice, this is crazy. You need money. I have plenty of money, more than I can spend in my lifetime. And trust me, I've tried. Let me help you out." Kat stared at me beseechingly. "Let me at least write a check to the school. Keep Liam and Bridget where they are, where they're happy and safe. We'll worry about the rest of it later."

I could feel my willpower begin to buckle. It was true, I wouldn't take a dime on my own behalf. But I would do anything for my children. Far more than just swallowing my pride.

"I'll pay you back," I said weakly. "I don't know how or when, but I'll pay you back."

Kat shook her head briskly. "Don't worry about that now. How much do you owe the school?"

"It's a lot, Kat. We have to pay them six thousand dollars by tomorrow."

Kat nodded briskly. "I'll make the check payable directly to the school. That way you won't have to wait for it to clear your bank."

"I don't know how to thank you." I watched her write the check, feeling equal parts of relief and shame.

"Don't say another word about it." Kat tore the check off and handed it to me.

I stared down at it, hardly believing what I was seeing. "This is made out for twenty thousand dollars."

"I know. I just wrote it."

"But we don't owe this much!"

"For now. But presumably you have another payment due next month. And the month after that. This saves time by taking care of the whole year now." The way she explained it made it all sound perfectly logical.

"This is too much," I protested, trying to give it back to her. Kat waved me away. "No, it's *way* too much. It's more than we owe for the whole year."

"Oh, please. Amanda went to private school. Class trips, laptops, there's always something. And this way, you and Todd can make a plan to go forward, get back on your feet, without at least this one thing to worry about."

I stared down at the check, hardly believing it was real and wondering if I could really accept it.

"I don't know," I breathed.

"I do," Kat said crisply. "And it's done. Now, first, let's finish this bottle of wine. And then let's figure out a game plan that doesn't include killing your husband, as tempting as that may sound at the moment."

14

Present Day

THE SUN WAS dazzlingly bright when we emerged from the Jupiter Island Public Safety Department. I blinked, and as my eyes slowly adjusted, I looked out at the lush green fairways of the Jupiter Island Club. A pair of golfers—one of whom was wearing plus fours—were just teeing off. This had to be the only police station in America set right in the middle of an exclusive country club.

"Nice day for golf," John Donnelly said cheerfully. "I wouldn't mind being out there myself."

"I'm not a golfer."

"Smart. It's a good walk ruined, or so they say."

"Did my husband hire you?" I asked, turning to look at him.

"A criminal defense attorney once told me he always instructs his clients that if they're ever pulled over by the police, they should take out his business card and stick it in their mouth," John Donnelly said, ignoring my question. "It never fails to surprise me how often otherwise intelligent people make the mistake of thinking they can talk their way out of trouble."

"I wasn't trying to talk my way out of anything," I said, stung at the mild rebuke. "The police told me they were only interested in my giving them background information."

"I hate to break it to you, but the police lie to suspects all the time. There aren't any rules against it. They can lie with impunity."

"But I'm not a suspect," I insisted.

Donnelly just looked amused. "Here's my card," he said, handing it to me. "The next time the police try to interview you, don't say a word until you talk to me first. Put it in your mouth if you have to. And plan on coming to my office tomorrow at two."

I looked down at the card. "Why?" I asked. "Do I need an attorney?"

"I know you have questions," Donnelly said, holding up a hand. "But this isn't the time or place. We'll get into it all tomorrow."

He turned and, hands stuck jauntily in his pockets, headed toward a large silver Mercedes sedan parked in front of the police station. I stood and watched as he pulled out, narrowly avoiding hitting a fire hydrant before he drove off.

I didn't check my phone until I was safely sitting in my car. Surely Kat must have called me back while I was being interviewed, or at least responded to my texts. But the only messages I had were several texts from Todd:

Are you still at the police station?

What's going on? Should I meet you there?

??

?????????????????????

I texted him back:

Everything's fine. Just leaving now. Why did you hire the attorney?

I wondered if I should try calling Kat again. The police hadn't told me not to speak to her—I doubted they had the right to—but I wondered if calling her immediately upon leaving the police interview would look suspicious. I didn't know how easy it was for them to access phone records, but I had to assume, going forward, that any contact between Kat and me might be monitored.

Screw it, I thought. I needed to talk to Kat. I needed to hear her voice, to ask how she was handling her newly widowed state. Most important, I needed to find out what she knew about the police investigation.

The phone rang several times before her voice mail recording was suddenly playing in my ear:

"Hi, this is Kat Grant of K-Gallery. Leave me a message and I'll call you back."

Her tone was light and playful and almost painfully familiar. It was the same voice she used when suggesting something decadent, like having champagne with lunch.

I left her yet another voice mail message:

"Kat, it's Alice. I'm just leaving the Jupiter Island police station, and I need to talk to you as soon as possible. Please call me back."

I hung up, set the phone down on the car's console and reversed out of my parking spot. I signaled left out of the parking lot, then right onto South Beach Road. I hadn't gone far when my phone rang. I grabbed for it, again hoping it was Kat. But, no, it was Todd. I swallowed down my disappointment as I accepted the call.

"Hi."

"Jesus, I've been worried. What's going on?" Todd barked in my ear. He always became angry when he was worried.

"I just sent you a text."

"I know. That's why I called. What did the police want?"

"They were mostly interested in getting background information on Kat and Howard. They asked a lot of questions about their marriage."

"What did you say to them?"

"Can I tell you about it this evening?" I asked. "My head is still spinning from all of the questions. I was actually glad to see the attorney you sent, because he got me out of there. Where did you find him, anyway? He was very slick."

Todd hesitated. "What are you talking about? I didn't hire an attorney."

"What do you mean? Who else would have hired him?"

"What's going on? This is crazy. Look, I'm heading home now. I'll meet you there, and you can tell me everything then."

Todd hung up before I could talk him out of coming home. The last thing I felt like doing right now was rehashing the past few hours. Instead I wanted to sit quietly, clear my head and try to piece together what was going on.

At least Todd missing work was less of a problem than it would have been in the not-too-distant past. After spending a year working in short-term contract positions with various architecture firms, mostly in Miami, Todd had decided to go out on his own. He'd opened Campbell Architecture four months earlier, with an office in a modern commercial strip building downtown and the obligatory black-and-white logo in Helvetica font. His new firm was getting a slow but steady drip of work, mostly referrals from clients he'd worked with in his S+K Architects days. We weren't wealthy, not by a long stretch, but for the first time in a long time, we were doing okay.

When I arrived home, I found Todd standing barefoot in the kitchen, reheating a mug of coffee.

"Why don't you make a fresh pot?" I asked just as he pulled the coffee out of the microwave.

Todd started, and the mug slipped from his hand. It fell to the floor, shattering on the travertine tile, splattering hot coffee everywhere.

"Damn it, you scared the hell out of me!" Todd ran a hand through his dark hair. "I didn't hear you come in."

"That was my favorite mug," I said, staring down at it lying in shards on our kitchen floor. It had been hand-thrown by my mother's husband, Robert, the white-bearded potter. They'd sent it to me the previous Christmas. I didn't normally like homemade pottery, most of which was too hippy dippy, and reminiscent of tie-dyed shirts and crocheted plant hangers. But this mug had been beautiful. It was dark purple and perfectly oversize.

"I'm sorry," Todd replied. "But you shouldn't have sneaked up on me like that. When did you turn into a ninja?"

I smiled despite myself, despite the morning I'd just had. "I didn't know I had developed ninja skills. It's good to know. They could come in useful."

"I'll make more coffee," he said.

"What I want is a stiff drink, but I'll settle for coffee."

Once the coffee was made—black for me, cream and sugar for Todd—we settled in at the kitchen table.

"How was your morning?" I joked with forced cheerfulness. "Anything interesting happen?"

Todd smiled faintly, but it didn't mask his concern. "What's going on? And why did you think I hired an attorney for you?"

"Because an attorney showed up while the police were interviewing me. John Donnelly." I laid the attorney's business card on the table and slid it over to Todd. "He barged right in and stopped the interview. And he wants me to come to his office tomorrow."

"Why was he there?"

"If you didn't send him, then by the process of elimination, Kat must have. She's the only other person who knew I was going in for the police interview."

"You finally talked to her?" Todd asked. "I thought she's been incommunicado."

"No, actually I didn't speak to her. I left her a voice message and sent her a text. I still haven't heard back." I frowned. "Actually, it is sort of weird, isn't it? Why wouldn't she at least text me back to let me know she'd sent a lawyer to help me? I know she's dealing with a lot right now, but still."

Todd got out his phone. After tapping and scrolling it, he handed it to me. "Is this the guy?"

Todd had pulled up the website of the law firm Donnelly & Buchanan. There was a picture of John Donnelly wearing a single-breasted dark suit, a silver tie and a matching pocket square.

"Yes, that's him. Why?"

Todd took the phone back and, frowning down at it, ran his finger over the screen, scanning through the text. "I don't think he's a criminal defense attorney. The firm's website says they specialize in estate planning and probate litigation."

"Assuming Kat did send him, maybe he's a friend or someone her family knows." I shrugged. "I guess I'll find out tomorrow when I meet with him."

"What did the police want to talk to you about, anyway?"

I sipped my coffee. It was bitter and too hot. I put down the mug and pushed it aside.

"The police have a theory that Howard didn't fall off the balcony," I told him. "They think he might have been pushed."

Todd stared at me, his eyes growing wide. "Seriously?"

I nodded. "They say they have a witness who saw it happen."

"But that would mean…they think he was *murdered*?" Todd asked. He shook his head. "Jesus. Did they tell you who the witness is? I wouldn't think that many people would have a clear view of the Grants' house."

"That's exactly what I thought. But the detective said it's a guy who lives on the other side of the Intracoastal, apparently some sort of amateur astronomer. He was out that night with his telescope, supposedly looking at the stars."

"But he had his telescope pointed at his neighbor's house? That sounds less like astronomy and more like someone hoping to see his neighbors having sex. But what does any of this have to do with you?"

"Apparently I'm one of the few people who knows how to access Kat's house," I said. "And it's true. I do. I know where she keeps the spare key and the code to their house alarm."

"How do the police know that?"

"I assume Kat told them."

Todd shook his head. "Let me get this straight… Howard's death might have been a homicide. And Kat told the police that you had access to her house. And then she sent in a lawyer to stop the police from interviewing you."

"Don't be ridiculous—"

"How am I being ridiculous?"

"You're making it sound like Kat's out to get me," I protested. "Nothing nefarious is going on here."

"Other than Howard being murdered, you mean."

"If he *was* murdered. I don't know that I would automatically trust the word of a Peeping Tom," I qualified. "And if Kat sent the attorney, I'm sure she was just worried about me. She probably feels bad that I'm being dragged into any of this."

"The only person Kat worries about is herself." Todd snorted.

"That's not fair," I said. "And it's not true."

Todd's lips twisted into a moue, and he shrugged. His opinion of Kat had soured over the years. At first it took the form of mild concern about how much time I spent with her, the long lunches that often extended well into the afternoon. But rather perversely, he'd become even less enchanted with Kat in the months since she'd loaned us the money. I didn't know why, exactly. Maybe he was even more uncomfortable than I was being in her debt.

"So, what now? Are you a suspect?"

"I doubt it." I shook my head. "But the police did ask me where I was that night."

"They asked you for an alibi?" Todd's voice rose with anxiety.

I nodded and lifted one shoulder in a shrug. "I suppose so."

"What did you tell them?"

I looked at him, surprised. "What do you think? I told them that you and I had an argument, so I left home and went for a walk on the beach."

"Jesus! Alice, why did you tell them that?"

"Why wouldn't I?"

"Because this is serious! It's now a murder investigation!"

"Exactly. So it seems like a bad idea to start lying about where I was on the night when the supposed murder took place," I pointed out.

Todd ran both of his hands through his hair, causing it to stand up on end in black spikes.

"I can't believe you are so naive," he said. "Innocent people get blamed, get *convicted* for crimes they didn't commit all the time!"

I stared at my husband. "Are you telling me I should have lied when I told the police where I was the night Howard died? Because if I did, and they caught me in the lie, it would look terrible."

"Yes, you should have lied!" Todd exclaimed, his voice

straining with frustration. "You should have told them you were home with me. That we were watching some shitty action movie on cable. I would have backed you up, and they would have moved on to the next person on their list of suspects."

I was touched, I truly was. I reached a hand across the table, which Todd took. I looked down at his hand, square and strong, and suddenly had a vivid memory of one of our early dates. Todd had brought me to a Habitat for Humanity work site where he'd been volunteering. He saw it as a way of giving back, of using his architecture degree for good. It had impressed me.

This is a good man, I remembered thinking.

Todd had handed me an orange hard hat and patiently taught me how to hammer nails into the standing studs. I'd watched him and noticed how capable and strong his hands were. I think that might have been the moment when I started falling in love with him. Later, after we shared a take-out Margherita pizza at my apartment, Todd and I had slept together for the first time.

"Don't worry," I told him now. "I'm sure they don't really consider me a suspect. Why would I want to kill Howard? It's crazy."

"Crazy or not, you're on their radar." Todd shook his head. "I suppose you can't call them and tell them you were mistaken? That you actually were home that night and it was a different night when you walked on the beach?"

I smiled. "I think changing my alibi would probably look just a little suspicious. Don't you?"

Todd shook his head, his eyes dark and fathomless against the ashen pallor of his skin. He still had a scrap of toilet paper stuck to his neck where he must have nicked himself shaving that morning.

"Why did you have to tell them we got into a fight that

night?" Todd asked, his voice thick with emotion and fatigue, and something else I didn't recognize. Regret, maybe. Or dread.

"Because it was the truth," I said. "And once you're caught telling a lie, no one will completely believe anything you say ever again."

15

Eighteen Months Earlier

"WE CAN'T ACCEPT THIS!"

We were sitting at our kitchen table, Kat's now slightly wrinkled check lying between us. Todd was eyeing it with a mixture of suspicion and fear, as though it weren't an overly generous and life-saving gift but instead an undetonated bomb.

It was late, well past dinnertime. Both children had gone to bed, smelling of raspberry shower gel and mint shampoo. Liam was reading a volume of *Calvin & Hobbes* comic strips, which was as far as he was willing to exert himself on any book not assigned by a teacher. Bridget was on a Laura Ingalls Wilder kick and was currently reading my personal favorite, *Farmer Boy*, with its wonderful descriptions of the wallpaper in the parlor and golden buckwheat cakes covered in maple syrup. No one in *Farmer Boy* ever discovered her husband had been spending the hours he was supposed to be at work knocking back overpriced lattes and probably flirting with the tattooed baristas.

"It's too late," I said. "I already accepted it."

"But it's ridiculous," Todd said. His lip was curled, causing him to speak in an unflattering sneer. I had never disliked him more than I did in that moment.

"How is it ridiculous?"

"It's more than we even owe the school."

"That's the point." I took a sip from my water glass, grateful for the cold, clear liquid. I'd had wine earlier with Kat, reasoning at the time that it was a crisis and any alcohol consumed was medicinal. Now my mouth tasted dry and stale, and I could feel a tension headache coming on. "It's supposed to give us some breathing room while we figure everything else out."

"It isn't Kat's responsibility to pay our children's tuition," Todd argued.

"No," I agreed. "It's *our* responsibility to do that. But you lost your job and didn't pay the school and then lied about it for months, which is how we ended up in this position. And I'll be damned if the kids are the ones left to deal with the consequences."

This, unsurprisingly, silenced Todd. He was naturally pale, possessing the sort of skin that never tanned but instead turned red and blotchy when he was out in the sun for too long. Tonight, however, what color he normally possessed had drained from his face, leaving him pasty and drawn.

"I'm sorry," he said quietly. "I'm sorry I lied."

I stared down at my glass of water. It wasn't. I didn't—couldn't—forgive him. Not yet, at least, and maybe I never would.

Every marriage had its ups and downs, and ours was no different. Todd and I had even been to see a marriage therapist several times over the past few months to work on our communication skills. Dr. Ian Keller, who was a master of the empathetic head nod, had advocated that we use "I" statements with one another. For example, at this moment, he'd urge me to say, "I feel sad when you're not truthful with me about our finances."

But I wasn't in the mood for "I" statements, especially now that I knew we couldn't afford what we'd paid out of pocket for those sessions with Dr. Keller.

It was the first time I had ever seriously contemplated leaving Todd. I was surprised by how empty and tired I felt at the idea. I had assumed marriages in trouble spiraled downward among shouting and dramatic scenes. That was certainly how my parents' divorce had played out, with dishes being thrown, locks changed. I was only eight when they divorced, but I had a very clear memory of finding my mother sitting on the living room floor, cutting up their wedding photos with a pair of scissors, the shreds of my relatives lying in scrap heaps around her.

No, I didn't feel like yelling or cutting up our wedding photos. I felt like crawling into bed and going to sleep for a long, long time. Maybe that meant Todd and I would make it, after all. Maybe you needed the rage to gain the necessary momentum to propel yourself through the drama of divorce.

"We could ask my parents for a loan. Or your parents," Todd offered meekly.

I nodded. We could. And they would probably help, if they were in a position to do so. But it would mean coming clean about our myriad financial problems, which neither of us wanted to do. Besides, I wasn't sure how flush either set of parents were. My dad and stepmother were retired, and Todd's father was in poor health.

My mother, Ebbie, and I had never been close. She had decamped to an ashram shortly after her divorce from my father, leaving me confused and scared at her sudden departure. When she returned six months later, she'd cycled through a few bohemian career choices, all of which failed, while dating a series of aging hippies, all of whom I disliked. I'd always assumed that my interest in math and logic problems was at least in part a reaction to her chaotic parenting.

Now Ebbie was married to Robert, a potter, and they lived in Asheville, North Carolina. She managed the store where they sold the mugs and platters he threw. We didn't see her very often. I had no idea how wealthy she and her husband were, but I'd certainly never ask to borrow money from them. My mother and I didn't have that sort of a relationship.

"We could just enroll the kids in public school," Todd suggested. "It isn't *that* terrible an option. We know people who send their kids there."

The truth was, we hardly knew anyone who sent their kids to the local public schools. Our friends and acquaintances were the parents of our children's friends, the people we'd met over the years at soccer games and dance practices and the volunteer shifts that were now mandatory at all private schools.

"I've heard that the trick to the public schools here is to get your kids placed on the honors track," Todd continued rationalizing.

I had heard the same thing. Then again, I had read in the paper that the kid who had been stabbed the previous week had been an honors student. His assailant—not an honors student—had cornered him in the bathroom, brandishing a knife while he demanded the victim turn over his pocket money. The victim had only seven dollars. Several editorials had questioned how the perpetrator had been able to smuggle the weapon into the school in the first place, as the kids had to pass through metal detectors to get inside.

Todd looked at me inquiringly.

"No," I said. "Liam's not going to that middle school. The elementary schools aren't as bad, I suppose, if only because the kids are too young to stab one another. But Bridget doesn't handle change well. She had a near panic attack just last week when the new soccer schedule came out and she'd been put on a different team than last season. How do you think she'd handle a whole new school, a new teacher, new classmates? It's in both the children's best interests to keep them where they are."

"Even if we can't afford it?"

"We can afford it with this loan from Kat. Or at least, they can stay where they are for the rest of the year. We'll worry about next year later. Maybe we'll be in a better financial position by then. If not, maybe we can look into getting them scholarships."

Todd perked up at this. "The school has scholarships? Can't we apply for one now, for this year?"

I shook my head. "No. Not midyear. Anyway, you're missing the point."

"Which is?"

"I have already accepted this money. I'm going to give the check to the school tomorrow," I said flatly. I stood up to refill my water glass. My head was now throbbing. I rummaged around the kitchen junk drawer, looking for a bottle of ibuprofen.

Todd shook his head helplessly. "We'll never be able to pay her back."

"Yes, we will. You'll find another job. I'll get more tutoring students. I've heard that SAT prep pays well. We'll make it work."

I didn't mention the telephone call I'd received that afternoon from a publisher in New York. I hadn't picked up, but she'd left a message on my voice mail saying she'd read my book of logic puzzles and wanted to see if I was interested in taking on a similar project. I hadn't called her back yet, but even so, I wasn't sure why I didn't tell Todd about it. Perhaps I didn't trust that anything would come of it. Or maybe I didn't think Todd deserved to hear my good news when he had hidden so much from me.

"I've sent out résumés. No one in town is hiring." Todd rumpled his hair with both hands. "I have a meeting set up for next week with a firm in Miami. They said they might be able to use me, although probably only on a contract basis. And it would mean a long commute."

"Not ideal," I agreed. "But it's better than nothing."

Todd shrugged and nodded. "I'll get something. I'm good at what I do."

I didn't doubt that he was a good architect, and it wasn't hard to believe that earnings were down so far at S+K Architects that they'd had to lay off Todd and two other junior architects. The real estate market had been in a slump for years. Todd's now former bosses had promised him a good reference, and they might even be able to hire him back if business picked up.

At least, that was what he'd told me. The problem with learning that your spouse has lied to you, and done so repeatedly, is the complete loss of trust. Maybe Todd's story of his dismissal was true. Or maybe he'd been caught slacking at his job or hitting on the receptionist or stealing office supplies.

Who knew what the truth really was?

The following day, I dropped off the check to the school bookkeeper, Patricia Davies, a middle-aged woman with a prematurely gray bob and oversize glasses. Ms. Davies held the check, blinking down at it, but refrained from commenting on the amount or signatory.

"I'll apply this to your account, Mrs. Campbell," she said.

"Thank you," I replied, feeling oddly hollow as her fingers began click-clacking on her keyboard.

I turned away, trying to shake the feeling that I had just done something very, very wrong. *Did I?* I wondered, but then I reminded myself, yet again, that I had not accepted this money on my own behalf. I was doing it for Liam and

Bridget so they could stay at their school and not have their lives shaken up midyear.

Neither a borrower nor a lender be. Who had said that? I wondered. Ben Franklin? Dr. Seuss? I couldn't remember, but it was stuck in my head and set on repeat.

When I got home, I tossed my handbag on the counter and headed straight for my laptop, which I'd left out on the kitchen table that morning. I'd been researching how to become qualified as an SAT prep tutor over a breakfast of Greek yogurt and stale granola.

Once my computer had whirred to life, I typed *borrower nor lender* into an internet search engine. The results popped up, and after a few simple clicks of the mouse, I learned it wasn't a Ben Franklin quote after all, but a line from Shakespeare's *Hamlet*. It was in a soliloquy by Polonius, offering advice to his son:

> Neither a borrower nor a lender be;
> For loan oft loses both itself and friend,
> And borrowing dulls the edge of husbandry.
> This above all: to thine own self be true,
> And it must follow, as the night the day,
> Thou canst not then be false to any man.

I felt a shiver of discomfort but kept reading. Polonius was later referred to in the text as a "tedious old fool" before being killed by Hamlet. This did nothing to soothe my frayed nerves.

Would this money, this incredible gift Kat had given me, turn out to be a curse? *No*, I thought. *Don't be ridiculous. I don't believe in curses.*

My phone rang, or rather, barked, startling me. I glanced at it and saw that the call was from the 212 area code. New York City. I suddenly remembered the voice mail message I'd received the day before from the editor. I'd meant to call her back that morning but had been so distracted I'd forgotten.

"This is Alice Campbell," I said, trying to sound professional.

"Hello, Alice, this is Lydia Rafferty. I'm an editor with Kidtastic Publishing," the voice on the other end of the line said. She spoke quickly but enunciated every word.

"Yes, I got your message yesterday. I was just about to call you back," I lied.

I quickly—and, I hoped, silently—typed *Kidtastic* into my friend Google. Google replied that in the world of publishing, Kidtastic was a Big Fucking Deal. Their real success came from direct-to-school marketing in the form of fund-raising book fairs and regular order forms. I had seen dozens of these over the years, crumpled up at the bottom of my children's backpacks. We had actually ordered our fair share of books through this program, which offered competitive pricing and free books to the classroom teachers with enough parent purchases. The books sold were mostly paperbacks, with the occasional book set or merchandising add-on thrown in.

"First of all, I *loved* your book," Lydia said. "The logic puzzles were great, it was easy to read, and best of all, it was educational. I think you'd be a great fit with Kidtastic."

"You mean you want to reprint my book?" I asked doubtfully. I couldn't remember the exact details of my publishing contract, but I was fairly sure I didn't have the ability to sign it over to another publisher. "I'll need to talk to my publisher. I didn't retain the rights to resell it—"

"Oh, no, I'm sure you didn't. And as wonderful as it was— as it *is*—" she corrected herself with an overemphasis on the word *is* "—we were hoping that you could do something *slightly* different for us."

"What do you have in mind?"

"I'm so glad you asked that," Lydia said excitedly. "*Well,* right now the supernatural is hot. Hot, hot, hot. Wizards, vampires, zombies, ghosts. Kids are clamoring for more fantasy books."

I was confused. "You want me to write a fantasy novel?" I asked, hoping I didn't sound as dubious as I felt. Fiction was hardly up my alley. I'd always preferred biographies and historical nonfiction to novels in my personal reading.

"No, no, nothing like that," Lydia reassured me.

"I'm not quite sure what you mean, then."

"We want you to write what you've already written—logic puzzles. But what we were thinking of—what *I* was envisioning—" Lydia paused to inhale "—is a series of books of logic puzzles with a magical background. Problem solving with wizards! Using logic to avoid the undead! It would be such a fabulous joining of the educational—and believe me, Alice, parents are only too happy to throw money at *anything* considered educational—while setting it in the fantasy worlds that kids love. I just know it will be a huge hit! And I want you—we at Kidtastic want you—to write this series. I can't think of anyone better."

I was speechless.

"Alice? Are you still there?" Lydia sounded concerned.

"I'm here. I'm just… Well, that sounds fantastic," I said weakly, knowing that I wasn't reaching the heights of appropriately enthusiastic. Ideally she'd chalk it up to my being overwhelmed, which was certainly true.

"I know! I think so, too," Lydia said triumphantly. "I take it you're interested?"

"Yes," I said. "I'm interested. Very, very, very interested."

Lydia's laugh was a low, deep rumble. "I thought you might be."

Lydia and I continued to chat—or, more accurately, she talked at great length about her vision for the new series, while I mostly listened and made the occasional upbeat response as needed. She wanted me to agree to write three books for

Kidtastic initially, and then more if they sold well. Lydia said they'd hire an artist to illustrate the books and asked how quickly I could write them, as they would like to release the books every two to three months.

"Kids have short attention spans," she explained. "And if they get hooked on a series, they'll want every book that comes out. Releasing them in quick succession helps keep the sales elevated."

Her enthusiasm was catching, and I found myself growing more and more excited at the prospect. I had enjoyed writing the first book of logic puzzles but had never thought I could turn writing into a career. But now, listening to Lydia's enthusiastic chatter, I started to believe that maybe I could make a success of this opportunity.

By the time we got off the phone, and I sat down to start sketching out my ideas for the first book in this new series, my worries about Kat's loan ebbed away. I had made the right decision to accept the money, I decided, and with this new opportunity, I might even be able to pay her back faster than I'd ever imagined.

And anyway, Kat was right. It was just money.

16

THE LAW OFFICES of Donnelly & Buchanan were located on the twenty-first floor of the Northbridge Center in downtown West Palm Beach. Locals referred to it as the Darth Vader building because of its imposing all-black glass exterior.

When I exited the elevator and pushed open the glass door etched with the law firm's name, I was surprised at how modern the office was. I had expected a law office that specialized in trusts and estates to be conservative, perhaps with leather wingback chairs and pictures of hunting scenes on the walls. Instead the reception area was decorated with low-slung tan leather Barcelona chairs, sleek aluminum tables and palm trees in square concrete planters. There was a large modern painting on the wall that I thought I recognized from K-Gallery. I looked closer at it and saw that the artist was Crispin Murray, whose work Kat often carried.

"May I help you?" the receptionist asked me. She was an attractive woman about my age with a sleek blowout and wearing a dark skirt suit.

"I'm Alice Campbell," I said. "I have a two o'clock appointment with Mr. Donnelly."

"He's expecting you." She stood. "I'll take you back."

I followed the receptionist down a long hall, admiring how deftly she navigated the dark hardwood floors in her cripplingly high heels. At the end of the hallway, she knocked on a door and then opened it.

"Mr. Donnelly, Mrs. Campbell is here to see you," she said, then stepped aside so I could pass into his office.

John Donnelly stood and smiled when I entered. "Hello again, Mrs. Campbell."

His corner office with two walls of floor-to-ceiling windows had an amazing view of the water and the island of Palm Beach beyond. After we shook hands, Donnelly sat down behind a large modular desk of dark lacquer that was bare except for a sleek tablet and gestured for me to sit in one of the caramel leather visitors' chairs facing the desk. An enormous modern painting of a horse rearing up hung on the wall. With its bared teeth and flaring nostrils, the horse appeared menacing. I looked away.

"Thank you for coming in this afternoon," Donnelly said. "Can I get you anything? Coffee, tea, mineral water...?"

"Water would be great."

"Evelyn, we'll have sparkling water," Donnelly said to the receptionist, who was still waiting at the door.

"Of course, Mr. Donnelly," she replied. She disappeared and then returned almost immediately with a tray with two chilled glasses and a large bottle of San Pellegrino. She set the tray down on his desk and then turned to leave.

"Hold my calls," Donnelly told her. He cracked open the cap, poured the water into the two glasses and handed one to me. I took a small sip to be polite—I detested sparkling water—and then set it down.

"I don't know how you can get any work done with this incredible view," I remarked, gesturing out at the panorama. The sun sparkled on aqua water, and a large luxury boat was making its way slowly down the Intracoastal. "I'd spend all day staring out at the water."

"That's the thing about life. You can get used to just about anything," Donnelly deadpanned. "And anyway, working my ass off is the only way I can afford the view." He winked. Even though this and everything else about him was borderline cheesy, I couldn't help being charmed by the attorney.

"Thank you again for your help yesterday."

"Don't mention it." Donnelly waved a hand at me. "And don't forget what I told you. If the police want to question you again, call me first."

"I'm assuming Kat sent you?"

"I've known Kat since she was a little girl." Donnelly smiled, his teeth gleaming like a toothpaste advertisement. "She was a precocious child, as you might imagine. One time when she couldn't have been more than five, I was meeting with her father at their house. She pulled me aside and asked what I was doing there. I explained that my job was to help people organize their family finances, while obviously doing my best not to mention death or anything else that might scare her. She looked at me with a very serious expression and said, 'Well, just so you know, my daddy loves me best. Much more than my brother.'"

I smiled. "Kat told me she's always been a daddy's girl."

"She definitely is that. And I think she was right. Her father always has favored her over Josh," Donnelly admitted.

This was not surprising. I'd met Josh only a few times, but whenever I had been around Kat's brother, I'd been struck by how pompous and self-congratulatory he was. He had the conceit to believe he had earned his place in the world, when in truth, everything he had in his life, from his two-thousand-dollar home espresso maker to his vanity job as a vice president of Wyeth Construction, had come directly from his father.

Donnelly was reading my mind. "Then again, who

wouldn't prefer Kat to Josh? She got the looks, the brains and the personality in that family. Kat has the whole package."

"Speaking of Kat, I've been having a difficult time getting hold of her," I said. "I'm sure she's just overwhelmed with the funeral and all the emotions and details involved with Howard's death. Will you please let her know I appreciate her sending you to help me out yesterday?"

Donnelly cleared his throat and folded his hands on the desk in front of him. "Kat didn't send me."

"She didn't?"

"No. Her father did."

I frowned. "But why would Mr. Wyeth do that? He barely knows me. How did he even find out I was at the police station?" But of course, I knew the most likely answer to this second question. Kat must have told him.

"Look," Donnelly said, his smile still in place, "I'm sure you're aware that Thomas Wyeth is a powerful man. He's unhappy that the police are investigating Howard's death as a homicide. It was hardly a secret that Howard Grant was a severe alcoholic. His death was obviously an accident. Everyone should just be glad that he wasn't driving that night and didn't kill anyone else."

"That would have been terrible," I agreed.

"Thomas is convinced that the police are pursuing this as a possible homicide only because of who he is. They don't want to be seen as giving favorable treatment to Kat just because she's Thomas Wyeth's daughter," Donnelly continued.

"Maybe. But the police told me they have a witness who claims he saw Howard being pushed off the balcony."

Donnelly shrugged, clearly not impressed. "If they ask around long enough, they'll find a witness who will say he saw a UFO land on top of the Grants' house and little green men came out and zapped Howard with ray guns. Witnesses are inherently unreliable."

"I don't disagree," I said. "I'm sure that's why they questioned me. I know they're trying to build a case. I'm just not sure whom they're building it against."

Donnelly nodded. "That's why I asked you to come in today. In the future, the Wyeths would prefer it if you didn't cooperate with the police investigation."

"I don't know what you mean by cooperating."

Donnelly raised both of his hands, palms out, in a placating gesture. "Don't misunderstand. No one's accusing you of disloyalty. But the family would like your assurances that you won't speak to the police again."

"I wasn't planning on it," I said, feeling a growing sense of discomfort. I wasn't sure what Donnelly was getting at. I didn't often find myself in the position of not grasping a situation. It made me uneasy. "But what if the police want to speak to me again?"

"Then you call me. I'll deal with it," Donnelly replied, smile back in place.

"Look, I appreciate your help yesterday, and I don't want to sound ungrateful. But the police weren't just asking me about Kat or about her marriage to Howard. They asked me if I knew how to access the Grants' house and they wanted to know where I was the night Howard died," I said.

Donnelly waved a dismissive hand. "They were just trying to scare you."

"Maybe. Or maybe they're treating me as a suspect."

"I doubt that," Donnelly said. "You don't have a motive."

"I didn't like Howard."

"No one liked Howard." Donnelly grinned. "Not to speak ill of the dead, but he was an asshole. If everyone who thought he was an asshole was a suspect, they'd have an overly large number of people to consider."

Despite my growing trepidation, I cautiously returned his smile. I could see why Donnelly would be successful charming clients through the otherwise unpleasant process of drawing up a will. Actually, I wondered how much of that he did these days. It was becoming increasingly clear that he was in Thomas Wyeth's inner circle. That in itself might be a full-time—not to mention quite lucrative—job.

"My point is, if there's any possibility that the police are going to look at me as a potential suspect, even if it's only a remote one, I don't think it's a good idea for me to retain an attorney who isn't obligated to put my interests first," I added carefully.

Donnelly tipped his head to one side. "What would make you think I don't have your interests at heart?"

I looked back at the attorney. Surely he didn't expect me to join in a pretense that his main objective here was to help me.

"Look." Donnelly sighed. "I know that Kat values your friendship, and I know you feel the same about her."

"Of course I do," I said, softening. The truth was, I missed Kat. The past few days had been stressful for me, and I could only imagine how much worse they'd been for her.

Donnelly folded his hands together, and he leaned forward slightly, like someone with a secret to share. "I've been authorized to tell you that the family will be generous."

This startled me out of my nostalgic reminiscing. "Excuse me?"

"Any consideration would have to wait until the police investigation is resolved, of course," Donnelly continued. "But once that's concluded and Kat is in the clear, they are prepared to make a significant settlement on your behalf."

A significant settlement. Translation: the Wyeths were offering me a bribe if I agreed to stay away from the police investigation. I stood. "I don't want their money."

"No, please. Sit back down. You're taking this the wrong way," Donnelly assured me, his tone soothing, a hand held up in protest.

"Am I? I don't think so."

"They aren't asking you to do anything illegal or even unethical. They just want you to know that your loyalty will be rewarded."

"I hope this is coming from Kat's father and not from Kat," I said. "If it is, I'll overlook how incredibly insulting it is, because I know that parents will do anything to protect their children. But please make it clear to him that I find his offer offensive."

Donnelly tapped his fingers on his desk, and for the first time in our short acquaintance, he looked serious. Finally he nodded. "I'll tell him, if that's what you want."

"That's what I want." I turned to leave, figuring we had said everything. But Donnelly called after me before I reached the door.

"Thomas just wants to make sure that Kat is safe," he said. "It's the only thing that matters to him."

I looked back at the lawyer.

"I hope she's safe, too. She's my best friend."

17

Twelve Months Earlier

IT WAS LATE, but I was still up working, my fingers flying over the keyboard. I was so, so close to finishing *A Zombie Bit My Math Teacher*, the first in the series of logic books I had contracted to write for Kidtastic. The book was set in the fictional town of Shrieksville, which had recently been attacked by a horde of the undead. The remaining survivors had to solve a series of logic puzzles to figure out who had been infected and who remained human.

The most challenging issue was to keep the zombie attacks bloody enough to capture the attention of modern-day tweens, already jaded by movie and video game violence, without alienating their parents by allowing the attacks to degenerate into an unacceptable level of blood and carnage. I thought I knew where to draw the line. A zombie could bite its victim, even hunch over a body it was feeding on. But agonized screams of pain, appendages ripped from bodies and pooling puddles of blood were over-the-top. My zombies might be deadly, but they weren't butchers.

The book had come together faster than I'd thought possible. I was even more surprised by how much I enjoyed working on it. Writing had become a haven away from all the problems—in my life, in my marriage—crushing me under their weight. I was yet again able to retreat into logic to soothe my mind, to order my world.

There was a soft knock on the office door.

"Come in," I said, expecting one of the children. Liam was still up, too, working on his science fair project on hovercraft. I had tucked Bridget into bed before retreating to the office, but she always had a hard time settling into sleep. It wasn't unusual for her to get up for a glass of water or to voice a worry about a strange sound she'd heard.

The door opened. I looked up from my laptop and saw my husband standing in the doorway, as though he wasn't sure he should cross the threshold. He had dark smudges of exhaustion under his eyes, and his green-striped tie was loosened and slightly askew.

"Hi," he said. "I just got home."

Todd was working on a contract basis with a firm in Miami. The job required long hours, bookended by a two-hour commute each way, so he would regularly get home after nine. We didn't see much of him during the week.

"Hi," I replied. "I made chicken for dinner. It's in the fridge, if you want to heat up a plate."

"Thanks, but I ate on the road." Todd nodded to my computer. "Are you working?"

"Yes. I want to finish writing the solution to this problem before I go to bed."

"Then I guess I'll leave you to it."

It was my turn to nod. This was what passed for our marital communications lately, ever since I'd learned about Todd losing his job. It was as though the lie had taken on a life of its own and was now spreading its tentacles into every corner of our relationship. Todd had once asked me, in an aggrieved tone, why I couldn't forgive him. I'd shrugged this question away. It wasn't that I couldn't forgive him. It was that I no longer trusted him.

Todd was closing the door behind him when I said, "Hold on a minute."

He turned back. "What's up?"

"Don't forget I'm going out of town tomorrow," I said. "I've arranged for Max's mom, Jennifer, to drive the kids home from school. Then Emma is coming over to babysit until you get home from work."

"Oh, right. The big Girls' Weekend Away." His tone was sour, and I could feel my spine straighten with anger.

I knew he was calling it that just to irritate me. Kat had invited me to go to Key Biscayne with her for the weekend. In fact, it had been her birthday present to me the month before. At first I had refused to accept it. We hadn't paid back a penny of the twenty thousand dollars she had already lent us, so I could hardly accept another extravagant gift from her. My advance and Todd's contract work were keeping us afloat, but we were hardly flush. I couldn't justify the expense of a vacation right now.

"I need to get away," Kat had said, trying to persuade me. "Howard and I are barely speaking, and getting the new exhibit installed at the gallery has been hideous. I'm so stressed out, I can barely breathe." This had surprised me. Kat never looked stressed out, and that day had been no exception. I figured she was just saying it to talk me into the trip. "Please, Alice! It would do us both some good."

I had finally given in and accepted, even though doing so gave me a slithering sensation of guilt. When had I become this person who allowed others to pay my way for me?

But now, with Todd looking down at me, disapproval etched on his face, I experienced a flash of self-righteous anger. The man who had gotten up every day and pretended to go to a job he'd been fired from while he cashed out his retirement account was going to judge me for going away for a weekend? That, I would not put up with.

"Something like that," I said coldly.

"How long will you be gone for?"

"I'll be back Sunday."

"Just promise me you'll be careful."

"What is that supposed to mean?"

"That you don't drink too much. Or let Kat drive you when she's been drinking."

My anger flared up again. "Stop talking to me like I'm a delinquent teenager. I can take care of myself."

"I know you can. It's just when you're with Kat—"

"What?"

"You drink more than usual."

"That's ridiculous." I gestured toward my laptop. "I need to get back to work. I have to finish this chapter before I can go to bed."

Todd stood there for a few beats, blinking at me, before he finally turned away. He shut the door quietly behind him.

"What did I tell you?" Kat exclaimed as we walked out onto the back patio of the Ritz-Carlton Key Biscayne. "Isn't this heaven?"

I had to agree. It was absolutely gorgeous, easily the nicest hotel I'd ever stayed at. There was an enormous pool surrounded by tables and chaise lounges. Dozens of tall, stately palm trees swayed gently in the breeze. I could see a large tiki bar where people were sitting on wicker sofas, sipping rum cocktails. Beyond that was the beach with powdered sugar sand and the aqua sea I remembered from my Miami days.

I inhaled deeply. Even the air seemed more luxurious as it filled my lungs. I could feel my body relax as tension I hadn't even noticed I was holding on to started to seep away.

"It's amazing," I replied. "It's *perfect*."

I turned to smile at Kat, who looked pretty and much younger than her age in a coral patio dress. For once, I was almost as well dressed as Kat. I had treated myself to a new dress from Nordstrom to bring on the trip. The navy blue silk shift had been on sale, of course, but it had still been a highly pleasurable purchase. I felt coolly glamorous in it. Like a totally different person, leading a totally different life.

Kat grinned back and squeezed my hand. "Shall we get a cocktail?"

We headed for the tiki bar, where we perched on tall stools that looked out at the ocean, calm today with only the occasional whitecap visible. The bartender was so handsome, and the waitresses so pretty and shapely, I wondered if the hotel had a policy of hiring only beautiful people to work there.

"What can I get you ladies to drink?" the bartender asked, setting cocktail napkins in front of us. He was wearing a name tag that read HUDSON. When he smiled, deep dimples appeared in his cheeks.

"What do you recommend?" Kat asked, smiling back at him.

"I don't want to brag, but I happen to make the best grapefruit-and-mint mojito you will ever have in your life."

"That's a pretty bold statement," Kat said, glancing at me. "What do you think, Alice? Should we see if his game is as good as his talk?"

"Why not?" I agreed.

But Kat's attention was so fixed on Hudson, I wasn't sure she'd even heard me.

"And what will you give me if it isn't the best mojito of my life?" she asked him, lifting her chin in a way that showed off her pale, slender neck.

Hudson tipped his head to one side as he considered this. "If it's not the best mojito of your life," he finally said, "I will stand on the bar and strip naked while singing 'Lady Marmalade.'"

Kat laughed and clapped her hands in glee. "And how exactly does that benefit me?" she asked flirtatiously.

"Well, you'd get to see that I have a terrible voice," Hudson said, matching her tone.

"Okay, then, challenge accepted," Kat replied. "Two mojitos, please."

"You won't be sorry," Hudson promised.

We watched him set about making the drinks, squeezing grapefruits and muddling the mint.

"Remember Awful Ashley, the sister-in-law from hell?" Kat asked, spinning her stool to face me. "When she heard we were coming here for the weekend, she said, 'How decadent. I'd love to have a weekend away on my own, but I'd rather have a happy marriage.'"

"As though the occasional weekend away from your husband somehow violates the sanctity of marriage?" I asked incredulously.

"Exactly. She's so ridiculous." Kat grinned. "Not that either of us is exactly the poster child for the happily married."

"True, but that happened well before we went away for the weekend," I said. "What's her deal, anyway?"

"She's always been a nightmare." Kat rolled her eyes. "I still can't figure out why Josh married her. She does that whole 'I'm just a little Southern belle' bit." As Kat mimicked Ashley, she inserted an extra twang in her accent. "All while retaining the personality of a pit viper."

"When I met her at your parents' Christmas party last year, I got the feeling she wasn't your biggest fan," I commented.

"God, no, she hates me. *Hates.*"

"Why?"

"Who knows? I think it's partly because she thinks I had some incredibly privileged childhood. Ashley's father was a

Baptist minister in rural Alabama. Her mama was a preacher's wife. They didn't have money for new clothes and birthday parties, much less riding lessons and sleepaway camp. Or maybe she hates me because Josh told her that I tried to talk him out of marrying her. The idiot. I don't know why he couldn't have kept that little nugget of information to himself." Kat shrugged carelessly as though she couldn't care less.

"Why didn't you want him to marry her?"

"You met her," Kat said. "Do you think it's possible that all the Botox she's injected into her head has made her even crazier than she was before?"

"I doubt it. If insanity was a side effect of Botox, every Floridian over the age of forty would be nuts."

"Who says they're not?" Kat countered.

"Here you are, ladies," Hudson said, placing tall frosty glasses in front of us.

"Cheers," Kat said, lifting her glass to mine. We clinked our glasses, then sipped our drinks while Hudson waited for the verdict.

"Oh, my God," I exclaimed. "This is fantastic!"

"It really is," Kat agreed. "This is the best mojito I've ever had."

Hudson beamed. "I told you."

"I guess that means we're going to miss out on your rendition of 'Lady Marmalade,'" Kat teased him.

"You never know." Hudson was grinning widely. I suspected his dimples were good for tips.

"When you see our drinks get down to here," Kat said, leveling her hand against the middle of her glass, "go ahead and make us another round."

Hudson saluted her. "Will do. Enjoy."

Kat turned back to me. "Where were we? Oh, right, Awful Ashley. When Josh met her, she was a waitress. You know the kind. Big boobs, small tank top. She was obviously rebelling against her Holy Roller parents."

"Just like in the movie *Footloose*."

"Right, except with chicken wings and hand jobs in the customers' cars instead of teenage kids dancing," Kat said.

"Seriously?" Kat enjoyed saying shocking things. I couldn't always figure out when she was telling the truth or just being provocative to amuse herself.

"Who knows? Anyway, Josh was smitten by her—" Kat rolled her eyes "—*charms*. They started dating, and six months later they eloped. Their first daughter was born a few months later. As you can imagine, my mother was horrified by the whole thing."

"But they've been married for a while, correct?"

"Over twenty years. Their oldest daughter graduated from college last year."

"Then there must be some substance to the marriage."

Kat shot me a strange look. "What does that mean?"

"Surely something more than an unplanned pregnancy must have kept them together all of those years."

"What kept them together was a quick succession of children, coupled with a lack of a prenuptial agreement." Kat shook her head and stirred her drink with her straw. "Why? What did she say to you about me?"

"What?" I asked, distracted by the thought of what it must be like to live all those years under such hostile familial scrutiny. I hadn't liked Ashley, but even so, spending two decades knowing your husband's family didn't think you were good enough for him seemed a horrible burden for anyone to bear.

"You said she didn't like me. What did she say?"

I hesitated. I didn't want to start off our weekend on a sour note.

"Just tell me," Kat insisted.

"It wasn't anything too terrible. She just made a comment

about how she thinks you use people. And she started going on about someone named Marcia something." I laughed. "I only remember that part because of *The Brady Bunch*. You know, 'Marcia, Marcia, Marcia!'"

"Marcia Grable? Jesus, I haven't thought about her in years." Kat shook her head. "I can't believe Ashley brought her up."

"Why? Who is she?"

"She's a yoga instructor. Or at least, she used to be. I have no idea what she's doing now." Kat sighed and shook her head. "I met her when I signed up for some classes at the yoga studio where she taught. We were friendly for a while. But then she began showing up everywhere I went. Restaurants, boutiques, even the grocery store. It started to get a little creepy."

"You were being stalked by your yoga instructor?"

"Yes!" Kat laughed. "I know, it's bizarre, right? Welcome to my life. But honestly, it was really weird." She shook her head and took a sip of her drink. "I tried setting limits with her. I thought she'd get the message and back off."

"But she didn't?"

"No, she did not. Instead she showed up on my doorstep on Thanksgiving Day holding a pumpkin pie, insisting that I'd invited her to dinner. When I told her I had no idea what she was talking about, she went hysterical. My entire family was there, including Awful Ashley. And there was Marcia, crying on her pie and saying something about how we were supposed to be best friends. She left only when I threatened to call the police."

"That passes weird and veers right into scary."

"Tell me about it." Kat shuddered. "I mean, I felt sorry for her in a way. She was obviously not well. But it was hardly my fault."

"No, of course it wasn't."

"My darling sister-in-law apparently thinks it was," Kat said, taking another sip of her mojito.

"Two more," Hudson announced, appearing with another round of fresh mojitos for us. I looked down at my empty glass in surprise. I hadn't realized I'd finished the drink.

"Excellent," Kat said, handing Hudson her own empty glass. "You are my new favorite bartender."

"I aim to please." Hudson winked at Kat, and she smiled a creamy, self-satisfied smile back at him.

Kat picked up her glass, ready for another toast. "To having the best damned weekend possible," she said, and I tapped my glass against hers.

We dined on carne asada and drank a bottle of pinot noir at the Cantina Beach, the hotel's restaurant overlooking the ocean. The food was delicious, although by the time we finished, the alcohol was causing my head to swim and I felt pleasantly drowsy.

"Do you feel like a nightcap?" Kat asked after she'd signed the bill, waving away my attempts to put my close-to-the-limit credit card in the leather bill holder. "They have a fabulous bar here, and you know how I feel about hotel bars. They're my favorite thing in the world."

I had noticed that alcohol never seemed to affect Kat, or at least not the way it affected everyone else. Her eyes might get brighter, her laugh a bit louder, but she never became sloppy. I thought about Todd's comment that I was drinking more since Kat and I had become friends. It had annoyed me deeply at the time, but partly because I knew he was right. Kat was always up for another drink, and another, and another. I needed to be more careful, and right now the last thing I wanted or needed was any more alcohol in my system.

"I think I've had enough to drink for the night, but I'll keep you company," I said.

The bar was pretty fantastic. It had a cozy, clubby feel, with red walls and leather armchairs and sofas. Next door, in the lobby lounge, a Latin band was playing. Couples started to dance, some of them surprisingly good. They took their salsa dancing seriously.

Kat sat down on an empty love seat, while I claimed the adjacent chair. When a waitress came over, Kat ordered us each a vodka martini.

"One straight up with a twist, one extra dirty with a blue cheese–stuffed olive," she said.

"No, thanks," I said. "If I have a martini, I'll pass out."

The cocktail waitress raised her eyebrows, unsure how to proceed.

"I'll just have a glass of water," I said.

"No, she'll have the martini." Kat's voice had an edge to it. The waitress hesitated but then nodded and left.

"Why did you do that? I really don't want a martini." I was starting to feel bullied.

"But I hate drinking alone," Kat said. She turned to smile at me, back to her usual charming self. "It's just like the night we first met, when we had martinis at the airport. You said you couldn't possibly, and then you proceeded to drink two."

"Only because you talked me into it," I said. "You're clearly a bad influence."

"I certainly hope so," Kat retorted. "I'd hate to die and have everyone stand around at my funeral, talking about what a saint I was. I'd much rather be remembered as a hell-raiser. This music is great, isn't it?"

"You should go dance."

"Maybe I will, if a handsome stranger asks me," Kat said. She stretched her arms up over her head and grinned. "I feel like dancing. I feel like dancing and flirting and making mischief."

"It's been so long since I've flirted with anyone, I probably wouldn't remember how."

"I have a hard time picturing you ever flirting with anyone. You're too collected, too analytical."

I arched my eyebrows. "I didn't just spontaneously burst into being as an adult logician. Believe it or not, I was once a teenager. I did all sorts of silly teenager things."

Kat snorted. "I don't believe it. I'm sure you were the quiet, serious type who got straight As and never went to parties. All of the boys had crushes on you, I'll bet, but you were so aloof and untouchable, they were afraid to approach you."

"Aloof and untouchable?" I repeated. "That's actually insulting."

"No, it's not. You're like the heroine of a Hitchcock movie."

"Hardly," I said, feeling secretly pleased at this description.

"No, you are. I would love to be seen as a beautiful ice queen," Kat exclaimed. "But I'm too much of a chatterbox to pull it off. Hitchcock heroines can't be bigmouthed broads. It's all wrong for the narrative."

I was rolling my eyes at this just as the waitress returned with our martinis. She'd carefully placed our drinks and a bowl of nuts on our table.

"Thank you." Kat picked up her drink and took a sip. "Mmm. This is delicious."

"What do you want to do tomorrow?" I asked. "There's a state park nearby, if you feel like hiking."

"Are you insane? If I want to go for a walk, I'll go to the mall," Kat said. "I'm planning to spend all day tomorrow in a lounge chair on the beach. They have little flags on the back that you can put up whenever you want a drink. It's fabulous."

I smiled and thought it did sound nice. I couldn't remember the last time I'd spent an entire day doing absolutely nothing. No writing or tutoring or dishwashing or laundry or homework assistance. It had been years, I thought, because even our sporadic family vacations didn't offer a break from the daily grind of parenting. But now I would have one day, one perfect day, when I wouldn't be required to do anything other than flip through magazines and reapply sunscreen. Despite my best intentions, I picked up the martini and took a sip.

"That does sound pretty fabulous," I said, leaning back in my squishy leather seat, drink in hand.

"Look who's here," Kat said. She sat up, her eyes bright, and smiled at someone. "It's the mojito man."

I turned my head and saw Hudson just as he spotted us. He waved and I thought he'd leave it at that—surely he was meeting friends closer to his age—but he surprised me by walking over. He stood in front of us, smiling his dimple-cheeked smile.

"How did I know I'd find you two ladies here?"

"Were you looking for us?" Kat asked.

"Definitely."

Hudson had changed out of his work uniform and was wearing a kelly green polo shirt, seersucker shorts and brown deck shoes with no socks. I wondered how old he was and thought he had to be in his late twenties or early thirties. Young enough to have a name like Hudson, anyway.

Hudson was looking down at Kat—who in her late forties was certainly attractive and smart and, yes, still sexy—with open, almost hungry interest. I was struck again by how handsome he was, with his boyish good looks, thick brown hair and square jaw. His eyes, which I had noticed earlier when he was working at the bar, were an unusual shade. I'd thought they were hazel at first, but now they looked almost green. He had them fixed on Kat now, while the corners of his lips were curled up in a faint smile.

I wondered at his motives. Was he focusing on Kat because he found her irresistible...or because she was wealthy? It probably wasn't hard for him to figure that out. Most of the guests at a hotel like this were well-off. And then there was Kat's credit card, an American Express Black Card, that Hudson had commented on when she paid for our drinks. He'd tapped it against a glass and laughed at the metallic clink it made.

"I was just telling Alice I was hoping a handsome man would come ask me to dance," Kat said now.

"It sounds like my services are required." Hudson held out a hand.

I choked back a laugh at this corny line, especially when I saw Kat light up, stand and take his proffered hand. I was mesmerized by both her easy acceptance of this flirtation and his lack of discomfiture. Kat glanced at me and gave me the ghost of a wink, which I wasn't sure how to take.

Hudson led Kat out to the dance area just beyond the bar. I sipped my drink while I watched them through the arched doorway, moving together, hips swaying in rhythm, hands clasped. Hudson was the better dancer, good enough that he was able to lead Kat through the moves. He spun her around at one point and Kat nearly lost her balance. She laughed up at him, her cheeks flushed.

Hudson suddenly pulled Kat closer to him. Keeping one hand on the small of Kat's back, cupping the other behind her head, he lowered his mouth to hers. I felt like a voyeur as I watched them kiss, standing still in the middle of the floor, while the other couples danced around them, but I couldn't seem to look away.

Kat, I thought, *I hope you know what you're doing.*

18

THE NEXT MORNING I woke alone in the hotel suite that Kat and I were sharing. I had my own room, and as soon as my eyes opened, I sat up abruptly. The air felt still around me. I swung my legs out of bed, stood and padded through the communal living room. Everything looked unchanged since I'd gone to sleep the night before, which didn't surprise me. I was a light sleeper and would probably have woken if Kat had returned to our room. Since I hadn't, I assumed she'd been out all night. Still, I hesitated for a moment. If Kat had come back, I didn't want to wake her. I pressed my ear to the door of her bedroom, but I couldn't hear anything from within. After a moment, I creaked open the door. I wasn't surprised to see that her bed was empty and still neatly made up.

I'd left Kat and Hudson still enmeshed together on the dance floor when I retired the night before. I assumed that wherever Kat was, she was with him. I checked my phone, but she hadn't texted or called.

I showered and dressed in a cotton embroidered tunic over an aqua bikini, then headed downstairs. The hotel served breakfast buffet style, and I had the choice of eating inside or out on the patio. It looked like a glorious day, so I opted for the alfresco dining option and requested a table for one. But when the hostess walked me outside, Kat was already there, sitting at a table with Hudson. She waved me over.

"Come sit with us," she called out, gesturing toward an open rattan chair.

Both Kat and Hudson were wearing their clothes from the night before, and Kat's face was scrubbed free of makeup. It seemed odd and vaguely uncomfortable to be sitting with my married friend and the man she had apparently picked up the night before. But as they didn't seem at all embarrassed, I tried to tamp down my own discomfort.

"Hi," I said, keeping my tone bright. "How's breakfast?"

"The eggs Benedict is fabulous," Kat replied. "You should try it. You have to order them from the waitress, though. They're not part of the buffet."

"Looks good." I glanced over at Hudson, who was not eating the decadent eggs Benedict. Instead his plate was filled with what looked like egg whites scrambled with peppers and onions and a side dish of cut fruit.

"He doesn't eat carbs." Kat shuddered. "Can you imagine such a bleak and horrible existence? No pasta, no bread. I wouldn't make it through a single day eating like that."

Although Kat was supposedly speaking to me, she was smiling coyly at Hudson. He grinned back at her, enjoying the attention. I was ancillary to the conversation. My presence, it seemed, was useful only to give them another topic to flirt over.

"How do you think I maintain my six-pack?" he bragged.

"I thought you must just do a lot of sit-ups." She laughed, reaching over to pat his flat stomach.

As if this display weren't nauseating enough, Hudson then murmured, "That, too," leaned forward and kissed her. When I caught sight of tongues flicking, I stood abruptly and headed inside to the buffet. I wished I had requested a table inside so I could have eaten my breakfast in peace. I certainly had no interest in trying to choke down a plateful of eggs while Kat and Hudson pawed at one another like horny teenagers.

I was also already resentful about this awkward situation being imposed on our plans for a day of beachside lounging. If Kat had wanted to have a revenge affair—if that was what this was—why did she have to pick *our* weekend away together to do it?

I got in line at the omelet station, although unlike Hudson, I ordered mine with whole eggs, cheese and bacon.

When I got back to the table, Hudson was gone. Kat was sitting alone, looking relaxed and happy while she sipped a mimosa.

I almost asked *Where's your boyfriend?* but managed to stop myself. I didn't want to sound as churlish as I felt. Instead I said, "Where did Hudson run off to?"

"He went home to shower and change. He has to work this afternoon," Kat said. She took a sip from her champagne flute. "Mmm, I love mimosas. You should get one. It's delicious. I swear, everything tastes better here."

I was starting to have concerns about how this trip would affect my liver.

"No, thanks" was all I managed to say between forkfuls of food.

Kat flagged down a passing waiter. He stopped at our table, smiling subserviently.

Kat ordered, "Two more mimosas, please."

"Right away, madam," he replied and hurried off.

"God, I hate being called *madam*," Kat said, making a face. "Can't we women band together and get that word struck from the English language?"

"Why did you order two? I just told you I didn't want one." I wasn't entirely sure why I was so irritable—whether it was Hudson or Kat's disappearing act the night before or the fact that she did not listen to me when I said I didn't want to start imbibing at nine in the morning—but I couldn't keep the sharp barb out of my tone.

Kat stared at me. "Well, excuse me. I thought we were on vacation, but you certainly don't have to drink it if you don't want it." She drawled out the words in an exaggerated way.

She sounded so much like a moody, hormonal teenager, I couldn't help smiling.

"You sound like you're fifteen," I said when Kat scowled at me.

My words dispelled the frostiness. Kat laughed, too, and pushed her sunglasses on top of her head.

"I feel like I'm fifteen," she confessed. "This is crazy, isn't it? But then Hudson touches me and I'm just—" She stopped and shook her head. "I don't know. Like I'm not in charge of whatever is happening. Does that sound silly?"

It did, but I shook my head. "No, of course not."

Kat smiled condescendingly. "I've shocked you. I had no idea you were so provincial, Alice."

My irritation flared back up. I was quickly losing patience with this situation. I didn't like Howard, but he was Kat's husband. She had chosen to marry him, and more to the point, she had chosen to remain married to him after he cheated on her. Even if she had her reasons not to divorce him—whether they were money or fear of being alone or simply not wanting to give up on the marriage—it had still been her choice. Yet here she was, acting selfish and silly, and she had the nerve to mock me for failing to embrace her adultery?

There was a brief pause while the waiter arrived with the two mimosas.

"You can do as you please," I said. I took another bite of my omelet, although I could barely taste the food. It felt as though the trip had already been soured. Despite the lavish accommodations and beautiful surroundings, I suddenly wished I was home—even if that meant another Saturday spent getting caught up on the laundry. Unfortunately, Kat and I had driven down together in her Porsche convertible. I was stuck here. Despite my earlier protestations, I took a sip of my mimosa.

"You're angry with me," Kat commented.

I put my fork down and looked at her. "I thought this was our weekend to get away. To relax and spend time together."

"We are! Look," Kat said, sighing, "I'm sorry I deserted you last night. I shouldn't have."

I nodded, accepting her apology. "It just feels…well, awkward, I guess. It's like I'm suddenly the third wheel on a very steamy first date."

Kat laughed and flushed slightly. "Yes, well, last night might not have been my best moment. And I *am* sorry that I left you alone—that wasn't cool, I know it wasn't—but honestly, I have zero guilt when it comes to Howard. I don't know what that says about me. Maybe it means I'm a horrible person, but I suddenly feel weirdly alive. It's like I finally woke up to the fact that I can have a life after divorce. I know that sounds trite, but whenever I've tried to picture myself leaving Howard, not being married, I just…shut down."

I softened. Maybe I *was* being too harsh, too puritanical. Kat had been through a lot with Howard, but she'd been married to him for more than half her life. Of course the idea of leaving him, of building a life for herself without him, would be daunting. Perhaps having a brief fling with a younger man would prove to be the catharsis she needed to move on.

"Although it's possible that thanks to Hudson, I now have an entirely unrealistic vision of what postdivorce life would look like," Kat continued, leaning in and lowering her voice. "Without going into too much detail, he was absolutely *amazing*."

I raised a hand, wanting to staunch this confessional flow. "It's okay. You don't have to go into detail."

Kat made a face. "I wasn't going to," she said. "And you really *are* a prude."

"No, I'm *not*."

"Yes, you *are*. Anyway, all I was going to say is that it's probably not very likely that my future will be filled with hot young bartenders."

"You never know," I commented. "There could be thousands of them out there, waiting for a beautiful divorcée to walk into their bars."

Kat shuddered. "I hate that word. *Divorcée*. Ugh. Never say that again. It's almost as bad as *madam*. Hurry up and finish your mimosa." She drained the last of hers. "I want to go for a swim."

Despite the rocky start, it ended up being a lovely day. We spent most of it on the beach, stretched out on lounge chairs, the sun warming our skin. Kat had gone up to our room to change. When she returned, she brought down a stack of fashion magazines. We paged lazily through them, reading actress profiles—all of whom claimed they never dieted and maintained their whippet-thin figures through yoga and healthy lifestyles—and articles advising the perfect shade of red lipstick for every complexion. When we got hot, we waded into the clear aqua ocean and floated on our backs while we gazed up at the cotton-ball puffs of clouds in the sky. When we were hungry or thirsty, we raised the flag attached to the beach chairs to summon a waiter. Someone would rush over to supply us with whatever we desired. Then, when we grew tired of being on the beach, we went up to our shared suite, where we each showered and changed before heading back down for cocktails.

We returned to the outside bar, where Hudson was working. He brought us our drinks and a plate of hummus and pita chips and stopped back to chat with us when he had a lull in customers. I had to admit he was a pretty charming guy, and it was less awkward talking with the two of them than it had been that morning.

Hudson had promised to find us after his shift, so I was surprised when later, just before dinner, Kat asked if I wanted to go back to the beach.

"It's so beautiful out," she said. "Let's go for a short walk. It will give me a chance to clear my head so I can figure out what I should do about Hudson."

I nodded, and we strolled back down to the beach, which was now deserted. The sun was setting, turning the sky into ribbons of pink and orange. The ocean was calm, its waves lapping gently onto the beach. Kat and I stood side by side and looked out at the water, neither of us speaking.

Finally Kat broke the silence. "As I'm sure you can guess, things aren't going well with Howard and me."

Kat rarely talked about the state of her marriage with me. I knew that right after she found out about Howard's affair, she had confronted him. He'd denied it at first, but once Kat showed him the pictures her private investigator had taken, he'd finally admitted to it. She said they discussed separating but decided to try to work things out, on the condition that he ended his relationship with the Alana Dupree. He'd agreed. Since then, she'd rarely mentioned him to me. This had struck me as odd, but I knew how painful his infidelities had been for Kat. I didn't want to press her. Anyway, I wasn't sure what working things out meant for them, since as far as I knew, they hadn't been to couples therapy or made an effort to spend more time together, nor make any other meaningful changes. Or maybe they had done all of those things and Kat just hadn't told me.

"Did something happen?" I asked.

"A few somethings happened."

Kat sounded so strange, her voice tight and higher than

usual. I turned to her, reaching a hand out, but she didn't seem to see me. Her face was blank and she had her arms wrapped around herself.

"Kat, what is it?"

Kat breathed in deeply, and when she exhaled, she puffed her cheeks out. I noticed then that tears were sliding down her face.

"Kat? Tell me."

"I'm sorry. I probably should have told you everything before, but somehow telling you makes it more real, I guess," Kat said. "Okay. There are actually two things I haven't told you about. The first is that I found out Howard is still having an affair with the bartender. Or maybe he never stopped the first time." She shook her head and laughed without humor. "And now I've gone and slept with a bartender. What do you think that says about us?"

"Oh, Kat," I said. I put an arm around her and squeezed her. She didn't resist, but she also didn't hug me back.

"I just feel so incredibly stupid." She exhaled loudly. "Why did I think he was suddenly going to start being faithful? Because he said so?"

"That is sort of how it's supposed to work," I said softly. "He says he'll be faithful and you believe him."

"Only if you're an idiot. Which apparently I am."

"How did you find out?"

Kat sighed again and kicked her sandaled foot into the soft white sand. "In the most humiliating way possible. I followed him."

"Oh, no."

"Yeah, there's nothing like finding out that you're a cliché." Kat sighed. "Anyway, he was apparently so looking forward to getting his dick sucked that he didn't notice I was driving right behind him. I followed him all the way to her condo."

"I'm sorry I was so shitty and judgmental earlier," I said. "About Hudson."

Kat shrugged. "You didn't know."

"But still. I should have given you the benefit of the doubt."

"The worst of it is, that's not even the worst of it."

I waited, dreading what was coming next.

"I didn't confront him then, in the parking lot of her building. It just seemed so...well, tawdry, I suppose. And I didn't want to give her the satisfaction of seeing me outside *her* apartment, yelling at *my* husband. So I drove home, and while I waited for him to return, I drank two large martinis."

I could picture her sitting alone in her beautiful kitchen, drink in hand, trying to stop herself from visualizing her husband romping with his girlfriend.

"Did he come back that night?"

Kat nodded. She was still looking out at the water, her arms still wrapped around her, as though by doing so, she was holding herself together.

"He did. And I told him that I'd followed him, and he... he hit me."

I inhaled sharply and turned to look at her. "Oh, my God, Kat. He *hit* you? *Where?*"

She returned my gaze, her blue eyes steady and sober.

"He backhanded me across the face." She shook her head like she still couldn't quite believe it. "He hit me so hard, I saw stars. You know, like in cartoons when little stars and birds rotate around a character's head?"

Kat laughed, and it was such a sad, broken sound that I nearly cried.

"Has he ever hit you before?"

"No. He's grabbed me a few times, you know, hard on the upper part of my arm," Kat said, demonstrating this by squeezing her own arm. "And he pushed me once, actually pushed me really hard, but he was so drunk that he didn't remember it the next day. So I'm not sure that counts."

I stared at her, dumbfounded. "What are you talking about? Of *course* it counts."

"No, I mean, I know it wasn't *right*, but I also don't think it was intentional. When he slapped me—" Kat stopped and shivered "—*that* was intentional."

I listened, trying to absorb what Kat was telling me. Of course spousal abuse occurred across the socioeconomic divides. I knew it did. It just had simply never occurred to me that anyone I knew—much less someone I knew as well as Kat—was being battered. It was like one of those terrible made-for-television movies, the ones with titles like *Abandoned and Betrayed*.

"What are you going to do?" I finally asked.

Kat looked at me blankly. "About what?"

"What do you think?" I said. "About *Howard*. You can't stay with him. You have to move out or get him to move out. Right away."

"I told you before, if I divorce him, he'll get half my money, half the house, probably even half of K-Gallery."

I could feel a flash of anger push up past my original shock at her sad confession.

"Kat, you can't stay married to someone who beats you."

"He doesn't *beat* me. He slapped me. It's not the same thing."

"It's still abusive," I argued. "Look, I'm not going to say the money doesn't matter. Of course it matters. But even if you had to give him half of everything, you'd still be an incredibly wealthy woman."

"But that's just it. Why should I have to give him half?" Kat asked, turning to me, her voice suddenly angry. "What has he done to deserve that?"

"I'm not saying he deserves it. But your safety is more important."

Kat looked at me, her expression so savage that she was almost unrecognizable. Her eyes were narrowed into slits, her lips pulled back in a snarl.

"I wish he'd just die," she said through clenched teeth. "That would solve everything."

"Waiting for him to die is not exactly a good action plan," I pointed out.

"Why not? Drunks die all the time. They get into car crashes, they fall down stairs." Kat spoke as though in a trance.

I wondered if this was an oblique reference to my brother-in-law's death. Brendon, the drunk who had died after falling down the stairs on Thanksgiving. I didn't like thinking about that night and pushed the memory away.

"You can't count on Howard having a car accident," I said.

Kat turned to stare back out at the water. The light was fading and the sky was turning smudged gray. But there was just enough light for me to see the tears still rolling down Kat's face. I wrapped an arm around her again, and she briefly rested her head on my shoulder.

"I wish he would die," she repeated. "It would solve everything."

19

Present Day

HOWARD'S FUNERAL SERVICE was set for ten days after his death at the Church of Bethesda-by-the-Sea on Palm Beach. It was the same church Kat and Howard had been married in, which I knew only because Kat had pointed it out to me a few years earlier, when we were driving by on our way out to lunch.

"That's where the shit show began," she'd joked. "For better or worse. Emphasis on the latter."

I still hadn't heard from Kat.

Instead I'd learned about the location and time of the service from Howard's obituary in the *Palm Beach Post*. I wasn't even sure if I should attend. Todd had argued against my going.

"I think you should stay the hell away from the whole thing," he said in a lowered voice the night before the funeral.

Todd and I were sitting on the couch, watching a movie with the kids. I'd made hot chocolate and popped a big bowl of popcorn. Liam and Bridget were lounging on beanbag chairs in front of the television, the popcorn between them. I glanced down at my children, hoping they hadn't overheard their father.

They appeared to be too absorbed in the movie, which was one of the seemingly endless superhero films Hollywood churned out. I had stopped paying attention within the first five minutes and was instead brooding on whether I should attend the funeral. Todd was apparently reading my mind.

"Something weird is going on," Todd continued. "And I don't like you being dragged into it."

"I'm not being dragged anywhere," I murmured back.

"You know what I'm talking about. Being questioned by *you-know-who.*"

This coded speech was for the benefit of the children, who didn't know about my meeting with the police.

"Are you talking about Voldemort?" Liam asked, not taking his eyes off the television screen.

"What?" Todd asked.

"You know, *he-who-must-not-be-named.* That's what they call Voldemort in the Harry Potter books," Liam said.

"Oh. No, I was talking about something else," Todd quickly replied.

"What?" Liam pressed.

I widened my eyes at Todd, trying to communicate silently that this clearly wasn't something we should be talking about in front of our children, even obliquely. People always underestimated how much attention kids were paying to what was being said. In my experience, they missed very little.

But Todd wasn't ready to give up the argument.

"Watch the movie," he urged our son. Liam lapsed into silence. Todd seemed to assume that meant Liam was following the directive. He leaned closer to me and said softly, "If Kat wanted you there, you would have heard from her by now."

"Maybe," I said, also speaking sotto voce. "I agree, it's odd I haven't heard from her. But it is possible that she's just been swallowed up by everything that's happened. Grief can make people act strangely."

Todd snorted. "I don't know that I buy Kat in the role of grief-stricken widow. She's too selfish, for one thing."

"You think she's selfish?" I asked, surprised. "She's one of the most generous people I know."

I didn't mention her loan to us. I didn't have to. The fact that we still hadn't paid Kat back weighed heavily on both of us.

"Not with money," Todd conceded. "But emotionally, absolutely. She always has to get her way, or watch the hell out."

I sipped at my hot chocolate, considering this. Usually when Todd made a disparaging comment about Kat, I became defensive. But in light of all that had happened in the days since Howard's death, I was suddenly more open to alternate theories on what sort of a person my best friend really was.

Todd was right. Kat *could* be selfish. Not when it came to things like writing us a twenty-thousand-dollar check, obviously. She was always quick to pick up the lunch check and had insisted on treating me when we went to Key Biscayne for the weekend.

And yet I had seen her become coldly furious when the car dealership wouldn't fit her in the same morning she called to make an appointment. And then there was the time she'd berated a sales clerk at Neiman Marcus when the young woman struggled to ring up the pair of shoes Kat was purchasing.

Kat had watched, growing increasingly impatient, as the girl looked blankly at the computer, clearly not sure how to operate it.

"What exactly is the problem?" Kat had asked, tapping her titanium Amercan Express Black Card against the counter.

"I think she's new," I'd whispered to Kat.

"Why should that be my problem? Good God. I thought Neiman Marcus was supposed to be known for customer service," Kat had snapped. She turned to the clerk, who looked close to tears. "If you don't know how to ring this up, can you please call someone over here who does?"

But the worst example I could remember was when Kat's housekeeper, Marguerite, brought her three-year-old grand-daughter with her to work one day. Neither Kat nor Howard was supposed to be home, so I'm sure Marguerite didn't think it would be an issue. Kat, however, had closed K-Gallery that day and returned home earlier than expected. When she walked into her kitchen and found the little girl sitting at the table, coloring on scrap paper, she had confronted Marguerite. The older woman had explained that her pregnant daughter-in-law had gone into labor and Marguerite's son had taken his wife to the hospital. There wasn't anyone else available to watch the little girl.

Kat listened to this explanation, then coolly told her house-keeper of eighteen years that she needed either to leave or to call her son immediately and have him pick his daughter up.

I hadn't been there when it happened, but Kat had casually recounted this to me a few days later when I met her for lunch.

"But why?" I'd asked. "Did she get crayon marks on your table or something?"

"No. But why should I have to deal with a noisy, sticky toddler running around? It's my house. Marguerite works for me," Kat had replied. "I never brought Amanda to the gallery when she was little. It's unprofessional."

This wasn't a fair comparison. Kat owned her business, and Amanda had a full-time nanny when she was little.

I offered the obvious explanation. "It sounds like they had an emergency."

"How was it an emergency? The woman had presumably been pregnant for nine months. It's not like they didn't know what was coming. They had plenty of time to arrange for alternative childcare."

I had opened my mouth to point out setting up a babysitter ahead of time might not have been possible. Or maybe they had made other arrangements that had fallen through. Or, just possibly, the young couple hadn't been able to afford to pay for childcare. But Kat clearly didn't care.

"So, what happened?" I'd asked instead.

"What do you mean? She called her son and he came and picked up the kid."

"He left his wife when she was in labor? Did he miss the baby being born?"

"I have no idea." Kat shrugged, losing interest in the discussion. "I think I'm going to get the Cobb salad. What are you having?"

Yes, Kat could be generous…but really, only when she wanted to be. Or when it didn't cost her anything she wasn't already able or willing to give up.

"Why don't you like Kat, Dad?" This time it was Bridget piping up, and she turned back to look at us, her face concerned.

"I like her just fine," Todd said, not sounding even the least bit convincing. Bridget obviously had the same opinion.

"Did she do something bad?" Bridget asked. "Was she mean to Mom?"

"If you're not going to watch the movie, why don't we turn it off?" I suggested. The kids, predictably, howled in protest and immediately affected deep interest in the movie. I glanced over at my husband and mouthed, *Later.*

In the end, I did go to the funeral. Todd wasn't happy about my decision, but he insisted on accompanying me. This both surprised and touched me. I hadn't told Todd this, but the truth was, I didn't want to go by myself. And after my meeting with John Donnelly, I wasn't entirely sure how welcome I would be.

Traffic was heavy on our way over to the island, and the service was just starting when Todd and I arrived. We hurriedly sat ourselves toward the back of the church just as the rector began with a call to worship. I obediently bowed my head while he prayed. Afterward the rector went on to describe Howard as a loving husband and father, a force for good in the community, complete with a list of charities he'd contributed to. He made Howard sound like a much nicer, better person than he had been, which I suppose was standard fare for a funeral. As he spoke, it was hard not to stare at the coffin positioned at the front of the congregation and think of the body within.

I gazed around the sanctuary, which was quite pretty. The church had been built in a Gothic style, complete with arches along the nave and beautiful stained glass windows. At first I didn't see anyone I recognized, but then, when I glanced back over one shoulder, I saw Detective Demer. He was looking right back at me so that for a moment our gazes were locked. My stomach gave a nervous lurch. But then he nodded pleasantly, and I responded with a thin-lipped smile before turning away.

Kat was sitting in the front row, so I could see her only from behind. She was wearing what looked like a white suit jacket, and her dark bobbed hair gleamed. She sat between her daughter, Amanda, and her father, and occasionally she lifted a tissue to her face, presumably to dab away tears.

The reverend finished and announced that Howard's daughter, Amanda Grant, was going to recite a poem. Amanda stood and made her way to the pulpit. She was a tall, slender young woman with a pale, serious face and straight dark hair that fell halfway down her back. Her dress was a severely cut black shift, and its simplicity suited her. I had met Amanda a few times over the years, and she'd always struck me as one of the most composed young women I had ever encountered. She was driven and studious, and certainly not one to giggle or zone out trancelike while staring down at her phone.

When Amanda took her place behind the microphone, she cleared her throat and looked out at the congregation. I was struck, as I'm sure everyone was, by the grief etched on her face.

"Howard Grant was not my biological father, but he was my father in all the ways that matter. He married my mother when I was a baby but did not adopt me officially until I was twelve. He said he wanted to wait until I was old enough to decide on my own that I wanted him to be my father legally. Since he was, and always had been, my father in my heart, this was an easy decision for me to make. I remember the day he adopted me. We went to the courthouse and stood before the judge, and I officially became Amanda Grant. I was so proud."

Amanda faltered and looked down for a moment, collecting herself. She took a few deep breaths before continuing.

"My father wasn't always an easy man. I'm sure most of you are aware of that. But that tough, brash businessman you all knew was not who he was with me. He was just my dad. He helped me with my math homework and never missed one of my volleyball games. He supported my dream of becoming a doctor and cheered me on whenever I became discouraged. He was always there when I needed him. Always. I loved him very much," Amanda said. "I'm now going to read a poem called 'Song: When I Am Dead,' written by Christina Rossetti."

She unfolded a piece of paper and smoothed it out on the pulpit, then began to read in a clear and steady voice:

"When I am dead, my dearest,
Sing no sad songs for me;
Plant thou no roses at my head,
Nor shady cypress tree:
Be the green grass above me
With showers and dewdrops wet;
And if thou wilt, remember,
And if thou wilt, forget.

"I shall not see the shadows,
I shall not feel the rain;
I shall not hear the nightingale
Sing on, as if in pain:
And dreaming through the twilight
That doth not rise nor set,
Haply I may remember,
And haply may forget."

The congregation was absolutely silent as she recited the poem. I was sure they were all struck by the beauty of the words along with Amanda's extraordinary self-possession.

For my part, I was simply stunned. I realized I had never seen Amanda and Howard together. Amanda was rarely home from school. The few times I had met her had been in passing. I'd have stopped by Kat's house or K-Gallery just as Amanda was leaving. Howard wasn't present on any of those occasions.

But one thing was suddenly very clear—Kat had deceived me about the nature of Howard and Amanda's relationship. She had repeatedly told me that they were not close, that Amanda would not have minded if she and Howard had divorced. According to Kat, Amanda had even on occasion asked her why she continued to stay married to such an unpleasant man. But now, sitting here, watching this composed young woman speak about Howard, it was clear there was nothing false about Amanda's grief. Her beloved father had died and her heart was broken.

Amanda returned to her seat, and after that, the service dragged. Howard was eulogized first by his business partner, then by Kat's brother, Josh. It seemed obvious to me that neither had liked him very much, as both speakers overcompensated by wildly praising his life and character. The reverend offered another prayer. Kat had foregone the modern tradition of playing a montage of photos of Howard accompanied by a sappy ballad, so we were spared that.

But I would have had a hard time concentrating no matter how short the service was. I was too distracted by one alarming thought:

If Kat had lied about the nature of Howard's relationship with Amanda, what else had she lied to me about?

20

AT THE END of the service, the pallbearers lifted the coffin off the fabric-draped dais and carried it out of the church on their shoulders. The family stood and, led by Kat and Amanda, followed the coffin down the aisle. Her arm linked through her daughter's, Kat looked wan, her normal vivacity drained away. She was wearing a tailored white pantsuit over a black silk blouse that I hadn't seen before. I wondered if she'd bought it for the occasion. As Kat approached the pew where Todd and I were sitting, I tried to catch her eye. But she either didn't see me or didn't want to acknowledge that she had.

Kat's mother and father, Eleanor and Thomas Wyeth, followed their daughter and granddaughter. Thomas was somber but pleasant, shaking hands with people as he passed. Eleanor looked austere, and other than the occasional gracious nod for a favored few, she kept her chin high and her eyes fixed straight ahead.

"What's next?" Todd murmured. "Is there a reception after?"

"I don't know. They didn't make an announcement. Maybe it's by invitation only." I nodded toward the line forming to exit the church. "It looks like they're having a receiving line. I'll ask Kat."

My pulse quickened at the thought that I'd finally get a chance to talk to Kat, if only for a moment. It was obviously not the time or place for an in-depth conversation, but at least I'd be able to get some sort of read on what was happening.

"Mrs. Campbell, how nice to see you again."

I turned and saw John Donnelly standing there. He looked especially dapper in a dark gray suit and pale yellow tie. He held out his hand and I shook it.

"Mr. Donnelly, this is my husband, Todd," I said. Then, turning to Todd, I explained, "Mr. Donnelly is the attorney who helped me out the other day."

I hadn't told Todd that the attorney had offered me what was, for all intents and purposes, a bribe if I agreed not to further cooperate with the police investigation. Todd was already worried about the entire situation. I didn't want to add to his anxiety.

"It's nice to meet you," Donnelly said cheerfully, shaking hands with Todd. "I thought the service was very well done. For a funeral, that is. Despite my line of work, I'm not a big fan."

"I don't know that anyone is," I remarked.

"You never met my aunt Tilly," Donnelly said, sticking his hands in his pockets. "She was a true aficionado. Never missed a funeral in the neighborhood if she could help it. She loved nothing more than coming back and telling anyone who would listen that the priest was a windbag or that the widow had chintzed out on the coffin."

"She sounds like a pistol," Todd said.

"Yes, well, you didn't have to spend Thanksgiving with her," Donnelly quipped.

Todd and I laughed politely, and Todd said, "It was nice to meet you."

But before we could turn and join the receiving line, the attorney stopped us. "Why don't you leave this way?"

"Excuse me?" I asked.

Donnelly gestured toward a side door at the back of the church, which had an exit sign hanging over it. "This way out is faster. You'll skip right by the crowd."

I glanced at Todd. He looked confused.

"Thank you, but we'd like to give our condolences to Kat and her family," I said, not sure why I had to explain this.

"Let me put it this way—the family would prefer it if you left through the side door." Donnelly shrugged and spread out his hands. "Don't make me be the bad guy here."

"Bad guy? What's he talking about?" Todd asked me.

Without taking my eyes off the lawyer, I replied, "I believe what Mr. Donnelly is saying is that Kat, or more likely her father, doesn't want us to go through the receiving line."

"Why?" Todd asked.

"Care to answer that, Mr. Donnelly?"

"I don't want to make a scene," the lawyer said.

"Neither do we," Todd retorted.

I glanced in the direction Detective Demer had been sitting during the service, hoping that he had already left. He hadn't. Instead he was standing, watching us. When he caught my eye, he raised his eyebrows. I felt a twinge of unease. I didn't know what was going on, but I was pretty sure it wouldn't benefit any of us to have the detective involved.

"Hello, Alice." Thomas Wyeth had appeared behind his lawyer, looking as genial and good-natured as he had been the night of the Christmas party. Mr. Wyeth was wearing a navy blue suit, but the jacket was open and his hands were stuck jauntily in his pants pockets.

"I was just telling Mr. and Mrs. Campbell that it might be easier for them if they left through the side door," Donnelly explained.

"Ah. Why don't I take it from here? I just saw Marilee. She was looking for you," Mr. Wyeth said.

John Donnelly affected a look of pretend horror. "My wife," he said, turning back to Todd and me. "I better go join her before she gets it into her mind to become the third ex–Mrs. Donnelly. That's something I certainly can't afford."

Donnelly turned and left through the same door he had been urging Todd and me to sneak out. Mr. Wyeth watched his attorney leave, then turned back to look at me. I tensed, feeling a bit like my namesake when she fell through the rabbit hole. I braced for whatever was coming next. I didn't know if I should expect outright hostility or more of this polite weirdness.

Thomas Wyeth's expression was benign. He smiled and looked at Todd.

"May I borrow your wife for a moment, Mr. Campbell?" Mr. Wyeth asked.

"Please, call me Todd."

"All right, then, Todd. Would you mind? I'd just like to speak to Alice privately for a few minutes. This is a difficult time for our family. I think it would help Kat tremendously if Alice would hear me out."

Todd glanced at me worriedly, but I nodded at him. I had no idea what Kat's father wanted, but I was a firm believer in getting as much information as possible. Even though I knew that Mr. Wyeth was playing on my loyalty to Kat, he was smart to do so. I did want to help Kat, even if I still didn't know what was going on or why she wasn't speaking to me. She was my friend, my *best* friend, no matter what had happened over the past week. Even if she had lied to me about her daughter's relationship with Howard. And anyway, maybe it hadn't been an intentional lie. Maybe it had been wishful thinking, a hope that their inevitable divorce wouldn't negatively affect her daughter. But whatever the truth was, I certainly didn't want to cause Kat any distress on the day she buried her husband.

"It's fine," I said, laying a placating hand on my husband's arm. "I'll meet you out front."

"You really want me to go out the side door?" Todd asked incredulously.

I glanced at Mr. Wyeth, and he gave an almost imperceptible nod accompanied by a slight shrug of his shoulders. *It's for the best*, he seemed to be saying. It occurred to me that Thomas Wyeth must be in his seventies, although despite the white hair and weathered face, he certainly didn't seem that old. He had a youthful vitality about him.

"I'll be right out," I promised. Todd nodded reluctantly, but he turned and exited through the same door John Donnelly had used a few minutes earlier.

"Shall we?" Mr. Wyeth asked. "The courtyard is beautiful. There's a koi pond."

I followed him across the nave, to a door on the far side that led out to the church's courtyard. Mr. Wyeth was right. The church's gardens were lovely. The koi pond was actually a long rectangular tiled pool, anchored on one end by a fountain and surrounded by walls of geometrically cut shrubbery. A grassy bridge arched over it, creating both a decorative touch and a footpath. As we drew closer, the koi swarmed toward us.

"Aren't they something?" Mr. Wyeth said. "I think they're hoping we've come to feed them. Do you have any idea what they eat?"

"No," I said. "My daughter had a goldfish once, but she just fed it fish food we got at the pet store. It was a lot smaller than these fish."

Mr. Wyeth chuckled. "I imagine it was. Do you think they're related? Are koi just goldfish on steroids?"

"I think it might be a little more complicated than that."

"Most things are." Mr. Wyeth smiled. "I thought the service was quite nice."

I nodded. "The poem Amanda recited was beautiful."

"She picked that out on her own. That girl is something. I love all my grandchildren and I'm proud of every last one of them. But Amanda has always been special."

"She's an impressive young woman."

"I'm sure you're wondering why I wanted to speak with you."

I nodded and waited. He glanced around as though wanting to make sure we were alone. Other than the fish, we were.

"I think it's best if you and Kat don't communicate. At least for a while," Mr. Wyeth said.

His tone was mild, but his words were chilling. I finally had confirmation, if I needed it, that Kat was actively avoiding me.

"May I ask why?"

"It's a difficult time for Kat, as I'm sure you can imagine. Howard's death was sudden, and now the police have gotten it into their heads that it wasn't an accident. On top of everything else Kat has had to deal with, the police keep asking her all kinds of invasive and upsetting questions." Mr. Wyeth shook his head as if he thought the police's investigation was in bad taste. "Everyone knows Howard had a problem with the bottle. He obviously had too much to drink that night and fell off his balcony. Instead of just accepting that, they want to turn this into some sordid crime. They're probably hoping that it will make them famous, that they'll end up being interviewed on the *Today* show."

"Mr. Wyeth, I understand this has been a difficult time for Kat. But I don't understand what that has to do with me or why you don't want me to speak with her."

"I believe the police consider Kat a suspect in Howard's death."

"She was out of the country," I pointed out needlessly. "As far as alibis go, that's about as foolproof as it gets."

"We both know that doesn't necessarily clear her." Mr.

Wyeth stared moodily at the fish, his customary bonhomie gone. "And I know you spoke to the police."

The sudden change in his manner unnerved me.

"They interviewed me, but I certainly didn't say anything to implicate Kat," I said carefully.

"You told them Howard was having an affair," Mr. Wyeth said. I stared at him, wondering how he knew this. He again seemed to be reading my thoughts. "The Jupiter Island Public Safety Department is hardly the FBI. You couldn't possibly have thought that what you said to them would remain confidential."

I actually was annoyed at how naive I had been. But at least I finally knew why Kat wasn't speaking to me, at least in the days since I'd spoken to the police. My telling them about Howard's affair was problematic for her in two ways. One, it established a clear motive for why she might want Howard dead. And two, it now looked like she had been hiding her knowledge of the affair from the police. Which, of course, was exactly what she had been doing. That still didn't explain why she had been avoiding me before the police had interviewed me.

"I had to tell them about the affair because Kat told the police that her housekeeper and I were the only two nonfamily members who knew how to access the spare key and house alarm. That made me a suspect." I knew I sounded defensive.

"I'm sure that wasn't Kat's intention," Mr. Wyeth offered.

"Of course it wasn't. I know that." I struggled to regain my composure. "But the fact is that there was at least one other person, possibly more, who might have had access to their house. Howard might even have let his girlfriend in that night. It seemed like a pretty important piece of information for the police to have."

"To protect yourself."

"Of course I want to protect myself."

"And therein lies our problem."

I crossed my arms in front of me. "Mr. Wyeth, I appreciate you're worried about Kat. I'm worried about her, too. And I'll do whatever I can to help—"

"I don't want you to help her," he cut in. "I want you to stay away from her. Kat wants you to stay away from her. Is that clear enough?"

Thomas Wyeth and I stared at each other for a few long beats.

I was suddenly reminded of a favorite toy I had as a child, an old-fashioned kaleidoscope. It looked like a spyglass. At least, that was what I'd liked to pretend it was. I'd look through it and see a colorful pattern made up of tiny glass pieces. But all I had to do was rotate it—*click, click, click*—and the first pattern would disappear, to be replaced by a different pattern made out of the same pieces. The affable man, beloved father to my best friend was gone, replaced by a formidable, ruthless man.

"Fine," I finally said. "I won't contact Kat if she doesn't want me to. But I'd like to hear that from her directly."

Mr. Wyeth's expression darkened. "Who the hell do you think you are?"

"I'm not sure what you mean."

"We've tried to deal with you pleasantly," Mr. Wyeth growled. "Donnelly made you a very generous offer."

"He tried to bribe me into not cooperating with a police investigation! What exactly was I supposed to have found pleasant about that?"

"In my experience, there are two main ways to achieve a goal," he said. "One involves a carrot. The other involves a stick. Which would you prefer?"

Mr. Wyeth took a step toward me so that he was suddenly standing far too close. I was very aware that we were alone, apart from the freakishly large fish staring up at us from their watery prison.

"Are you threatening me?"

Mr. Wyeth's smile was chilling. "Take my recommendation however you'd like."

Before I could respond, we were interrupted.

"Is there a problem here?"

We both turned and saw Detective Demer walking toward us. Relief flooded through me.

"Not at all, Detective," Mr. Wyeth said, his tone suddenly back to its usual conviviality.

Demer looked at me, his dark eyes concerned. "Is everything all right, Mrs. Campbell?"

I nodded. "Yes, it's fine. Mr. Wyeth was just showing me the koi pond."

"It's an incredible sight," Mr. Wyeth said. "If you'll both excuse me, I need to rejoin my family. This has been a difficult day for all of us."

He nodded at the detective and then smiled at me. His pleasant mask was back in place, but I could see something cold and hard behind his eyes.

Detective Demer and I watched Thomas Wyeth walk away. The detective gave a slight shake of his head before turning back to me.

"They are an interesting family," he remarked. "What's that old saying about the rich being different from you and me?"

"I used to think that wasn't true," I said. "Or at least, I thought it wasn't universally true. I assumed good and bad people come from all walks of life, and it's not useful to make generalizations."

"You don't believe that anymore?"

I considered this. "I don't know. That's the problem with my line of work. People are more complicated than logic allows. They certainly aren't reliably consistent."

"It's not too late for you to cooperate with our investigation," the detective said.

I glanced up at Demer, who was looking as rumpled as ever. I couldn't read his expression. I'd had the sense since our first meeting that he wanted to help me. Or, more accurately, that he wanted to cause the least amount of disruption to my life possible. I think he believed I might be someone with information about a possible crime, but not a criminal myself. Still, it would be naive to believe that he was on my side, especially since Thomas Wyeth had just told me that someone had leaked the contents of my interview with the police.

"I'll keep that in mind," I replied. Then I turned away and walked out of the garden.

21

THE DAY AFTER Howard's funeral, I did an internet search for Marcia Grable, Kat's former yoga teacher/stalker. She was still in the area, now running her own studio called Lotus Yoga.

Kat had told me Marcia was mentally unhinged. And yet the yoga teacher was the only other person I knew of who had been excommunicated by Kat. I sat staring at my computer, tapping my fingers on the table, trying to decide what to do. Go over there and meet her or drop it altogether? But I needed answers, and Kat had made it clear—or at least, her father had—that she wasn't going to speak to me.

I couldn't leave it alone. I stood, grabbed my handbag and headed out the door.

I arrived at Lotus Yoga just as a class was ending. Dozens of sweaty women streamed out of the studio, each clutching a rolled-up yoga mat. Once the crowd had thinned, then disappeared, I headed inside.

The yoga studio was clean and open and smelled like oranges and mint. In the front there was a small shop that sold yoga mats, blocks, straps and fifty-five-dollar sweatshirts emblazoned with the Lotus Yoga logo. In the back, past the shop area, there was a large space with hardwood floors and mirrored walls. I looked around, but there didn't seem to be anyone on duty.

"Hello?" I said. My voice sounded small and tentative in the open space.

"I'll be right out," came the perky response. A moment later, the owner of the voice appeared from a back room I hadn't noticed.

"Hello," she said, smiling warmly. "I'm Marcia. How can I help you?"

Marcia Grable didn't look like a crazy stalker. Then again, I wasn't sure what a crazy stalker was supposed to look like. Marcia was absolutely gorgeous—tall and very lean with long blond hair, caramel tanned skin and excellent posture.

"Hi," I said. "I'm…" And then I stopped. Somewhat unlike me, I hadn't planned on what I was going to say. *Did you really stalk my best friend? You look far too chilled out to be a stalker.* It didn't seem like a great conversation starter.

The woman waited, smiling patiently.

"Alice," I finished lamely.

"It's nice to meet you, Alice. Are you interested in signing up for a series of yoga classes?"

"Yes," I said and then immediately felt guilty for the lie. "Well, actually no. That's not why I'm here."

Marcia looked at me curiously.

"I'm not sure how to say this in a non-weird way. But do you by any chance remember Kat Grant?"

The Zen disappeared from Marcia's face, replaced by a wary, watchful expression.

"What do you want?" she asked. Then she shook her head and said, "Actually, never mind. I don't care what you want. I'd just like you to leave."

I held up my hands, fingers spread. "No, really. I'm not here to bother you."

"It's too late for that." Marcia picked up a cordless phone. "Do I need to call the police?"

Until recently my only interactions with the police involved the occasional parking ticket. Now the mere mention of the police made me deeply uneasy.

"I'm sorry I startled you. I'm not here to upset you," I quickly added.

"Then why are you here?"

I hesitated. Marcia lifted the phone again, her finger hovering near the talk button.

"I'm just looking for some information."

Marcia crossed her arms, still holding on to the phone. "What kind of information?"

"I know Kat," I said. "She's my friend. Or she *was* my friend. I don't know if she still is or what to think. It's just her sister-in-law mentioned your name to me once, when she was warning me about getting too close to Kat… Something's happened, and… Anyway, I thought you might be able to help me. I'm so sorry if my coming here is an imposition."

To my surprise, Marcia smiled. She also set the phone down on the counter near her cash register.

"Do you want to go get a chai tea?" she asked.

We headed to a nearby Starbucks, where Marcia ordered her chai tea. I opted for a latte.

Marcia looked around. "Let's sit over there." She nodded to a corner of the coffee shop.

I was glad she had picked a table that was somewhat private. Jupiter was a small town in many ways. I had already recognized a mother from Seaview Country Day sitting across the coffee shop, immersed in a conversation with a friend. I also suspected that a few of the women wearing tank tops and cropped yoga pants had come here straight from Marcia's last class. I doubted she was any more eager to have our conversation overheard than I was. Actually, the very fact that the coffee shop was so crowded, with raised voices bouncing off the tiled floors and walls, worked in our favor. An eavesdropper would have to work hard to overhear what we said.

Marcia popped the plastic top off her tea and poured in two packets of sugar. I must have looked surprised—I would have pegged her for one of those healthy types who viewed sugar as a form of poison—because she looked vaguely guilty.

"I have a sweet tooth," she explained, stirring her tea with a wooden stick. "So, Kat Grant. I haven't seen her in years, and suddenly her name keeps popping up everywhere."

"It does?" I asked, wondering if the police had spoken to Marcia, too. It was possible. Kat might have given Marcia's name to the police. That would make sense if Marcia had really stalked her. But I didn't want to bring up the police investigation and risk spooking her.

"You didn't hear that Kat's husband died? It was on the front page of the paper last week," Marcia said. She narrowed her eyes. "I thought you said you were good friends with her."

"Oh, no, I did know that. I went to his funeral yesterday," I told her.

"I'm not exactly sure what you want from me," Marcia said.

"I was hoping you'd tell me your version of what happened between you and Kat."

"And why should I do that?"

I drew in a deep breath. "Because I'm starting to wonder how well I know the person I thought was my best friend."

Marcia laughed without humor and took a sip of her tea. It apparently wasn't sweet enough, because she tore open another packet of sugar and added it to her cup.

"My guess is that you don't know her nearly as well as you think you do," she said. "But if you're looking for answers about what makes Kat tick, I'm not sure I can help you."

"What happened between the two of you?"

"I met Kat years ago, when I was working as an instructor at Bliss Body Yoga," Marcia said. "Kat would come in two or three times a week. She made a point of telling me I was her favorite teacher, which was, of course, incredibly flattering, since I was a fairly new instructor at that time." She stopped and thought about this. "Actually, I think that's part of Kat's appeal, right there. It isn't just that she flatters you. People throw around compliments all the time. 'I like your hair' or 'Your dog is so cute.' But Kat's different. It's like she can almost instantly figure out what's most important to the way you see yourself, then she compliments you on that."

I thought uneasily about the many times Kat had praised my intelligence. *You're the smartest person I've ever met, Alice. You have the most extraordinary mind.*

"It may sound silly, but at that time, I had a lot of anxiety about teaching yoga," Marcia continued. "I'd get incredibly nervous before every class, to the point that I'd hide in the bathroom, trying not to throw up. I was always worried my clients would be thinking the whole time that I didn't know what I was doing or that I wasn't as good as other yoga teachers they'd taken classes with."

"It doesn't sound silly at all. I used to teach. It's hard standing up and speaking in front of people, being the authority," I agreed.

"Especially when you're starting out." Marcia nodded. "And I don't know what you taught..." She paused.

"I was a college professor," I said. "I taught in the math department."

"Oh. Wow." Marcia blinked a few times, then returned to stirring her tea. "Well, that's different. You probably had a degree and credentials. I mean, you go through training and certification to teach yoga, of course, but even so, I felt like a fraud at first. So when Kat told me how great my classes were, it made me feel terrific. Like I was doing what I was meant to do." She looked up at me. "It was pretty powerful."

"And, of course, you started feeling happier and better about yourself when you were around Kat," I said slowly. This was starting to sound alarmingly familiar.

"Exactly. I mean, don't get me wrong," Marcia said, raising a hand, "your friends *should* make you happy when you're around them. That's the point of having friends. But with Kat...it's different. When she does it, it's to *manipulate* you, because she wants something from you." She stopped and shook her head. "Even after all this time, I'm still not entirely sure what it was she wanted from me. Or maybe it's just that I still can't believe what she wanted."

"What do you mean?"

Marcia breathed in deeply. "Okay, but I'm warning you— this is going to sound a little crazy."

I actually hoped it *would* sound crazy. That Marcia's friendship with Kat wouldn't remind me—more than it already had—of my friendship with her. But I smiled and said, "I'm sure it won't."

"Kat wanted me to have an affair with her brother," Marcia said.

I was wrong. It sounded completely bonkers. A small part of me was disappointed that I wouldn't find answers to my many questions here, but mostly I was relieved. Kat was right. Marcia *was* disturbed.

Just then, one of the baristas dropped something behind the coffee bar that clattered loudly to the floor. Everyone looked up, startled by the noise. The barista flushed with embarrassment, while her coworkers began to tease her for her clumsiness. I used the brief interlude to think of an excuse to extricate myself from this conversation and leave Marcia to her overly sweet tea. Nothing came to mind.

"I knew you'd think it sounds nuts," Marcia continued. She laughed without humor.

"I didn't say that," I said carefully.

"Okay, look, you wanted to know," Marcia said. "And that's what she wanted. She couldn't stand her brother's wife."

"Ashley."

"Right, Ashley. Awful Ashley. That's what Kat called her. She used to joke that Ashley lived on a diet of wine and bitterness," Marcia recalled.

She suddenly had my attention again. This was *exactly* how Kat had described Ashley to me.

"She was convinced that Ashley had trapped her brother... I can't remember his name," Marcia said.

"Josh," I supplied.

"Right, Josh. How could I forget?" Marcia said, shaking her head. "I think I've been trying to repress the whole thing. Anyway, Kat wanted to break up their marriage."

"What?" This was starting to sound contrived. "Why would she want to do that? And even if she wanted to, how would she manage it?"

"The why is easy. She hated Ashley and she wanted her out of the family."

I didn't doubt that Kat disliked Ashley—she had admitted that to me herself. But I had a hard time imagining her plotting to break up the marriage. Marcia read the skepticism on my face.

"I thought it was crazy, too," Marcia said. "I told Kat that she shouldn't get involved. Besides, Josh and Ashley have, what, two or three kids together? And this was almost ten years ago, so they were still pretty young at that point. Kat didn't seem to care that her plan would have meant those kids, her nieces and nephews, would have their family broken up."

I hadn't intended to interrupt her—especially now that she was talking freely—but I couldn't help myself. "Wait..."

I splayed my hands in front of me, nearly knocking over my latte. I pushed it to the side. "She had a plan? An actual plan to get them to divorce?"

Marcia straightened in her seat, tucking her hair back over her shoulders. "She wanted me to seduce Josh."

"But...how?" Then, worrying she'd take offense, I added, "I mean, you're obviously gorgeous."

Marcia laughed. "Don't worry, it's not like men just see me and divorce their wives on the spot. Hardly. I mean, hell, if I had that sort of power, I'd head to Silicon Valley and pick off a billionaire."

"I'm sure you could."

"That's very kind, but no. That's not what I meant. And it's not what Kat had in mind," Marcia said.

"What did she have in mind? I don't mean to pry, but this just sounds..." I was going to say *crazy*, but I stopped myself.

"Crazy. I know, I told you it would." Marcia inhaled deeply through her nose, then exhaled loudly and almost instantly looked calmer. When she saw me watching her, brow furrowed, she smiled and said, "It's *ujjayi pranayama*. We use it in our yoga practice as a way to calm the body and mind."

"Maybe I should sign up for some classes."

"Maybe you should." Marcia smiled. "Anyway, it all started because Kat was having a lot of conflict with Ashley around that time. They were planning a party for Kat's parents' wedding anniversary together, and Kat pretty much hated everything Ashley suggested. I remember Ashley wanted there to be a theme—I think it was Cherry Blossoms in the Spring or something like that. And Kat kept saying, 'It's an anniversary party, not a fucking high school prom!'"

Marcia had an uncanny ability to mimic Kat's fast-paced speech.

"And then she'd say something like 'I wish Josh had married someone like you, Marcia. Someone calm and grounded.'

She'd say that a lot. Like, if she could go through a catalog and handpick her future sister-in-law, she would have chosen someone more like me. Which, okay, I know that sounds a little odd, but I have to admit, it was flattering."

I nodded. "Of course."

"But it was also harmless. Or at least, it was at that point. Kat and Ashley were just spending too much time together, and it did seem like Ashley was going out of her way to be annoying. She'd say stupid crap, probably just to wind Kat up. I thought Kat was just venting," Marcia said with a shrug. "The way people do."

"But at some point it presumably moved past venting."

"Yes." Marcia looked down at her tea cupped between her hands. "This is the part where it starts to get really weird. Kat invited me to go away for a weekend. To Amelia Island. Have you ever been there?"

I nodded. It was a resort island in northeast Florida. Todd and I had once taken the kids there for a week. "Yes, it's beautiful."

"It is," Marcia said. "And it was Kat's treat. Which was... Well, I didn't have much money at the time. So even though it felt weird letting her pay for everything, I was excited to get away."

Yet another similarity to my friendship with Kat, I realized with growing unease.

"She booked us in at a beautiful hotel right on the beach," Marcia continued. "And the weekend started off great. We hung out by the pool, went to dinner and then had cocktails at the hotel bar. That's when Kat told me her brother was there."

"Where? At the same hotel?"

Marcia nodded. "Yep. He was there with some of his friends for a guys' golf weekend."

"Did Kat know he'd be there ahead of time?"

"Of course. That was the whole point of our being there,

although I didn't know it at the time. Anyway, I asked if we shouldn't go say hello or invite him to join us for a drink. She said no, it would be much more fun to play a practical joke on him."

"What sort of practical joke?"

"She said, 'Wouldn't it be funny if when he went back to his room, you were naked and waiting for him?'"

"Jesus," I whispered.

"I know. That was her plan."

"And you went along with it?"

"God, no! Of course not. But we were drinking a lot that night—wine at dinner, cocktails at the bar. There was something about Kat that made me...I don't know, want to please her, I guess. She was paying for this whole weekend, after all, and I didn't want to be a killjoy. So I laughed and pretended I thought her plan was funny." Marcia blushed and looked down at the table. "I know how dumb that sounds. Trust me, I've spent a lot of time regretting that I didn't tell her right then and there I didn't want anything to do with it."

"Why? Did something happen?"

Marcia's laugh was a sad, broken sound that made me dread what she was about to tell me.

"I was pretty drunk, and honestly, there's a point when I don't remember anything," Marcia said. "I've always wondered if Kat might have drugged me. It certainly would have been easy enough for her to slip a date rape drug into my glass. I know, I know. It sounds crazy. But one minute we were in the restaurant, the next...I woke up in her brother's hotel room. Naked."

I stared at her, at a loss for words. "So you went through with it?"

"No!" Marcia said, holding up both hands. "I didn't sleep with him."

"It's actually none of my business," I said.

"No, it's not, but I'm telling you anyway—I didn't fuck him," Marcia said. "Or maybe it would be more accurate to say he didn't fuck me, since I was obviously not in control of the situation."

"So what did happen? How did you even get into his room?"

Marcia shrugged. "I have no idea. I assume Kat got a key somehow. She has a talent for convincing people to do things for her. Or maybe she just bribed someone who was working in reception. It probably wasn't that hard. Anyway," she continued, "when I woke up, Josh was there. He was sleeping sitting up in an armchair. Fully clothed. When he woke up, he started crying."

"Josh was crying," I repeated. I couldn't picture it. The few times I'd met him, he'd been so smug, so self-conceited.

"He was really upset and worried his wife would find out about it, my being there in his room overnight." Marcia shook her head and her face softened. "I hadn't even been attracted to him before, but I actually was a bit then, seeing how in love with his wife he was."

"Did you tell him that Kat had wanted to play a practical joke on him?"

"Yes, of course. I had to explain why I was there. And he said—" Marcia stopped, waiting for an older couple to move slowly by our table. The man walked with a cane and gripped his wife's arm to steady himself. Once they passed, Marcia twisted her head from side to side, checking over her shoulder to ensure no one could overhear, before lowering her voice to a whisper. "Josh said, 'I should have known that fucking cunt was behind this.'"

"He said that about his sister?"

"He knows her better than anyone, right?"

For some reason, this was the most chilling thing she'd told me yet. I shivered and looked down to see that the fine hairs on my arms were standing on end.

"What did you do then?"

"What do you think I did? I dressed and I got the hell out of there," Marcia said. "And that's when it got really weird."

"Weirder than waking up in Josh's room?"

"Yes, even weirder than that." Marcia drained the rest of her tea.

"Do you want another?" I asked, gesturing to the paper cup, but Marcia waved me off.

"No, thanks. Anyway, I went back to the room that Kat and I were sharing. She was wide-awake and waiting for me. She'd even ordered room service. She was dying to hear what had happened."

"Between you and Josh," I clarified.

"Yes. I know, I thought it was gross, too. But she wanted every detail. And the creepiest part, the part where I said I couldn't remember anything, seemed to excite her. Not sexually. At least," Marcia said with a shudder, "I hope not. But it was like the amnesia made it an even better story."

"I still don't understand how this was supposed to end his marriage. Was she hoping he'd confess the infidelity to Ashley? Or that he'd want to see you again and you'd end up having an affair?"

Marcia shrugged. "I'm not sure. Maybe it was part of a larger plan. I know she had a private detective working for her, someone she'd hired to follow her husband when she thought he was cheating on her. Maybe she was planning to hire him to follow her brother and have him take photos of Josh with me or someone else. Or maybe she just wanted to throw a grenade into their marriage to see what would happen."

"All this because she didn't like Ashley?" It was hard to keep the skepticism out of my voice.

Marcia looked at me. "All because she *hated* Ashley,"

she corrected me. "And she wanted her out of the family. I thought you were friends with Kat. Haven't you figured out that she always has to have her way? *Always*."

"What did she say when you told her you didn't have sex with Josh?"

"Oh, she was pissed off. She kept saying, 'Well, you were really drunk, how do you know?' And I pointed out that there weren't any—" Marcia paused "—um, fluids. She just laughed and said he probably wore a condom. I mean, do you get how weird this is? I'm a grown woman. If I drink too much, it's my own responsibility, but at the same time…if a man had sex with me and I wasn't conscious while it was happening, that would be rape. Remember, this was the person who was supposed to be my best friend, and she was basically *hoping* that was what happened."

"But you weren't raped," I said.

"No. I'm one hundred percent sure, thank God. But still. Isn't it seriously screwed up that she wanted that to happen?"

She stared at me as though waiting for an answer.

"I don't know what to think." The Kat I knew would never have done such a thing. A part of me was still hoping that the entire story was bullshit. That all it would take was a few days of digging and I'd find out that Kat and Marcia had never gone on the trip or, if they had, that Josh and Ashley had been in Paris that weekend.

I'd find out that this woman really was delusional. That Kat really wasn't a monster.

"You don't believe me," Marcia said. She shook her head again and looked disappointed. "I knew you wouldn't."

"I didn't say that," I protested.

"You didn't have to." Her blue eyes were hard, like chips of glass. "I guess it's a good thing I saved all of her texts, isn't it?"

22
―――――

DESPITE A LOOMING deadline for *I Think My Dad Is a Werewolf*, my latest installment for Kidtastic, I didn't get any work done that afternoon after I returned home from meeting with Marcia. Instead I sat in our home office, reading through the pages of texts Marcia had screen-capped and forwarded to me from her phone. It certainly looked like the texts she'd saved were from Kat, although I had no idea how hard it would be to fake that. If Marcia did make it up, she would've had to put an enormous amount of work into the forgery. There were hundreds of texts back and forth between them.

Most of them read like the usual exchanges between two friends. Texts like,

Kat: Free for lunch tomorrow?

And,

Marcia: R u coming to class tomorrow?

And,

Kat: What's the name of that eye cream you were telling me about

They were as trivial as most texts, but I found them noteworthy—and a little chilling—when I realized that here, at last, was the absolute proof Kat had lied to me. She and Marcia had been friends—close friends, even. They had lunched together frequently, had inside jokes at the expense of a few regulars at the yoga school—one who took phone calls during class, another they'd nicknamed Stinky Girl—and had spent a lot of time discussing the various men Marcia dated. For example, after a particularly disastrous date, Marcia had texted,

Marcia: Ur lucky ur married.

Kat: Only because extracurricular activities are SO much more fun.

Marcia: Hahaha. You're terrible. What if H finds out?

Kat: He never has before ☺

I read this exchange again. Was this Kat confessing to an affair or a series of affairs? She had never mentioned anything to me about having past affairs, but then again, she'd also told me that she'd barely known Marcia, who, Kat claimed, had gone on to stalk her. These texts, sent from Kat's cell phone to Marcia's, seemed to prove otherwise.

And then I remembered our trip to Key Biscayne, when Kat had spent the night with Hudson. She'd led me to believe it was the first time she had ever been unfaithful to Howard. She had even made a compelling case that Howard deserved to be cheated on. I had thought at the time that she was awfully relaxed about the infidelity. It had been me, not Kat, who had been uncomfortable breakfasting with Hudson the morning after. Was that because Hudson hadn't been her first extramarital dalliance?

My stomach gave a sour twist of unease. Yet more evidence that I didn't know Kat as well as I'd thought.

Kat and Marcia texted about Ashley frequently, and Kat's growing irritation at her sister-in-law became evident.

Kat: Awful Ashley wants us to commission a portrait of all of us incl spouses and kids for my parents' anniversary. Not a photograph, which would be bad enough, but a fucking painting.

And,

Kat: If Ashley suddenly disappeared off the face of the earth, would I be a suspect? Wait, don't answer that. I'd be suspect numero uno.

And,

Kat: Ashley the Asshole. Wait. Ashhole? Assley? Anyway, AA just told me we need a color theme for the party. Like: MAROON. Or: HOT PINK. SMFH.

I was clearly behind on my texting acronyms and so had to look SMFH up. It meant Shaking My Fucking Head.

The texts after they'd returned from the disastrous Amelia Island trip, when Marcia failed to seduce Josh, seemed to signal the end of their friendship.

Kat: I don't know why ur so upset. It was supposed to be a joke. I told you, Josh and I have a long history of playing practical jokes on one another.

Marcia: I was sexually assaulted when I was younger. This brought back a lot of bad memories. I'm not sleeping well.

Kat: Jesus, you said you didn't sleep with Josh and now suddenly he raped you?

Marcia: No, of course not. But it's dredged up some scary memories for me.

Kat: You're being way too sensitive.

That was the last text Kat had sent Marcia. Marcia had fired off nearly a dozen more, along the lines of:

Marcia: I thought we had lunch plans today? Where R U?

Marcia: Did you get the messages I left you?

Marcia: Why aren't you returning my calls?

Marcia: Kat? What's going on?

Presumably it was sometime after her last text went unanswered that Marcia had appeared on Kat's doorstep, pie in hand, and Kat had threatened to call the police on her. Assuming that part of Kat's story was true. Who knew what strands of truth were woven in among all the lies?

I remembered a story I'd read in a magazine a while back about a phenomenon called ghosting. It apparently involved cutting off all contact with someone without explanation. The story had been about a famous actress ghosting her equally famous actor boyfriend, so I had assumed it was something that mainly happened among the romantically involved. But it seemed remarkably similar to Kat's cutting off all contact with Marcia. Kat had ghosted her.

And now Kat was ghosting me.

I leaned back in my chair while I processed this new information. Though I didn't want to believe it, though I looked for an alternate theory of what was going on, I kept coming back to the same conclusion.

Kat was not the person I thought she was.

Suddenly I was questioning everything she had told me. Had Howard been abusive? Was her marriage troubled? Had she truly been my friend?

I had a sudden, vivid flashback to a conversation Kat and I had the weekend we spent at Key Biscayne. It was the day of the uncomfortable breakfast with Hudson, but before Kat told me she wished Howard were dead. We were down at the beach, reclining in side-by-side lounge chairs, looking out at the ocean. The water was still, and there was a paddleboarder passing serenely by, making the exercise look far easier than it probably was.

"I wish I could do that," Kat said, shading her eyes as she looked out at the paddleboarder.

"Why can't you? You live on the water. You could launch right off your dock."

"I know. But it wouldn't be the same as here, would it? She looks so peaceful," Kat said in a dreamy voice.

I nodded but said, "That's because she's all the way out there. Everything looks better from a distance. Close up, she's probably a hot mess. In fact, she's probably stopping every few strokes to shoot up heroin."

Kat burst out laughing. "She is not! Where would she keep it? She's wearing a bikini, for God's sake."

I shrugged. "I have no idea. Maybe her bikini has pockets. Junkies are resourceful."

"I'm glad we came," Kat said. She closed her eyes, drew in a deep breath and let it out slowly. "Thank you, Alice."

"What are you thanking me for?"

"For being my friend," Kat said. "I don't know how I ever managed without you."

I shaded my eyes to look at her, sensing her mood had shifted.

"I'll always be your friend," I said. "You know that."

Kat's lips curved up into a sad smile. "You may be the first person in my life who truly loved me for me, and not just because you had to."

"I'm sure that's not true," I protested.

"Isn't it?" It was Kat's turn to shrug. She dropped the magazine she'd been paging through to one side and impatiently pushed her sunglasses up on her head. "I think it's the story of my life."

"What are you talking about?"

"Do you remember I once told you that when I was young, my mother constantly warned me about whom I was friends with? That she told me over and over again anyone who wanted to get close to me was only doing so because of who our family was?"

I nodded. How could I forget something so creepy?

"I lied to you when I told you that," Kat said.

"You did? So your mom was okay with your having friends?"

"No, that part was true. I lied when I said I already had a group of friends I could trust. I never did. I wanted to, but whenever I started feeling like I could be close with someone, I'd hear my mother's voice in my ear," Kat said. She imitated Eleanor Wyeth's voice with chilling precision. "'You can't trust anyone, Katherine. You think they're your friends, but they're all users, looking for what they can get from you.' I was ten. After she told me that, I had a hard time trusting anyone."

"Jesus," I said. Revulsion churned in my stomach, partly because of how ugly the word *users* was, but also because if I was here, at this beautiful hotel, on this dream of a weekend, all on Kat's dime, what did that make me? Was I just another of the users Mrs. Wyeth had warned Kat about?

"Well, Eleanor will never win any awards for Mother of the Year, that's for sure." Kat picked up the sunscreen, squirted a blob of it onto her hand and began rubbing SPF 55 over her arms.

"Pass the sunscreen," I said. Once Kat handed it over, I began slathering it over my limbs, which were already looking suspiciously pink. Like most redheads, I didn't tan or even freckle. I burned. Whenever I was at the beach, I had to hide under large floppy hats and sun umbrellas, and constantly reapply my sunscreen. "What did your mother do?"

Kat laughed, but it was a cynical laugh without much humor. "What didn't she do? She tried to control every single aspect of my life. What I ate, what I wore, whom I associated with. She picked my hairstyle, my extracurricular activities, even the boys I eventually dated."

It was not hard to picture the Eleanor Wyeth I'd met as an iron-fisted control freak.

"When I was fifteen, my mother decided I needed to lose ten pounds," Kat continued. "I wasn't even overweight. I just wasn't rail thin. So she put me on a diet, then harassed me and bullied me and berated me until I lost the weight. She used to force me to go out on runs in the middle of the day in the summer because she believed that I'd sweat out more fat. I passed out once and woke up on a neighbor's lawn with the yard man standing over me with a rake in one hand."

"Like in a creepy way?"

"No, I think he was actually trying to be helpful. He pulled me up and got me a glass of water. When I recounted it to Eleanor later, she told me to stop being so dramatic. I just needed to be more disciplined. Then, to draw a line under this point, she gave me a salad for dinner with one slice of tomato and no dressing."

"That's abusive."

"It definitely was," Kat said. "The worst, though, were the put-downs. I have never been pretty enough, thin enough, smart enough to please her. Not by the standards my mother set. And she let me know it every single day of my life."

"Have you ever talked to anyone about this?"

"Like who?"

"A therapist or your father—anyone?"

"My father." Kat shook her head. "I asked him once why he didn't take my side in the endless battles with my mother. He told me, 'You'll leave in a few years, and then it will be just your mother and me left here at home. That's why I have to take her side.'" Kat laughed her mirthless laugh again. "Typical of my father. Brave when facing anyone and every-one except my mother. Then he turns into a spineless shit."

I turned to look at my friend, who suddenly appeared small and hunched up on her lounge chair.

"Are you okay?" I asked, extending an arm in her direction.

"You know me. I'm always okay," Kat said. She arched her back to roll her shoulders and then reached out to raise the flag behind her chair. "But I do need a drink."

The beach attendant raced over. "What can I get you?"

"I'll have a vodka and soda with a splash of grapefruit juice," Kat said. She looked over at me, her eyebrows raised.

My plans to teetotal that day evaporated. "I'll have the same," I said, trying not to think about what a beachside drink here would cost.

"I love this flag," Kat said. "Do you think I can get one for my house?"

"Of course. But to recreate this, you'll also have to hire

someone who runs over to take your order when you raise the flag."

Kat snapped her fingers. "Foiled at every turn." She shifted on the chaise. "Will you toss me back the sunscreen? I'm going to look like a tomato if I get any more color. You were smart to bring a hat. I should go in and buy one in the gift shop."

I handed her the bottle. She squirted the lotion into her hand, and the chemical scent of fake coconuts filled the air.

"Why do you think your mom did that to you?" I asked.

"Who knows? Maybe she was threatened by the fact that she was getting older, and suddenly had a young, pretty daughter to compete with," Kat said, carelessly dropping the sunscreen down onto the hot sand. "Or maybe she's just always been bug-fucking nuts. That gets my vote."

I thought about my relationship with my daughter. Any fears I had about Bridget growing older, entering puberty, becoming a sexual being were focused on her being victimized by the predators of the world. Everyone loved a pretty girl, especially the freaks and deviants. I had certainly never been threatened by her youth, or viewed her as my competition.

"How did you cope?" I asked.

"I don't know. How do kids ever cope? Aren't we all, in the end, a product of our parents' bad parenting?" Kat asked flatly. "I'm the person my mother created. It's all her fault."

I considered this. I knew my own family dynamics—my parents' divorce, my father's remarriage, my mother's haphazard parenting—had formed me, molding me into the remote, analytical adult I now was. It wasn't hard to see that as a result of the chaos, I had craved order, had even made it my career.

Our drinks arrived then, this time hand-delivered by the dimpled Hudson. At his appearance, a light switched on inside Kat. I could almost see her mentally cast aside her sad reminisces and revert back to her usual effervescent self. Even after Hudson left, returning to the tiki bar, I didn't have the heart to bring up her childhood again, or to ask Kat what she meant when she said it was her mother's fault she had turned into the person she was today.

Maybe I should have.

My doorbell rang, and I started. I'd lost track of the fact that I was sitting at my desk, staring into space. I closed my laptop, stood and arched my back to alleviate the tightness caused by hunching over my computer for so long. I headed to the front door, expecting to find a Girl Scout hawking Thin Mints or a neighbor asking me to sign a petition against the pollution of our local waterways.

But as it turned out, it was neither.

Instead, for the second time in a little over a week, Detective Demer and Sergeant Oliver were standing on my front step. Oliver looked smug, which should have tipped me off that something unpleasant was about to occur. But I was distracted by the sky, which had turned gray and ominously dark. I'd been so immersed in reading the texts between Kat and Marcia, I hadn't noticed a storm was rolling in.

"Mrs. Campbell," Detective Demer said in his calm, deep voice, "can you please step outside?"

"Why?" I asked.

"You're under arrest for the murder of Howard Grant."

23

THE NEXT TWENTY-FOUR hours were a nightmare.

Detective Demer and Sergeant Oliver transported me nearly forty-five minutes north to the Martin County Sheriff's Office. When I asked why I was being taken out of Palm Beach County, Demer explained that the Jupiter Island Public Safety Department didn't have a jail and the Grants' house—and the scene of the alleged crime—was located in Martin County. All pretrial detainees were booked into the Martin County Jail.

He'd allowed me to call Todd before we left my house. Oliver had protested this.

"Why should she get special treatment?" the sergeant had snapped.

But Demer had looked down at me, and for a moment I had the oddest feeling that he didn't want to arrest me. That in some way he was sympathetic to what I was going through.

"Please," I'd said. "I have to let my husband know he needs to pick our children up from school."

Demer had nodded. "Go ahead."

I'd called Todd, but maddeningly he didn't pick up. The call went to voice mail.

"I'm being arrested," I said, surprised at how steady my voice sounded. "I need you to pick up Liam and Bridget from school, and then hire a criminal defense attorney. Not John Donnelly. Someone else. One of the school dads, Alan Feldman, is a tax attorney. Call him. He might be able to recommend someone." I'd hesitated, then added, "I love you."

After I hung up, Sergeant Oliver read me my rights, simultaneously taking out her handcuffs.

"I don't think cuffs are necessary," Demer said.

"It's protocol," Oliver snapped.

Demer did instruct her to cuff my wrists in front of me instead of behind my back like she wanted to. My comfort was not at the top of her concerns, but she acquiesced.

Oliver drove, heading north on US 1. Demer sat in the passenger seat, while I rode in the back, my handcuffed wrists resting on my lap. For a while, we passed by the strip malls, restaurants, car dealerships and marine supply stores that made up the main commercial area of Jupiter. I wondered if I'd be spotted in the back of a police car by anyone I knew.

"We have some time on our hands," Demer said, breaking the silence. "Is there anything you feel like talking about?"

I ignored him and continued to stare out the window. The Intracoastal Waterway came into view. Across it, I could just glimpse Jupiter Island.

"For example, we could talk about why you lied about where you were on the night of Howard Grant's death," the detective said in a conversational tone.

"What?" I couldn't help but say. "I didn't lie."

"You said you were walking on the beach. But one of the traffic cameras took a photo of you on South Beach Road heading toward Jupiter Island," Demer said.

"Which has beaches. That's where I went to walk."

"There's a beach less than a half mile from your house. You

would have had to pass right by it on your way to Jupiter Island. Why wouldn't you walk there?"

"I don't know. I didn't put a lot of thought into it. I was angry, so I left my house. I drove around for a while. Then I decided I felt like taking a walk. Why does it matter where I accessed the beach?"

"It matters, because it puts you within a few miles of the Grants' house on the night Howard Grant was murdered," Demer explained.

"That's why you arrested me? Because I walked on a beach that was a few miles away from Kat's house?" I was incredulous.

Sergeant Oliver had been quiet until then, but she obviously couldn't help herself. "You can cut the innocent act. We know Katherine Grant gave you twenty thousand dollars."

For a moment I felt like I couldn't quite breathe. They knew Kat had loaned us that money. A loan we hadn't paid back. But, wait...*how* did they know? And why was it even relevant? She had given me that check over a year ago. Unless it finally gave the police a missing piece in their theory. Kat wanted Howard dead. And Kat gave me twenty thousand dollars.

I was beginning to understand why they had arrested me. *Breathe*, I thought. *Think*.

"Have you heard from Katherine Grant?" Demer asked.

"Excuse me?"

"The day we interviewed you, you said you hadn't spoken to Mrs. Grant since she returned home from her trip to London. I was wondering if you'd gotten back in touch with her." Demer's tone was conversational, as though we were casual acquaintances discussing whether it was likely to rain later in the day.

"I'm not going to say anything without my lawyer present."

"Okay," Demer said. "Let me know if you change your mind. We do have some time to kill."

I pressed my lips together and looked back out the window.

When we got to the Martin County Jail, the following things happened:

Sergeant Oliver removed my handcuffs. Then she and Demer handed me over to a female uniformed Martin County Sheriff's deputy who didn't bother to introduce herself. She was short, with a muscular build, large brown eyes and unusually shiny dark hair. Under different circumstances, I would have asked her what hair products she used. As it was, I was too focused on trying not to throw up.

This new officer brought me into another room, this one small and windowless and furnished with only a utilitarian bench. She closed the door to protect my privacy, which was pretty much the high point of what happened over the next ten minutes.

I was instructed to take off all my clothes, including my underwear. I did so, folding them neatly and placing them on the bench as though I were just at my gynecologist's office and the nurse had asked me to disrobe. Any delusions I might have had that this search would be anything nearly similar to a gynecological exam were quickly dispelled.

The deputy picked up my clothes. She first shook them out, then ran her hands over all the seams, apparently checking for drugs or needles or God knows what, while I stood there, naked, trying to cover myself with my hands.

The deputy then told me to lean forward and run my fingers through my hair. Then she snapped on a pair of latex gloves and issued a set of terse instructions, which I did my best to follow.

"Pull your ears forward."

"Open your mouth and move your tongue from side to side."

"Tip your head back."

She checked all of these spaces, as well as my armpits and under my breasts. Then came the most humiliating part of the examination. I was instructed to spread my legs, bend over, and, finally, to squat and cough. It was awful and humiliating, and by the time it was over, my eyes were stinging with tears.

How has this become my life? I wondered, swallowing back the sob building in my chest.

At least the deputy hadn't made it worse than it had to be. She wasn't rough with me or unnecessarily cruel. If anything, she seemed almost bored by the exam. But then, unlike me, she probably did this every day.

Once she'd ascertained that I wasn't carrying any contraband inside my body, I was given back the underwear and sports bra I'd been wearing earlier, along with a set of dark green scrubs and plastic shower slides.

"Put these on," the officer said. She stood and waited while I dressed in the scrubs, then escorted me out to the main booking room.

The rest of the booking process reminded me of waiting in line at the Department of Motor Vehicles, only with the horrifying addition that at the end of it, I was going to be imprisoned. They were processing quite a few people that day, so at each station—intake, fingerprints, photos—there was a line. While we waited our turn, we sat in a holding room behind a heavy sliding door. There was an officer present, watching over us. Not everyone was handcuffed, although I was, probably based on the severity of the charges against me. I did my best not to make eye contact with him or any of my fellow arrestees.

One of the men also waiting to get processed was watching me. He was heavily tattooed and had a goatee and shaved head. The weight of his stare felt dirty.

Finally he said, "Hey, there, Ginger. Does the rug match the curtains?"

This earned him a chuckle from a few of the others. Encouraged, he stuck out his tongue and waggled it in my direction.

"Knock it off," the attending officer said in a bored voice.

I folded into myself and wished I could become invisible.

One by one, we were called out for the various phases of booking, then sent back to the holding area to wait some more. I was given a wristband with a number and my photo on it. It reminded me of the ones I had worn at the hospital when I was giving birth.

I noticed that the deputies in charge of shepherding us through the booking procedures were not in any obvious hurry to process the prisoners in the most efficient way possible. Instead they stood around cracking jokes and talking about the latest episode of *The Voice*. I was fairly sure that one of the deputies, an overweight man with a cherubic face, had a crush on the woman who had strip-searched me. He kept attempting to engage her, while she smiled with polite disinterest.

I tried to do as I was told, determined not to ask too many questions. But finally I couldn't stand it any longer, and I asked the deputy taking my fingerprints what would happen next.

She paused as though considering whether she wanted to tell me. But maybe the desperation in my voice moved her, or maybe it was just the fact that they hadn't found any drugs inside my anus.

"You'll be brought before the judge tomorrow. He'll make a decision on bail then," she said.

That one word—*tomorrow*—was so horrifying that for a moment I couldn't even breathe.

"Tomorrow?" I repeated. "What about *tonight*?"

But the talking part of our interview was over. She pursed her lips and pressed my fingertips against the blotter.

I was brought back to a pod. That was what they called the prisoners' living area—a *pod*. It consisted of a brightly lit central room built out of cinder blocks and painted a dirty cream with a jaunty dark green stripe around the middle. It reminded me of the common room in my freshman dorm at college, although here, the only furniture in sight was a group of tables and benches, all of which were bolted to the floor. There was also a television suspended from the ceiling, tuned to a game show, and a shelf that held a battered-looking assortment of board games. The room smelled terrible, a combination of locker room funk and bleach. The pod was filled with women, most of whom were younger than me. They barely looked up as the deputy and I passed, which I took as a good sign. I didn't want to attract any attention.

Surrounding the pod, like spokes on a wheel, were the prisoners' sleeping quarters, each of which were large enough to house two inmates. The deputy escorting me led me to my room, which consisted of a set of metal bunk beds, a toilet and a tiny corner metal sink. The bottom bunk bed in this quarter had clearly been taken, while the top bunk had a bedroll and pillow. My stomach turned again. I had a roommate.

"This is yours," the deputy said, handing me a flimsy plastic sleeve that contained a toothbrush, a travel-size tube of toothpaste and a bar of soap.

Something about these spare toiletries caused me to panic.

"Wait!" I pleaded just as the deputy was turning to leave.

She turned to look back at me. She had a plain, fleshy face devoid of makeup and wore her hair in a long braid down her back. "What?"

"You can't just leave me here," I said. "I need to see a lawyer! I have rights!"

She actually smiled. "That's what every first timer says." She turned to leave.

I was left alone, standing in my cell. Just outside, past the open sliding door, were a few dozen criminals. Although I was pretty sure that they were, like me, pretrial detainees. I knew from somewhere—Political Science 101?—that they weren't allowed to house pretrial detainees with convicted felons. And, I thought, the pretrial detainees were probably somewhat safer to be around. Surely they wouldn't want to make things worse for themselves before they went to trial.

The full realization that I was trapped here, locked up like a criminal, suddenly hit me.

They were keeping me away from my children. Liam and Bridget needed me. I couldn't stay here.

But I couldn't leave.

My breath shortened and my heart began to pound so quickly that I could hear the blood thrumming in my ears. My chest began to hurt. I wondered if it was possible that I was having a heart attack.

"My God," I whispered. "What's happening?"

I realized distantly that I was probably having a panic attack. Bridget suffered from them occasionally, and her doctor had taught us how to cope with them. I closed my eyes and forced myself to take a deep breath, hold the air in my chest for a few beats, then slowly exhale through my mouth. I repeated this several times while trying to picture the ocean on a calm day. The water lapping serenely…a lone pelican gliding low over the waves…the warmth of the sand under my bare feet.

My heart rate slowed, and fear began to recede, retracting its twisting, barbed tentacles.

Once the panic attack had subsided, I decided that the only way I would get through this would be to break down everything into manageable tasks.

First I would make up my bed. I had to perch on the metal edge of the bottom bed frame to reach it. But the extended time I was spending in the sleeping quarters had apparently piqued my new roommate's curiosity.

"What the fuck you doing?" a voice said from the doorway.

I smoothed the blanket over my bunk, then stepped down and turned to meet my roommate. She was a scrawny woman with short, spiky peroxide-blond hair showing black roots and a truly impressive number of tattoos. She had a vine of flowers sprouting from one foot and extending all the way up to her neck, and a series of words and symbols inked on both her arms.

"I'm Alice."

"Okay, Alice," she repeated, nodding, "what the fuck you doing?"

My roommate's name was Kayla. She had been arrested on drug charges, but other than insisting that the charges were "fucking bullshit" and that she'd been "set up by a fucking whacked-out meth-head whore," she said she didn't want to talk about it. At least, not for the first five minutes of our acquaintance. After that, it was all she wanted to talk about.

"I didn't even buy the drugs," Kayla complained. We had moved out to the common room and were sitting together on hard plastic chairs. "I mean, I gave Spring my money, but I was arrested before I got the Oxy. So if I never had it, how can I be guilty of buying it? It's like you go into Best Buy to get a fucking TV or whatever, you haven't actually bought it until you check out and leave with your merchandise, right?"

"Who's Spring?" I asked.

Kayla snorted and rolled her eyes. "She's a fucking bitch, that's who she is. She used to be, like, my 'best friend.'" Kayla made quotation marks with her fingers. "But then she got busted for possession, and if she'd just shut the fuck up, they wouldn't have known about me. But, no, she was whacked out and started running her mouth. Shit. Now I'm here."

"The Prisoner's Dilemma," I said.

Kayla squinted at me. When she frowned, her eyebrows, which had been plucked into thin lines, formed a startling V shape.

"Huh?"

"It's a famous logic puzzle." I waved a hand. "Never mind. It's not important."

"I like puzzles," Kayla said. "When I was a kid, I used to do those puzzles where you find the words hidden in a square of letters. I was good at them, too."

"This is a different kind of puzzle."

But Kayla wasn't ready to give up. She nodded her chin at me. "Tell me, but don't give me the answer. I want to see if I can figure it out on my own."

"Okay." I swallowed a sigh. After all, there wasn't anything better to do. The television show currently playing at a too-loud volume was some sort of talk show on which people yelled and swore at one another, their nonstop expletives bleeped out. It was impossible to understand what any of them were saying, and listening to it was giving me a headache. "The Prisoner's Dilemma involves two people who have been arrested for committing a burglary."

"What are their names?" Kayla asked.

I shrugged. "It doesn't matter. Let's call them Bert and Ernie."

"You mean like from *Sesame Street*? No, my daughter hates that show."

"You have a daughter?" I asked, surprised. Kayla was very young, probably no older than twenty. "What's her name?"

"Beyoncé," Kayla said proudly.

"Oh, that's very—" I hesitated "—original."

"I know, right? Anyway, Bey thinks *Sesame Street* is stupid. I don't blame her. That little Elmo is annoying as fuck," she said.

"What show does she like?"

"I guess *Dora the Explorer.* That's her favorite."

"Okay," I said. "So, we'll call our two suspects Dora and Diego."

"Yeah, I like that better. Dora and Diego." Kayla laughed. "That's funny as shit. Anyway, go ahead."

"Okay." I took a deep breath and gathered my thoughts. "The police believe that Dora and Diego committed a burglary, but they don't have any evidence to prove it. So in order to make a case, they need Dora and Diego to testify against each other. They put each suspect into a separate interrogation room, then ask them to testify against the other."

"Why would they rat on each other?" Kayla interrupted. "No one does that, other than meth-head whores like Spring."

"They're offered an incentive to talk," I said. "The police give both suspects the same deal—if you testify against the other, you'll walk free, and your accomplice will spend ten years in jail."

"So what's the catch?"

"The catch is that if neither one of them testifies against the other, they both walk free. But if they both agree to testify against each other, they'll both have to serve five-year jail sentences. So without speaking to one another, Dora and Diego have to decide what to do. If you agree to testify, you'll either walk free or, at worst, serve five years in jail. But if you remain silent and your accomplice testifies against you, you'll go to jail for ten years."

Kayla was silent for a minute, considering this.

"That's fucked up," she finally said.

I shrugged. "That's the problem. It's a game of trust. What would you do?"

"I don't know. If I'm Dora, then Diego's my homey," Kayla said. "I wouldn't want to betray him and shit. Like Spring did to me, that little bitch."

"Okay, so imagine Diego's not your friend. You'd never met him before the night of the burglary."

"I don't know. I guess you sort of have to do the testify thing, right?" Kayla said. "Because that way you might go to jail, but it wouldn't be for no ten years."

"That's exactly right," I said. "Anyone acting in their own self-interest will always choose to testify."

Kayla grinned broadly. "So I got it right? Really?"

"You got it right."

She let out a whoop and thrust a fist in the air. "I told you I was good at puzzles!"

"So is that what happened with you and your friend?" I asked.

"Who, Spring?" When I nodded, Kayla shrugged and said, "Nah, it wasn't anything like that. The police popped her for buying Oxy, and so she became a narc for them. She brings in enough people for them to arrest, she gets off."

"And she gave them you? Her best friend?"

"I told you, she's a fucking bitch." I knew Kayla was trying to sound tough, but the betrayal was clearly hurtful. She ran one hand through her spiky hair while the other tapped out a beat against her leg. *Tap-tap-TAP. Tap-tap-TAP.*

"I'm sorry she did that to you," I said. "She wasn't a very good friend."

Kayla shrugged, looked down at her tapping hand.

What are you going to do? that shrug seemed to say. *There's no true loyalty in the world.*

I knew how she felt.

"Alice Campbell? Your lawyer's here," one of the officers called out.

24

THE GUARD LED me through a sliding metal door out of the pod, then down a short linoleum-floored hallway through yet another sliding door. The doors opened and shut with thunderous clangs, the noise echoing off the cinder block walls. I had been hearing the doors slam shut all day, the noise competing with the inmates' shrieks and laughter for which could be the loudest. I hoped the arrival of my attorney meant I was getting out of jail immediately. I couldn't imagine ever falling asleep in this place.

The guard ushered me into a room, larger than I had expected, with four round tables, each surrounded by chairs. A woman dressed in a severe gray pantsuit was sitting at one of them.

"Alice Campbell?" She stood and held out her hand. "I'm Grace Williams. Your husband hired me to represent you."

Grace Williams was almost absurdly pretty. She had large green eyes, shoulder-length blond hair and fine, symmetrical features. She wore chunky tortoiseshell-framed glasses in what was probably a failed attempt to detract from her model good looks.

"Thank you for coming, Ms. Williams," I said, shaking her hand. Her grip was firm and cool.

"Please, call me Grace. We're going to be spending quite a bit of time together, so there's no need for formalities."

The guard left, and Grace gestured for me to sit.

"Your husband filled me in on the basics, and I have to say, I'm surprised the state has brought charges against you. They don't have much to go on," Grace said. "But before we get started on that, do you have any questions for me?"

"How soon can I get out of here?"

"You'll have a hearing tomorrow morning in front of Judge Wilkinson, where we'll argue for bail. You have no priors and you have substantial ties to the community, so despite the severity of the charge, I imagine you will get bail," Grace said.

My entire body went cold. I looked down to see that my hands were shaking.

"So I am going to have to spend the night here," I said, trying to sound calm, but failing. My voice was strangled somewhere low in my throat. I had hoped that the appearance of my attorney meant that the Sheriff's deputy had been wrong, and that I would be released immediately.

Grace looked at me over the rim of her glasses. "I know it's distressing, especially if you've never been in jail before. But look at it this way—it's just one night. What we really need to focus on is keeping you out of jail for the next thirty years."

She was right—this did put one night of jail into stark perspective—but it was hardly a calming thought. I could feel my heart rate accelerate again, the now familiar pounding filling my ears.

"Oh, God," I whispered.

"Don't panic," Grace said, holding up a hand, her palm facing out.

I took a few deep breaths and tried to calm down. Panicking was not going to help anything. I rolled my shoulders back, forcing the muscles to relax, and managed to get a grip on my emotions before they started to spiral.

"Do you know how much the bail will be?"

"Unfortunately, because of the severity of the crime you've been charged with, it will almost certainly be high. At least $100,000, and possibly as much as $600,000. But you won't have to pay that out of pocket. I'll put your husband in touch with a bail bondsman."

I desperately wanted to return to the world I had lived in a few short weeks ago, one where I had blithely assumed that I'd never see the inside of a prison, or need the services of a bail bondsman.

"Before we begin discussing your case," Grace continued, "know that anything you say to me is protected by attorney-client privilege. That means I will keep whatever you tell me confidential. However, you should also know that I'm bound by a series of ethical rules, so don't tell me if you're guilty. It could limit the type of defense I can put on for you."

"But I'm not guilty!" I protested, fear turning my voice high and tinny.

"All right," Grace said. Her smooth expression didn't change. I wondered if she believed me. Maybe all her clients claimed they were innocent. "Please tell me what happened in as much detail as you can."

I told Grace about Kat and Howard, and how I had come to know them, and what I knew about their marital problems and Howard's alcoholism. I also recounted in depth my initial interview with Detective Demer and Sergeant Oliver and how at first I believed they were building a case against Kat. But then they arrested me.

"They said they had a photograph from a traffic camera that showed me heading toward Jupiter Island the night Howard died," I told her. "And they told me they knew Kat had given me a large amount of money."

Grace had been busy jotting down notes on a lined yellow notepad with a Montblanc pen. Now she glanced up at me.

"How much money?"

I hesitated. "Twenty thousand dollars. But it was a loan. Kat lent it to me over a year ago because we fell behind on our children's school tuition. I didn't want to accept it, even as a loan, but if I hadn't, the children wouldn't have been allowed to stay at their school." I could feel myself flush with embarrassment. "The money had nothing to do with Howard or his death."

"Who would have known that she gave you that money?"

"Lent, not gave. I'm not sure. My husband knew, of course, and since Kat made the check payable directly to the school, the bookkeeper there would have known."

"What's the bookkeeper's name?"

"Patricia Davies. It was an unusually large check, even for the school, so it wouldn't surprise me if she remembered it."

"I'll have my investigator speak to her. If the police did interview her, it may be helpful to know what they asked her," Grace said, making a note. "And you said they had a traffic camera photo placing you near Jupiter Island on the night of Howard Grant's death?"

"Yes," I said. "But it was taken at an intersection several miles away from the Grants' house. When the police first interviewed me, they asked me for an alibi for the evening Howard died. I told them that Todd and I argued, and I left and went for a walk on the beach."

"Why did you argue?"

"Is it important?"

Grace shrugged. "It could be."

"My husband and I have had some financial difficulties over the past few years."

"What sort of difficulties? Anything illegal? Drugs, that sort of thing?"

"Oh, no. God, no. But I found out that day my husband had gotten a new credit card without telling me and had run up a balance." I sighed and pressed a finger to each temple. "Just garden-variety overspending. Living beyond our means. My husband, unfortunately, is a spendthrift. If he wants something, he buys it, even if it isn't logical to do so at the time. It's the cause of about ninety-five percent of our marital disagreements."

"Okay. So you fought. Then what happened?"

"I left. I didn't want our children, Liam and Bridget, to overhear us arguing. It upsets them, especially Bridget. She's—" I stopped and inhaled deeply again. I hoped the extra oxygen would wake up my brain, which after four hours in prison felt like it was already atrophying. "She's highly strung. So I drove around for a while, then decided I felt like going for a walk."

"But why Jupiter Island? Why did you decide to go there?"

"I didn't decide," I said. "That's just it. I was upset. I was driving aimlessly. I'm not sure why I headed toward the island. It was probably just mental muscle memory, since I've driven there so many times to see Kat. At the moment I decided I wanted to get out and walk, the Jupiter Island beach was the closest place to stop. There wasn't anything nefarious about it. It's just a horrible coincidence."

"Did anyone see you at the beach? Maybe in the parking lot?"

I shook my head. "I didn't see anyone. It was late by then, after ten. I stopped to wonder if it was stupid to walk in the dark by myself, but ironically enough, I decided it would be safe because it was Jupiter Island, where there's hardly any crime." I laughed without humor. "It would almost be funny if the whole thing hadn't turned into this nightmare."

Grace didn't smile back. She continued taking notes on her yellow notepad. "I'll have my investigator look into whether there were any cameras at the beach parking lot. That would verify your alibi."

"I can't believe the police honestly think I'd kill Howard," I said. "What would be my motive? I didn't even know him very well. Kat's the one I was friends with."

"My guess? They don't think you're guilty, but they're hoping that by arresting you, they'll put enough pressure on you that you'll agree to testify against your friend."

"But that's horrific," I exclaimed. "They're putting me through this just to coerce me?"

"The police don't always play fair," Grace said. She looked up at me, her pretty eyes keen and focused. "What else can you tell me?"

I told her the rest—about John Donnelly's proffered bribe, Thomas Wyeth's veiled threats. I even told her about my talk with Marcia Grable and her belief that Kat was a sociopath.

"Do you agree with her?" Grace asked.

I shrugged, suddenly feeling exhausted. "A few weeks ago, I would have said no way. But now, who knows?"

"The police arrested you at least in part because they found out Kat Grant had given you a large amount of money," Grace pointed out. "I'm sure she wasn't the one who told them that. It would make her look guilty. If you pay someone to kill for you, it's still considered first-degree murder."

I shook my head. "That money had nothing to do with any of this. I wish I had never accepted it."

"Is there anything else you can think of?"

"The witness who claims he saw Howard pushed off the balcony," I said. "He's the only reason the police think Howard was killed. If he's lying or mistaken, they don't have a case. I think he might be the key here."

Grace nodded and jotted down another note. "We'll find out who this supposed witness is and then check his bank records."

"You think someone paid him off?"

"Maybe. It's worth checking out."

"But who would do that? The Wyeths have the means to pay off anyone, but like you said, how does that benefit Kat? If they think I killed Howard because Kat paid me to, that would put Kat in legal jeopardy." I considered this. "Unless that's the point? What if someone set me up because they want to hurt Kat?"

"Who would do that?"

"I have no idea. Everyone loves Kat. Well, except for Marcia Grable. And Kat's sister-in-law."

Grace took off her glasses and pressed her fingers to her temples.

"Is that information overload?"

Grace smiled. "No, but the reality of my job—and that of any other defense attorney—is that we like simple narratives. They're easier to sell to juries. All these speculations and cross-hatches and conspiracy theories don't make for a clean defense."

"Sorry," I said.

"No, don't be. I asked you to tell me everything. It's just that there's more than I anticipated. But don't worry. I'll sift through it and find the right narrative for us going forward."

Her words, which made her sound like a political commentator spinning on a cable news show, had a chilling effect.

"I don't want a narrative," I said. "I want the truth to come out."

Grace looked almost amused. "I think you need to understand something. It's not my job to find out the truth about who killed Howard Grant. In fact, I don't care who, if anyone, killed him. It's up to the state's attorney to make a case that you're guilty of the crime, and it's my job to blow as many holes in their evidence and arguments as I can. Our only objective here is to get you an acquittal, and keep you out of prison. Do you understand?"

It was the most reassuring thing she could have said to me.

I nodded. "I'm sure you'll do a great job."

★ ★ ★

I was right. I didn't sleep that night. The pod was too loud, even when the doors weren't clanking open and shut. I could hear the other prisoners talking and coughing and crying. Kayla had a nightmare that caused her to thrash around her bunk and mumble incoherently. But even if it had been quiet, I couldn't have gotten comfortable on the thin foam acting as my mattress. However I positioned myself, rolling from one side to the other, my body would start to ache from the lack of support and cold metal below the mat. And the terrible smell seemed to have infiltrated everything—my hair, my polyester scrubs, my nostrils.

By the time the morning dawned, looking gray and bleak through the tinted windows of the pod, I was exhausted and my brain felt foggy. I had already learned that we ate all our meals in the pod. Breakfast consisted of a tray of lukewarm oatmeal, a bruised banana and a small plastic cup of something that purported to be orange juice. I ate with a subdued Kayla at one of the round tables. No one spoke to either of us. I couldn't swallow the oatmeal, which stuck in my throat, but I drank the juice and nibbled at the flavorless banana.

Grace had told me that my first appearance would take place that morning, but she had neglected to tell me that I wouldn't be transported to the courthouse, as I had assumed. Instead bail hearings took place at the jail via a video hookup similar to the Skype program that Liam and Bridget used to talk to their grandparents.

Liam and Bridget. I could almost keep it together as long as I didn't think of my children. It was bad enough that I had been taken away from them for one night. What if I was convicted and kept away from them for twenty years or more? The thought caused the bile in my stomach to churn as another wave of nausea swept over me. I swallowed, willing myself not to throw up, as I was led into the room where video court was held.

I was told to sit, along with eight detainees of both genders—including the tattooed man who'd waggled his tongue at me the day before—on a row of chairs set up behind a podium. In the front of the room was a television on a rolling cart with a camera mounted on top. We could see Judge Wilkinson, a heavyset man with dark hair and an extravagant mustache, enter the courtroom. He took his seat at the bench and began calling up the cases one at a time. Most of the charges were drug related, along with one assault and a DUI. All of them were represented by the public defender on duty.

When it was my turn to appear before the Skype judge, I was escorted to the podium, where I was joined by Grace. She looked sharp and well rested and was dressed in a sharply tailored navy skirt suit. I felt shabby standing next to her in my unshowered state, wearing the same prison scrubs I'd slept in.

"Case number 16-00756, State versus Alice Campbell, one count…capital murder," the judge said. He perked up a bit at the severity of the charge and looked at me. "Are you Alice Campbell?"

"Yes."

"And is this your attorney?" Judge Wilkinson asked.

"Yes. Grace Williams for the defendant, your honor."

"Ms. Campbell, do you understand the charges that have been brought against you?"

I glanced at Grace. She nodded.

"Yes," I said.

"And are you planning to proceed with Ms. Williams as your attorney, or do you need one appointed to you by the court?"

"I've hired Ms. Williams to represent me," I said. "I don't need a court-appointed lawyer."

"What is the state's position on bail?" Judge Wilkinson asked.

The state's attorney on duty, a serious young man wearing

an ill-fitting suit and a tie that looked like it had been bor-rowed from his father, stepped forward. This was probably his first job out of law school.

"Your honor, due to the seriousness of the charges and the threat to the community that the defendant poses, the state believes that Alice Campbell should be held without bail."

"What?" Grace exclaimed.

The judge turned his head in her direction. "Ms. Williams, what do you have to say?"

"First of all, the charges against Mrs. Campbell are lu-dicrous," Grace stated in a strong, clear voice. "The state didn't even have enough evidence against Alice Campbell to be granted an arrest warrant, so they instead arrested her on trumped-up probable cause. The reality is that they don't have a case. There is not one single scrap of physical evidence tying Alice Campbell to the death of Howard Grant. It's our position that the police arrested Mrs. Campbell in what is a frankly despicable attempt to frighten her into cooperating with the police investigation."

The state's attorney looked shaken by the force of Grace's argument.

"Your honor, the state believes very strongly in the, um, strength of our case," he said, his voice high and unsure.

"What case?" Grace shot back. "Name one shred of evi-dence you have that proves my client committed this crime."

"Simmer down," Judge Wilkinson said. "Counselor, as you know, we don't deal with probable cause issues at a first ap-pearance. You'll need to take that up with the felony judge. File your motion and have it set there. We're dealing strictly with the issue of bail. I take it you are arguing that your cli-ent qualifies?"

"Yes, your honor," Grace said. "Alice Campbell is a model citizen. She's a married mother of two, has a PhD in mathe-matics and is a notable writer. Most important, she does not have a single prior arrest or conviction. She owns a home, and all of her ties are to this community. She is deeply motivated to prove her innocence in this case."

"Your honor," the state's attorney started to say, but the judge raised a hand.

"Save it," he said. "I'm setting bail at $500,000, cash or bond. Surrender your passport. Next."

Grace smiled, pleased at her victory. I was reeling at the astronomical number. I was pretty sure our house wasn't worth $500,000, even without the mortgage on it.

"That went well," Grace whispered as we turned away.

"Did it? That's a lot of money!"

"Everything's all set. Your bond has already been arranged—"

"It has?" I was confused. Grace had already explained the way bonds worked, and that Todd would not have to come up with the entire $500,000. Still, he would have to make a substantial deposit to a bail bondsman. Where would he have found the money to do that? Our finances had certainly improved, but we weren't flush.

"It will take a few hours for them to process you out of here. We'll speak tomorrow," Grace said, and then she turned and strode off before I could ask her any more questions.

I was told to sit back down while the remaining detainees had their video appearances. Once we had all been processed, the officers took us back to our pods.

It was excruciating being stuck in my pod without any word on what was going on or how much longer it would be until I was allowed to leave. There was nothing to do other than listen to the never-ending blare of bad daytime television intermingled with the endless complaints of my fellow pod mates. They carped on and on about how bad the food was or how uncaring their families were or how incompetent their attorneys were, and they did so loudly and enthusiastically. I longed for a comfortable bed and a few hours of quiet away from this noise so I could rest and clear my thoughts.

Then finally, just when I didn't think I could stand the interminable boredom for one more minute, a guard showed up.

"Alice Campbell, come on down," the guard said in a bored voice.

She escorted me to the same room where I'd been processed upon arrival. She cut my wristband off and gave me back the clothes I'd arrived in. I changed and was then escorted down a hallway, through several sets of the sliding metallic doors clanging open and then shut behind me. Finally I was decanted into the lobby, a depressing space filled with rows of industrial chairs welded together at the base, and walls decorated with posters advocating the benefits of drug rehabilitation.

And then I saw him. Todd was standing there, looking so familiar and safe. Unexpected tears stung my eyes. Todd held his arms open as I rushed to him. He pulled me close so that my cheek was pressed against his shoulder. I hugged him back fiercely. I couldn't remember the last time we had clung to one another like this.

The day Meghan died, probably.

"I've never been so glad to see anyone in my life," I said, my voice muffled against his chest.

"I didn't want to bring Liam and Bridget," he said. "I hope that was the right decision."

"Thank God you didn't. I wouldn't want them to see me in here, to see me like this." I thought again about what would happen if I were convicted, if I had to spend the rest of my life in prison, and I sagged in my husband's arms. If he hadn't been there, holding me up, I might have collapsed under the weight of my fatigue and strain and fear.

"Thank you for getting me out," I said, looking up at him. He had tears in his eyes, too. "How did you afford the bond?"

Todd hesitated and drew back. "There's something I have to talk to you about," he said, keeping his voice low. His face looked tense and worried. "I'm pretty sure you're not going to like it."

"It can't be worse than being arrested for murder and spending a night in jail," I said weakly.

Todd smiled, but it didn't erase the concern shining in his eyes. "Probably not quite that bad."

Todd stepped to one side, putting a supportive hand on my lower back. I saw then that he hadn't come alone to the police station, after all.

"Hello, Alice," my mother said.

25

I HADN'T SEEN my mother in over three years. Meeting her in the waiting area at the Martin County Jail was surreal, especially after everything I'd been through over the past twenty-four hours.

"Ebbie?" I said blankly.

My mother—Elizabeth Sheehy, née Conners, known to one and all as Ebbie—smiled, her eyebrows arcing. "What kind of a greeting is that? Come give me a hug."

She held out her arms. She was wearing the flowing clothing she'd always favored. A long tunic over an even longer skirt, both in a purple-and-gray bohemian print. I moved woodenly toward her and allowed her to put her arms around me. She leaned back to eye me.

"You look terrible," she concluded.

"Thanks."

"Don't be like that. You know what I mean."

"I've been in jail, Ebbie," I said. "Not a spa."

My mother looked great, but then, she always did. Ebbie had been a beauty when she was young, with her luminous, faintly freckled skin and long, thick red hair. Even now that she was well into her sixties, and her hair was streaked with gray, she was still a striking woman. Annoyingly, she had always discounted her genetic good fortune and insisted that her appearance was the result of whatever her fad du jour was practicing—like Buddhism or guided meditation or chakra alignment.

"What are you doing here?" I asked.

"I heard you'd been arrested, so I flew down late last night."

"Ebbie put up the money for your bond," Todd told me quietly.

I glanced at my mother. "You did?"

"Why do you sound so surprised? You're my only daughter. And besides, I have a very generous heart. People are always telling me that."

I wasn't shocked that she would want to help. My mother, for all her faults, had never been miserly. I'd just never known her to have much money. Perhaps a hand-thrown pottery studio was more lucrative than I'd thought.

"I don't know what to say," I said. "Thank you."

My mother squeezed my arm. "Don't mention it. And I don't want you to worry about a thing. I plan on staying with you throughout this entire ordeal. Now, let's get you home. You look like you could use a shower."

She hooked her arm through mine and pulled me toward the glass front doors. I was so tired, I let myself be swept along, even as her words started to sink in. I looked back at Todd, trying to communicate silently, *What was that she just said about staying with us throughout?* I saw my dismay mirrored in his expression.

I'm so sorry, he mouthed.

I fell asleep in the car on the forty-five-minute trip home. I awoke just as Todd turned onto our street. There were three news vans parked in front of our house.

"What are they doing here?" I asked.

The reporters and their cameramen had been milling

around, chatting with one another or tapping on their phones. But as soon as they saw our car approach, they quickly mobilized. The reporters swarmed toward Todd's Honda Accord, yelling out questions, while the cameramen hoisted bulky cameras to their shoulders and began to shoot footage of my homecoming. Todd ignored them and pressed the button to open the garage door. While we waited for it to rise, I could hear them calling out.

"Why did you kill Howard Grant?"

"Did Katherine Grant pay you to kill him?"

"Are you and Katherine Grant lovers?"

I looked up at this last one, shocked by the suggestion.

"Ignore them," Todd said, pulling into the garage and closing the automatic door.

"Did you hear what that reporter just asked me?" I demanded. "What the hell is going on?"

Todd looked grim. "Your arrest has been a big story."

"It's how I found out," Ebbie piped up from the back seat. "I saw it on the internet when I logged on to my email. Children's Writer Arrested for Murder. I almost fell out of my seat when I saw your picture! Who is this Kat person, anyway?" She lowered her voice to a breathless hush. "*Were* you lovers?"

"Ebbie! God!" I exclaimed. The worst part was, my mother probably would have been thrilled if I'd had a lesbian affair. It had always annoyed her that I'd opted for a staid life in the suburbs.

"Don't be so judgmental," Ebbie chided.

I drew in a deep breath, held it for a few beats and exhaled. "What have Liam and Bridget heard?" I asked Todd as I climbed out of the car. I could still hear the reporters outside, yelling questions. Their presence was unnerving.

"They know that something's up, obviously. But I kept them home from school today and turned off their broadband access." He got out and walked around the car to take my hand in his. "We'll have to tell them something, but I wanted to wait until you were home."

"Thank you. I appreciate that." I squeezed his hand.

"You have to tell them the truth," my mother said, slamming her door shut behind her. "It's important to be honest with children about everything."

Ebbie once told me, in far too much detail, about the first time she'd had sex with a man after divorcing my father. I was ten at the time. Needless to say, I had not appreciated her honesty.

Todd knew my family history all too well, and he looked at me worriedly. But I was too tired and too relieved to be out of jail to rise to her bait.

"Let's go inside," I said wearily.

Liam and Bridget were in the living room, curled up on opposite ends of the couch, watching one of the Harry Potter movies. They jumped up when they saw me, and I hugged them tightly, tears stinging my eyes.

"I missed you so much," I said, wrapping an arm around each of them.

"Where were you?" Bridget asked.

"Yeah, why didn't you come home last night?" Liam chimed in.

"I'll tell you about it later," I said. "I need to shower and change and to lie down for a little while. What are you watching?"

"*Harry Potter and the Deathly Hallows: Part 1*," Liam said. "We decided to have a Harry Potter marathon today, since we didn't go to school. We're going to watch *Part 2* next."

"TV rots the brain," Ebbie said, hands on her hips. "The children should be outside, breathing in the fresh air, feeling the sun on their faces. That's the problem with modern parenting. You all have your children hooked up to tablets or cell phones. No one experiences nature anymore. Let them live and explore and embrace life! Let them go fish, go to the beach and ride their bikes around having adventures until it's too dark to see!"

I stared at my mother in disbelief. Had she already forgotten the news vans parked in front of our house? Forgotten that I'd spent the past twenty-four hours in jail?

"A Harry Potter marathon sounds perfect," I said, turning back to my children. "I'll make some popcorn for you later."

My children's cheers drowned out their grandmother's tut-tuts, which I considered a victory of sorts.

"You've never listened to me," my mother said testily.

I was too tired to argue. "I'm going to go wash up" was all I could manage.

In the bathroom, I peeled off my clothing, which now smelled like the jail, and threw the garments in the small trash can next to the sink. I turned the shower on as hot as I could tolerate and stood under the water until it started to run cold, only then soaping myself up and scrubbing the grime off my body. When I was done, I pulled on my soft white terry cloth robe and padded into our bedroom. Todd was there, lying on the bed, reading his emails on his phone. He looked up and smiled when he saw me.

"Hi," I said, lying down next to him. Despite my short nap in the car, I was still exhausted. It reminded me of the scratchy-eyed, never-ending fatigue I'd experienced when my children were newborns. I knew I was going to have to sleep soon just to clear the fog from my mind. "How are the kids, really? Have they been upset?"

"Bridget had a hard time sleeping last night," Todd admitted.

I wasn't surprised. Bridget's anxiety was always worse at night, when she was tired and her resistance low. I hated to think of her lying in bed worrying about where I was.

"What did you tell her?"

"Just that you had a late work meeting."

"And she bought that?"

"I'm not sure. But I made her some cocoa and read with her. Eventually she got back to sleep."

My world tipped and slid as I imagined a future in which I was convicted of murder, spending the rest of my days in prison. And not, as I gleaned from the previous night, in a place as cozy as the Martin County Jail. The state prisons were, according to the other prisoners, much less pleasant. And while I was there, living with murderers and addicts and gangbangers, my children would grow up without me. Todd was a good father. But could he do the work of two parents? Would he make their lunches every day and change their sheets regularly? Purchase Halloween costumes and fill Christmas stockings? Could he be me?

No. I was pretty sure he couldn't. Which meant that I couldn't go back to jail. Not ever, not even for one night.

"How are you feeling?" Todd asked.

"I'm pissed off."

He laughed. "That wasn't what I expected you to say."

"Actually, I think, in a way, this has been a good thing. It's better to be angry and ready to fight than to bow down to this bullshit." I shook my head in disgust.

"Fight?" Todd asked. "Fight who?"

"Anyone who wants to keep me away from my family." I was more specific in my thoughts. *Thomas Wyeth. John Donnelly. Kat.*

"What was it like in jail?" Todd asked, turning to face me. "Was it scary?"

"At first." I drew in a deep breath, remembering it all—the body cavity search, the time I spent in the pod, the hopeless despair that weighed down the prisoners. "And then it was mind-numbingly boring. And noisy. It's never quiet. And it's never dark."

"Isn't that a good thing? I would think bad things could happen in the dark," Todd said.

"I'm not sure. I was in a pod with other pretrial detainees. It's in everyone's best interest at that point not to cause trouble. Physically, I was mildly uncomfortable. Mentally, it was a struggle."

"I'm glad you're home and safe." Todd reached for my hand, folding it in his.

"I'm fine. Or I will be once I get some sleep." I yawned. "I like Grace. She seems very competent. She's convinced that the arrest was the police's attempt to bully me into cooperating with their investigation."

"Yes, I spoke to her this morning. She seemed very confident that they'll drop the charges eventually. Anyway, she came highly recommended. And she was expensive, if that's any indicator," Todd said.

"Did you have to pay her a retainer?"

Todd nodded. "I did, but I don't want you to worry about that."

"Telling me not to worry is like telling me not to breathe."

Todd smiled and held open his arms. I curled into him, resting my head on his shoulder and feeling the rise and fall of his chest. I couldn't remember the last time we had lain like this. It was nice. Surprisingly, my night in jail was proving more effective than all our marital therapy sessions put together.

"I wasn't sure what to do about Ebbie," Todd murmured. "She just appeared out of the blue last night and offered to write a check. We needed the help. But then she announced she was moving in, and I didn't know what to do."

"That's Ebbie. She comes at a price." I shook my head. "I sound ungrateful. Coming here and offering this money is actually the nicest thing she's ever done for me. In the past, she would have just sent me an email saying she was meditating on my finding peace and happiness."

"Maybe people really do change," Todd said.

"I'm too tired to be that optimistic."

I took a long nap that afternoon and emerged from bed just in time to stop Ebbie from making a vegan mushroom-and-lentil shepherd's pie for dinner.

"Liam and Bridget will never eat that," I said.

"Don't be silly. They'll love it," Ebbie insisted. "Children need to be exposed to new flavors."

"Mushrooms make me gag," Liam announced. He'd found a Frisbee somewhere and was twirling it on one finger. "Like, if I even see one anywhere near my food, I would probably hurl all over the table and on everyone's plates and everywhere within ten feet."

"Thank you, Liam, for that incredibly vivid image," I said. "We'll order pizza."

"But I have everything I need to make the casserole," Ebbie complained.

"That's very nice of you, but Todd's allergic to mushrooms," I lied.

"He is?" This was Liam.

In my exhaustion, I had forgotten that children are natural truth detectors.

"Yes," I said firmly. "He is."

"Cool. Maybe I am, too." Liam flung the Frisbee up so that it bounced off the ceiling.

"Liam, knock it off," I said.

"Take it outside," Ebbie suggested.

"No!" My voice shook. "Not outside. You can go play the Xbox if you want."

Liam hurried off, not waiting to see if Ebbie could talk me out of letting him have the additional video game time.

"They've been inside staring at the television all day," Ebbie protested.

I turned to her. "The reporters are still out there."

"So? They're not going to bother the children."

"Don't be so naive," I said. "And besides, I used to watch television for hours when I was his age."

"No, you didn't."

"Yes, I did. You were always off with your friends, doing whatever it was you did, and you left me home alone all the time," I said. "What did you think I was going to do?"

"That's very disappointing to hear." Ebbie made a moue of disapproval. "I would have hoped you'd use that time to improve yourself. To read poetry or learn to play a musical instrument or write in your journal."

"Seriously? Mom, I was a teenager," I exclaimed. "You're lucky I wasn't smoking pot and getting pregnant."

"Am I?" Ebbie tipped her head to one side. "I'm not so sure about that. You might have benefited from some non-traditional life experiences."

"So, pizza for dinner?" Todd asked, walking into the kitchen, before I could respond. Which, under the circumstances, was probably a good thing.

"Yes. Will you call it in?" I turned to him, happy for any excuse not to continue this conversation with Ebbie. "Get a veggie one for my mom, and then whatever the kids want. They usually want a supreme."

"The children can eat vegetarian pizza," my mother interjected. "All that meat isn't good for them."

I closed my eyes for a moment and took a few deep breaths. *Don't react*, I told myself. *Stay calm.*

"Just get a veggie and a supreme," I said.

Todd went out for the pizzas. His departure caused a brief stir among the press still staked out in front of the house, but they quieted down quickly. I wondered how long they'd stay there. It struck me then that the press monitoring the comings and goings of my family was the least surreal thing to have happened over the past few days. My life had become unrecognizable.

Todd returned with the pizzas twenty minutes later and set the steaming cardboard boxes on the counter. I put out plates and napkins, and everyone helped themselves. Once we were seated at the table, I knew that it was time to tell the kids what was going on, or at least a version of it. I would have liked to do so without Ebbie present, but I didn't see a way around it.

"I know you're probably wondering why you stayed home from school today," I began once I'd chewed and swallowed a bite of veggie pizza. I would have preferred the supreme myself, but the children certainly weren't going to touch the veggie, and I'd already saddled Todd with a fake mushroom allergy.

"It was awesome!" Liam exclaimed. "Can I stay home tomorrow, too?"

"I don't know." I looked at Todd. "They have to go back at some point, right?"

"Just one more day? I have a science test tomorrow I'd like to skip," Liam said.

"You're not staying home just to miss a test," Todd told him.

"Then why did we stay home today?" Bridget asked.

"That's what I want to talk to you about," I began again.

"Your mother had some issues she needed to work out," Ebbie interrupted.

"Thank you, Ebbie, but I can handle this."

"If Gram is your mother, why do you call her Ebbie?" Bridget asked.

Ebbie smiled fondly at her granddaughter. "You can call me Ebbie, too. I've never been comfortable with the labels or relationships our patriarchal society imposes on us."

Bridget looked at me, confused by her grandmother's rhetoric. I drew in a deep breath, pushing down my irritation that in the middle of everything I was going through, my mother's presence was forcing me to deal with her tiresome, never-ending political posturing.

"Gram doesn't like being called *Mom*," I said. "She believes it devalues women by emphasizing childrearing as their most important contribution to society."

"So should I call you Alice from now on?" Liam asked.

"No," I said. "You will continue to call me Mom."

"Yes, your mother has always been very clear that she has no wish to follow in my footsteps," Ebbie said, dabbing at her mouth with a paper napkin. "She's always disparaged my beliefs."

I put down my pizza. "That's not true. We're just very different people."

"Exactly. I'm open to the world and all its experiences," Ebbie said.

"Which makes me what, exactly?"

Ebbie sighed. "I love you dearly, Alice. But you've always kept your feelings closed off."

"That's not true," I said, bristling. "The fact that I don't feel the need to talk about my feelings all the time doesn't mean I don't have them."

"Why don't we get back on topic?" Todd suggested mildly.

I glanced at the kids. Liam had folded his slice of supreme pizza to make it that much easier to wolf down. Bridget, as always, had removed all of the toppings from her pizza and was eating it backward, crust to point.

"Where were you last night?" Liam asked.

I nodded and pushed my plate to one side. My appetite had disappeared.

"I'll tell you. But first, I don't want you to worry," I said, looking at Bridget. I could instantly tell that this was the wrong way to begin. Telling my daughter not to worry just caused her to worry preemptively about whatever was coming. "Everything is going to be fine. But the truth is…I was arrested yesterday. I spent the night in jail."

My children stared at me with such identical wide-eyed shock that I almost smiled. I didn't often think the two of them looked alike, but every once in a while, there would be a moment when, with an expression or gesture, they seemed so similar.

"Cool," Liam said.

"It certainly was not cool," I said.

"You were in *jail*?" Bridget asked, her voice rising on the last word. She burst into tears.

After that, it took a few minutes to calm her down. She eventually crawled into her grandmother's lap, even though she was far too big to do so comfortably. Ebbie didn't seem to mind. She rocked Bridget as though she were a baby, stroking her hair and patting her back. Liam used the interlude to eat another piece of pizza, then fetch a third from the cardboard box on the counter.

"Don't eat too much," I cautioned him. "You'll get a stomachache."

"No, I won't. I could eat that whole pizza all on my own," Liam bragged. "Why were you arrested? Were you drinking and driving?"

"Of course not. Why would you ask that?"

"Because Mason's dad did and he got arrested. I don't think he had to spend a night in jail, though. I'll ask Mason about it."

"Please don't." I drew in a deep breath. "I wish I didn't have to tell you this, but the police arrested me for murder."

This bald statement silenced everyone, even Bridget's weeping.

"You *killed* someone?" Liam asked.

"Of course she didn't," Todd said loudly.

"I don't think the police even believe I had anything to do with it," I said, hoping I was striking the right tone to reassure them. "My lawyer doesn't think they do. She thinks they are just trying to pressure me so that I'll cooperate with their investigation."

"But why would they do that?" Liam asked.

I looked at Todd. Despite my nap, I was still tired, and my brain felt like it was stuffed full of cotton. Why hadn't we made a plan for what to tell the children? This wasn't a conversation to wing.

Todd nodded at me and said, "The truth is, and this is very unfortunate, the police sometimes use their position of authority to bully and intimidate."

"That's what they're doing to Mom?" Bridget asked from her perch on Ebbie's lap.

"You're crushing your grandmother," I told her.

Ebbie smiled and cuddled Bridget closer. "No, she's not."

"Who do they think you killed?" Liam asked.

Todd and I exchanged a look. I shrugged. It wasn't like Liam couldn't find out in five minutes on the internet.

"Kat's husband. Howard Grant."

"No way," Liam said to me, his mouth dropping open like a cartoon character's.

"Well, it will all be cleared up shortly," I said. "But we didn't want you to go back to school without knowing what was going on."

"Do I have to go back to school?" Liam asked.

"Yes," I said at the same time Ebbie said, "Of course not."

I looked at my mother. "What did you say?"

Ebbie rolled her eyes dramatically. "It's not like the sixth grade is so important that he can't miss a few weeks."

"Seventh grade," Liam said.

"Whatever," Ebbie said.

"Bridget, Liam, if you're done eating, please clear the plates, then go to your rooms," I said.

"I'm not done eating," Liam said.

"Yes, you are," Todd said.

"I don't want to go," Bridget moaned and snuggled into Ebbie's arms.

"Bridget, do as your mother told you," Todd said sharply.

Bridget gave him a hurt look but slithered out of Ebbie's arms and stalked out of the room. Liam followed her, swiping a piece of pizza as he went. I was too weary to call him back.

"Ebbie..." I turned to my mother. "I appreciate your help, but please do not undermine me in front of my children."

She looked surprised. "What are you talking about?"

"Don't you understand that this situation is already difficult enough without you saying things like school isn't important?" It was hard to keep my growing frustration out of my voice. "Of course it's important. Not just the learning part, although that's the biggest reason. But even more important is the stability and sense of routine it gives them."

"And what about when their classmates ask them if their mother is a murderer?" Ebbie asked.

"Ebbie, please," Todd said.

"You know it will happen. What then?" she persisted.

"They'll have to deal with it if and when it does," Todd said. "We'll talk to them. Coach them on the best response."

Ebbie looked at me. It was a coldly appraising look, as though she were seeing something there that she hadn't before. "Did you have anything to do with it?"

"With what?"

"This man's death."

Todd inhaled sharply as though someone had punched him in the stomach.

I stared back at my mother while an icy fear seeped through

me. Ebbie and I had never been close, but she was still my mother. If she didn't believe I was innocent, who would?

"Ebbie, that's out of line," Todd said, suddenly furious. His hands were clenched into such tight fists, the veins in his arms were standing out.

Ebbie didn't seem to hear him. She continued to gaze at me with that peculiar expression. And for my part, I found I couldn't look away. I felt like she was slicing me open, revealing what I'd rather have kept hidden.

"You were always an odd child," Ebbie said. Her voice was so eerie, the hairs on my arms and the back of my neck stood on end. "You had a different sense of right and wrong. You were never bad, but you could be…*cold-blooded* is the only word for it. Like the time you found that baby rabbit the cat had gotten at and played with but hadn't killed. Do you remember? It was clearly going to die from its injuries. You said we had to put it out of its misery. I couldn't bear to do it. So you went and got the shovel and…just took care of it. Like it was nothing."

The memory swam back. I did remember killing the rabbit, but it hadn't been nothing. I couldn't stand seeing it suffer, and Ebbie hadn't been any help. After I'd euthanized it, I'd gone straight to the bathroom and thrown up until my stomach was empty. Even now the thought of it made me feel sick.

"Jesus Christ," Todd exploded. He stood up, pushing his chair back so angrily that it almost toppled over. "That's *enough*, Ebbie. Alice has been through *enough*. Look at her. She's as white as a sheet! If you can't be here without upsetting her, then you need to go."

Ebbie shook her head slightly as though waking herself up, and then she gazed at my husband as though just hearing his words. "What? Oh, no. That won't be necessary. I'm here to help out, not to cause any distress."

I stood, my legs shaky. "I'm going back to bed," I said. "I'm still very tired."

Todd moved around the table to put an arm around me. "Are you okay?" he asked, his voice softening.

"I'll be fine."

"Call if you need anything," he said.

I nodded and walked stiffly out of the kitchen.

"Good night, Alice," Ebbie called after me.

I didn't answer. I was still trying to process the chilling fact that when my mother looked at me, she saw a potential murderer. I heard Todd mutter something in a low tone to her. Ebbie responded with a predictable shrill indignation, but I couldn't make out what they were saying. That was probably for the best, I decided.

I retreated to the sanctuary of my bedroom, where I lay down on our soft king-size bed and stared up at the still overhead fan. My brain was fatigued, but it fought at the numbness, too anxious to shut down. I reached for my phone on my bedside table, where I'd plugged it into its charger. It, too, had spent the night in jail.

I was surprised that my phone hadn't blown up. I had twenty-three text messages. Most of them were nice. Or nice-ish. A sample:

Omg. R u ok? Lmk if u need me 2 cover school pickup.

Hope everything ok. Call if u need anything.

Just kill yourself now and save the taxpayers the cost of a trial, you evil freak of nature.

The supportive ones were from friends and parents of my kids' friends, and many of them made awkward yet touching offers to help. The threatening and insulting ones were from unknown numbers. I wanted to delete them but thought I should probably show them to Grace first.

I also had a number of voice mails. These were mostly from the press, asking for an interview or giving me a chance to comment on a story or asking for my reaction to a story they had run without first asking for my comment. I listened to each one before deleting it.

And then, from a number I didn't recognize:

"Hi, Alice, it's Kat." Pause. "I hope you're okay. Please be okay. Anyway…we need to talk, but somewhere where no one will see us. I'll meet you at the Jupiter Lighthouse tomorrow at 9:00 p.m. It's closed then, but I used to sneak up there when I was a teenager, so I know how to get in. No one else will be there. We'll be able to speak in private. I know that sounds paranoid, but with everything that's going on, I *am* paranoid. I borrowed this phone, so don't call me back on this number. If you can't make it, I guess I'll try to get in touch with you some other way." Another pause. "I miss you. I'm so sorry about…everything."

The message ended there.

26

Three Months Earlier

I WAS SAUTÉING chicken on the stove while simultaneously helping Liam with his literature homework. He was holding a worn hardcover school copy of *Where the Red Fern Grows* and looking peevish.

"I'm supposed to compare a time in my life to when Billy in the book buys his two coonhounds," Liam said.

"And you can't think of anything?" I asked, adding sliced onions and green peppers to the pan.

"No, nothing. I've never even had a dog," Liam said grumpily.

"I don't think you have to be quite that literal. Just try to think of a time when you got something you'd been hoping for."

"Or we could just go get a dog. Then I would know exactly how Billy felt," Liam suggested.

The dreaded dog conversation. Liam had been begging for one for years. Just recently he'd enlisted Bridget in the cause, so now I was hearing it from both of them.

My phone rang. I glanced at it and saw it was Kat.

"Hey," I said to her. "You just saved me from having to

come up with yet another excuse for why we're not getting a dog."

"I heard that," Liam said.

"You were meant to," I called back.

There was a ragged intake of breath on the other end. And then what sounded like a sob being suppressed.

"Kat? What's wrong?" I asked. There was no response. "Are you there? Hello?"

I heard her breathing again, sounding hard and labored. "Something's h-happened. Can you come over?" Her voice broke on the word *happened*.

I looked at the stove, where my family's dinner was half-cooked, then at Liam, who was paging through his book. "Right now? This isn't the best time."

"Please," Kat said, her voice high and thin. I had never heard her like this. "I need you."

I glanced at the clock. It was already after six. Todd should be home soon, and he could take over on the domestic front.

"Okay. Give me half an hour, and I'll be over."

Kat exhaled a long, shaky breath. "Thank God."

"Can you at least tell me what's going on?"

There was another silence. It went on for so long, I thought Kat had hung up. But then, finally, she said, "It's Howard. He just... *Oh*." She sobbed again. "I'll tell you when you get here."

Kat had refused to say any more over the phone, except to assure me that she wasn't in any immediate danger and that, no, she absolutely did not want me to call the police. I waited anxiously for Todd to get home, but I put the time to use finishing the chicken and putting out all of the taco toppings while distractedly answering Liam's homework questions.

"You're not even trying," I finally snapped at him. "You just want me to give you all the answers."

"I am too trying! This is really hard," Liam complained.

"Hello, everyone. What's going on?" Todd walked in.

"The daily homework battle," I said. "Did you have three hours of homework when you were in seventh grade? I didn't."

"I can't remember that far back." Todd gave me a kiss on the cheek, which was what passed for physical intimacy in our marriage these days.

Todd set his leather architect bag on the table, like he always did when he came home from work. I responded as I always did.

"Please don't leave that there. Dinner's almost ready. Liam, set the table, please." Then, turning to Todd, I said, "I have to go out for a bit tonight."

"Where to?"

"Kat called. She was upset about something and wants to talk."

Todd's expression soured. "Of course. Kat crooks her little finger and you go running over to her."

Anger flared in my chest, hot and tight. "Being a good friend is not a character flaw."

"It is when you put your friend ahead of your family," Todd fired back.

"I've cooked dinner. I've helped Liam with his homework. I've driven Bridget back and forth to soccer practice. What else do you want from me?" I asked. "Am I supposed to scrub and scour the floor while singing along with my little talking mouse friends?"

"Are you going to eat dinner with us?" Todd's voice spiked with anger.

"No, I'll eat later."

Todd flung his hands up as though this made his point. "Perfect."

"What the hell is your problem?" I threw the spatula I'd

been holding into the sink with more force than necessary, then turned toward Todd, hands on my hips.

"Me? You're the one racing out of here, leaving your children behind."

This just served to enrage me more. But before I could respond with a barbed comment of my own, Liam interrupted.

"Stop fighting!" he yelled, standing up, his hands balled into fists at his sides.

Liam never raised his voice. He had always been the happiest, most easygoing of children. When he was a baby, he grinned and gurgled and held out grasping starfish hands to everyone who came near. He had carried this natural bonhomie throughout his childhood and into the teenage years. And now my breezy, easy boy was standing before us, rigid with unhappiness, tears gleaming in his eyes.

"Honey," I said, turning to him.

"Liam, it's okay," Todd said at the same time.

"It's *not* okay," Liam bellowed. "It hasn't been okay for a long time! You're always mad at each other and I'm sick of it!"

He stalked out of the room, leaving Todd and me behind to stare at each other.

"I'll go talk to him," I said.

"No, I'll do it," Todd said. "You go ahead. And I don't—" he held up a placating hand "—mean that in an ugly way."

I nodded but hesitated. We weren't through here. "You know, you play tennis in the evenings twice a week, and I don't hassle you about that."

Todd dipped his head and rubbed the back of his neck. "I know. And it's not about the time away. It's about..." he began but stopped.

"Kat," I said.

"Kat," he agreed.

"Is this because of the money she lent us?" I asked. "I talked to Lydia Rafferty at Kidtastic yesterday. She said the series is selling well. I think we'll be able to start paying her back soon. Once we're caught up."

"No. Maybe. I don't know." Todd shook his head and looked weary. "I appreciate what she did. Don't look at me like that. I really do."

"Then what is it?"

"You've been different ever since you met Kat. Ever since the two of you became friends." Todd looked at me, holding my gaze. "You do see that, don't you?"

But I wouldn't have agreed with anything he said at that moment, let alone something so damning.

"No. I don't see that at all." I picked up my bag nestled on one of the kitchen chairs. "The dinner stuff is all out. You and the kids can serve yourselves."

And then I turned and left.

The sun was sinking in the sky as I pulled into Kat's driveway, my tires crunching against the gravel. Her house looked imposing and silent as I made my way up the walk, but the light by the front door was on. I rang the doorbell. Nothing happened, so I rang again, this time holding the doorbell down longer. Still nothing.

I peered inside the window beside the front door, cupping my hands around my eyes. The house looked still and empty, and there weren't any interior lights on that I could see. I tried to fight back a feeling of unease.

I walked around the house, letting myself through a side gate and glancing around to see if anyone was watching me. The last thing I wanted was for the police to show up and arrest me for loitering. But I needn't have worried. As I turned around the back corner and headed toward the patio, I saw Kat sitting on one of her cushioned wicker chairs, glass of wine in hand, feet tucked underneath her. She looked wan tonight, dressed in all black—a mock turtleneck workout shirt over yoga pants—and somehow smaller than usual.

She turned, then started as I approached.

"Oh!" she said, lifting a hand to her heart. "You scared me."

"I rang the doorbell a few times," I said, sitting down in the chair opposite her. "What are you doing out here?"

Kat shrugged listlessly. "I felt like I was suffocating inside, so I came out here to get some fresh air."

"Good thing I looked back here," I said. "I didn't think anyone was home."

"Sorry, I should have realized I wouldn't hear the doorbell. Do you want some wine?" Kat asked. She picked up a bottle and waved it at me.

I nodded. Kat stood and went to the poolside bar to get an extra glass. She filled it and handed it to me.

"What's going on?" I asked.

Kat inhaled deeply, then sighed. "I shouldn't have bothered you. It's not like you can do anything to help."

"You never know. Maybe we can figure it out together."

Kat's face suddenly crumpled. She covered her face with her hands. Her shoulders shook silently.

"Kat? Are you okay?" I sprang out of my seat to crouch next to her, my hand on her shoulder.

"I'm sorry I dragged you over here. I shouldn't have," Kat said, her voice shaky and muffled by her hands.

"Don't apologize," I said. "Just tell me what happened."

Kat finally lowered her hands and looked at me with watery red eyes. And then, without speaking, she pulled at the collar of her mock turtleneck, hooking it with one finger and pulling it down to reveal the skin over her lower neck and sternum, mottled with a ring of dark bruises.

I gasped, dropping my wineglass. It shattered, the pale pink wine pooling on the patio.

"Did Howard do this to you?" Without waiting for a response, I stood, grabbing her hand and gently pulling her up, too. "Come on. We have to get you to the hospital."

"No," Kat said harshly, wrenching her hand away from me. "I'm *not* going to the hospital."

"You have to. You need to get checked out. Make sure there isn't any serious damage."

Kat laughed without humor. "It's a bit late for that." She waved me down. "No, I'm fine. I will be fine. My throat just hurts a little."

"Where's Howard?" I asked, the anger burning hot and white inside me. If he thought he could get away with this, he was very, very wrong.

Kat shrugged. "I have no idea. We fought. This happened—" she gestured at her neck "—and then he left. Probably off to see his girlfriend."

I stared at Kat, at a loss for what I should do or say. Logic would say that she should get the hell away from here, away from this house, away from Howard, and, once she was safe, call the police. Lounging outside by the pool, wineglass in hand, made no sense at all.

"Come on, Kat. We have to go before he comes back," I insisted.

"Go where?"

"Anywhere. Come stay at my house tonight," I said, even though I knew she'd never agree to that. Kat didn't enjoy spending time at my house, with its confined spaces and resident raucous children. "Or if you won't go with me there, let me take you to your parents' place. Or a hotel. You could check into The Breakers. It would be like a mini vacation."

Kat laughed her hollow, humorless laugh. "Thanks, but no, thanks. I'm not exactly in the mood for a vacation."

"You're just going to sit here and wait for him to come back and hurt you again?" I asked angrily.

After our trip to the Keys, when Kat told me that Howard had hit her, I'd read up on domestic abuse, especially when it occurred among the wealthy. The women in those situations had a habit of hiding what was happening, embarrassed for any of their social peers to find out. But Kat wasn't a trophy wife, skulking around a mansion, worried about what would become of her if she blew the whistle on her abusive, bread-winning spouse. Her family's money had bought this huge house, and she had the security of a well-connected family to look after her. She might face some minor public scrutiny—people loved to gossip—but surely nothing she couldn't deal with. Kat was a Wyeth. That alone gave her an unusual measure of protection.

"No. I'm going to finish off this bottle of wine, then possibly open another. And while I sit here and drink my wine and look out at the water, I'm going to figure out how to make that fucking asshole pay for what he did to me," Kat said, her voice suddenly eerily calm.

I sat back on my heels, my hand still on her shoulder.

"You can't stay here."

"Want to bet? This is my house," Kat retorted.

"Which won't matter if he kills you," I pointed out. I began picking up the shattered fragments of my wineglass.

"Leave it. Marguerite will clean up tomorrow."

I ignored her, piling the pieces of glass in a napkin. I stood and went to the bar to get another wineglass, before returning to my seat. Kat passed me the bottle, and I poured myself a glass. After Kat's disclosure, I needed it. "You need to tell me what happened."

Kat drew in a deep breath. "Howard came home after work. We'd made plans to eat here. I'd bought a couple of fillets that I was planning to cook. But he announced that he had to go back out to a work meeting. Which was obviously bullshit."

I nodded. I wouldn't have believed him, either. "You thought he was meeting the bartender?"

"Her or whoever else he's fucking these days. Someone he felt the need to shower and change for, something he wouldn't have done if it really was a late business meeting." Kat shook her head. She looked more tired than sad. "So I confronted him. I told him that I knew what he was up to, that if he planned to see her again, he should pack a bag, because he wouldn't be welcome back here."

I nodded.

"And then he just lost it," Kat said. "I could tell he'd been drinking—his eyes were red, and anyway, I could smell the scotch on his breath—and he just came at me. Got right up in my face and started yelling that he would not be told he couldn't return to his own house. I told him that since I'd bought it, it was actually *my* house. Then he just…lunged at me."

Kat stopped and raised a hand to her throat, her fingers gently brushing against the fabric of her shirt.

"That's when he choked you?"

Kat nodded, took another large gulp of wine.

"Kat." I sighed. "You have to call the police and file a report. Or, if you won't do that, you have to leave. It's not safe to stay here without doing anything to protect yourself."

"No," she said, turning sharply in my direction. "I will not let him run me off. Besides, he won't be back tonight."

"He's going to stay out all night?"

She shrugged. "It wouldn't be the first time. Especially if he's on a bender."

I rubbed my face wearily. Kat could be incredibly stubborn.

"Have you ever tried talking to him about not drinking so much?"

"It's pointless. He wouldn't listen. He did actually go to rehab once."

"He did? What happened?"

"He lasted fourteen hours, then called a cab."

"They let him leave?"

"They didn't have a choice. He checked himself in, so he could check himself out. Anyway, at this point, I don't think it would make much of a difference."

"I don't know. Adding alcohol to marital conflict is like throwing gas on a fire, at least in my experience," I said, remembering too many arguments Todd and I had engaged in after cocktails had been consumed.

"No, I meant, even if he sobered up, this was the final straw. I mean, he choked me. He put his hands around my throat and squeezed until I started to black out." Kat lifted her own small, pale hands up to her neck to demonstrate. "And I saw it in his eyes. There's something feral and rotten inside him. He wanted me to die. He was *hoping* I would die."

I shivered and took a sip of wine. "What stopped him?"

"I don't know," Kat said, the fire leaving her voice. "Certainly not any concern on my behalf. Probably fear that he'd spend the rest of his life in a jail cell. Howard might hate me—it's obvious he does—but he wouldn't survive in jail. He's too soft. He likes his luxuries too much."

"He isn't worried you'll call the police about what happened tonight?"

Kat shook her head. "Probably not. Although I should."

"You definitely should."

"Do you know what would happen if I did? It would be on the front of the *Palm Beach Post* tomorrow. Developer's Daughter Revealed to be a Battered Wife."

"So?" I said. "There are worse things that can be said."

"Not to me," Kat retorted. "All the Palm Beach bitches would be gossiping about it for years. God, I hate them."

I could feel my patience slipping again. "Why do you care what they think?"

"Because I do!" Kat flared up. "And if you're not going to help, you might as well leave."

"I am trying to help," I said, stung.

"Telling me over and over to leave my house is not helpful." Kat's words were slurred around the edges, and I wondered how much wine she'd had before I arrived.

There probably wasn't any point in continuing this conversation. I could sit with Kat and eventually get her to go to bed, but then what? Should I sleep over at her house, just in case Howard came home? That might be the most prudent course of action—I doubted he'd pick up where he left off if I was there—but it would certainly cause tensions to escalate at my house. And even putting Todd's irritation aside—something I was all too willing to do—it would stress out my children.

Kat was my friend and she was in trouble. But Liam and Bridget depended on me.

I set my mostly untouched wine down and clasped my hands together. "What do you need, Kat?"

She laughed bitterly. "A different life."

"Then let's make that happen."

"You make it sound so easy."

"No, not easy." I shook my head. "Of course it won't be easy. But you can't stay here, rattling around this big house, waiting for your husband to come back and possibly hurt you again. And I can't stay here on guard duty. We need to come up with a plan."

Kat looked warily at me. "What sort of a plan?"

"I think the best course of action would be for you to check into a hotel tonight and go see a divorce attorney tomorrow. I'll go with you," I offered.

Kat shook her head mulishly. "I already told you, I'm not going anywhere."

I swallowed back a sigh. "Then let me call your parents or your brother. Maybe one of them can come over."

"If you call my parents, I will never speak to you again," Kat said sharply.

"Come on, Kat," I said, wearying of her petulance.

"You think I'm kidding? I'm not. You'll never hear from me again. You won't be the first so-called friend I've had to jettison."

That was it. I'd had enough.

"Fine," I said, standing. "Then I'll leave you to it."

Before I could go, Kat was on her feet, grabbing at my arm.

"Don't go," she begged. "I'm sorry. I shouldn't have said that."

Kat looked at me pleadingly while tears slid silently down her face. My anger drained and I patted her arm.

"Take a deep breath," I said soothingly, as though I were talking Bridget down from a panic attack.

Kat tried to inhale, but it was choked off by a throaty sob. "I can't believe I've become this person. Afraid of my own husband."

"Well, this has to stop," I said firmly. "It's time. You need to take action."

"Yes," Kat said, slowly lifting her head to look at me. Her eyes, usually a vivid blue, looked dark in the twilight. "It's time I do something."

A shiver of apprehension passed over me. "You'll go see a lawyer tomorrow?"

Kat shook her head slowly. "No, that's not what I mean at all. Howard needs to be stopped."

"What are you talking about?" I asked cautiously.

"Never mind. I'm not dragging you into this."

Fear flashed through me. I could feel my heart start to beat faster.

"Into what?"

"Just promise me this," Kat said. "Whatever happens, promise me you'll be on my side."

"Of course I'll always be on your side," I assured her.

"No matter what?"

The words were loaded, edgy with unspoken meaning. I wasn't sure what she was asking of me. I looked at her, waiting for clarification, but Kat just stared back at me.

I thought about Todd and his accusation that I put Kat before our family. And I thought about Liam and Bridget and how much they still counted on me. Once you became a mother, you lost the right to put yourself in danger voluntarily.

But then I looked at my scared, battered friend and knew that if I didn't help her, something bad would happen. Howard was too volatile, his hostility fueled by alcohol and resentment. The next time he went after her, he might kill her.

Finally I nodded. "No matter what."

In the looming twilight, already alive with the sounds of cicadas, frogs and other creatures that roamed the night, the words sounded like a promise. Like an oath.

The truth was, it frightened me.

27

Present Day

I WAS DREADING my meeting with Kat.

After everything that had happened since Howard's death and all that I had learned about her, I didn't know what to expect. Would she be the same Kat who'd been my best friend for the past three years, or would I be meeting a virtual stranger? This thought unsettled me for most of the morning. But I had to go. I needed to find out what was going on.

I also wasn't crazy about the idea of meeting at the Jupiter Lighthouse, a popular local tourist destination. I'd visited the lighthouse once before, chaperoning Liam's class on a school field trip. It was a long climb to the top, and once you made it, you were rewarded with a scenic view of the Intracoastal Waterway and the Atlantic Ocean. But the lighthouse would be closed at nine o'clock at night, so we would be trespassing if we met there. I'd already been arrested once that week and wasn't eager to repeat the experience.

I finally decided that my best course of action would be to go early, while the lighthouse was still open to visitors. I'd buy a ticket for the tour, then try to find a spot where I could hide and wait for Kat to arrive. I was probably being overly cautious, but something about this meeting was making me edgy. I needed to be prepared for whatever might happen.

There were still a few problems I had to solve beforehand. And for that, I'd need Ebbie's help.

I found my mother in the kitchen, sitting at the table, working on a sudoku puzzle. This was a sight so shocking, I stopped abruptly and stared at her.

Ebbie looked up, peering at me over the top of tortoise-shell readers. "What?"

"You're working on a puzzle?"

"And why is that such a surprise?"

"Because you hate puzzles. You've told me that for years. Pretty much every time I've talked about my career in your presence."

"No, I haven't," Ebbie replied.

"Yes, you have. When I told you that I was writing a series of books of logic puzzles for tweens, you scoffed."

"I never scoff at anything. I'm open to all of life's many experiences." Ebbie took off her glasses, letting them hang down around her neck, secured by a chain.

"Your exact words were 'I don't know how you can do that. I hate puzzles. My brain doesn't work that way.'"

"I *never* said that."

I could feel my inner fifteen-year-old rising to this bait. Ebbie *had* said that, almost verbatim, and it was annoying listening to her pretend she hadn't. She'd always thought if she simply denied saying or doing something, that would magically make it true. I took several deep breaths and fought down my irritation. I had larger issues than a narcissistic mother to deal with at the moment.

"Do you know what your problem is?" Ebbie asked. She leaned back in her chair and crossed her arms.

"Living under a cloud of suspicion? The threat of spending the rest of my life in prison for a crime I didn't commit?"

My mother ignored my sarcasm. "You're far too rigid. You always have been, even when you were little. You don't allow people to change and grow."

I poured a cup of coffee from the carafe and sat down across the table from my mother.

"Is that what this is?" I asked. "Changing and growing through sudoku puzzles?"

"Maybe," Ebbie said.

I sipped my coffee. It tasted slightly scorched. "I need your help. I have to go somewhere this afternoon. I'll be gone for a while. And I don't want Todd to know where I am."

"That sounds very mysterious. How can I help?"

"The first problem is getting past the reporters outside. If I drive myself, they'll follow me."

"I'll drive you," Ebbie offered. "They won't follow me."

"How can you be so sure?"

"Oh, I know how to deal with them. Leave it to me. You can hide in the back seat. We'll find a way to camouflage you."

"Okay." I was pleasantly surprised at Ebbie's sudden burst of helpfulness. "If you think that will work."

"I'm sure it will."

"Now I just need to figure out what to do about Todd."

"Why don't you want him to know where you're going?"

I smiled ruefully. "Because he wouldn't approve and would probably try to stop me."

Ebbie nodded. "I'll think of something to tell him."

"Like what?"

"I'll say we're going to the grocery store," Ebbie suggested.

"And when I don't return home for six hours?"

"You're going to be gone that long?"

I nodded.

"Well, he probably won't buy that you spent so long buying groceries. I'll try to come up with something else. I wonder if he'd believe me if I told him you were at a meditation center, processing your feelings about the arrest," Ebbie said. "Probably not."

"Probably not," I agreed. I reached out and rested my hand on her arm. "Thank you."

Ebbie patted my hand and smiled. "Anytime you need to sneak away for a secret assignation, I'm here to help."

I'd never been on a stakeout before, but I assumed there would be two major challenges—not being seen and overcoming the boredom. I dressed for comfort—leggings, a long-sleeve sweat-wicking shirt, running shoes—and pulled my hair back in a low ponytail. My picture had been on the front page of the *Palm Beach Post* that morning, so there was a risk someone might recognize me. I decided to wear a baseball hat and a pair of large sunglasses and hoped they would be enough to conceal my identity.

Next I loaded a backpack with bottled water, granola bars, bananas and a paperback novel I'd been meaning to read for a while. I also brought my wallet, my cell phone—the volume muted—and, just in case, a can of pepper spray.

One piece of good luck was that Todd decided to go into his office after lunch. He hadn't been there since he first found out about my arrest, and he had to pick up the partially completed blueprints for a house he'd been hired to design.

"You don't mind, do you?" he asked before he left.

"No, of course not."

"I won't be too long," he promised. "I'll work here."

And I won't be here when you get back, I thought. I knew Todd would be upset when he returned home and found me gone. I hated to cause him additional stress and worry after everything we'd been through over the past few days. But there was nothing I could do about that now.

I read on the Jupiter Lighthouse website that the last tour of the day was at four o'clock, so I asked Ebbie to drive me over there at three thirty. I brought a throw blanket from the living room out to the garage, and after I lay down in the back of my Volvo station wagon, Ebbie arranged it over me.

"Well?" I asked.

"As long as you stay still, I think it will work," Ebbie said. "Are you comfortable?"

"Not really."

"You'll have to stay back here only a few minutes, just until we get past the reporters."

Ebbie closed the tailgate, and a minute later I heard her open the driver's-side door.

"Are you ready?" she called back to me, starting the car.

"I guess."

"What?" Ebbie asked. "I can't hear you."

I yanked the blanket off my face and said, "Let's go."

Ebbie opened the garage door, and I pulled the blanket back over my face. I could feel the car back down the driveway, followed by the shouts of the reporters. One or two of them were brazen enough to pound on the car. I was shocked to hear Ebbie roll down the automatic window.

What the hell is she doing? I wondered.

The reporters were thrilled at the interaction. I could hear them swarm toward the car, shouting out questions, and the sound of camera shutters whirring. I held my breath and tried to keep my body as still as possible.

"Hello," Ebbie said in her friendliest voice. "How are you all doing today?"

If the reporters were put off by this unusually friendly

response to their swarming, they quickly bounced back. They began shouting questions at Ebbie.

"Why did your daughter kill Howard Grant?"

"What is your reaction to the rumor that Katherine Grant paid Alice Campbell to execute her husband?"

"Is it true that Alice Campbell is on a suicide watch?"

This last question startled me.

Suicide watch? I wondered. *Where'd they get that?*

But Ebbie just chuckled, as though the reporters were delightful scamps.

"All of you have far too much negative energy. I'm going to the grocery store, and while I'm there, I'm going to buy some sage. When I get back, I'll do a cleansing ritual on all of your news trucks," Ebbie said. I couldn't see what their reaction was, but from the silence, I thought they were probably momentarily stunned, as Ebbie added, "Free of charge."

"Thank you, ma'am, but that's really not necessary," one of the reporters said in a faltering tone.

"Don't be silly. I insist," Ebbie said. "Sage cleansing ceremonies are wonderful for clearing bad energy out of spaces and bringing us all closer to the Goddess of Earth."

This seemed to result in more stunned silence. Then one of the braver reporters said, "Where are you going?"

"Publix," Ebbie said. "Do you want to come along? I can show you all of the herbs I need to buy, and I'll explain how they're used in various rituals. No? Suit yourself. I'll see you all when I get back. Bye!"

I felt the car move forward and heard the sound of Ebbie's automatic window whirring back up.

"All clear," Ebbie called out a few minutes later. "No one followed us."

I pulled the blanket off me and sat up. "You were taking an awfully big risk there."

"Inviting them to come watch me buy herbs?" Ebbie

laughed. "No, I wasn't. The last thing any of them would ever want to do is hang out with an old hippie who wants to teach them about herbal cleanses."

"Do you really know how to cleanse negative energy?"

"No idea," Ebbie said. "I made it up. I'm surprised they bought it."

I shook my head but smiled. My mother was still capable of surprising me.

Hunched low in the back seat, I directed Ebbie to the lighthouse. She pulled into the visitors' lot, which was half-full.

"Here?" Ebbie asked. "Are you sure about this?"

"Yes," I said. "The person I'm meeting will be by the lighthouse, but not until nine."

"Why do you need to be here so early?"

"An abundance of caution," I said. "You don't mind making dinner for the kids?"

"Not at all."

"Great, thank you. There's pasta and a jar of sauce in the pantry. And you'll come back to get me later?"

"Yes, what time?"

"I'll text you." It occurred to me that I had never received a text from my mother. I wasn't entirely sure she understood how to send one. "Do you know how to text?"

"Don't be so condescending," Ebbie retorted.

"Is that a yes?"

"Yes, I know how to text. What time should I plan on?"

"Probably nine thirty, maybe even ten." I hesitated. "What are you going to tell Todd?"

"I thought I'd tell him you were having cabin fever, so you decided to go to the movies," Ebbie said. "Will he buy that?"

"Probably not, but it's as good an excuse as any. And far more believable than telling him I'm hanging out at a meditation center." I picked up my backpack and reached for the door handle.

"I don't know what you're doing or who you're meeting, but, Alice...please be careful."

"I will," I promised.

Ebbie nodded. I could tell she was reluctant to leave me, and to be honest, I wasn't thrilled at being left there for the next six hours. I didn't know what to expect, and not knowing unnerved me. But I had to speak with Kat, and this might be my only chance.

"I'll be fine." I opened the back passenger door. "Don't worry about me."

"There's no such thing as a mother not worrying," Ebbie replied. "I would have thought you'd have figured that out by now."

28

THE VISITOR CENTER and museum for the Jupiter Lighthouse were housed in an older white clapboard building with a wraparound porch. I walked inside into a small room with creaky, uneven floorboards that served as both the museum store and the ticket counter. Passing by the display stands stocked with T-shirts, stuffed marine animals and souvenir seashells, I headed to the counter, which was manned by an older woman with very straight posture and short white hair.

"I'd like to buy a ticket for the lighthouse tour."

"You're just in time," the woman told me. "The last tour is at four o'clock. One adult?"

"Yes, please." I fished my wallet out of the backpack.

"That will be ten dollars."

I paid cash for the admission and was given a sticker to put on my shirt. I thought the woman looked at me oddly, and for a moment I was worried she had recognized me from the news stories about my arrest. I tried to tell myself she was probably just wondering why I was wearing my sunglasses inside on an overcast day. Still, I quickly turned away and headed toward the gate, where she'd told me the tour group was gathering.

The last time I'd been to the lighthouse, a few years earlier, I'd accompanied a class of enthusiastic ten-year-olds. This time, the tour group—which, at twenty strong, was larger than I had expected—was older and less rowdy. It was made up mostly of adults, and judging by their ages, mostly retirees. I waited quietly to the side, pretending to read the lighthouse brochure and hoping no one would recognize me.

A petite young woman with a long ponytail and wearing a Jupiter Lighthouse T-shirt arrived.

"Hi, everyone. My name is Cassie. I'll be guiding the tour up to the lighthouse today," she said. "I'll tell you about the lighthouse's history as we walk up the hill."

She unlocked the gate and began to lead us up the winding gravel path.

"The original plans for the lighthouse were drawn up by Lieutenant George Gordon Meade in 1854. However, construction wasn't completed until 1860," Cassie detailed. She walked backward so that we could hear her as we ascended the hill. "The lighthouse is one hundred five feet tall, and it stands one hundred fifty-three feet above sea level."

As Cassie rattled off her list of facts, I tuned her out while I looked for the best place to hide and wait for Kat. I needed to pick a spot where I was completely concealed, but where I could still see anyone approaching the lighthouse. The path wound up a hill, and we passed the original lighthouse keeper's house to the left and a large outdoor tiki hut to the right, which the museum used as an educational center. I discounted both spots as being too out in the open.

Finally we reached the steps that led up to the red lighthouse with its black top. I had grown so used to the sight of the lighthouse on the vista, a backdrop to our daily domestic life, that I barely noticed it anymore. So now, looking at it, stretching over a hundred feet high, I was struck by just how impressive it really was.

"Before we begin our climb up the lighthouse, turn your attention to the banyan tree. It was planted by Captain Seabrook in 1931, and as you can see, it's still thriving today," Cassie said.

To the right of the steps was a large banyan surrounded by a deck. I smiled. The tree had multiple twisting trunks and low swooping branches. It would be the perfect place to hide. The center trunk was so wide, I could crouch behind it and be completely concealed from anyone approaching the lighthouse. I just needed to get away from the rest of the group.

"And now, if you'll come this way, up the stairs, we'll go into the lighthouse," Cassie continued.

The group herded toward the steps leading up to the base of the lighthouse and formed a line. They slowly made their way into the tower, disappearing one by one, until only Cassie and I were left on the deck next to the banyan tree.

"After you," Cassie said, turning toward me with a swish of her ponytail.

"I've changed my mind," I said. "I'm afraid of heights."

Cassie frowned, her forehead wrinkling. "It's not that bad. And the view is totally worth the climb."

I shook my head. "No, I really can't do it. It makes me feel sick just thinking about it."

"I'm not supposed to leave anyone alone down here," Cassie said.

"I think I'm going to throw up," I said, sinking down onto a bench. I bent over, pressing my hands to my temples, looking, I hoped, like someone on the verge of a panic attack. "Don't worry. I'll just sit here and wait for you to come back down."

"Okay, but please stay here and don't wander off. We'll be back in twenty minutes," Cassie said.

I nodded weakly. Cassie turned and headed into the lighthouse.

I waited for three beats, then stood and quickly slipped into the small wooden shack next to the lighthouse. Cassie had said it was the electrical room, and it housed a large generator, coils of electrical wires and an assortment of tools. The little shack was hot and airless, but I was concealed for the moment. I just hoped Cassie wouldn't think to look for me in here.

I waited for what felt like much longer than twenty minutes, but finally I heard voices again. The tour group had returned. And Cassie had noticed that I was missing.

"I told her to wait here," she said, sounding fretful. "We're not supposed to let people wander off on their own!"

"She probably went back down to the visitor center," one of the others said. "Especially if she wasn't feeling well."

"I guess," Cassie said. "I just hope my supervisor doesn't find out. Anyway, let's go down the hill, and I'll take you through the house where the lighthouse keeper and his family used to live."

I looked at my watch. It was quarter to five. I decided to stay in the electrical shack for an hour, well past the time that the lighthouse and visitor center closed, just in case Cassie or someone else came back to look for me.

The next hour felt like one of the longest of my life. I was wedged between the electrical equipment and a rough wall, sitting on a hard cement floor, and I had to keep taking deep breaths, trying to calm the claustrophobic impulses that made me want to bolt back outside to the fresh air and spaciousness.

Luckily Cassie didn't return. When the time was finally up, I stood and stretched my stiff muscles, then stepped outside. It was nearly six, and the sun slanted down at a sharp, blinding angle. I slid my sunglasses and hat back on and headed toward the banyan. I picked out a spot at the base where I could sit without being seen by anyone approaching the lighthouse on foot.

Then the real wait began. Kat would arrive in three hours. Or she wouldn't. Those were the only two choices. One, we were still friends, still allies. The other, we were playing a very different game, and I didn't know the rules to it.

I read for a while, although I had a hard time focusing on my book. My eyes kept sliding over the words without taking them in. Finally I gave up and checked my phone. Todd had called a few times and left messages. He'd also sent a text:

Where r u? Ebbie said ur at a movie, but I don't believe her. Please call me back, I'm worried!

I exhaled while I considered my reply. There had been a time in our marriage not too long ago when Todd's feelings would not have been at the top of my concerns. It was different now. I had been through a lot over the past few weeks, and Todd had been my champion throughout, his support never wavering. And this was how I paid him back—evading him about my whereabouts, stranding him at home stewing in worry.

I replied,

Am fine. I'll explain everything when I get home. Try not to worry, everything will be all right.

Actually, I had no idea if everything would be all right, now or ever again.

Time ticked by. I was glad that I had not opted for a career as a private detective. Stakeouts, especially ones conducted sitting outside, leaning against a hard and bumpy tree, were no fun. I had anticipated boredom and hunger, but I hadn't thought of the other inconveniences, like a full bladder and stiff muscles.

The sun set just after seven thirty, leaving behind a hazy purple sky in its wake. As the sun drifted down, the lighthouse suddenly lit up. No one had come, so I figured it must be on an automatic switch. The light was comforting, especially as night fell, but I was glad that my chosen spot was still covered in darkness. I would be able to see anyone approaching the lighthouse—Kat, ideally—but I would remain hidden as long as I stayed where I was.

Finally, at eight forty, I heard a noise, something distinctly different than the chorus of frogs I'd been listening to. Footsteps against the gravel. Someone was coming up the hill. I tensed and, crouching behind the banyan tree, twisted in the direction of the path and waited for the person to come into view.

It wasn't Kat.

At first I could tell only that it was a man, which was enough to make my pulse quicken. Was he a security guard, or worse, a police officer? Had someone seen me?

As he drew closer and stepped into the pool of light cast down from the illumination of a thousand watts, I could see him more clearly. I didn't recognize him, and he didn't appear to be a police officer or security guard. He was wearing a T-shirt and jeans, not a uniform. He was a young man in his twenties with a square, muscular build, a closely trimmed goatee and tattoos winding around his arms and neck. His expression was hard, and there was something menacing about him that frightened me. I instinctively knew to stay hidden.

He walked over to the deck between the lighthouse and the banyan tree and sat on the same bench where I'd feigned illness a few hours earlier. He took out his phone, checked it and then put it back in his pocket. He was fidgety and restless, but one thing was clear—he was waiting for someone.

29

THE BENCH WHERE the man sat was about twenty feet away from my hiding spot. I was completely concealed in the darkness, but if I moved or made any sound at all—a sneeze, a gasp, anything—he would probably hear me.

I had no idea who the man was or why he was here, but I certainly had no intention of alerting him to my presence. For now, we waited. I waited to see if Kat would show up, and he waited for whomever he hoped to see. Maybe he was meeting a lover, or maybe he was a drug dealer waiting for a customer.

Or maybe Kat had arranged for him to be here.

I huddled against the tree, my pulse racing, as I considered what I knew.

Kat had set me up to be here, isolated and alone. This man had shown up at the very time and spot she'd arranged for us to meet. And Kat was nowhere to be seen.

Was it possible that my best friend had sent this man to scare or even hurt me? A week earlier, I would have said no, never. But now I wasn't so sure. I certainly didn't know Kat as well as I'd thought I did.

I might not know her at all.

★ ★ ★

I didn't dare look at my phone to see how much time had passed. It could have been anywhere from twenty minutes to an hour. The man occasionally took out his phone and checked it.

Just as I was starting to feel the strain in my muscles from staying so absolutely still, the man stood. He looked around, and for one heart-stopping moment he stared right in my direction. I held my breath. But then he looked away, and I realized that he had not heard me or sensed my presence but had been looking at the waterway beyond.

He turned toward the path. He was leaving. I watched him, backlit by the bright pool of light shining down from the lighthouse, and suddenly had an idea. It might be foolish, and yet I thought it might be beneficial someday.

I slid my phone out of my pocket and, cupping my hands over it so its light wouldn't give me away, opened the camera app and checked to make sure the flash was turned off. Moving very slowly, I lifted the phone and took several photos of the man in the seconds before he turned and headed back down the hill and into the darkness.

After he left, I checked the time on my phone. It was nearly ten o'clock.

Kat was clearly not coming.

Still, I waited another half hour before texting Ebbie. I wanted to make sure the man was gone before she pulled into the parking lot. Finally I texted,

Can u pick me up now?

Ebbie texted back immediately,

On my way.

I took out my pepper spray, just in case, and crept slowly down the hill. When I reached the gate, I saw that it was unlatched. The chain had been cut and was lying on the ground. I glanced around but didn't see or hear anyone. Still, I couldn't be sure that he wasn't waiting for me somewhere close by. I tried to move as stealthily as possible until I reached the parking lot and saw that it was empty. Relief flooded through me. The man, whoever he was, appeared to have left.

A minute later, Ebbie drove up in my car, headlights shining in the unrelenting darkness. I ran out to it and quickly opened the rear door and got inside.

"I've been worried sick!" my mother said. "You were so much later than I thought you'd be! Did you at least get the information you were hoping to find?"

"Not exactly," I said, tucking the pepper spray back into my bag.

Ebbie looked back at me. "Are you okay?"

"Yes," I said. "I'm fine."

Or I would be, once I figured out what Kat was up to.

When we got back to the house, Todd was waiting in the living room, watching the Tennis Channel with the volume off. He had a bottle of beer in his hand, and his wavy dark hair was sticking up on end as though he'd been running his hands through it.

"I'm going straight to bed," Ebbie said from the doorway. She looked tired, and I felt a stab of guilt at keeping her up so late.

"Good night," I said. "And thank you again. For everything."

Ebbie smiled. "Good night."

When she had left the room, I sat down on the couch next to my husband, tucking my legs underneath me. He was still staring at the television.

"Hey," I said.

He nodded and took a sip of his beer.

"Aren't you going to say anything?" I asked, reaching out to rest my hand lightly on his arm.

"What would you like me to say?" Todd sounded tired and tense, but not mad. I was glad. I wasn't up to facing his anger.

"I'm sorry I left the way I did. I know that I worried you," I said. "And I know you've been through a lot lately."

Todd finally turned to look at me. "I wasn't worried. I was scared out of my mind. Two days ago you were arrested for murder. Tonight you disappeared for hours without telling me or even Ebbie, apparently, what you were doing. What was I supposed to think?"

"I had to do something."

"So I gathered."

I knew I couldn't tell him that Kat had asked me to meet her at the lighthouse or that she hadn't shown up or that she possibly had sent the tattooed man after me. Todd would insist on going to the police, which I had absolutely no intention of doing. I hadn't trusted the police even before they arrested me for murder.

Instead I'd have to lie to my husband. If I dressed it up in a half-truth, maybe he'd even buy it.

"I got a text message from someone who said he had information about the witness who claimed to have seen Howard pushed off the balcony," I said.

"Who?"

"I don't know, he didn't give me his name. In fact, I'm not even sure it was a man. But whoever it was wanted me to meet him at the lighthouse after hours, so I went and waited. But he didn't show up."

"You did what?" Todd practically shouted.

"*Shh,*" I said. "You'll wake up the kids."

"What were you thinking?"

"Please stop shouting."

Todd set down his beer bottle with unnecessary force on the side table. "But that's crazy. It doesn't make any sense. You were gone for, what? Six, seven hours? Just to meet someone you don't know?"

"He said he had information for me. I couldn't just ignore that."

"Let me see the text," Todd demanded with his hand out.

We looked at one another for a long moment. Todd was upset, yes, but there was also something in his expression I couldn't quite read. A wariness I hadn't seen before. I wondered if he knew I was lying.

"I deleted it," I said quietly.

"What the hell is going on, Alice?"

"I've told you everything I know."

Todd closed his eyes. "We can't get through this if you don't trust me."

"I do trust you."

"Then tell me what you were doing tonight."

"I already told you. I was meeting someone I thought wanted to help me. But I was wrong. That person didn't show up." This, at least, was the truth. "If he had, and I could have used his help to clear my name, it would have been worth it."

Todd shook his head, picked up his beer and took a long drink from the bottle. I knew he still wasn't sure he believed me, but I could tell he was softening. Finally he reached out and took my hand. "I know you're scared and worried, but please promise me you'll never do anything like this ever again."

"Believe me," I said, turning to look at the silent tennis match, "I learned my lesson tonight."

I didn't get any sleep that night. I lay in our bed, listening to my husband's soft snores, while I tried to figure out what

Kat was up to. Had she simply been unable to show up? If so, it was an awfully big coincidence for that man to be at the closed and gated lighthouse at the exact time Kat and I were supposed to meet there. But if Kat had sent him in her place, what had she been hoping to accomplish? It was hard to believe that he had been there to deliver a benign message. Had he been sent to scare or even hurt me? And if so, what would Kat do when he told her I didn't show up?

Finally I gave up on sleep. I crept out of our bedroom without waking Todd and padded to the kitchen. I made chamomile tea and sat down at the table, my hands cupped around the steaming mug, while I tried to think about what I should do next.

I turned my laptop on and opened a blank document.

Then I began to type.

30

I WAS STILL sitting at the kitchen table in front of my laptop when Todd came in, clean-shaven and dressed for work. I had long since finished writing the document I hoped would keep us all safe. Now I was sipping coffee, reading the headlines of the news online and contemplating how thankful I was to be alive that morning.

"Did you get any sleep?" Todd asked, leaning over to brush his lips against my cheek.

"A little."

"I forgot to tell you when you got back last night—Grace called while you were out. She wants us to come into her office this afternoon."

"Did she say why?"

"No, but she said she hoped to have good news for us. She needs to talk to the prosecutor on your case this morning, and then she'll meet with us after that."

"I could use some good news," I said with a wan smile.

"What good news?" Liam asked, bounding into the kitchen. He was still wearing his pajamas, and his hair was sticking up. "What's for breakfast? Are you going to make eggs?"

"No, let your mother rest. Have some cereal," Todd said.

"It's okay. I don't mind." I stood and stretched. My muscles felt stiff and sore from the hours of sitting uncomfortably against the banyan tree.

"Am I going to school today?" Liam asked.

Todd and I exchanged a glance. He shrugged. "I don't think another day off is such a bad idea."

"I agree," I said. "Let's keep the kids home today, at least. We'll know more about what we're dealing with after we talk to Grace."

"Come in," Grace Williams said, waving us into her office. Unlike John Donnelly, Grace didn't have a corner office with a water view. Her law office was located in a two-story building on North Dixie Highway just down the street from the courthouse. But it was an open, airy room with stylish touches, like a demilune desk with curved legs and a leopard-print rug. There was a large table to one side covered in file folders and stacks of paper.

"I know, it's a mess," she said, waving at the piles. "But there is a method to the madness. Or at least, I know where everything is. Please sit down."

Todd and I sat side by side on cream upholstered French armchairs. He reached over and took my hand in his. The gesture reminded me of a frightening moment during my pregnancy with the twins. The doctor had ordered an amniocentesis, and when Todd and I were brought in to be given the results, we'd sat just like this. Now, as then, we were hoping for the best but bracing for a potentially life-altering blow.

Grace sat down behind her desk and laced her fingers together. "I have good news."

Todd and I glanced at one another.

"Let's hear it," Todd said.

"The prosecutor is dropping all of the charges," Grace said. "The paperwork is being processed as we speak."

I gasped and covered my mouth with my hands. Todd raised his hands in triumphant fists and said, "That's fantastic! What happened?"

"It was actually Alice's idea," Grace said, nodding approvingly in my direction. "And you were absolutely right."

"About what?"

"That the key to the whole case was the witness who claimed he saw Howard Grant pushed over the balcony," Grace said. "I sent my investigator to meet him."

Todd looked over at me. "Does this have anything to do with your meeting last night?"

Grace frowned. "What meeting?"

"Nothing," I said, shaking my head at Todd before turning back to Grace. "Who was the witness?"

"His name is Ronald Shaw," Grace said. "Apparently he's a bit of a character."

"And this man, Mr. Shaw, said he didn't see anyone push Howard after all?"

Grace shook her head. "No, he still claims he saw someone that night. He was quite insistent. He said that he had a clear view of the Grants' house through his telescope, and he saw a woman push Howard Grant off a balcony."

Todd and I exchanged another perplexed look.

"Then why are they dropping the charges against Alice?" Todd asked.

"Ronald Shaw has Alzheimer's," Grace said. "He's lucid at times, but during the course of the interview, he lost track of what year it was and who the president was."

"That's very sad," I said.

"Sad for him, yes, but good for you," Grace said. She shook her head. "Mr. Shaw's wife told my investigator that the police officer who interviewed her husband showed him a photo lineup and put a lot of pressure on him to identify Alice as the person he saw push Howard Grant. Someone named Sergeant Sofia Oliver."

"I'm not surprised. She's not my biggest fan," I said drily.

"In any event, Mr. Shaw is not competent to testify against you. And without a witness, the state's attorney doesn't have a case. They can't even prove that Howard Grant was murdered," Grace continued.

"I can't believe it," I said, feeling dazed. "After all of this, after everything I went through, it's just...over. Just like that."

"It's good news, Alice," Grace said.

"The best news," Todd added.

"In fact, if you're interested, I think you have grounds for a lawsuit," Grace began.

"What kind of lawsuit?" Todd asked.

"False arrest. False imprisonment," Grace said crisply. "If the police had done their job and investigated properly, they would have known that their main witness wasn't of sound mind. In fact, it sounds to me like Sergeant Oliver seriously overstepped by putting so much pressure on Mr. Shaw to identify you in the photo lineup. They should never have arrested Alice."

"No," I said quickly. "I don't want to sue the police. I want to put all of this behind me."

Grace nodded philosophically, although I thought she looked a little disappointed. "It's your choice, of course."

"What happens now?" Todd asked.

Grace went over the basics in her fast, bullet-point way of talking—the clerk of court would record the dismissal of the case, and Grace would petition to have the arrest expunged from my record. I sat still, trying to absorb all the information, while Todd nodded along.

Grace finally paused to take a breath. "Do you have any other questions?"

"No, I think that's everything." Todd slapped both hands against his legs. He looked to me. "Do you have any questions?"

"Actually, there is something I want to talk to Grace about," I said. "But I need to speak to her privately."

"I can't hear what you're going to say?" Todd asked, surprised.

I was sorry to hurt his feelings, but it couldn't be helped. The stakes were too high.

"It's nothing to worry about," I assured him. "I'll be only a minute."

Todd stood. "I guess I'll wait for you outside."

Once Grace and I were alone, she looked at me with her cool, calculating gaze. "What's up?"

I pulled a manila envelope out of my bag.

"You said that the attorney-client privilege covers all communications between us. I need it to cover this." I held the envelope up for her to see.

Grace nodded. "Is that something you want me to read?"

"No," I said. "And I know this is going to sound a little melodramatic, and maybe even a little crazy, so I apologize in advance. But I need you to hold on to this for me. Please don't break the seal while I'm alive. But if something happens to me—if someone kills me, or if I die in an accident or apparent suicide—open it then. Read it and then give it to the police."

To give her credit, Grace's expression didn't change. "Okay," she said slowly. "Is there an end date?"

"What do you mean?"

"Will there come a time when you'd prefer I destroy the contents of this? Without opening it?"

I considered this. "Five years. If I'm still alive in five years, I'll contact you and ask you to destroy it."

I handed the envelope to Grace. She looked down at it and nodded. "Until then, I'll keep it in my file."

"Thank you."

"You're very welcome." Grace hesitated. "I don't want to know what's in here, do I?"

"No," I answered. "Probably not."

31

THINGS WENT BACK to normal surprisingly quickly.

The reporters staking out our house disappeared. The *Palm Beach Post* ran a short story under the headline Local Writer Cleared of Murder Charges.

The children returned to school.

Ebbie returned home to her bearded potter.

Todd returned to work.

No one tried to kill me.

Kat and I had still not spoken. The day after the charges against me were dropped, I sent her a brief text telling her we needed to meet. I set a time and day the following week. She didn't respond, but I had a feeling that this time she'd show up.

To prove how serious I was, I sent her one of the photos I'd taken of the man at the lighthouse.

After dropping the kids off at school on their first day back, I laced on my sneakers and headed out for a run. I hadn't gone jogging for a while and it was a long, tough slog, especially in the early-May humidity. I hoped summer wasn't arriving early in South Florida. When I finally turned back onto our street, I saw Detective Demer standing in our driveway, waiting for me. I slowed to a walk as I approached him. He was tall and formidable, although his suit was rumpled as usual, and there was what looked like a coffee stain on his yellow tie.

"I didn't know you were a runner," Demer said.

"I'm not," I said, trying to catch my breath. My T-shirt was soaked with sweat, and I plucked it away from my chest. "I'm trying to get back in shape."

"Good for you," Demer said. "I keep thinking I should start working out again. But I've always hated exercising so much, I never stick to it."

I nodded without comment. I was sure the detective had not come here to discuss his exercise habits with me, and I was eager for him to get to the point.

"What's going on?" I asked. "Are you here to arrest me again?"

Demer smiled. "No, not today. I just stopped by to say goodbye. I'm going back to Tallahassee this afternoon."

"The case is closed, then?"

"It is. The only reason it was pursued as a homicide was the witness. Now that we know the witness is incompetent, there's no way to prove that Howard Grant was murdered," Demer said.

"Sergeant Oliver must be crushed."

The detective smiled. "I think she'll bounce back. There's been a spate of golf cart thefts on the island. That will keep her busy for a while."

"Does she believe that the witness was incompetent?"

"No," Demer replied. "She thinks he made an accurate report of what he saw, and she tried to argue that he'd still be a persuasive witness if the case ever went to trial."

"You don't agree?"

"It doesn't matter if he's persuasive. The man has advanced Alzheimer's. He doesn't know where he is most of the time. No state's attorney is going to take a case to trial with such an unreliable witness. Any halfway decent defense attorney would destroy Ronald Shaw's testimony." Demer shrugged.

"I wish you'd figured that out before you arrested me."

The detective nodded. "You may not believe this, but I didn't want to arrest you."

I looked at him for a long moment. "Actually, I do believe that. Is that why you came here? To tell me that?"

"No..." Demer hesitated. "Or at least, not entirely that. I came to warn you."

"About what?"

"There are rumors that Thomas Wyeth has some dubious business associates," Demer told me. "No one's ever been able to make a case against him—he's too careful for that—but there's talk that he has links with an organized crime syndicate in South Florida."

I nodded. Nothing about the Wyeths would have surprised me at this point. And if Kat had sent the tattooed man at the lighthouse after me, she certainly hadn't found him in the Yellow Pages.

"These are dangerous people," Demer continued. "Not the sort you want to get mixed up with."

"I'll be careful."

Detective Demer looked at me for a long moment. He seemed to be weighing whether to tell me something. I waited.

"Do you know anything about sociopaths?" he finally asked.

"Not really. Why?"

"They've always fascinated me. Pure evil under a charming exterior."

"You mean like serial killers?"

"Not necessarily. In fact, most of them aren't killers. Those are just the ones that get featured on news shows. Sociopaths can just be charismatic and manipulative people who go through life without being weighed down by a conscience. Not caring who they hurt along the way. Does that sound like anyone you know?"

I nodded slowly. "It might."

"Please take care of yourself. I'd hate to be back here investigating another homicide." Demer checked his watch. "I should get going."

"Safe travels," I said. "And don't take this the wrong way, Detective, but I really hope we don't meet again."

Demer smiled, his teeth flashing white against his dark skin. "If I had a dollar every time I heard that. And they say dentists get depressed because everyone hates seeing them. They should try working as a homicide detective."

I laughed. Under different circumstances, I probably would have enjoyed getting to know Detective Alex Demer.

"Goodbye, Mrs. Campbell," he said, touching his fingers to his temple in an ironic salute.

32

A WEEK LATER, I sat on a bench near a playground where I used to take my children when they were little. It featured a huge plastic jungle gym in the shape of a castle, along with swings and slides and assorted climbing apparatuses. It was a gorgeous Saturday afternoon, warm but with a slight breeze that kept it from being too hot. It had the feeling of being the last day of spring before the sweltering summer heat would arrive, engulfing us for the next four months. The playground was crowded, teeming with children, while their parents—mostly mothers, with a few dads sprinkled about—sat on benches, armed with juice boxes and bags of Goldfish crackers.

"Alice," a familiar voice said.

I looked up, shading my eyes with one hand, and smiled when I saw who it was.

"Hello, Kat. I'm glad you could make it."

Kat did not return the smile. "You didn't give me much choice. You said you'd go to the police with what you know if I didn't. Why did you want to meet here, of all places?"

I'd forgotten that small children irritated Kat, almost to an irrational degree, but it was a bonus to having chosen this spot.

"I thought after how things went the last time we were supposed to meet, it was probably a good idea to pick a public place," I commented. "Who was the man you sent to the lighthouse that night?"

Kat sat down next to me. She was wearing a loose cotton blouse, skinny jeans and enormous sunglasses. She crossed one leg over the other.

"I have no idea what you're talking about." She was uncharacteristically terse, her usual vivaciousness set aside for the moment. "And how do I know you're not wearing a wire?"

"I'm not, but feel free to pat me down if you want."

Kat shook her head. "That's okay. I certainly don't plan on saying anything that would incriminate myself. Why did you want to meet?"

"I'd like some answers. I think I deserve them after everything that's happened."

"You can ask what you like." Kat tossed her hair back. "But I'm not promising I'll answer."

"Why did you have me arrested?"

"Have you arrested?" Kat laughed, but it was a mirthless sound. "You did that to yourself."

"Excuse me?"

"You told the police Howard had been having an affair. That just fueled their suspicions of me." Kat's tone was sour. "The detective, especially. He suspected me right from the beginning."

"I had no choice. I told them about Howard's affair only after you told them I was one of the only people with access to the house. Howard's girlfriend would have had access to the house, too."

"I didn't know that pervert across the Intracoastal would be watching my house through his telescope," Kat snapped. "Or that the police would be so fucking incompetent, they wouldn't manage to figure out a little sooner that his brain had turned to Jell-O. Christ, it would have saved us both a lot of trouble."

I was determined to stay calm, but this rankled. "Both of us? You weren't the one who was arrested for murder *and* had to spend a night in jail."

"You should have kept your mouth shut," Kat said in a hard, cold tone of voice I'd never heard her use before. "And since you didn't, I had to give them an alternate suspect. By the way, that female cop? She really didn't like you. In fact, she *hated* you. She was all too willing to believe that you killed Howard, especially after I hinted that you might be in love with me. You should have seen her. She ate that up."

Fury washed over me. "You told her I was in love with you? You know that's not true."

Kat sighed as if I had disappointed her. "You're entirely too caught up in worrying about truth and lies, Alice. The reality is, no one cares." Kat shook her head. "Life goes on."

"It doesn't go on for Howard."

"People die all the time. And trust me, no one is mourning Howard. Except maybe his girlfriend, but probably not even her. He wasn't that good a lover."

"What about Amanda? She was heartbroken that her father died," I snapped. I didn't want to give Kat the satisfaction of knowing she was getting under my skin, but her callousness was hard to take.

Kat stiffened but then waved a hand as though she were swatting away a fly. "Howard wasn't her father. And if she was upset at the funeral, it's because she was romanticizing his role in her life. God, I was dumb to get knocked up by her real father. I thought he was going to be someone, and instead he was just another weak, stupid man. Do you know that when I told him I was pregnant, he started to cry? It was embarrassing."

"He was probably worried his wife would find out and it would end his marriage." I shook my head, wondering how

319

I'd managed to spend so much time with Kat without ever really seeing her for who she was. What she was.

"It was supposed to. That was the whole point of my getting pregnant in the first place. He wouldn't leave his wife for me, so I had to give him a nudge. But instead of being strong and doing the right thing, he started blubbering and begging me to get an abortion." Kat shook her head with disgust.

"Why didn't you?"

"I'm not sure. I certainly didn't have any deep maternal instincts at that point." Kat exhaled deeply. "But it seemed like the best play at the time. And if he had gone on to run for president like he planned, I would have had quite the little poker chip in my pocket."

I still didn't even know who this mystery politician was. Or if he was even real. I wouldn't have put anything past Kat at this point.

"Amanda's real father wanted to run for president?" I didn't bother trying to keep the skepticism out of my voice.

"Oh, he tried, but it turned out he wasn't as talented a politician as he thought he was. He crashed and burned right out of the gate. And then it was too late. Amanda was already born," Kat said. She waved her hand again. "Enough about that. It's in the past. Are we done here?"

"No. I have more questions."

"Like what?"

"Like, did Howard really strangle you?"

I remembered every moment of that night. The night she'd begged me to help her. The night everything had changed.

"Just promise me this," Kat had said. *"Whatever happens, promise me you'll be on my side."*

"Of course I'll always be on your side," I'd told her.

"No matter what?"

"No matter what."

But the conversation hadn't ended there.

"He told me he's going to kill me," Kat had said. *"He told me so tonight."*

"He was drunk," I'd said. *"People say stupid things when they've been drinking."*

"He meant it. I could see it in the way he looked at me. His eyes were so cold, so...evil," Kat had said, and she'd shuddered then, wrapping her arms around herself. *"I'm telling you, he's going to kill me. And he'll figure out a way to do it without getting caught. He'll make it look like an accident."*

"I won't let him hurt you," I'd said.

Kat had suddenly reached out, twisting her fingers around mine. *"You could kill him for me, Alice. No one would ever suspect you. You're the smartest person I know. You're the only one I know who could get away with it."*

Kat had lapsed into silence. I guessed she was weighing the pleasure of gloating over her machinations against not wanting to give me any more ammunition against her.

I thought back to all of the stories she'd told me over the years about her marriage to Howard. She'd effortlessly woven truth and lies together to create the semblance of a monster. And I'd believed her.

"So did he really strangle you, or was that just another lie?"

"I already told you—you can ask what you want, but that doesn't mean I'm going to answer." Kat smiled her little devious, self-satisfied smile. I wanted to slap it off her face.

"And his affairs? Did you make those up, too?"

"God, no." Kat laughed. "Howard was never very good at staying faithful."

"But you didn't care," I said flatly.

"Oh, I did at first, although I have to admit that I was more angry than brokenhearted. I'm Thomas Wyeth's daughter. Howard was damned lucky to have me, to have married into my family. How dare he cheat on me! But, no, by the end, I was well past caring about who he stuck his dick into," Kat agreed.

Her lack of remorse chilled me to the core. "Do you want to know what happened that night?" I asked.

After a long, charged pause, Kat said, "Not really."

But I had no intention of letting her off the hook that easily.

"I picked a fight with Todd over a credit card bill. I'd known about it for a while, but I put off confronting him about it until that night so I'd have a good excuse to storm out. I drove over to your house and let myself in with the key you left. The alarm was off, which was helpful. I was hoping Howard wouldn't hear me, but I brought my pepper spray with me just in case. You were right, by the way. Howard was already really drunk. When I found him, he was lying on top of your bed, still fully dressed and snoring. At first I was worried that he was unconscious and I wouldn't be able to wake him up. I shook his arm. When he opened his eyes, I told him you needed to speak to him."

Howard had been confused when he woke to find me peering down at him. He'd left the lights on, so he couldn't tell what time it was. He smelled of scotch and sweat, and his forehead was damp as though he'd been out running and not just sleeping off a bender. But he was so drunk, he hadn't questioned why I was there in his bedroom, jostling him awake.

"Kat needs you," I'd said.

"Kat?" Howard looked up at me, his eyes bleary and unfocused. When he spoke, he slurred his words. *"She's not here, is she?"*

"She is. She's outside, waiting for you. She needs you, Howard. You have to get up. Now."

He struggled to get out of bed. I rested a hand under his elbow and steadied him as he got shakily to his feet.

"Where is she?"

"Outside," I said, gesturing with one hand toward the balcony. *"Out there."*

Howard staggered out there. *"Kat,"* he called. *"Kat?"*

"She's down by the pool," I said. *"Look down and you'll see her."*

"She is? I thought she was somewhere else. Out of town." Howard lurched toward the balcony, gripping the metal railing with both hands.

"No, she's home, of course," I said in the same soothing voice I used with Liam and Bridget when they were babies and getting fussy. *"She's down there. Can't you see her?"*

Howard clung to the railing and leaned over it, peering down at the patio with landscaping lights that shimmered and reflected on the surface of the pool.

It wasn't as difficult as I had expected. I pushed him with both palms splayed, hitting his upper back. He fell forward, throwing his arms out to regain his balance. But it wasn't enough. He swayed for a moment, confused about what was happening, but not capable of resisting, either. I pushed him again, harder this time.

For a long moment, Howard was almost all the way over the railing but hadn't yet fallen. He made an odd noise, like an injured animal crying out in pain. His hands grasped for the railing, trying to hold on to it.

He looked at me then, his expression one of fear and confusion.

"Please," he said.

I stepped forward and gave him one final push.

And then he was gone.

There was a terrible *thunk* that reminded me of the sound of a coconut falling from a tree and hitting the pavement below.

I looked over the railing at Howard's body lying prone on the tiled deck. A stream of blood was trickling away from his body toward the still, aqua water of the pool.

★ ★ ★

"I didn't think he could survive the fall," I said now, glancing over at Kat. She looked pale, I thought, but otherwise hadn't reacted to my retelling of the events of that night. At least, not that I could see. She was still hiding behind her sunglasses. "But I thought I should make sure. A job well done and all that."

"What do you want, Alice?" Kat asked abruptly.

"Want? I don't *want* anything." Then I considered this. "Actually, that's not entirely true. I don't want you to send another thug after me like you did that night at the lighthouse. That's why I decided I need an insurance policy."

Kat shrugged. "That picture you took doesn't prove anything."

"I don't know about that. The picture, combined with your voice mail asking me to meet you that night… I think I could make a pretty compelling case to the police that you sent him after me. But to be honest, I'd rather not involve the police, for obvious reasons. So I made other plans."

Kat tipped her head to one side. "Like what?"

"If anything happens to me, if I'm hurt or if I disappear, I've arranged for evidence to surface that you paid me to kill Howard."

Kat inhaled sharply, which, I had to admit, was gratifying. I had succeeded in rattling her.

"What evidence?" she asked. "And who has it?"

I laughed. "As though I'd tell you that. But if anything happens to me, you'll have a lot to answer for. You'd better hope I live a long and peaceful life."

"It may surprise you, Alice, but I don't want anything to happen to you. In fact—" Kat reached into her purse and pulled out a piece of paper "—this is for you."

She handed it to me. I looked down at it. It had two lines

of text on it, mostly numbers, interspersed by a string of random capital letters.

"What's this?"

"It's the access information for an offshore bank account in the Caymans," Kat said. "There's a million dollars. It's all yours."

I looked at this paper with its sequence of numbers and letters, all containing a future Todd and I had never imagined.

Or a future of trouble and possible incarceration, depending on who was watching.

I folded the paper in two and handed it back to her.

"No, thanks."

"Take the money," Kat insisted. "I know you can use it."

I shook my head. "I don't want your money, Kat. I never did."

Kat pushed her sunglasses on top of her head and looked directly at me for the first time since arriving at the playground.

"You never really did care about the money, did you? I always found that strange."

I shook my head. "No. I was friends with you because of you. Or at least, the person I thought you were."

"You know, it—the money—impresses most people. Even though it's all just bullshit. But you already know that. You always did."

I nodded. "Yes, I like to think so."

Kat tucked the paper back into her handbag and stood. "I think we've said all we need to."

I reached out and grabbed Kat's wrist, stopping her. Her wrist was small, dainty even, and I could feel the fine bones under her skin. I squeezed tightly, causing her to inhale sharply.

"How did you know?"

"Know what?"

"That I'd do it?"

Kat looked down at my hand still gripping her. She was deciding whether to tell me this last secret between us.

"I see people," she finally said. "I see them for who they truly are. It's my one true gift in life. Although, to be honest, sometimes it feels more like a curse. I have to admit, you weren't the easiest person to read. Not at first."

I stared up at Kat, not quite sure I could believe what I was hearing.

"I'm right, aren't I?" Kat asked.

"I have no idea what you're talking about."

Kat smiled. "Fine, if you want to play it that way. You're the one who's always insisting on the truth. Are you going to let me go now?"

I opened my hand, releasing her. Kat rubbed her wrist.

"Goodbye, Alice," Kat said. "I don't imagine we'll meet again."

She pulled her sunglasses back down, then turned and walked away from me. And as I watched Kat's retreating figure—her head held high, her dark hair glossy in the sunlight—I finally knew without a doubt what she was. Kat was a knave, a liar through and through.

She might even manage to one day convince herself to forget the night she'd told me Howard had threatened to kill her. The night she'd begged me to kill him before something terrible happened to her. She'd had quite a bit to drink, after all. Or maybe she'd remember it just enough to justify that she hadn't meant it, that I must have been crazy to have taken her seriously. It was also how she'd justify cutting me out of her life, like a surgeon slicing out a tumor. Maybe she'd even turn fanciful, and the art curator in her would imagine me as a Picasso in which the parts were all there but didn't line up quite right. An eye too high, a nose too far to the side, a soul too fragmented. She'd tell herself I was both damaged and damned to hell.

But as I sat on the hard bench and watched the children play, I knew Kat was wrong to think that. I wasn't damaged, and I certainly didn't believe in hell.

I believed in logic. The clean, clear sorting of facts. And when you stripped away those things that confuse the facts—passion and anger, sorrow and fear, love and hate—the logical conclusions are often breathtakingly simple.

Some people do not deserve to live.

Take Howard, for example. He had been a sadistic, bullying drunk who had contributed little to the people and world around him. Even if he hadn't yet physically abused Kat, he probably would have eventually. He might even have killed her if he could have figured out how he could get away with it. His death was a benefit to everyone who knew him. Except, perhaps, to Amanda. She was the one good thing Howard had left behind.

If I'd known then that Kat had been manipulating me, I wouldn't have killed him. But I also wasn't going to pretend that he was an innocent.

And then there was Brendon, Todd's older half brother. Early in our marriage, Todd had told me about an ugly footnote in his family's history involving Brendon when he was a teenager. Todd hadn't known the details, only that there had been an accusation that Brendon had hurt a younger female cousin. It was only many years later, when Todd was an adult, that he figured out the assault had been sexual in nature. She was a troubled girl who grew up to be an even more troubled adult—drugs, commitment for her mental illness. Todd wasn't entirely sure what had happened as they'd lost touch over the years. No formal complaints had ever been filed against Brendon.

But years later, after the children were born, we'd spent Thanksgiving weekend at Todd's parents' house in St. Augustine. Brendon, who lived in Gainesville, and whom I'd never before met, had shown up unexpectedly for Thanksgiving dinner. He was in his late forties by that point and had not taken good care of himself over the years. He was overweight, with puffy, pallid skin and the sour smell of someone who didn't wash as often as he should. I could tell that Todd's mother—Brendon's stepmother—was not happy to see him, and even less happy when he asked to spend the night on the sofa after drinking too much to be able to drive home safely. I had also noticed during dinner that Brendon's eyes kept drifting toward Bridget, then seven years old and beautiful, with her large eyes and long curls.

Long after Todd fell asleep, I stayed awake, listening. Just past midnight, I finally heard the footsteps creaking on the stairs. I slipped out of bed and opened my door in time to see Brendon reaching for the doorknob of the guest room my children were sharing.

I stepped out into the hall, and he, sensing the movement, turned and saw me. For a few seconds, we stared wordlessly at one another, predator and mother of the prey. Brendon's hand dropped from the doorknob, and he began shuffling toward the staircase, which was located in the middle of the hallway, equidistant between where he and I stood.

I moved quickly, surprising myself.

Surprising him.

But then, Brendon was drunk, and I was not.

Just as he reached the stairs and was about to descend, I gave him a good, solid push from behind. I had slipped into Todd's and my bedroom and back into bed next to my sleeping husband before the sound of Brendon's body hitting the floor below wakened anyone else in the household.

Would Todd have made the choice I had if he'd been the one to see Brendon poised at our sleeping children's door? Perhaps. And yet somehow I doubted it. People like Todd and Kat might believe a person deserved to die, might even want someone dead, but that didn't mean they were capable of that final push. The action that sent a body tumbling off a balcony or down a flight of stairs. Even when that push was the only logical solution to the problem.

And then there were the times logic pointed to death not as a punishment but as a release. A kindness. A gift born of love.

Like when a mother sees her infant daughter dying in increments, her tiny body working against her gossamer-thin will to live. The doctors spoke words of hope to the mother, assuring her they were doing everything they could. Later, when she was feeding quarters into the vending machine for a cup of the acrid coffee that would keep her alert as she stood vigil over her tiny charges, she overheard those same doctors discussing how bleak the situation really was. How the hemorrhage was not resolving on its own. How even if the infant did survive, which had become increasingly unlikely, she had almost certainly suffered severe brain damage. The baby would face a life not worth living. They would have to prepare the parents for the bad news, for the terrible weeks or months to come. Before they told her this, the mother did the only thing left she could do for her daughter.

As they sat together in a rocking chair under the dimmed lights of the deserted neonatal intensive care unit, the mother allowed her daughter to slip peacefully out of the world while being held in the arms of the person who loved her best, one hand pressed gently over the baby's rosebud mouth and tiny nose.

I stood suddenly, blinking back tears. I'd always hated crying, hated its pointlessness. I was suddenly eager to leave the playground. I was tired of sitting on the hard wooden bench, tired of listening to the children, who were worn-out from their day of play and growing peevish. I was tired of how illogical the world could be, full of its frustrating inhabitants, people who claimed to want one thing and then changed their minds once they got it. Most of all, I was tired of Kat and her unrelenting selfishness. I was glad to be rid of her.

I turned and walked away from the playground, heading toward the parking lot. I was suddenly eager to be at home myself, to see Todd and the children. Maybe we'd go out to dinner. Liam and Bridget both loved the Japanese steak house, where the hibachi chef put on a show, his knife moving lightning quick to carve up the meat that would become our dinner.

Soon the sun would start its slow descent, leaving behind an inky dark sky. This day would be over.

A new one would dawn tomorrow.

There was no point in dwelling on the past.

★ ★ ★ ★ ★